GAMBLING LION

Part 1 of The Pride of Lions

ANTOINETTE GEORGE

This series of books is dedicated to my late father.

History always fascinated him and I believe that's where my love of the subject comes from. He always encouraged me to read anything and everything, just as he did, and he was a fount of knowledge on all sorts of random subjects.

I'm not sure what he would have made of all my books, but he was always supportive of everything I tried to do and I like to think they would have amused him no end.

It's many years since he passed, but I still love and miss him a lot.

The Granville Legacy: Set Two

THE PRIDE OF LIONS

Nicholas de Bresancourt was an aristocratic but penniless refugee of the bloody French Revolution from which he'd escaped as a four-year-old orphan, thanks to Francis Granville and his friends. Nicky had lost everything: family, estate and fortune, and grew up hating those responsible in France for ending countless innocent lives on the guillotine and then Bonaparte, whose megalomania had put his country through so much further upheaval and war. With no other means to support himself or earn a living, and his pride refusing to allow him to accept the charity of his wealthy adoptive family, Nicky has joined the British army, keen to serve and help end the interminable war in Europe.

With Francis as a mentor, Nicky has matured into a charismatic, capable man and a clever fighter, as well as a lover of many women. He is also trilingual, thanks to growing up and being educated at an English school with a Spanish step-mother and French step-father. He is therefore ideal material to work undercover and put his talents to use on behalf of his adopted country. First, as an agent liaising with the Spanish rebels and guerrillas as the British endeavoured to drive the French out of Spain during the Peninsular War, and then as a full-blown spy for an anonymous Whitehall Department and Wellington, on the trail of a dangerous and ruthless French agent operating in both Spain and France: a man with a long-standing, personal vendetta against The Shadow, the man he suspected had caused the death of his father.

Part 1: Gambling Lion

London. June 1812.

He was carrying important dispatches from the British Army HQ in the Peninsula to the War Ministry in London and hadn't been home for over a year.

While waiting for confidential and urgent documents to take back to the Army high command, Nicholas de Bresancourt is ordered to meet an inscrutable gentleman in the innocuous-sounding Department of Information in Whitehall. Lord Ashcroft wants to utilise his talents to track down a dangerous French agent who has been causing trouble for those still battling Bonaparte across Europe, and has now turned up in Spain. Meanwhile, Nicky also takes the opportunity to catch up with his adoptive relations, including the dying family matriarch, the nearest thing he's ever had to a grandmother, as well as the wife he was inveigled into marrying and now wants rid of.

Unsurprisingly, being Nicky, he decides to take a few hours off for a bit of personal R&R from the stresses of family matters and work. Good looking, charismatic and a consummate lothario, he heads out on the Town with a few regimental friends and they take him to a new gambling salon in Mayfair which is all the rage: *Le Lion D'Or*, owned by a mysterious masked woman who calls herself *La Lionesse*. Inexplicably fascinated by the lady, who in turn seems very taken with the handsome soldier, she asks him up to her private quarters to continue their game of cards and he accepts, and that's when she raises the stakes...

Historical Landscape

Dear Readers,

If you're following the continuing saga of the life and times of Francis Granville, I hope you're going to enjoy this sequel story about Nicholas de Bresancourt, Duke of Valenciennes, adopted son of Edouard and Carlotta de Mornay. The twisting and turning plot is full of even more adventure and drama, love, passion, steam, fascinating characters (some new and some familiar) and of course, a really evil villain! And lions.... Rawwwwr!

But it's also based on what I think is a fascinating period of history, both English and European. If you aren't very familiar with this era, its revolutions and wars, or it's been too long since you were at school (!), I thought I'd give you a brief overview which will help put the events in the story into perspective. There are a couple of maps here as well (in case your geography is also a bit hazy) to help you understand what was going on in Spain while the British army was there, and then back to southern England and northern France where of course the main characters have their roots.

Historical enemies down the centuries, probably since William the Conqueror invaded England back in 1066, and the English controlled part of France during the Hundred Years War in the Middle Ages... during the 1700s, Britain and France were yet again involved in significant wars both in Europe and far from their shores. From the beginning of the century in 1704 when John Churchill, Duke of Marlborough, (the ancestor of Winston Churchill), resoundingly defeated the forces of French King Louis XIV and his allies at Blenheim, the old rivalry continued unabated. Both nations vied with each other for supremacy as they sought to either influence who ruled the various countries of Europe, or colonise new territories around the globe, in North America, Africa and the Far East, seeking both power and influence as well as new trading opportunities.

By this time, Great Britain, or more specifically the all-powerful British East India Company, controlled large areas of the Indian subcontinent as it expanded its commercial interests across south-east Asia. Army units fought various wars in alliance with local rulers until eventually, the decisive battle between the British and the French at Wandiwash in 1760 cleared the way for Britain to become the main European power in India and it became a springboard for further expansion of trade and influence throughout that part of the world, all the way down to Australia where the first convicts landed from a small fleet of British ships in Botany Bay in 1788. A penal colony was subsequently set up near there and thus began the colonisation of Australia by the British (who incidentally just beat the French to it; they landed in Botany Bay 6 days before the French expedition arrived.)

Although a British commanded army continued to have a significant presence in India after 1760 and be involved in local battles well into the 19th century, the focus of the British and French animosity turned west and both countries became embroiled in the American Revolutionary War from 1775-83.

France's help was a major contribution towards the United States' eventual victory and resulting independence. However, as a cost of participation in the war, France accumulated over 1 billion *livres* in debt, which significantly strained the nation's finances. The French government's failure to control spending compounded many other growing social problems and led to serious unrest in the nation which eventually culminated in the Revolution in 1789.

Thereafter, while Britain came to terms with the loss of its American colonies, France was in turmoil and descending into anarchy.

At the start of 1791, the other monarchies in Europe became concerned at the serious Revolution happening on their doorsteps and they considered whether they should intervene: either in support of King Louis XVI, to prevent the spread of revolutionary fervour across the continent to their own countries, or to take advantage of the chaos in France to expand their own borders. By 1792, France found itself at war with its neighbours and after a series of small victories, a series of defeats followed and this downturn allowed the radical Jacobins to rise to power and impose the Reign of Terror. This inevitably led to Louis XVI and Marie Antoinette, along with large swathes of the French aristocracy and upper classes, meeting a grisly end on the guillotine. Tens of thousands were either executed or murdered across France in under a year during this most bloody period of French history.

From 1794, the war situation turned again and improved dramatically for the French. A hitherto unknown officer from Corsica, one Napoleon Bonaparte, had been rapidly rising through the ranks. Appointed Brigadier General in 1793 at the age of only 24, he began his first full campaign in Italy in April 1796. Within a year, French armies under Bonaparte were overwhelming their enemies and one by one the European states sued for peace.

By the start of 1800, Britain was becoming ever more alone in its successful resistance to Bonaparte. Its maritime supremacy was of growing importance as a series of naval victories secured control of the Mediterranean while it endeavoured to blockade France by sea. There was a brief peace and break in hostilities in 1802, but inevitably it didn't last.

Bonaparte's star continued to rise, he was an extremely capable military general and his victories made him increasingly popular in France where he continued to consolidate his own political power. In 1804, he was crowned Emperor Napoleon I as his armies continued their conquest of Europe. However, at sea, Britain reigned supreme and Nelson's famous victory at Trafalgar in 1805 decimated the French and allied Spanish navies and prevented a potential invasion of England itself.

Fuming and frustrated by the old enemy across the Channel and hoping to isolate and weaken Britain economically, as she was trying to do to France through her naval blockade, in 1806 in retaliation, Bonaparte introduced and tried to enforce his 'Continental System'. This was a large-scale embargo on British trade, and even the post, which forbade the import of British goods into any European countries allied with or dependent upon France. But it was ineffectual as smuggling became rife and trade simply continued through Portugal, Spain and Russia, much to his irritation. As a result, Bonaparte launched an invasion of Portugal, the only remaining British ally in continental Europe. After occupying Lisbon in November 1807, he seized the opportunity to turn against his former ally, deposed the reigning Spanish royal family and declared his brother King of Spain in 1808. The Spanish and Portuguese revolted, and Britain supported them, and so began the Peninsular War.

Bonaparte did well when he was in direct charge, but problems and losses followed his departure from Spain to re-focus his attention on subjugating and controlling central and eastern Europe, leaving his Marshals to run the campaign. He severely underestimated how much manpower would be needed, and the effort in Spain was a drain on that as well as money and prestige, and ultimately failed. Especially once an able British commander, Sir Arthur Wellesley, was put in total charge of the British army, supported by the Portuguese and Spanish rebels and ruthless guerrillas. Wellesley had recently arrived after a victorious tour of duty in India. His success in the Peninsular War saw him elevated to become Duke of Wellington and eventually the two opposing military leaders faced each other at the epic Battle of Waterloo in 1815. After that, Europe enjoyed nearly a century of relative peace and prosperity.

Against this background, England in 1812 was itself experiencing a difficult year.

The war against Bonaparte and the French seemed never-ending and was a constant drain on the country's finances. In particular, action in the Peninsula was at a critical point as Wellington's fortunes continued to ebb and flow in his efforts to push the French out of Spain and back into France. In Europe, meanwhile, Napoleon's ego had made him cast his eyes east and the French were now marching on Russia. There seemed to be no stopping his megalomania. On the domestic front, the Government continuously watched public feeling, wary of radicals who sought social change and in May, to the shock of the country, the Prime Minister, Spencer Perceval, was assassinated in Parliament, in the lobby of the House of Commons. And if all that wasn't enough, tensions with the new United States caused an outbreak of hostilities between the two nations in June, known as the War of 1812 (which actually lasted until early 1815) with Britain subsequently having to defend its colonies in Canada from American incursion.

And the middle of 1812 is where Pride of Lions starts. So read on and find out what Nicky, Francis and their eccentric family and friends get up to as their tale continues some 20 years on from where Behind the Shadow finished in 1792…

Apologies for the boring history lesson, I trust it hasn't sent you to sleep! But I hope you move on and enjoy the fiction story now as much as I enjoyed writing it. And if by chance you are interested in little historical anecdotes related to events in my books, keep an eye on the blog on my website where I occasionally write further musings: https://antoinettegeorge.com/blog/

Antoinette…

Channel Coasts of England & France,
1790-1816

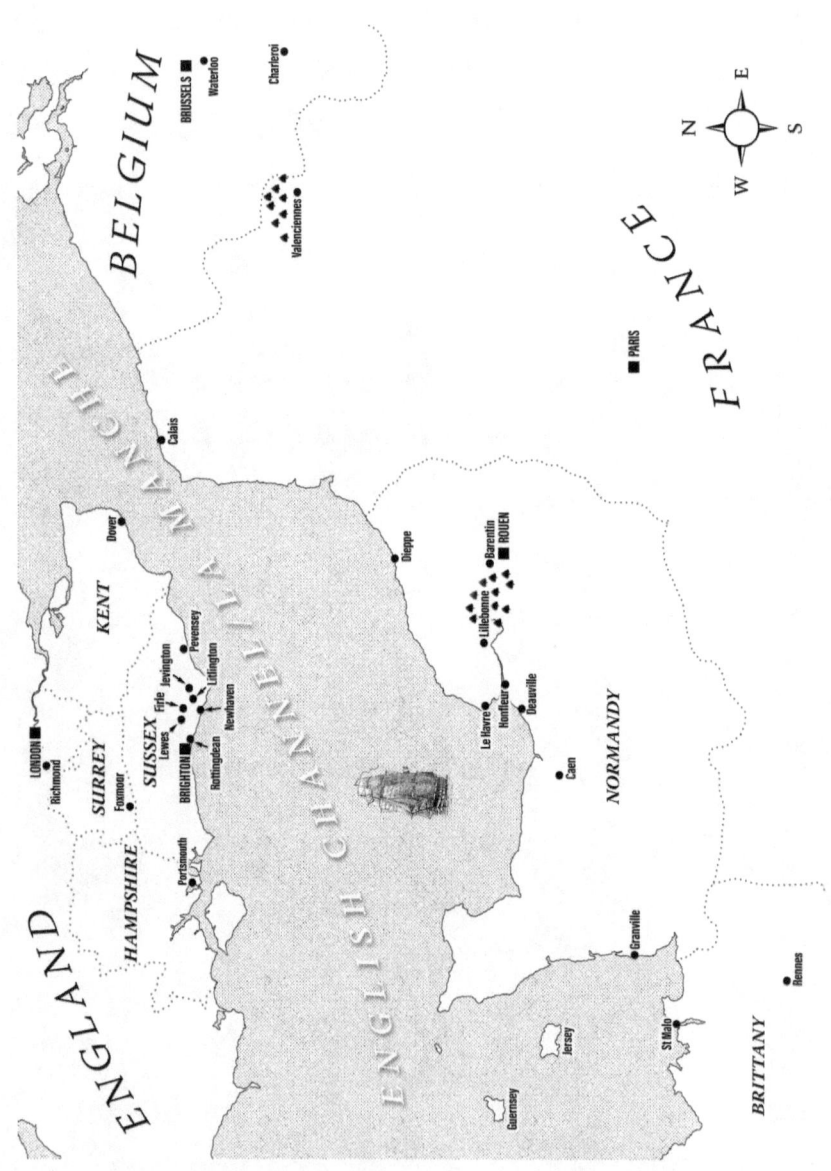

ENGLAND

BELGIUM

FRANCE

LA MANCHE

ENGLISH CHANNEL

BRUSSELS · Waterloo
Charleroi

Valenciennes

PARIS

Calais

Dover

KENT

Dieppe

Barentin · ROUEN

Lillebonne

SUSSEX
Pevensey
Friston · Jevington
Litlington
Newhaven
LONDON
Richmond
SURREY
Lewes
BRIGHTON
Rottingdean
Fanmore

HAMPSHIRE

Portsmouth

Le Havre
Honfleur
Deauville

Caen

NORMANDY

Granville

Rennes

Jersey

St Malo

Guernsey

BRITTANY

N E
W S

Southern France, Spain & Portugal with the
Main Battle Sites of the Peninsular War

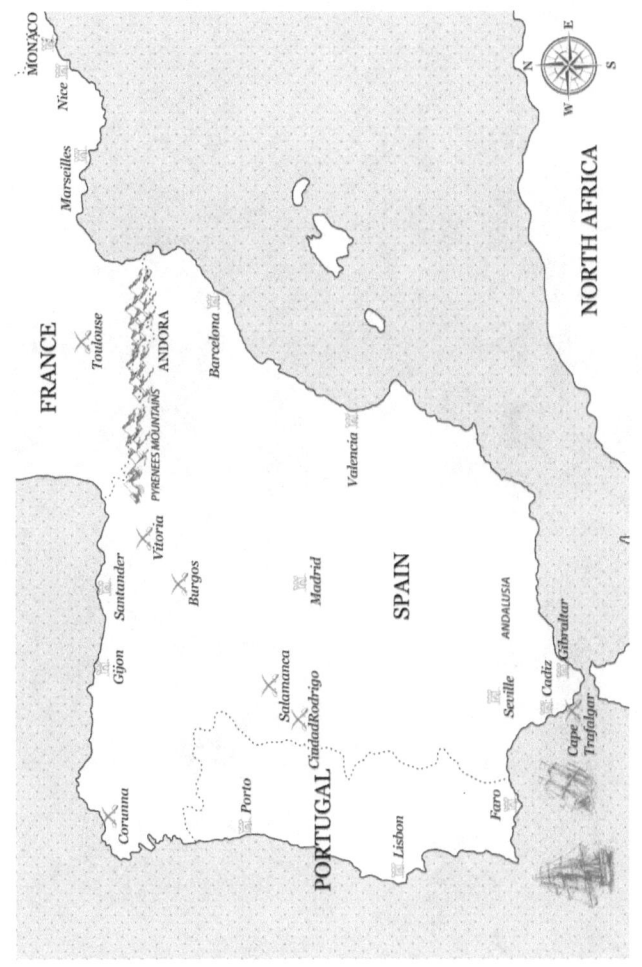

Prologue

La Lionesse - the proprietress of one of London's latest, most select and upmarket gaming saloons sat at a baize table in the main card room, toying with the stem of her glass of white wine and studied him through narrowed eyes.

Nicky. She hadn't seen him in nearly a year and was taken aback by his unexpected appearance at *Le Lion d'Or*. He was wearing his dress uniform, not evening clothes, so that presumably meant he'd been to his barracks and not yet gone back home to Firle House, although she'd been busy doing the accounts at *Le Lion d'Or* all afternoon, so wouldn't have seen him. He looked so handsome, sprawled in his chair and lounging like a predatory lion across from her. The high collar of his braid-trimmed jacket accentuated the tan he'd picked up in the Peninsula; even more sun-dyed blond streaks shone through his light tawny hair, which waved artistically across his forehead, definitely in need of a proper cut and styling. His bewitching golden eyes sparkled as he bantered with his fellow Hussar officers and *La Lionesse* breathed unevenly as she felt a deep curl of unexpected lust spear her belly.

However, despite her overwhelming pleasure and relief to see him safely back in London, sitting in front of her, another part of her was fuming that he'd chosen to go to the barracks and then come straight out on the Town, instead of heading home to see her or his family. As she drank her fill of the sight of him, she determined to teach him a lesson and a dangerous smile curved her lips.

Leaning forward and keeping her voice low and hoarse, the woman wearing the ornate lion mask that covered all her face barring her lips, topped by an ornate wig resembling a large mane, looked around at the group of handsome young officers in their striking uniforms, and her lips curled.

"Puurrrrrrrrr," she growled seductively, curling her fingers into claws to paw the air like a playful cat. "So, Gentlemen, *Le Lion d'Or* is delighted to welcome you to our new establishment. Would you permit me to offer you some wine on the house and join you for a few rounds of cards? I always enjoy entertaining our brave soldiers."

As she expected, they almost fell over themselves in their acceptance and with a flick of her hand, glasses and a couple of freshly opened bottles appeared by their table, along with a sealed pack of cards.

Over the next hour or so, Arabella de Mornay, known by her family and friends as Bella, toyed with them all, ensuring one or other of the group won a round from time to time, while a hovering waitress kept their glasses refilled. So far as she was able, she ensured that Nicky never managed to win anything.

After an hour, as her own glass was being refilled, she whispered some brief instructions in the waitress's ear. Shortly after, in a natural break in the game, a gong sounded and a footman announced a late supper was being served for those who wished to partake of some refreshment. The group rose to their feet to adjourn but, as the table broke up, she put her hand on Nicky's arm to detain him momentarily and whispered in his ear, "I am so sorry you didn't manage to win a round. Perhaps you would care to join me for an opportunity to win back some of your money? Just while your friends go and find some supper, er…unless you are particularly hungry, that is?"

Nicky smiled knowingly at the masked woman. He knew an 'interesting' offer when he heard one, so he merely nodded his head as she put her arm through his and led him off through a curtained doorway, out of the gaming room and away from the gambling throng. Once through the doorway she merely beckoned him to follow her as she made her way down a long corridor and up a couple of flights of stairs, then through into what were obviously her private apartments. As he followed her up the stairs, he watched the lion's tail swing to and fro below her waist as her bottom swayed seductively in front of him. A lecherous smile illuminated his handsome face as he thought his luck had finally changed that evening.

Not sure what to expect as he walked through the doorway, Nicky was slightly taken aback to find himself in a tastefully and luxuriously decorated sitting room where a low fire was burning in the grate of an elaborate fireplace, to keep off the unseasonably cool summer evening chill. Oil lamps and candelabra glowed softly, revealing French Louis XVI furniture, subdued cream curtains and matching furnishings. Through an open alcove into what had obviously been a smaller room at one time, a large desk sat in the window embrasure and overlooked what he presumed to be a courtyard or the street below. Similarly, another open alcove led through to a dining area with more windows and filled with more French furniture. Altogether, the private accommodation was quite large and would be light and airy during the daytime.

As they entered and she closed the door behind him, the masked woman told Nicky to open the bottle of champagne standing in an ice-bucket on the sideboard alongside some glasses, while she went through and cleared the papers on her desk, tidying them into the drawers below. Then she pulled a small card table over towards the fire and indicated to him to bring near two upright armchairs. As he took a seat in one, she went over to an ornate cabinet and took a couple of new packs of cards from a large pile he saw stored inside. She returned to take her place opposite him and for a few seconds they sat and looked at one another. The silence in the room was only marred by the quiet ticking of the beautiful French ormolu clock on the mantelpiece over the fireplace.

Her lips curled in a smile, "*Alors, Monsieur, nous voilà.*" Bella didn't know why she'd addressed him in French, it just popped out and she reminded herself to be careful. "Would you care to introduce yourself? I should like to know with whom I am playing," her voice a hoarse whisper in the quiet room.

"Nicholas de Bresancourt, *à votre service, Madame.*" Nicky stood briefly to click his heels and make an extravagant bow. "So you speak French?" he enquired as he sat down again. "Are you French? Hmmm, I don't somehow think so?" he queried musingly, his head cocked on one side considering her accent, both French and English, both of which everyone else thought perfect, as he raised an enquiring eyebrow at the woman opposite him.

"No, I am not French, I was born here in London, but I do have, ah...French connections; though no love for Bonaparte or erstwhile Revolutionaries, I do assure you. My connections are, were, *emigrés*, from the Revolution you understand, back in the nineties."

"*Emigrés*? I'm glad to hear it," Nicky nodded. "And what should I call you? *Madame? Mademoiselle?*" Nicky's lips slowly curved in a tantalising, questioning smile as he decided there was no obvious ring on the finger of her left hand under her tight glove.

"Call me, *Lionesse*," came the purred response. "Are you French, then?"

"Yes, originally, but I've lived in England virtually all my life, since I was small. I was lucky to escape before the Revolution did its worst."

"Are you an aristocrat?" she asked curiously.

He waved his hand in the air dismissively, "Oh, very minor, nothing to mention, but the fanatics over there in the early nineties weren't fussy whose head they chopped off once they got a grip of the country, as I'm sure you know from your connections."

She was fascinated to hear the dismissal of his ducal title and inference he was nothing more than an insignificant noble. Once more, silence fell on the room as they looked at each other. "Are you going to take your mask off now we' re alone? I like to see who I'm playing against," Nicky finally asked.

"Oh no, I couldn't possibly do that. I never take it off," she purred back.

"Never?" he asked suggestively.

"No, never in public, only when I go to sleep."

"So, you sleep alone then?" he teased.

"Unfortunately, yes," she whispered.

"No current lover or husband?"

"Not at the moment," she replied, almost hesitantly.

Another silent pause. "Well, perhaps I could remedy that? Lovely *Lionesses* should never have to sleep alone." His soft voice crawled over her suggestively as he lounged back, sipping his champagne.

Bella dug her fingernails fiercely into the palms in her lap in an effort to keep her temper. Her husband had just offered to sleep with a strange woman he'd barely known a few hours. He hadn't been back in England even a day, let alone come and see HER. After all, she was only his wife! Her stomach roiled with anger and her brain seethed with the need for revenge and how she could pay him back for his infidelity. She'd originally intended to lure him to her sitting room to gamble further and win as much money from him as she could. Now, however, as she sat in the silent room, watching him watching her, other feelings came into play.

As her emotions see-sawed she felt her rage almost boil over, but at the same time the rational part of her brain was candid enough to acknowledge she'd tricked him into making their marriage real. He'd never wanted nor asked for it and he'd been furious at how she'd trapped him. After all, he'd only offered to marry her in the first place, a few years previously, at extremely short notice, when there'd seemed no other options to facilitate the acquisition of her inheritance. He'd expected the marriage to be quietly annulled as he didn't want a wife, especially not HER. Therefore, how could she realistically blame him for living the life he wanted? Nevertheless, his behaviour still rankled, even if she knew she was being irrational.

The problem, overwhelming everything else, was that she wanted HIM. She'd loved him for a long time, now more than ever. Her relief that he'd safely survived another tour of duty in The Peninsula had almost made her break down and weep when he'd walked in that evening. As it was, she'd hurriedly gone out into the hallway for a few moments to breathe deeply and collect herself from the shock of seeing him so unexpectedly. But this lust, now suddenly engulfing her senses, was a new experience for her. That one brief night, over a year ago, had been an all too short tantalising window to the passion she wanted to share with him. Seeing him again now, sitting opposite her, relaxed, oozing charm and too handsome for his own good, she wanted to have him kiss her, caress her and bring back those sensations he'd aroused in her before, those regrettably unconsummated feelings. Her restless dreams were nothing to the reality facing her. She wanted to reach out and touch him, feel his hard body next to hers, experiment with everything she'd read about but had yet to experience.

Bella mentally shook herself as she tried to get a grip on her emotions and decide what to do. She took another sip of champagne and watched him look at her expectantly, waiting for her answer; then the germ of a wicked idea crept into her mind and leaning forward, she tipped her head to one side and answered him.

"*Eh bien, Milor,* Nicholas," the lips curled below the mask, "I have a proposition for you." She picked up the pack of cards and started to peel off the wrapping. Opposite her, Nicky's eyes flashed and his indolent posture changed to one more alert as he sat up.

"We shall play cards. Then, I will see how tired I am." She shrugged her shoulders suggestively and licked her lips, knowing he was watching her closely. "Why do you not undo your jacket, take off your neckcloth and make yourself more comfortable, hmmm?" She appeared all polite yet seductive complaisance.

Slowly, his eyes never leaving her masked face, Nicky shrugged off his pelisse and unpicked the gold-braided clasps and hooks until the stiff Hussar jacket was open half-way down. Bella could see a fine white linen shirt revealed beneath and she watched as he slowly unwound his neckcloth. In response, she slowly pulled off the long, elbow-length gloves she was wearing, the fingers of which had designs on which made them resemble lion claws. Her costume was nothing if not appropriate and intriguing, tantalising and yet classy, as befitting the owner of the establishment.

"Now then, how much would you be willing to wager against me?" she whispered as she tapped her beautifully buffed and manicured fingernails on the tabletop. "Unlike downstairs, there is no limit up here."

Nicky looked at her again. "A thousand guineas? Would that suit you?" His words were like a caress.

Bella was stunned. She didn't think he could afford to lose so much money, but of course, she mused, she didn't know him well at all these days and had no idea what he'd been doing over the past few years. No idea, to be specific, if he'd made any money, in addition to his army pay, to bolster the small income he received from his holdings in the East and West Indies and Americas, carefully nurtured and grown by his stepfather, her own father. But, still, that wager wasn't what she'd expected at all. After his offer to sleep with her and the lascivious way he'd been eyeing her, she'd thought he'd offer a different type of wager altogether. She wondered what he was playing at. So she looked back at him and allowed her lips to pout seductively, "I have a better, more interesting proposal for you; money is so boring after all," she bantered back.

Nicky's lips curved into a wicked smile. He knew it, she wasn't interested in money; she wanted him. Deep down, he breathed a sigh of relief. A thousand guinea wager was way beyond what he could afford to lose, but as always, he'd gone with his gut-instinct, which was rarely wrong, especially where women were concerned. This was definitely going to be an interesting evening.

Bella took a deep breath and continued, "If you win, *Milor*, I shall pay you a thousand guineas, but if I win, you may grant me a little favour."

Nicky looked back at her, smiling, almost but not quite smirking. "And what sort of favour would that be, *Lionesse*?"

"Oh, I don't quite know at this instant, but I am sure I shall think of something. An evening at Vauxhall perhaps? A picnic in the country? Perhaps a visit to the Menagerie and the lions in the Tower? I think you could be quite amusing company and, regrettably, I do not have the opportunity to get out much." She spoke slowly, precisely and politely, doing her best to disguise her voice and usual manner of speaking to him, her family and close friends, when she normally gabbled on nineteen to the dozen.

She hadn't been able to resist the quip about the lions in the Tower of London. It had been a longstanding family joke about Nicky's obsession with the wretched creatures when he was a little boy. Until he was about ten or eleven, he'd driven his adoptive relations mad, insisting on visiting the place over and over again, endlessly fascinated by the big cats which were inextricably linked to his family name and coat of arms. She watched his face and knew that wasn't what he was expecting; she laughed to herself and waited for his response.

Nicky was slightly taken aback as he hadn't been expecting something so innocuous. He gazed at the woman opposite him and wondered again what she looked like. Her figure was perfect, just as he preferred in a woman. Tall and slender, full but not too full in the right places and her smooth expanse of skin, exposed in the almost shoulder-baring, empire line dress, looked soft and creamy and without any blemish. He longed to touch it and explore her body further. There was something suggestively sensuous about her in the elegant way she moved and carried herself and he thought again momentarily of the swinging tail on the back of her gold-coloured dress.

He narrowed his eyes as he contemplated her more closely. She wasn't very old, he was sure; he wondered what she was doing running an establishment like a gaming saloon. All he could see of her face were her lips. Deep pink, ripe and luscious. He felt himself harden slightly as he wondered what it would be like to kiss them, or to feel them on his body. He shook himself and forced his mind to pay attention. Even though he couldn't see her eyes nor her expression under the slits of her encompassing lion mask, he could have sworn she was considering an offer to take him to bed; not to go to the Tower of London or on a damn picnic. But the night was young and the prospect of winning a thousand guineas off her was also worthy of his best concentration. He hadn't been very lucky so far this evening, but as he'd suspected when he'd followed her up the stairs, his luck had turned. It had been quite a while since he'd bedded an Englishwoman, or any woman for that matter – and he was up for it.

"Very well, *Lionesse*, I accept. Shall we start?"

Bella smiled at his easy acceptance and handed a pack over to him to cut the cards to see who would deal. A consummate gambler at one time, her father had taught them both to play chess, draughts, dominoes and backgammon as children, as well as all sorts of card and dice games, saying it would help them think in different ways and train their brains. Although Nicky was a competent if conservative player, never reckless in his gambling, he lacked the extraordinary instant memory and ability to calculate the odds rapidly that both she and her father had, so he'd never managed to beat either of them. Not that anyone had ever beaten her Papa. In fact, other than herself, the only person who'd ever come close was her Great Aunt Elizabeth, her Uncle Francis's grandmother. She'd been trying for over twenty years and although now extremely old and very ill, she still muttered about beating him before she died.

She kept Nicky's glass filled with champagne but was abstemious in her own consumption to keep her mind alert. After an hour's play, he undid the rest of his jacket and took a long drink. All was quiet in the room as they both concentrated. The logs in the fireplace popped occasionally, just staving off the chill of a cool summer night; the clock ticked and periodically tinkling chimes broke the silence. After another hour, he sat back and looked at her. He'd won a mere handful of rounds and knew he was never going to beat her that night. He'd watched her deal and play, but was sure she hadn't been cheating and a surreptitious, close inspection of the cards revealed no hidden nicks or marks.

Nicky concluded Lady Luck was not on his side after all, so he might as well give in gracefully and kiss his thousand guineas goodbye. Still, he reflected thankfully, he hadn't lost more than a few guineas downstairs earlier in the evening. He laughed to himself as he couldn't miss what he'd never had in the first place. Now he was in the army and serving abroad, the other little money-making sidelines he'd quietly indulged in before joining up, those which relied on his good looks had perforce fallen by the wayside and his income was constrained, to put it mildly. He sighed to himself at the loss of that little income stream but reminded himself it would be easy to pick up again once this interminable war was over and he returned to London permanently.

Bella sat back and smiled like a cat in front of a bowl of cream. Nicky was always so easy to beat at cards, she almost felt sorry for him. But now, she licked her lips and put her mind to a much bigger gamble. Could she pull it off? The odds on that would require somewhat different skills to card counting and calculating. She looked over at him as he tipped the remainder of his glass of champagne down his throat and then lolled back indolently in his chair, watching her and laughing. He now looked like a large, recumbent lion and her belly somersaulted as desire coursed through her. She wondered what he was laughing at.

"Why are you laughing? Did I miss something here?" she tilted her head to one side.

"Not at all, I was just thinking of all the things I could do with a thousand guineas."

She sat forward, concerned, "Oh dear, are you in debt? Did you lose much downstairs? That's why we have a limit here."

He laughed, "No, no, nothing like that. I'm not quite destitute, yet. Though I think I might well be if I played cards with you for any length of time."

Bella laughed back at him, "Oh no, you were just unlucky, *Milor*. Sometimes the cards simply do not go your way," she shrugged.

Nicky looked back at her assessingly. "Somehow, I think there was slightly more than my bad luck going on here. You're quite some player for a woman, but then, you own this." He waved his hand around. "I suppose it's to be expected." Amusedly, he shook his head and held out his glass, "Shall we finish off the champagne and you can tell me what I owe you?"

She tipped the remains of the bottle into his glass, trying to speak nonchalantly, "Let me make a suggestion, *Milor*. I shall get another bottle, you may go and, ah, refresh yourself and meanwhile, I will ponder over my little favour."

Nicky rose, tipped his head politely towards her and sauntered over towards the door, pausing as she said, "You will find a closet at the end of the corridor, or go back downstairs if you wish a breath of air. I'm afraid it is rather warm up here but I lit the fire as the last couple of evenings have been a trifle chilly when I've come to bed in the early hours and I wasn't expecting to entertain visitors…"

As soon as he disappeared through the doorway, Bella shot to her feet and rushed through to her adjacent bedroom suite with its own small sitting area, dressing room and bathing room. Glancing hurriedly around, she made sure any incriminating evidence – the precious painting of her father and mother, any odd ornaments he might recognise – were hastily thrust into the back of an armoire in her dressing room. The bare wall without the picture looked a trifle odd but she could always say the painting normally there was being cleaned or replaced, if he did mention it. Then she rushed through to her bathing room and water closet to refresh and tidy herself and rummage through a large chest of drawers for a particular item she wanted, leaving it on the top. Hurriedly straightening the bed as she raced past, she went back into her sitting room and the cork on a new bottle of champagne had just popped out when he sauntered in again.

Acting for all the world as if she'd spent the past minutes idly waiting for him and not stressing over whether she could carry out her outrageous plan, she poured them both a fresh glass of champagne and raised hers in a toast. "Rawrrrrrr," she growled softly, "better luck next time?" and she tilted her head. Although she owned two gaming saloons, this enormous and risky private gamble was going to be the biggest of her life, *if* she could pull it off. Games of chance she was an expert at, what she was about now needed experience and expertise that she seriously and unfortunately lacked.

"To a better player, I think," he winked back at her and sat back in his chair, waiting for her next move.

He hadn't bothered to do up his heavy regimental jacket and as he lounged back, watching her and waiting, his eyes sparkling and full of expectation, Bella stared at the tanned column of his throat and let her eyes wander down to where his fine, soft shirt was now open at the neck, giving a tantalising glimpse of the hard chest beneath with its fine covering of tawny, sun-bleached hair. She licked her lips as her mouth suddenly went dry, but taking a deep breath she sat forward and steepled her fingers under her chin as she spoke softly and hoarsely.

"So, *Milor*, Nicholas. I have been considering what sort of little favour you could do for me."

Nicky didn't move. At last she was finally getting to it, he thought, smiling to himself, noting the slight tension in her shoulders and the way she bit her lip anxiously before she started speaking. In his line of work, watching someone's body language was critical as well as listening to what they were saying. It had saved him from all kinds of mishaps and miscalculations, learning the hard way sometimes. So, although he gave an outward appearance of relaxed indolence, drinking his champagne, he was watching her every move extremely closely, including any expression he could see under the bottom of the mask. He had been all evening; that was why he was positive she hadn't been cheating. He was surprised at her nervousness; owning a gaming establishment such as this, he'd presumed she was a woman of the world and would have no hesitation in asking for whatever she wanted; such as a new lover, him hopefully; but obviously not. She was intriguing. He therefore sat patiently, waiting.

"I thought about going to Vauxhall," she started to muse, "but in reality, although I love fireworks, I do so hate the crowds. Then I thought about a picnic and, don't get me wrong, I love the countryside, even the seaside, but the weather has to be right and it has been unseasonably cold and wet lately. And then there are the lions, but I am informed they are quite old and mangy now. Of course, I HAVE seen an elephant... and when one has seen one elephant," she languidly waved her hand in the air, "one has seen them all."

He couldn't help it, Nicky laughed out loud at her droll humour. Dear God, he wondered, how long was she going to string him out like this? He wanted to take her to bed, right then and there, to rip that damn mask off her face so he could look into her eyes when he touched her and kissed those tempting lips, to find out what colour her hair was under that mane of a wig. He'd been taking bets on that with himself all night. But he controlled his lustful urges and continued to sit patiently.

"So," Bella continued softly, "I can live without fireworks and crowds, countryside and picnics, lions and elephants...but tonight," she leaned forward towards him as she growled seductively again, then purred, "I do not think I can live without YOU." She reached out her hand across the table to grasp one side of his jacket and pull him towards her. "YOU, *Monsieur* de Bresancourt, are my favour!" she finally whispered as she took hold of one of his hands, pulled it to her lips and placed a moist kiss in the palm, letting her tongue run a little circle round it for just a brief moment.

Why the hell did he think she was nervous, he wondered, sensing his whole body jump as if it had been hit by lightning at the feel of her lips and tongue on his palm.

Bella felt the sparks course between them too. She momentarily sat still, watching Nicky as if stunned, his hand still grasped in hers. Then, without a word, she picked up the bottle of champagne, slowly rose to her feet and strolled over to open a closed door at the other end of the sitting room. He could see it led through to a bedroom suite. As she walked through, he watched the swishing tail as she subtly wiggled her bottom, then she half turned her head to look over her shoulder seductively and lifted one hand, crooking her index finger to beckon him to follow. Nicky needed no second invitation. Card games might be *Lionesse's* forte, but this was now his territory and he was a consummate expert. Picking up the two glasses he rose and strode after the mysterious and tantalising woman…

Chapter One

The fast British naval sloop made its way out of Portsmouth and through the western reaches of the English Channel, It headed around the Brittany peninsula and then headed south towards the northern Spanish coast, rolling through the choppy waters of the Bay of Biscay.

A tall, striking-looking man was standing on the deck in his shirt-sleeves, lost in his reflections as he stared across the endless blue horizon towards France, his birthplace, the strong sea breeze blowing his thick tawny hair around his head. Nicholas Antoine de Bresancourt, *Duc de Valenciennes*. It was a title he rarely, if ever used; partly because it was French and his adopted country had been at war with France for years, and partly because it was an empty one since there were no longer estates with tenants to care for them, a grand chateau with servants, and certainly no family fortune to go with the dukedom of which he was the last direct heir in a long line.

There had been '*Lions de Valenciennes*' – tall, strong, independent noblemen with their unusual tawny colouring which gave them their

nickname – at Valenciennes, in the region known as Hainault, since before the Hundred Years War with England. The Baron de Bresancourt at the time had earned a reward and his grander designation for helping Joan of Arc and the French army lift the Siege of Orleans in 1429, thereby defeating the hated enemy from across *La Manche*, the English Channel. It had been the turning point in the long war and finally enabled Charles VII to be crowned King in Rheims, who duly expressed his gratitude to his various loyal nobles with their personal units of fighting men, noblemen such as Geoffrey de Bresancourt.

Thereafter, the de Bresancourt *Ducs* revelled in their elevated aristocratic title, indulging their vanity by embellishing and extending the small but beautiful family chateau and surrounding fertile estates in the remote countryside of north-east France. This was despite the fact that Valenciennes itself was not officially part of France's domain at the time, given the city and region's location on the borders of the Southern Netherlands.

Over the centuries the area had sustained many overlords, but the de Bresancourts were only concerned with protecting themselves and making enough money to maintain their lifestyle and holdings, and generally kept their heads down, out of local politics, religious conflicts and sundry small civil wars which were rife in France at the time between the competing royal heirs to the throne; they tried to avoid attention unless it was to their financial advantage. To keep their chateau, lands and independence safe from marauders or other envious nobles and overlords, the early Barons had always maintained their own small but capable fighting force and would occasionally offer them as mercenaries if the payment was enough recompense and they weren't needed at home. This practice finally reaped its reward at Orleans where Geoffrey de Bresancourt accepted a Dukedom in lieu of monetary reward for his assistance, and gambled that Charles VII of Valois would assert his dominance over his Burgundian cousins, who were overlords of Hainault at the time and become king. Geoffrey loathed the Burgundians and suspected them of being behind the mysterious death of his father and coveting the de Bresancourt lands. His gamble paid off and the family never looked back.

After the armies of Louis XIV finally conquered the city in 1677 and the area was incorporated into northern France, the *Ducs de Valenciennes* began to attend Court and thereafter spent most of their time enjoying the delights of Versailles. They continued to ensure the family fortunes were kept well topped-up to finance their lives of luxury and pleasure by marrying wives with large dowries, trying to find tall, blonde and beautiful ones if possible, to match their own stature and appearance and thereby pass these traits on to their progeny. Down the years, the strategy worked well as the de Bresancourt men continued to sport their unusual colouring and good looks to go with their title. They left the toiling, poor tenants and peasants on the ducal estates to maintain them, thereby supporting their sybaritic lifestyles, with little regard for their wellbeing or welfare.

Unfortunately, this disregard contributed to their downfall and the seething peasants took their revenge when Antoine de Bresancourt fell victim, along with his family, to a venal and cunning Government official who was taking advantage of the upheaval caused by the Revolution in 1789. He hauled the family off to prison on trumped-up charges of 'treason' in an attempt to appropriate the famed Valenciennes golden fortune for himself. The starving and downtrodden peasants all cheered when they heard the proud, disdainful Duke and his selfish, uncaring wife were dead and ransacked the beautiful chateau until it was a virtual ruin and the estate was left to rot. Thereafter, the lands were seized by the Revolutionary government and the de Bresancourt family faded into distant memory, unloved and unmissed. No one knew nor cared what had happened to any of them, including the small, only son of the Duke whom most assumed had died in prison along with his parents.

Of course, Fate had intervened and Nicholas Antoine de Bresancourt was still very much alive and carried the striking stature and looks of his forebears. He had escaped, purely by chance, and was adopted by a kind and loving family who brought him up in England, safe from all the horrors the Revolution had wrought on his fellow French aristocrats. Now, ironically, he had chosen to fight in this current War for the other side, for England, France's historical and hated enemy.

Nicky gripped the ship's rail as the vessel ploughed through the swell and tossing waves, sunlight glinting on the gold signet ring on his little finger with its rampant lion coat of arms. His mind kept going over the events of the previous week in London. His unexpected and strange 'affaire' with the owner of the gaming saloons seemed quite surreal, bizarre even, but as his hand strayed up to the open neck of his shirt, he felt the loss of his precious lion necklace keenly. His last remaining link with the father he barely remembered before he'd escaped from the forbidding fortress prison where they'd been incarcerated and tortured.

He also missed her. *La Lionesse.* There was something about her that had connected to a deep part of him and he knew he'd not forget her any time soon. The passion they'd shared had been stunning and surprising. He would simply have to find her when he got back to London because he wanted her for himself, irrespective of what she looked like, his mysterious, faceless lover. He knew if he had the time it wouldn't be too difficult to find out who she was. Yet again, he cursed that he'd had so little opportunity in London and that he'd also been forced to leave so abruptly. He cursed Bonaparte and the wretched War that had ruined or interfered with so many lives across all of Europe, not just in England.

Nicky thought back to the private conversation he'd shared with his uncle about his unwanted marriage and his desire for an annulment or divorce, with his promise to think about if he genuinely wanted it arranged. He'd been so certain, he hadn't needed to think too hard. Now he just felt confused. He decided to put the subject out of his mind for a while and return to it in a few weeks' time, when he'd calmed down and could rationalise more sensibly and logically.

Sighing, he closed his eyes and raised his face to the sunshine, feeling the hot rays warm his skin. Unbidden, a picture crawled into his mind of a faceless woman in a short, gold-coloured lace shift, long black wavy hair streaming down her body. It was going to be a long time before he forgot her.

Finally, the sleek ship hove to in a deserted cove on the northern Spanish coast near the fishing village of Gijón, not far from the port at Santander. A lone man made his way ashore in the dead of night in a small longboat. As he waded through the inky, rippling shallows to the beach, carrying his boots to keep them dry along with a well-worn portmanteau, the strap of a heavy leather document bag slung across his chest, the longboat quickly disappeared back into the darkness. It returned to its mother ship, with every light doused to avoid detection, only the hint of moonlight between the scudding clouds outlining its ghostly shape in the shadows. Then, as quietly as it had appeared, the sloop hauled anchor and pulled out to sea again to continue its journey south to the safety of its Portuguese destination.

From the beach, the man, keeping his eyes peeled constantly for marauding bands of Frenchmen or Spanish guerrillas, headed inland to find a horse and then made his careful way south across country, to find and rendezvous with Wellington's camp which he'd discovered was currently somewhere near Salamanca.

Arthur Wellesley, lately elevated from Viscount to Earl of Wellington following the splendid British victory at *Ciudad Rodrigo* in January 1812, was now playing cat and mouse with Marmont's French army, which was located in the vicinity. The two opposing forces had been harrying each other for weeks as the French tried to repeatedly threaten Wellington's supply line.

Having made his way through the British encampment, the man handed over the urgent dispatches and other confidential documents he was carrying to Wellington's Chief of Staff, then met the Commander of the British Forces himself in his tent for a quiet conversation a couple of hours later. Wellington was seated at a small desk, reading through various reports, maps scattered across most of its surface. He leaned back, steepling his hands under his chin as the courier, who wasn't just a courier, entered and bowed; he was not wearing a uniform despite being a British officer.

"So, de Bresancourt, you've seen Ashcroft, I understand?" queried Wellington, looking at the younger man assessingly down his aquiline nose.

"Yes, Sir, he has concerns about the gold shipments from Rothschild and the activities of certain French agents who are now operating here in Spain."

"Quite so," murmured Wellington, "quite so. He seems to think you can ensure the safety of our next delivery and deal with these vermin?"

His visitor coughed, the expectations of this aristocratic man and the mysterious Ashcroft back in Whitehall in London looming hard over him. "I will do my best, Sir," he muttered.

"Quite so, quite so," Wellington repeated. "We expect nothing less. Have you any intelligence as to where these men are currently located?"

"Just before I left London, Ashcroft received word the particular man I'm after was possibly spotted near Madrid, so I intend to head off in that direction as soon as I'm able and see what information I can gather. However, whether it actually was him remains to be seen, given his description appears to cover half the male population of Spain, as in slim, light olive skin, dark haired with dark eyes." He tried not to sound facetious, merely hoping to keep Wellington's expectations at a manageable level.

"I see," Wellington mused thoughtfully. "Well, there's going to be a battle soon, here or hereabouts. Marmont's moving his troops around trying to outmanoeuvre us as well as cause supply problems, so I was considering pulling back towards the Portuguese border again. However, I have his measure, simply need an opportunity to turn and fight. I suggest you wait here for a few days and see what other intelligence comes in. Then, if we do fight and can rout Marmont, it will be an ideal opportunity for you to make your way towards Madrid while they regroup. I want to reach Madrid myself; it'll put the wind up the French and upset Bonaparte."

He paused, then mused again, "I personally think he's made a grave mistake going east. He crossed the Neman in June while you were away in London and the Russians won't be the pushover he obviously thinks they are." Wellington took a considering breath, then looked directly at the other man. "But that's not my problem at the moment, the Tsar can deal with him if he gets too near Moscow. Marmont, Soult, Joseph and Suchet are my problem, and pushing the French out of the Peninsula, once and for all. Your problem is dealing with the French agents undermining our efforts and threatening the Spanish, also ensuring the gold we need gets through."

Nicky looked back at the man opposite him thoughtfully. "If you don't mind, Sir, I'd rather make my way towards Madrid now, or in a day or two. Time is of the essence and if you beat the French and head that way yourself, my man may well disappear. Vague though my lead may be, I don't want to lose any opportunity to pick up his trail. He could decide to lay low for a while, but if I DO manage to locate him, at least I can find out who he's working with. Stealing a gold shipment will need quite a few accomplices and no little planning."

"Hmmm, quite so. Maybe that would be a better idea after all. But you'd best be careful, the French are everywhere at the moment between here and Madrid."

"Yes, I know, Sir, but I'll keep my head down, you can rest assured." He smiled carefully, "When is the next shipment due by the way, do you know?"

"I'm not sure, to be frank," replied Wellington. "Within the next couple of months. In time to pay the men and the Spaniards, to keep both happy over the winter."

"Very well; at least that gives me a bit of time to find some of my contacts and make enquiries."

The two men continued to talk intently for a short while concerning Wellington's campaign strategy and Nicky's plans to work undercover and how he could get urgent messages through, if necessary, should he find himself on the wrong side of the French army. Finally, he stood up and with a quick bow, headed towards the tent exit. As he lifted the flap he turned and grinned at Wellington. "See you in Madrid then, My Lord. I hear the *tabernas* and *señoritas* are quite delightful: nice wine, black hair, dark flashing eyes..."

Wellington merely gave him an icy stare and shook his head at the young man's frivolity. He didn't know him well but had received excellent reports of his undercover and liaison work with the Spanish rebels and had met him a couple of times previously to discuss that and get his views on a couple of matters relating to their Spanish and Portuguese allies. He'd received a separate message from Ashcroft about the man and his mission; he wondered about Ashcroft's assessment of the young officer. Charming, good looking, subtly facetious to Authority and with a devil-may-care attitude; he was apparently also proud and extremely bitter about those in France who had deprived him of his birthright. Ashcroft was concerned that he was not unemotional or ruthless enough to kill anyone who got in his way, no matter who they were, when he had to cover his tracks. Dead men told no tales in this line of work when few could be trusted. However, he seemed intelligent and could speak French and Spanish like a native, so that was his real asset for working undercover. Wellington had a high opinion of Lord Miles Ashcroft and his agents, also the work of his anonymous Department; not least, he was invariably and uncannily right in his assessment of men's characters and capabilities.

Nicholas de Bresancourt was an odd mixture, thought Wellington, as he watched the tawny-haired man depart, but he'd proved his worth many times over during the past couple of years on Army missions near or even behind enemy lines. Also, apparently cleverer, more innocuous-looking men, Ashcroft's usual type of undercover agent, hadn't made much progress in dealing with that Bernheim creature, so maybe this humorous charmer could do better. Wellington pondered as he stared at the tent flap. He, too, was generally a good judge of character and suspected the officer had hidden depths and might well come good. He had often seen men cover their intelligence, or a ruthless and determined persona, with a veneer of playful idiocy, humour and indolence, so maybe de Bresancourt was the same? Wellington was prepared to give him the benefit of the doubt. He and Ashcroft had no other choice and there was a lot at stake.

Chapter Two

Back in his quarters, Nicky retrieved a pack of cheroots and a couple of flagons of local wine and strolled off outside the camp to find a peaceful spot to think about his options and what to do next.

Nicholas de Bresancourt, the displaced French *Duc de Valenciennes*, currently an officer in a British Army Hussar regiment but now 're-assigned' and under orders from 'The Department of Information', had the latest information on the whereabouts of one Reynard, a wily gypsy clan chief, long time and trusted associate of some of the older members of his adoptive family back in London. Especially his mentor and friend, Francis Granville, Duke of Firle, a man who was more like a wise older brother to him now than someone he'd called 'uncle' when he'd been a little boy. Now, as he meandered along, Nicky thought about the usefulness of paying the gypsy a visit. Unfortunately, he was currently nowhere near Madrid, indeed he was far to the east, close to the coast and Nicky was unsure if he would have any useful information to make the dangerous journey there worthwhile.

Having found himself an ideal quiet and deserted spot, Nicky sat down under the intermittent shade of a withered olive tree, the hot afternoon sun percolating through its dry, wilted foliage. He kicked off his boots and undid the lacings of his shirt as the heat and hot dry wind raised a soft sheen of sweat across his body. He uncorked a flagon and swigged from it, periodically lighting and smoking a cheroot. He contemplated his pale-coloured feet and his tanned hands, knowing he'd have to remedy that contrast if he was going to be taken for a swarthy, native Spaniard and he grinned to himself. Slouching back against the tree trunk, he let the warm wine relax him and his mind drifted over his situation and his mission. Eventually, the heat and effects of the wine made him drowsy and with his strategy now formulated, he let his eyes close and sleep take over.

His last thoughts were of a faceless woman with her long, curling black hair and wicked smile, a woman who'd knocked him sideways during his quick visit to London a few weeks before. *Lionesse.* He didn't know her real name, nor what she looked like, but she'd still affected him more than any other woman he'd ever known; he had no idea why.

The following morning Nicky called on Major George Scovell, an officer of the British Army's Intelligence Branch, gifted linguist and codebreaker for Wellington. Scovell was in charge of a motley assortment of men whose task it was to intercept and decipher messages sent between the French forces. Although no codebreaker, Nicky's linguistic skills had brought him to Scovell's attention. From time to time, he'd been called upon to help the man and his little team, responsible for stealing messages from couriers and small forces of French troops he had helped ambush whilst working with bands of local Spanish partisans and guerrillas. They were harassing the enemy wherever they could as part of the Allied mission to force the French out of Spain. Various ribald greetings were thrown at Nicky as he strolled into their tent and he spent a useful fifteen minutes with Scovell getting an overview on where the man and his team thought the outlying bands of French might be lurking on the main roads between Salamanca and Madrid.

Armed with this information and some detailed maps of the area,

Nicky packed up some food and drink in a knapsack and disappeared off to another quiet, remote place on the nearby riverbank, well away from the encampment. Having found a peaceful, sandy spot, right by the river's edge, he stripped off his clothes completely and lay down in the hot sunshine to toast his whole body, periodically turning over like a hog on a spit, relieved by a breeze from the nearby river and then escaping into the cooling water or to a shady area not far off when the heat of the strong Spanish sun got too much. He studied his maps and started to plan a circuitous route which would take him to Madrid via assorted villages and hamlets where he hoped to glean information about the man he sought, or discover the whereabouts of any marauding French units he needed to avoid.

Nicky repeated this pattern for the next few days, calling in to Scovell's tent on his way out to check if there was updated intelligence on enemy movements. As he lay almost comatose under the sun, he either slept or let his mind rove over his other problems and what had happened during those few eventful days on his last, hasty visit to London. It had impacted on him in so many ways. Not just the woman he'd briefly become involved with, but the mysterious man who had recruited him to work for his Department in Whitehall, adjacent to the Ministry of War, clearly not remotely resembling the inane name it operated under; the man who had given him information about an individual which had stunned him. As Nicky had reflected during his brief voyage on the ship back down to Spain, everything about that week seemed slightly surreal; except it was real, very real…

Chapter Three

Inside the bedroom of her private apartment above the gaming rooms on the ground floor, Bella felt as if some other person had taken over her mind and body. Her pulse was racing, her heart was thumping and she felt like a totally different woman: alive, aware, lustful; wanton, even. She could feel heat pooling and pulsing between her legs at the excitement of what she was doing. It was a heady and unaccustomed feeling and all because of the man now following her.

She sat down on one side of the bed: a large, ornate, gilded four-poster set up on a dais, decorated with cream voile and silken hangings. It was a very feminine boudoir. Champagne in hand, she patted the space next to her. Nicky joined her, held out the two glasses he was carrying and she filled them. Putting the bottle down on the nightstand, she raised her glass to him once again. "To my favour. Tell me, *Milor* Nicholas, do you make love better than you play cards?" she purred teasingly.

Nicky's eyes roved her body as the tip of one tantalising finger traced a slow line down her neck, across her collarbone and roamed to the valley between her breasts. His lips curved amorously as he felt her shiver. "That's for me to know and you to find out. You can tell me in the morning," he whispered seductively as he leaned his head forward to plant a light, moist kiss at the base of her neck. She felt his tongue tickle her skin and Bella gasped as a frisson jolted its way straight down to her belly.

"My, my, *Chérie*, you're very responsive," he leaned forward to nibble her neck again, leaving a trail of seductive kisses down and across her collarbone. She gave a purring moan and arched her head back. "Mmmmm," he muttered. "You taste like strawberries and cream. I've been wondering all night, do you taste as delicious as this all over?"

Bella felt her face flame under the mask as her body went hot and cold at his suggestive words and she had to put her glass down before she spilled its contents. Nicky leaned past her to put his glass next to hers before starting to investigate the strings of her mask and the thick wig.

Quickly, she pulled his hands away and turned to face him. "Oh no, I told you, you can't do that," she whispered. "Remember, I never take it off in public."

"But we're not in public now, *Chérie*," he spoke softly. "How can I make love to you properly with your mask on and all those feathers and whiskers, not to mention your wig?" He grinned at her wickedly then leaned down to whisper in her ear, "And besides, I want to see your eyes when I make you climax...every time." Nibbling her earlobe, his hands crept upwards towards the mask strings once more as he heard her gasp at his words.

Bella scrambled up the bed away from him, her heart pounding. Momentarily stunned by his words, she realised she didn't know this Nicky at all. She was used to brotherly teasing and taunts, shared jokes, childhood adventures and challenges, someone she could confide in and a shoulder to cry on when needed. Five years her senior, her stepbrother had first been her playmate, then girlish crush, then her hero – and now, as he approached his late twenties, he was her ideal and perfect man. However, this amorous and obviously experienced lothario was something else; dangerous, quite lethal to women, she decided. Sensual, disarming charm oozed from his pores; his mere touch made her skin burn, she couldn't think straight when he looked at her and, he still hadn't kissed her properly yet. She cast her mind back to when he'd kissed her before. She'd thought then it was wonderful, intoxicating, had made her heart feel like it was bursting with love for him. But they'd been mere innocent kisses at Christmas under the mistletoe. Even when he'd taken her virginity, he'd been so deadly drunk he hadn't kissed her properly. Now, she just knew, when he kissed her she would quite possibly go up in flames.

For a moment, she wondered if she should simply take off her mask and reveal herself to him – but she knew if she did, apart from his anger at being tricked again, he'd run a mile and she wouldn't see him for dust. This was her chance to have him to herself for a night, satisfy her bedroom curiosity and lust; she'd worry about talking to him sensibly about their marriage when he came home officially the following day. Decision reached, she took his hands in hers and took a deep breath. "I cannot possibly let you see me, that would never do," she tutted mischievously in the put-on, careful, low and husky voice she'd adopted all evening. "But if you want to make love to me – after all, you lost, so it is MY favour – you have to do it my way or not at all and I promise, I will take my mask off. So," she breathed seductively, "*Milor* Nicholas de Bresancourt, *oui ou non*? Yes, or no?"

He was fascinated, he couldn't help himself. One minute the seductive wanton, the next it was as if she was almost frightened of him, but he had no idea why. She'd tied him up in knots for sure, but one taste of her skin and he knew he had to have her. Her response to his playful kiss on her neck had been stunning, so what would she be like once he had her naked in his arms? There was no other possible reply, "The answer is *oui*, yes, *absolument, bien sur*; absolutely, of course *Lionesse*, whatever you want. *Ce sera mon plaisir*, it will be my pleasure, yours too, I promise." He picked up one of her hands and kissed it on the knuckles, then over on her palm, then on the inside of her wrist and then gradually, tantalising butterfly kisses up her arm until he reached her elbow. "Oh, by the way, my family, friends...and lovers," he winked enticingly at her, "call me, Nicky." The mixture of whispered, seductive French and English in the accent she knew he was deliberately putting on and the saucy wink, was completely irresistible.

Bella sat back against the pillows, almost overcome with how much she wanted him. Her arm still burned where he'd kissed it and she felt out of her depth, in uncharted sexual territory. He was sitting, watching her, waiting for her to say something and she blurted out first thing that popped into her head, "Come on then, take your clothes off and let me see what favour I'm getting." The carefully modulated, ladylike language had vanished; the saucy, sometimes bossy little girl in plaits she used to be had taken over, but she was so bemused, her demand unintentionally emerged in a husky whisper, enticing and sensually inviting.

Her words were music to his ears; this was his game and he was a master at it, just as she was a master at card games. Nicky smiled knowingly at the masked woman and stood up to comply. They were now seriously getting down to business, he decided, determined to give her exactly what she obviously wanted, and more. Enticing, seducing, entertaining and amusing women, especially in the bedroom, was his speciality; he had it down to a fine art. If he hadn't been a soldier, one could almost call it his profession.

Tugging off the tight-fitting, braided uniform jacket, he turned to hang it over a nearby armchair then spun back to face her as he slowly, teasingly, undid the lacings on his shirt and pulled it out of the almost indecently tight military pantaloons, running his hand caressingly over the front of them to draw her attention to the bulge she could already see outlined there. Relatively ignorant or inexperienced in some of these matters, even if she was well aware of the theory in detail, it didn't take much for Bella to realise he was deliberately and erotically stripping for her. She was riveted and boggle-eyed behind her mask as she recognised what a rogue he was. She'd thought disrobing entic- ingly was something women did for men, especially prostitutes or exotic dancers. She had no idea men did it for women or how erotic it could be…

As his lips curled, Nicky's suggestive smile tantalised her as gradu- ally, with more subtle yet deliberate caresses of his chest and abdomen, he peeled the shirt up and down his tautly muscled torso a few times, exposing more flesh each time, then from each arm in turn before finally pulling it over his head and dropping it carelessly on the floor. He ran the fingers of one hand through his hair and the now tousled and practised seducer curved his delicious lips in her direction again, slowly running the end of his tongue over them before blowing her a kiss with a burning look.

When he sat on the bed to bend forward and pull off his boots, Bella caught sight of the little gold lion dangling on its chain around his neck. She knew it was his most precious possession and he never, ever, took it off. It had been given to him by his father when he was not quite five years old, the last time he'd seen him in the former grim fortress in Rouen, Normandy, where they'd been imprisoned at the start of the Revolution. It was before he'd been rescued by her mother, Aunt Cat and Uncle Francis and brought safely to England. Looking at the golden, sun-kissed streaks in his thick tawny hair and his golden, lightly tanned torso, she reflected he'd truly grown into a golden lion himself, the living embodiment of his inheritance and family name and crest. He was indeed Nicholas Antoine de Bresancourt, Duke, *Le Lion de Valenciennes*.

Tossing his boots aside, Nicky slowly returned to his feet and facing his rapt audience once more, one hand idled down his bare chest and progressed to the fastenings of the skin-tight pantaloons while the other suggestively and caressingly stroked up and down his torso and ripped abdomen, teasing his own nipples. He closed his eyes and sighed, rolling his head at the self-induced pleasure, licking his lips again. This man knew exactly how to set a woman's senses on fire and make her want him; urgently. He undid more buttons and fastenings, one by one, tantalisingly slowly, now pausing momentarily to stroke the hardness the clothes concealed. So engrossed was she in watching him, Bella subconsciously bit her lips and his eyes flared with lust as he noticed her reaction to what he was doing.

As her eyes roved over his muscled biceps, tanned chest and abdomen, Bella's fingers twitched with the urge to run them through the golden hairs that covered the taut, rippling muscles of his upper body. There wasn't an inch of spare fat and she was almost salivating at the prospect of touching him and caressing that flawless torso. Totally unaware of her tongue licking her lips, she could feel the heat rising in her face as she watched his eyes flare and he finally, slowly, peeled down his pantaloons, bent slightly to undo the fastenings down his calves and then pulled them off. There was nothing underneath.

Everything he did was seductive, graceful yet manly. He turned and stood in front of her, feet slightly apart, now completely naked, well over six feet of masculine perfection, almost like a living Grecian statue. Then, very slowly, to her shock and complete fascination he meandered his hand slowly down the centre of his muscled torso following the line of golden hair, sensually, invitingly. As it reached below his navel, it hovered tantalisingly before he let his fingers run up and down his stunning erection, stroking and teasing himself from the base to the tip. When his long, elegant fingers reached the top and swirled around the tip, she saw the tiny pearl of moisture leach out as he closed his eyes and dropped his head back with a small moan of pleasure. Erotic had nothing on what he did and the way he did it; and he was quite some man; a woman's dream, a fantasy come to life and made for her pleasure.

Bella was completely transfixed and felt hot moisture drool between her legs at the suggestive performance in front of her, her body twitching restlessly. "Do you like what you see, *Lionesse*?" he whispered hotly as he continued to stroke himself, his eyes burning towards hers in the masked face. "Do you want this? Am I big enough for you? Long enough? Thick enough? Imagine it, throbbing deep inside you, filling you completely, pleasuring you intensely, making you moan with the sensations it will create. Fast or slow, hard and demanding, teasing and drawn out, and so much else. Whatever you like I can and will do, with this, my mouth and my fingers…and I can last long enough to make you climax over and over…and then repeat the entire exercise until you're mindless, limp and exhausted with the pleasure. So, am I man enough for you, *Lionesse*?" The stroking and commentary continued as he subtly swivelled his hips and thrust suggestively. "Just think, if you'd lost our game, you would have had to pay a thousand guineas for this instead…"

She'd never heard anything like it and Bella was speechless, an extremely rare occurrence. She swallowed and managed a strangled, whispered answer. "As I said before, money is sooo boring, although it does have its uses," and she rose up off the bed and went to stand in front of him.

Nicky was completely still as she reached out and put her hands on his bare shoulders, revelling finally in the feel of his warm, smooth skin. She breathed in his scent: he smelled of soap and a fragrant, woodsy, musky cologne which tantalised her nose. Slowly, she ran her fingers down his muscled arms and then across his broad, ripped chest. He gasped softly as they grazed his now stiff nipples and instead of continuing their journey downward, she returned them there to tease and caress him, remembering what he'd done to himself, watching as he closed his eyes and let his head fall back again. On impulse, she leaned forward and licked first one nipple then the other, then even as she felt him gasp again, he suddenly wriggled and laughed and she realised the feathers on her mask were tickling him.

"You HAVE to take that off, *Chérie*," he chuckled, "or we're not going to get anywhere. I'm terribly ticklish, I'm afraid." Nicky grinned at her and for a brief moment Bella's mind flew back to their childhood and the numerous occasions they'd fought and wrestled playfully and despite being half his size and nearly six years younger, she'd always managed to win or escape his clutches simply by tickling him mercilessly. She couldn't resist the temptation now and her fingers reached round to the sides of his ribs where she knew he was most vulnerable and wiggled and teased. "Aaaaaaah, noooooo, mercy, please," he cried out, laughing and doubled up with mirth before collapsing on the bed. As he rolled back on the covers, Bella bent down and tickled under his feet which brought forth more cries and gales of laughter. She stood back completely stunned, fascinated by yet another facet to him. He was totally unselfconscious, uninhibited about his naked and aroused state and was rolling around on the bed in happy abandon and hilarity, just like he had when he was ten or eleven years old, but without the arousal. She thought her heart would burst with love for him, realising those feelings were now inextricably entwined with her uncontrollable desire and lust. She knew she was completely lost.

As Nicky finally recovered and stopped laughing, he sat up on the bed and chuckled at her, shaking his head. "Don't you think you've got too many clothes on *Chérie*, or have I got to make love to you with your petticoats on too?"

Bella paused. She realised he was expecting her to do what he'd done and entertain him with her own little striptease. He might be completely unembarrassed by parading his aroused body to tease and tempt a female audience, but she wasn't ready for that yet. It had taken all her nerve to climb into his bed a year previously and seduce him in the dark, falling down drunk as he'd been. To stand in front of him now and take all her clothes off, let alone caress herself while his hot eyes burned into her, she simply couldn't. Instead, she leaned across him and whispered in his ear, "In a moment, *Mon Cher*, be patient; anticipation is everything…" and she bent to kiss him on the back of his neck, little nibbling kisses that ran from the back of his ear down to his shoulder. As she walked towards her dressing room, he groaned theatrically, muttering something about provoking women and threw himself back down across the covers. She laughed.

She returned in seconds, a long length of golden silk in her hands and told him to sit up. He eyed the item suspiciously. "So, Nicky, you want me to take off my mask and wig?" He narrowed his eyes at her. "Well, I will, but we have to do this my way," and before he could say anything, she'd climbed on the bed and knelt behind him and wound the long, wide silk sash from one of her gold *Lionesse* outfits around his eyes several times and tied it tight. He froze.

She leaned down and whispered in his ear, "If you don't like it, just say and I'll take it off, but then I'll keep my mask and wig on. However, if you're happy to keep it on, then I'll take EVERYTHING off. It's your choice, *Milor*, Nicky…" and she sat back, resting her hands on his shoulders then idly caressing his skin, running her fingers up and down his neck and into his hair, waiting for his decision.

He didn't like it one bit, for many deep and personal reasons he would never dream of revealing to anyone and was about to object, when he felt the caress of her hands. He was desperate to see what she looked like and hadn't expected this turn of events at all. It had occurred to him she may have some sort of disfiguring scar on her face, like his stepfather, which would explain her reluctance to take off the all-encompassing mask, but some deep intuition told him that wasn't the case. For whatever reason, she simply wanted to keep her identity a secret. As Nicky felt her hands rove across his back and up his neck, he took a deep breath and made himself relax, realising how much he still desired *Lionesse* and that this would be the only way. It would be impossible to make love to her properly with that mask on. Damn, he hadn't even been able to kiss her delectable lips yet. If he'd wanted a quick or passing fuck, it wouldn't have mattered, but that was the point...he didn't. He wanted far more than that.

As Nicky considered his predicament, subconsciously toying with the lion charm that dangled from his necklace, he told himself how erotic it would be to make love to her without actually seeing her and he wondered if she was deliberately teasing him. Anyway, he could always pull the encompassing blindfold off later and once he did that, there'd be no going back for her. So, mind made up, he bent his head in acquiescence. "I don't like it, *Chérie*, but I want to make love to you tonight and if that's what it takes, I'll do what you want; as you said, it is YOUR favour. However..." he paused for a moment to make it clear, "just so you know," and he put up a hand to grasp hers where he felt it on his shoulder, "I'm not the submissive type." He smiled, not knowing now if she could see him or not, "I'm more than happy to play games and indulge your little idiosyncrasies or fantasies, but I'm not into pain, humiliation or serious perversion. Those are my terms, *Lionesse*."

Bella wasn't quite sure she understood everything he was referring to, though she had an inkling, but content he was happy to go along with her, she breathed an enormous, silent sigh of thanks. She undid the strings of her mask and, with relief, pulled it and her wig off. She rapidly removed the pins from her hair and shook her head to let the long, thick curls fall down her back, rubbing and scratching her scalp with a sigh of pleasure.

Nicky had rolled over onto his stomach and was resting his head on his folded arms. As he heard her sigh he turned at the sound. "What are you doing, *Chérie*?" he asked curiously.

"I've just taken my mask and wig off; aaah," she sighed again, "it's such a relief to let my hair down again."

"Come HERE, *Chérie*," he crooned softly. "Mmmmm, I can smell your scent on the pillows, but I can't come and get you."

Bella was just about to take off her dress but went over to the bed instead, concerned he'd attempt to take off the sash covering his eyes and she leaned down over his back, kissing his neck. She ran her hand across his wide, muscled shoulders and then let her fingers caress and drift down to his tight, firm buttocks. She couldn't help but notice his skin below the waist was paler than his tanned back and her hand roamed over his bottom and lower to his hard thighs and tautly muscled legs, covered in a smattering of tawny hair; the muscles were a testament, she presumed, to long hours spent in the saddle. He was a cavalry officer, in one of the British army Hussar regiments.

In his blind state, his other senses were far more alert and as he felt her hair tickle across his skin and her hand caressing his back, Nicky sighed with pleasure and rolled over. A strong arm snaked out around her body and he pulled her down onto the bed next to him. He let his fingers rove up to find her face and as they gently felt their way across her forehead then down to her nose and lips, he confirmed to himself there was no scarring she wanted to hide. Her skin felt like a ripe peach and he leaned his head and lowered his lips to kiss smooth cheeks until they found her mouth. With a soft sigh, he kissed her softly and nibbled her lips gently, encouraging them to open to him. As they parted his tongue crept inside and hot passion exploded between them.

Bella had suspected when he kissed her now it would be different to before, but nothing had prepared her for the overwhelming eruption of fierce desire that shot through her entire body like a volcanic wave. His tongue danced with hers and roved around her mouth, tasting, teasing and driving her wild. His hands scorched down her body, caressing and moulding her full breasts through the thin material of her evening gown, making her nipples swell and throb. One hand roved lower, pulling up her dress and petticoats and in moments she felt it sear up her leg as his fingers probed and brushed her sex. She writhed and moaned, totally lost to the maelstrom of sensations consuming her body.

"*Mon Dieu*, you're so wet for me already," Nicky groaned as he momentarily pulled away from her hot mouth to suck air into his lungs and get a grip on his runaway lust. This erotic game of hers had him strung out already. He could feel her writhe beneath his questing fingers and her soft sighs and moans were like fuel to the fire raging through his veins. He swore as he struggled to push her dress off her shoulders, unable to see where the fastenings were and then grappling with knots, bows and hooks when his fingers finally located them. His arousal was almost incendiary and he was desperate to get his hands on her body, to feel her soft skin next to his.

His muttering and frustration finally percolated her fogged mind and Bella struggled to sit up. Gently she pushed his hands away and knelt beside him to undo the rest of the lacings on her dress, corset and undergarments, pulling them off her body haphazardly, and throwing them onto the floor. She never got a chance to remove her stockings before he pulled her down again and his mouth returned to hers in another blaze of carnal desire. How she'd unintentionally wound up his lust in her little plan to keep her identity a secret, she had no idea. Slowly he moved from her mouth to her throat and then down to her breasts, his lips and tongue leaving a scorching trail over her skin wherever they touched it. *"Fraises et crème,"* he sighed. "Strawberries and cream, so sweet." His lips found her nipples and he licked and nibbled, then pulled first one then the other into his mouth to suck gently and then more forcefully as he felt her response.

As Bella felt his mouth tease and suckle her nipples, a white-hot shaft of lightning zigzagged low in her belly and she cried out, digging her nails deep into his shoulders. His mouth moved further, licking and sucking down her abdomen to her navel and then, in shock, she felt his lips go lower, even as she felt his fingers stroke and caress her and a questing finger crept up inside her, creating waves of tormenting pleasure. "Aaaaaaah, Nicky, noooooo," she muttered, scandalised, trying to pull away from his seeking lips.

But he held her fast, pulling her legs further apart. "Let me pleasure you, *Lionesse,*" he crooned in French. *"Mon Dieu,* your body feels so beautiful, your perfume is everywhere, your skin so soft, you taste *délicieuse,* quite delicious. Let go, relax and let me love you, you're so wet, so near the edge, I can feel it," and as he continued to kiss and caress her, back and forth across her sensitive folds and right at her core, his tongue licked, sucked and teased until, recovering from her shock, Bella abandoned her inhibitions and gave in to the building waves of intense pleasure coursing inside her, sending her completely mindless.

The spiral of feeling wound tighter and tighter until he could feel her tense and then he licked and sucked hard and his tongue thrust inside her and she cried out, "Nickyyyyyyyyyyyy, aaaaaaaaaah…" her back arched off the bed as her body jerked.

Bella had never known or felt such intense pleasure or feelings like it. She felt mindless, limbless, overcome, actually quite shocked at what she'd let him do to her; but oh, those feelings. It was beyond her brain to describe them and finally, she knew what it was like. She'd read about it but now she understood what an orgasm was all about. Indescribable. As her mind tried to recover some semblance of normality, she felt Nicky crawl back up the bed and pull her into his arms. As he kissed her mouth in a long, drugging kiss she knew she could taste herself on his lips and, amazingly, she revelled in the carnal, lustful feeling that gave her. His hands stroked down her arms and back and, as they moved round to cup her breasts, he placed one over where her heart was still thumping in response to the climax she'd just experienced. He chuckled as he bent down and placed his lips where his hand had been. "You see what happens when you give yourself over to my tender care, *Chérie*? I rather think you enjoyed that, hmmmmm? And we've only just started. Does having me blind like this make you as hot as it makes me? Do you drive all your lovers wild making them do this?" As his head came down to kiss her nipples again, those seeking fingers returned to their stroking once more and she gasped as she felt a renewed spasm of pleasure curl insidiously inside her and more moisture pool between her thighs.

She was incapable of sensible speech, not that she could answer him, other than muttering his name again, over and over, as she simply lay there and gave herself up to the wash of feelings, grasping his shoulders as if she would never let go. As his fingers teased her to fever pitch once more, she writhed around them helplessly, pleading with him to enter her. She could feel his throbbing hardness against her thigh and though she tried now to move her hands down to caress him, he pulled them away, laughing ruefully. "*Aaah, non, Chérie*, it's too much, you're too much; it's been too long since I was last with a woman and there's only so much a man can take; but later, you can work your magic on me with pleasure. My body is at your disposal, all night."

She was going to ask him how long it had been, but the thought was lost as he kissed her hungrily and moved up and over her, poised at last to end his teasing torment. Her hands moved around to his back, running up and down his spine and clasping and caressing his buttocks, pressing him wordlessly to take her.

Finally, Nicky groaned as if he could take no more self-imposed delay and with one hard thrust he impaled himself deep inside her. As she throbbed around him and gasped, he seemed momentarily stunned. "*Mon Dieu*, you're so tight! So hot, so damned tight, almost virginal," he moaned as he pulled back slowly and drove into her again, harder, deeper, filling her completely, the feeling almost blowing his head off it was so sublime.

"Do you want me to withdraw, *Chérie?* Tell me quickly so I know, or I can't promise if you leave it too late?"

She was beyond comprehension, thinking he meant to stop and start teasing her again. "Aaah, noooooo, noooo," she moaned as she pressed him more deeply into her, writhing against him.

Momentarily surprised, but relieved at her answer as he wasn't sure he'd actually be able to do it, aroused and so near the edge as he now was. It really had been a long while since he'd been with a woman, so Nicky gave in to the driving need that had overtaken him and once started, he simply couldn't stop. He lost control and gave in to the desire that had held him in thrall ever since he'd sat down in her sitting room and started to play cards, the desire that had infected him when she sat down at his card table earlier that evening.

Bella was moaning beneath him, squirming and writhing, her whole body on fire, feeling the spasms get more intense as that spiral started to wind up once more, except now it was impossibly intense, making her pant and cry out incoherently, pleading with him, her nails digging deep in his back.

Nicky was lost as the fiery passion exploded between them, moaning with her, driving and thrusting hard and wildly to pleasure her and himself, angling his body to rub against her sensitised flesh just where she needed it...and then she went over the edge, screaming and crying out his name, her head thrown back, eyes closed as her body rocked and bucked and she experienced the seismic emotions and waves that completely overwhelmed her.

As he heard the scream of pleasure and felt the climax overtake her, and as she spasmed and throbbed around him, Nicky cried out as his own release exploded out of him in endless streams, deep inside her before he collapsed on top of her for several stunned moments, then rolled off her onto his back, heart thumping almost out of his chest, totally overcome with the erotic experience to which he'd just submitted himself.

As they lay together in the silence, panting and overwhelmed by what had just passed between them, Bella turned and rolled into his arms which curled round her of their own volition. Kissing his sweat covered chest, she felt hot salty tears roll down her face. Tears of love, desire, anger, remorse and confusion. A whole gamut of emotions assaulted her as she lay there in her husband's arms... knowing he didn't know who she really was and it was simply too much for her shattered nerves.

Sensing her distress and at a loss to understand it, Nicky gently pushed what felt like copious coils of hair away from her face and leaned over to kiss her, feeling the tears on her cheeks. As he gently wiped and kissed them away he whispered, "What is it, *Chérie*? Did I do something to upset you? Did I hurt you? Was I too rough, too wild? Or are you feeling as overwhelmed as I at what just happened?" He paused and swore under his breath and went to pull the blindfold off, but Bella stopped him just in time, hastily trying to gather her wits and put her emotions back on track.

As she pulled his hands away from the sash, she whispered softly to him, "Oh no, you can't do that, it would spoil everything. Stay in the dark and let me keep my secret, please?" she leaned up and kissed him sweetly, caressing his face, running her fingers over his lips. "That was, incredible, *incroyable*. I'm overwhelmed, that's all. Silly, I know," she laughed gently and continued to whisper, "but promise me, please, please, give me your word, as an officer and a gentleman, you'll leave it for the rest of the night? Nicky? Please?" she pleaded.

Relieved that her tears were nothing to do with anything he'd done to her, Nicky was still unsure it was just reaction to that stunning bout of lovemaking that had distressed her. He'd heard the emotion in her voice and suspected there was more to it. "Are you sure, *Lionesse*? I'm not some callow, inexperienced youth. I know what you just experienced seemed to overwhelm you, both times. Even if I couldn't see it, I certainly heard and felt it. So are you sure there isn't something else?"

Bella heard the curiosity in his voice, looked at him and realised that he was no fool, even without his sight. But she was determined not to give herself away, not now, not after that momentous event she'd just enjoyed for the first time. She wondered if she could persuade him to make love to her again before he left. She truly had been overwhelmed, nothing had prepared her for the intensity of her response to him, what he would actually do to her, then how he made her feel. Nothing in the books she'd read came close to describing it and she wondered, her heart breaking, did he have this effect on all the women he loved when he was away? Taking a deep breath, she settled back down in his arms and whispered, "No, *Mon Cher*, there's nothing else. I was truly overwhelmed. You're a very talented lover and, it's been a long time for me too."

"Mmmmm, I could tell," he answered softly, idly winding her hair round his fingers, trying to guess how long it was. "You were so tight when I entered you, almost virginal. *Mon Dieu*, I nearly lost myself before I even started," he chuckled, "but you're such an attractive woman, even with the mask on, why haven't you got a lover or a husband? Or are they blind too?" he laughed at his own joke. "Do you, *Chérie?* Have a lover or husband? Or perhaps," he became serious, "have you lost one?" He rubbed her arms comfortingly, "I didn't see a ring," he finally whispered.

"Yes – and no," she sighed. "I mean, I have a husband but he's away and, he doesn't want me anyway." He felt her shrug.

"Whaaat?" Nicky couldn't believe what he was hearing. "You have a husband but he doesn't want you? Man's a fool," and he tightened his arms round her.

"Mmmmm, maybe, but it's complicated and I was lonely," she rubbed herself up against his body. "But never mind that now, I don't want to discuss it, not when I have YOU here," she ran her fingers up his arm, across a hard shoulder and up his neck. She caressed his face, tracing the line of his lips and gasped when he bit the tip of one, raising his own hand to grasp hers and kiss and suck each finger in his mouth, making her shiver as he murmured suggestively to her in French in between fingers.

"You're quite something you know, almost impossible to resist, but I suppose you know that? I would bet the women fall at your feet." She kissed his chest, nuzzling her nose in the soft hair there, "I wanted you the minute you walked into my little establishment tonight," she grinned, knowing he couldn't see. That at least was the complete truth, though so was most of the rest of her story she also realised.

His lips curled wickedly and he kissed her on the nose, but he persisted with his questions, still curious about her. "Is that why you wear a mask all the time? So you won't be recognised? Does your husband not know about all this?" and he raised his hand to wave it around vaguely.

"Something like that. But it's not just him, I'm a very private person. I would rather keep my identity quiet, a secret. It's safer for me too and in fact, makes things easier all round."

"Hah! A passionate woman with secrets. Irresistible!" he kissed her, feeling the coils of desire thrum in his blood again and he hardened despite the incredible release he'd experienced only a short while before. "I will find out who you are, y'know, my curiosity won't let me rest and I've already told you I want to watch you when you climax. Tell me again, *Chérie*, what colour are your eyes? I want to imagine them next time."

"You are a completely charming rogue, but my eyes are my secret. You won't find out who I am unless I choose to tell you." She kissed him back, nibbling his lips as he'd done to hers; she learned fast. "As for next time," she whispered saucily, "I only asked for ONE favour."

"Well, consider this a bonus, or my stake for our next game."

"Our next game?"

"Oh yes," he crooned seductively. "I only have a few days in London as I have dispatches to collect. Unfortunately, I'm not on any extended leave, but I'm not going back to Spain without seeing you again and this time, I do mean SEE you. I want to remember what you look like when I sail away."

"Hmmm, I don't know about that, I'll think about it," she whispered.

"I can be VERRRY persuasive," he started to kiss her neck, biting and nibbling at the sensitive juncture with her shoulder he'd discovered affected her so much and, as he felt her jerk and shiver in response, he grinned wickedly and chuckled, "See what I mean?"

"Don't be so sure of yourself. I can be very resistant to all sorts of flattery and attention," she purred, "but tell me," she had to ask, "are all your women as overwhelmed as I was when you make love to them?"

He burst out laughing. "A gentleman never discusses the ladies in his life, *Chérie*, but I can assure you that much as I would like them to be, I don't think many have been as responsive to me as you were, are, not that I can see you of course, but I can sense, feel and hear you," he whispered.

"Is there anyone waiting for you back in Spain then?" She had to know and held her breath.

"What a curious puss you are, *Lionesse*," he chuckled, "but no, there's no-one waiting in bed for me anywhere. Will that do?"

"It will have to, I suppose," she sighed, the prospect of knowing he had someone waiting in Spain to enjoy the pleasure she'd just discovered with him was more than she thought she could cope with.

"Good. I WILL persuade you before I go. I'm determined to see who you are, you're a challenge I can't resist."

Bella knew better than anyone how he relished a challenge; they'd spent their entire childhood and teenage years trying to get the better of each other. "Well, don't bank on it. You couldn't beat me at cards so don't think you can work your wiles on me either," she poked him playfully in the chest and laughed hoarsely. "And another thing, you still haven't given me your word you won't take this off tonight," she ran her hand over his sash covered eyes, "if you don't, you'll leave instantly, no matter how much I want you to make love to me again," she whispered seductively. "I mean it, Nicky," she finished assertively.

Nicky hesitated, but she had him. He wanted her again too and she knew it. So he sighed, "Very well, you win. I give you my word, but I can't believe I'm letting you do this to me. I must be out of my mind, obviously too long without a woman," he muttered to himself and shook his head in disbelief. Then he paused as he thought of something. "Oh, one thing, *Chérie*, I have no idea what the time is. The daylight usually wakes me but now it won't and I HAVE to be back at my barracks early. I've military matters to take care of and have to be... er... on duty for nine o'clock." He certainly wasn't going to tell her he was actually due at the Foreign Office and War Ministry for important briefing meetings concerning Wellington's plans in the Peninsula. "So, you will wake me in good time, please? Promise, *Lionesse*?" He held out his hand, "This is as important to me as your identity is to you."

This was something very serious. She knew him so well and could tell when he was withholding something. Bella realised she didn't know why he was in Spain, obviously not just soldiering she suspected, as they never got letters about manoeuvres, skirmishes or battles, unlike the families of other officers they knew. And no mention from him of going to see his family either, let alone his wife, so she merely answered, "Very well, I promise...and thank you," she whispered and kissed his nose. She intended to find out more when he finally came home, or she would tackle Uncle Francis; she was sure he knew more of what Nicky was doing than he let on and now SHE wanted to know. The prospect of him in danger even more terrifying to her than before, if that was possible. However, she pushed that to the back of her mind for now as she laughed and caressed his face, letting her hand roam down his body, "But it doesn't look to me like you're not enjoying yourself, *Milor*."

"Whoever said I wasn't enjoying your game, or you, You Baggage?" and he rolled over on top of her and started kissing her passionately and soon they were both lost once more.

Bella had no idea what time they'd finally fallen into an exhausted slumber. She stretched lazily, feeling the pull of slightly sore muscles, aching all over from the unaccustomed activity as her mind roved back over the previous evening. Nicky had made love to her on and off all night and she'd merely followed his seductive encouragement. Now, with the dawn sun streaming in her window, she could look her fill in daylight at his still sleeping body, sprawled out across her bed in abandon. Remembering suddenly her promise to wake him in good time, she looked over to the clock on her mantel and saw she still had a few minutes to have him to herself.

The whole night had been a revelation. Not just the lovemaking, though that had stunned her more than anything. That she was capable of such passion was also astounding and she couldn't believe all those desires and sensations had been dormant inside of herself, in her own Pandora's box waiting to be opened and set free. She blushed to the roots of her hair at the memory of Nicky's mouth and hands all over her body, bringing her to climax after climax as she'd wantonly begged for more, making him laugh wickedly and tease her further. Even as she remembered, she felt the stirrings of arousal once more and she was shocked at herself. She thought it must be the hot Spanish blood she'd inherited from her mother and she giggled; vague childhood memories of her parents kissing came to mind, revealing that her dear Papa was not quite the quiet, reserved individual most people took him to be. She knew they'd loved each other passionately and Papa was lost now without her mother even though it had been quite a few years since her untimely passing. As she lay there reflectively, her hand gently stroking the hair on his chest, Bella wondered if Nicky would ever look at her and kiss her the way her father had done with her mother. She sighed.

She also wondered if Nicky would genuinely want to come and visit *La Lionesse* again and deep down, she knew he would. Apart from the passion that had exploded between them, he wouldn't be able to resist the challenge of getting her to reveal herself. Part of her was angry that he'd prefer to spend his few short days in London with a mistress, owner of a gambling house and therefore completely unacceptable to Society, rather than stay with the real her, but then she was his unwanted wife and she'd already had that discussion with herself and achieved nothing. Besides, she wanted him to love her as she loved him. She couldn't bear the thought of him being with her reluctantly, then growing to resent and hate her for it. But now that she'd let him make love to her, how could she face the prospect of letting him go? She felt herself well up with tears as she realised the mess she was in, loving him and desiring him so desperately.

Perhaps, she thought, if he spent time with *La Lionesse* and their relationship deepened, she would reveal herself to him and gamble that he'd realise he could have all that with her, officially, as she was his wife already. Pigs might fly she thought. He'd be even more angry than he was before at another trick she'd played on him. And it still wouldn't make him love her. But he was here in London, now, if only for a few days and she wanted to be with him. She couldn't contemplate the dangers he faced in Spain with the interminable war against Bonaparte – waiting here in England with little or no information for months and years was a constant torment and she knew her family felt the same.

So, she decided, she'd carry on with her game. She had nothing to lose and everything to gain from a few stolen days with him. What she did at the end of the few days, she'd decide later, as she currently had no idea. In the meantime, she had to persuade him to return to her as soon as his military duties were over, after he'd been to visit the family. She was sure he wouldn't spend his entire time in London without letting them know he was in the country – even Nicky wasn't that callous. But how to persuade him? She couldn't go to him or be seen anywhere out with him; she had to make him come to her, here at the gaming house.

Bella lay there, pondering her problems as the clock slowly ticked and she watched Nicky's slow breathing. Her hand was still roaming over his chest and, as she gazed down at him, a shaft of dawn sunlight caught on his necklace, making the little golden lion gleam. She gazed at it absentmindedly, thinking again how apt his ducal title was with his stunning leonine colouring and also how precious that simple necklace was to him, more than anything else he possessed. Suddenly she sat up; that was it! She had her answer.

Carefully leaning over him she gently lifted the chain, looking intently for the little clasp, praying desperately she could undo it without waking him up. Slowly and cautiously, she felt her way along the links until her fingers felt what she sought, buried deep in the hair of his chest, next to where the little lion rested. Very gently, she prised the stiff clasp open and slowly, imperceptibly, pulled one end of the chain out from under the back of his neck.

Breathing a sigh of relief that he slept on, Bella carefully slipped off the bed, pulled on a dressing robe lying over a chair and went through to her sitting room, silently pulling the door closed behind her. Carefully moving her fingers along the stonework, she found and pressed a hidden spring under the mantelpiece of the fireplace. With a scraping sound, part of the masonry slid back to reveal a large hiding place containing documents, papers and a number of metal boxes which she knew held a very large amount of money, the latest profits from her little business enterprise. Pulling a soft handkerchief from her pocket, she carefully wrapped the precious necklace in the scrap of lace and put it in the hidden cavity, before pressing the spring again and ensuring the stone slid back into place.

Smiling to herself, she crept back into the bedroom, took off her robe and climbed back into bed. Wild horses wouldn't keep him away from her again that evening if she promised to return his necklace after another night in her bed – with or without the added challenge of a game of cards as well. Or maybe she could tempt him with a game of chess? She laughed to herself, she could toy with him even more playing that. Poor Nicky!

As she snuggled up next to his warm body, a strong, muscled arm curled around her protectively. She looked at the clock again – it was still only just after five o'clock – and he apparently didn't have to be back at his barracks on duty until nine. Her hand roved downward to gently clasp the source of her pleasure, watching in fascination as it instantly hardened under her gentle caresses. A pleasured sigh escaped his lips as he half woke and muttered to her, "Mmmmm... and what are you doing? That feels so good... but what time is it? I can't be late..."

"Oh, don't worry about that, it's still dark outside, you've got plenty of time," she purred, grinning wickedly as he rolled over and started to kiss her.

By the time they'd made love slowly and leisurely in the morning sunlight and she'd climbed out of bed to don her big mask and wig before removing his blindfold, he was of course late back to the barracks. He'd noticed his missing necklace instantly, but being in such a hurry and swearing vociferously at her in voluble French for delaying him, she'd merely tweaked his nose, an old childhood habit when he'd been in a snit if she'd beaten him at one of their games, laughed at his panic and said it was probably lost in the bed, she'd find it and keep it safe, she promised, so he'd have to come back and collect it from her later. Still muttering to himself, she'd sent him on his way grinning from ear to ear, knowing he'd be back as sure as chickens laid eggs.

Chapter Four

Nicky sat in the hackney on his way to the Foreign Office and reflected it was lucky he hadn't gone home to change before going out the previous evening and it was a good job he kept a change of clothes in a trunk at his barracks. Although in his dress uniform, he was at least properly outfitted for his military meetings, albeit unshaven, but he thought he could just about get away with that as he'd shaved the previous evening before going out and he passed a hand over his slightly rough jawline with yet another muttered oath. He also needed a haircut, but he could get both remedied when he finally got home and borrowed his uncle's valet. He threw his head back against the seat and mulled over the quirk of fate which had taken him to *Le Lion d'Or* the previous evening.

His ship had docked in East London in the early afternoon and he'd gone straight to his barracks to deliver the urgent dispatches he carried for the senior officers there and for the War Ministry. After that, he'd fully intended to make his way home to Firle House, see his family and spend a quiet evening with the Duke, updating him on the situation in the Peninsula. Francis Granville, Duke of Firle, was the only other person apart from his superiors on Wellington's staff in the Peninsula and in the Ministry in London, who knew the true nature of his work. The Duke had his own informal network of contacts in Spain, mainly among the gypsy fraternity, mainly for business reasons, but they kept him updated on events and Nicky had taken advantage of these contacts on several occasions. A personal friend of many senior Government ministers, past and present, any information the Duke picked up was also passed along direct to the appropriate military quarters. They never asked how he came by his intelligence and he never revealed his sources, but the occasional information was valuable and appreciated.

However, as often happened, Nicky had bumped into a group of old friends, fellow officers home on leave through battle injury or sickness and now fortunately recovered. Before he'd had a chance to object, they'd dragged him off for a reunion drink and persuaded him to join them on a visit to the new gaming establishment that was all the rage. When he heard the serving girls had their faces painted like jungle cats with whiskers, all dressed in costumes accordingly, complete with tails and furry ears on their heads, he'd laughed uproariously and happily agreed to join them. The Duke and his family could wait until tomorrow. After all, it was only a few hours and he felt he deserved a night out after so many months of living with danger and constant stress.

And so fate had taken him to *Le Lion d'Or* and as soon as he'd seen her, he'd been fascinated with the Proprietress. His friends said she very rarely appeared in person and then always dressed in her outrageous disguise, different from her girls and boys who merely painted their faces and wore amusing lion, tiger, leopard or panther costumes, whereas she was masked and bewigged and her gold coloured outfits were more decorous, albeit still very alluring, complete with a lion's tail as well which she was known to pick up and swish around in the air. Everyone assumed this was simply part of the entertainment and uniqueness of the establishment – apart from the strict limits on the tables – something they all appreciated, knowing they could drink and gamble safe in the knowledge they wouldn't be drawn into betting and possibly losing the large sums as often happened to many young men at the more insalubrious gaming hells around Town, or even at the refined St James's gentlemen's clubs like Whites or Brooks's or Boodles. *Le Lion d'Or* had set out to be different and was all about sophisticated, amusing entertainment for its well-to-do patrons, not losing one's fortune or estate.

Nicky had watched *La Lionesse* from a distance all evening, entranced by her disguise and some vague feeling he'd seen her somewhere before. But he'd merely laughed that off, even when she'd sauntered over to their table, tail twirling in one hand, and sat down to join them and he'd taken a closer look at her. She'd invited herself into their game in that laughing, sensually hoarse voice and he was sure he'd remember if they'd ever met somewhere else, so dismissed the feeling simply as mistaken identity. When she'd asked him to join her after for a private game of cards, he knew she'd also felt the pull of attraction between them, so he had followed her eagerly, sure he was going to end up being entertained in a far more interesting fashion than a mere card game. However, nothing had prepared him for what had followed.

He still wasn't one hundred percent sure her unusual stipulation of keeping him blindfolded was really to keep her identity a secret or she was just playing erotic games with him. Either way the night had been astounding. He couldn't remember many with a woman when he'd been so continuously aroused and overwhelmed by his response to her. Although he'd sensed her apprehension, even nervousness at first, which had surprised him for a woman in her position, she'd eventually relaxed and given in to the heady passion that seemed to have exploded between them, taking them both by surprise.

He'd already decided he would return again that evening to *Le Lion d'Or*, pulled by the curiosity to find out who she was and what she looked like, but now, he also had his mislaid necklace to retrieve. Unbidden, his hand went to his chest, feeling lost without the reassuring presence of his little charm. He was alarmed to discover it had come off – he never, ever, removed it and it had survived all manner of personal fights, military battles and energetic romantic interludes. As soon as he got it back, he would take it straight to a jeweller and get the clasp changed to something more secure, unless the chain itself had broken, in which case he'd get that replaced. Not that he'd discard the original, its sentimental value was too important. In the meantime, he had a morning of interminable military debriefings to sit through and then an afternoon with his family... and Bella.

That was another problem he had to deal with and he was determined to sort the whole matter out with her once and for all, hopefully without any further arguments, so they could both move on with their lives. As the carriage made its way towards Whitehall, an image of her came unbidden to his mind.

She'd changed and grown up so much in the years he'd been away. She wasn't the little freckled hoyden in pigtails he'd been used to, who followed him around when they were younger. Far from it – she had turned into a real beauty, so much like her Spanish mother. But she still felt like his sister and discovering he'd had intercourse with her had shocked him terribly. He'd reconciled his conscience, knowing it would never be repeated, but not his anger at being tricked into it; hell, what had she been playing at? She knew full well he'd only married her as a convenience and he didn't understand why she wouldn't let the annulment go through. It would have to be a divorce now, a very quiet one for her sake, unless Francis could finagle something else, as after all no one but the close family knew they'd spent a night together. Bella would be able to deal with her lack of virginity with whomever she ended up marrying, somehow, he was sure. Nicky knew nothing about the finer points of annulments and divorce but decided to talk to Francis about the entire matter that afternoon. The Duke of Firle could solve a lot of difficult problems with money and a word in the ears of the right people in the right places. In any case, Bella had caused her own problem, so she would have to deal with it!

His cogitations came to an abrupt end as the hackney drew up outside the Ministry building and he leapt down and hurried inside, his mind now turning to the situation in the Peninsula and Wellington's strategic options.

The meetings droned on endlessly and while Nicky gazed out from the high windows of the Ministry building, his mind drifted to the previous night, his eyes closing as he remembered the delicious feel and taste of *La Lionesse*. He felt his body harden in response before a sharp voice barked him out of his reverie.

"...de Bresancourt!? Did you hear me? You'll come back in two days to collect the dispatches to deliver to Wellington and get further instructions to deal with the problem we seem to be having with troublemaking French agents down there."

"Yes, Sir. Of course, Sir." Rising rapidly to his feet, Nicky stood to attention and bowed as the various Generals and their intelligence advisors left the room.

"NICKYYYYYYYYY!" his exuberant Aunt squealed as she picked up her skirts in a most indecorous fashion and ran down the hall of Firle House to pull him into a tight, emotional hug and kiss him all over his face. "When did you get back? Thank God you're safe! I worry about you constantly... Francissssssssssssssss! FRAN-CISSSSSSSSSSSSS!? Where are you, You Useless Man? Look who's arrived... FRANCISSSSSS!" She literally pulled Nicky across the foyer and headed towards the Duke's study back down the long hallway she'd just raced along, shouting at the top of her voice. "BROWNING!" she then called to the bemused butler over her shoulder, "Go and find Miss Arabella at once and tell her to come here THIS INSTANT, and please tell Mary to bring Elizabeth. She's got to meet her new uncle immediately!"

Chuckling at his excited Aunt's very unladylike behaviour as she ran along and shouted instructions left, right and centre to send servants scurrying for food and drink, to air his rooms and lay out his clothes as she dragged him down the hall in search of the Duke, Nicky reflected on how good it felt to be home. As they burst through his study door, Francis was already halfway across the room, an enormous smile on his face before pulling him into a tight bear hug, full of emotion, as he too kissed him on both cheeks. "Nicky! Welcome home! By God, it's good to see you're still in one piece, in spite of that bastard

Bonaparte's best efforts." Francis chuckled and turned to his wife, "Oh Cat, let him go for goodness' sake! Give him a chance to catch his breath. Come on, out of here, into the family room with you all…"

Nicky was still laughing as he let himself be pulled over to a sofa and his Aunt plumped herself down next to him, grasping one of his hands firmly in hers as she started a torrent of questions: "When did you get back? How long can you stay? Have you been in many battles? You weren't injured were you? Have you sent a message to Eddie? He's buried down at Arlington with Charlie, as ever, but he'll come up to Town at once, of course, when he knows you're back, or shall we send someone down there straight away? And I've got SUCH a surprise to show you…" she paused momentarily as the butler came in, preceding a footman carrying a large tray with tea and pastries and an enormous, white, long-haired dog brought up the rear and padded over to greet the newcomer and get his ears scratched.

"Ah, your pardon, Your Grace," the butler intoned, "but it appears Miss Arabella is not at home. Monique says she has gone shopping and will be back later this afternoon," and he bowed, awaiting further instructions.

"Oh botheration!" exclaimed Cat and she turned to Nicky, "Never mind, you'll see her later, now then, what would you like for dinner? Just say what you've missed most and I'll tell Cook to get on with it. Oh, Bubbles, do stop licking him to death, he's got nothing to eat in his pockets! Nicky, my love, come and have a nice cup of tea and I'll…." but she never got any further.

"Good God, Cat, you'll drive him mad with your questions and what the hell are you doing offering him tea?" Francis raised an eyebrow at Nicky and his uniform. "I take it you've been in the Ministry before coming here? Therefore, I suspect you must be in need of a very large drink after a morning with those old farts," he grinned. "In which case, wine? Brandy? What's your poison?" he strolled over to the long sideboard and picked up a decanter of brandy in expectation.

Grinning back at Francis, "Brandy, a very LARGE brandy if you don't mind," Nicky gratefully accepted the glass and downed a mouthful, profoundly relieved he wouldn't have to see Bella for the first time in front of Cat and Francis.

Taking a deep breath he started to answer Cat's questions one by one, pausing only for her to arrange for a fast messenger to be sent off post-haste to summon her brother, his step-father, to Town as quickly as possible, followed by another interruption as a maid came in carrying a large bundle which she carefully handed to the Duchess. Beaming, Cat pulled back a soft shawl and Nicky stared in amazement at a sleeping baby. "You have another little cousin at last, Nicky. Meet Lady Elizabeth Granville. Finally, I have another woman to help me manage Francis," and she promptly placed the child in his arms with an enormous, self-satisfied smirk.

Nicky gazed at the infant lying in blissful slumber and gently stroked her downy cheek and mop of black hair, smiling up at Cat, "She's beautiful. I had no idea. It's absolutely wonderful, especially after so long and your miscarriages; I knew you'd virtually given up on having more children, especially a little girl. Oh, I'm SO happy for you," and he looked over at Francis who was smiling, besotted, at his wife. "I see you finally remembered how to do it again, You Useless Bugger," and he winked.

Francis chuckled at Nicky, "How I'm going to cope with the pair of them I've no idea; she was only born barely three months ago and the whole house is in turmoil already."

The baby stirred and opened her large sky-blue eyes, peering up at the strange face above her and waved two tiny fists in the air. "She's got your eyes and hair," Nicky said to Francis, fascinated, as Elizabeth decided to exercise her lungs with a piercing howl.

Francis covered his ears. "Mmmmm, I know. My grandmother is beside herself with delight, seemingly even more so than when both sets of boys arrived," he shook his head in smiling puzzlement. "Needless to say, it's her family colouring, so I suppose she fancies a little Granville girl will grow up to be like her, heaven help us, but as you can hear, like her mother she has plenty to say for herself!"

He pulled a face as another wail rent the air. "I'm actually thinking of emigrating to Scotland for the next few months as she screeches like that from dawn to dusk and then half the night. She never seems to sleep for more than five minutes and she makes more noise than her four brothers put together; I'm sure the whole of Mayfair can hear her. The doctors say there's absolutely nothing the matter with her, she's just attention-seeking and making her presence felt and will grow out of it. I sincerely hope so or God only knows what she'll be like when she gets older," and he rolled his eyes theatrically.

Nicky burst out laughing and tried to shush the screaming infant, rocking her in his arms and crooning.

"Oh ho," laughed Cat, "so the special Nicky touch doesn't work with her; well, I suppose it's because she's definitely not a DUMB animal," and they all laughed. "Oh, give her to Francis, for heaven's sake, so I can have my tea in peace. He's the only one who can make her calm down," she sighed. "The infamous Firle charm does have its uses sometimes, especially at two in the morning," and all three of them laughed again as Nicky handed over the squalling, red faced infant who immediately quietened as soon as she looked up into her father's face. "See what I mean?" grinned Cat as she sat back and drank her tea.

Nicky spent a happy hour with Cat and Francis, periodically entertaining the demanding baby, and updating them on his adventures and explaining he only had a few days in London before he had to return to Spain. Cat was devastated on learning he wasn't on proper leave, but after relating some humorous stories about life in the Peninsula for his Aunt's benefit to cheer her up, she rose and took her leave, saying she had to supervise the nanny with the baby and get ready for dinner. As she bent to kiss his cheek lovingly with another emotional hug, she told him, "The boys are up at Oxford or at school and will be beyond cross to have missed you. They're so bloodthirsty, they all want to join the army and go off to fight Boney and kill every Frenchman in the Peninsula with you leading the way!" She shook her head and laughed before pausing for a few moments, finally saying quietly as she touched his hand, "Carlotta would have been so proud of you, My Love. I'm so relieved you're safe; I'm sure she's still looking after you from Heaven." Wiping a solitary tear from her cheek, she quietly left the room.

Nicky and Francis sat in silence for several seconds before Francis shook himself and got up to get the brandy decanter and refilled their glasses. He offered Nicky a cheroot as he took one himself and lit it from the low fire in the grate. Then he sat down, leaning back in his chair comfortably. Looking across at the younger man, he spoke quietly. "So, now you can tell me what you've really been up to since we last saw you...."

Chapter Five

Bella knew she couldn't stay out any longer. Nicky would be at home by now and she had to face him sooner or later. She tried to imagine how she would have greeted him if she hadn't known he was back and hoped her acting skills were up to the mark. Despite her lion mask and wig, she was terrified he'd still recognise her and it was with fingers crossed that she knocked on the door to his room shortly before they were all due downstairs for dinner. She had to see him alone, not in front of her Aunt and Uncle.

"Come." She heard the command and she nervously turned the handle and opened the door.

"Hello, Nicky," she said quietly as he turned to face her, abandoning the struggle to tie his cravat in an elaborate fall after nearly a year without having to wear one.

"Hello, Sooty," he spoke gently and was again taken aback by how stunningly lovely she looked. Her hair was piled high in a Grecian fashion, green ribbon threaded through it and long dark ringlets hanging over her shoulders and down her back. Her simple Grecian style, empire line dress of pale green silk brought out the colour of her eyes. He realised he'd missed her, both her laughter and her companionship, despite their angry parting and the cause of it. He simply couldn't stay cross with her and held out his arms, inviting her to give him a hug.

A big smile lighting up her face she rapidly crossed the room and let him envelop her in his arms, revelling in the feel of his body through the thin linen of his shirt as she lay her cheek against his heart. "I'm so pleased you're home safe," she mumbled into the warmth of his chest. "Every single day we worry word will come that something terrible has happened to you," and she looked up into his eyes, "I don't know what I'd do if it did, I couldn't bear it."

"Don't be a silly girl, I'm very careful," he smiled down at her as he kissed her cheek. "Anyway, I spend most of my time running errands for Wellington around his headquarters and doing paperwork, I'm never near any real danger."

Bella was astounded at his lie and pulled out of his arms to stand back and stamp her foot. "If you think I believe that tarradiddle, you're being an even bigger moron than usual," she blazed at him, hands on her hips. "You've no idea what's it like being here week after week, month after month, with no word, no letters, never knowing where you are, what you're doing, if or when you are ever coming back!" The pent-up angry words of concern poured out of her. "And it's not just me; Papa worries all the time and so does Uncle Francis. I know he hears things that he doesn't tell us and sometimes when Aunt Cat and I are out and we see some wounded or crippled soldiers, especially when they're begging for alms because they're too injured to work or fight any more, or have anyone to care for them, we just burst into tears thinking it could happen to you too. Some of their injuries…. lost arms and legs, blind or disfigured… it's all so terrible…"

Nicky went back to her and pulled her into a hug. "Oh, Sooty, I'm so sorry. Don't be cross with me, please; I don't mean to worry you all, surely you must know that, but it's so difficult to write sometimes when I'm in the field, the post isn't like here."

"Ha! You've just contradicted yourself seeing as how you said two seconds ago that you spend most of your time doing paperwork at HQ!" She looked up into his eyes again, her own suddenly glassy with tears, "We're not fools, Nicky, we know you're in danger. We hear about the skirmishes, the sieges, the battles and the terrible numbers of casualties at some of them. Just a note, even a line, now and again would at least let us know you're still alive or not terribly wounded. Please," she begged, tugging his shirt, "please remember that; we all care for you so much."

He sighed, "I know, I know," Nicky looked down at her, cuddled in his arms, her own wrapped around his waist and a great feeling of tenderness washed over him. He'd always felt so protective of her and he realised he'd never given enough thought to what she, indeed everyone here at home, was doing in his absence. He made a mental note to try and comply with her request, but he knew it wouldn't be easy when he often spent months undercover pretending to be French or Spanish in order to infiltrate behind enemy lines.

In the distance, the dinner gong sounded, bringing an end to their conversation. Nicky pulled away and turned again to the mirror to tie his cravat, swearing under his breath when it wouldn't go right.

"Oh come here, let me do it," Bella tutted. "I'll tell Benjy to get you organised tomorrow when he's sorted out Uncle Francis; he obviously didn't realise you were here and needed valeting." She picked up a freshly ironed neckcloth and proceeded to tie it in an artfully knotted creation, making a mental note to get her uncle's valet to lend some assistance the following evening. When she'd finished, she helped him into his waistcoat and a tightly fitting black evening jacket, smoothing the creases out and dusting off invisible bits of dust, until he stood back and expressed himself satisfied with his appearance, a pleased smile on his face.

"I knew I'd missed my calling. Perhaps I should get myself a position as a valet to while away my days when you're gone again," she joked at him. "And by the way, you need a haircut. Would you like me to oblige?" she giggled.

Nicky grinned as he looked at her in the reflection of the mirror, standing behind him, clothes brush in hand. "I don't think so, you and scissors are a definite no-no as far as I'm concerned. I'll get Benjy to do it," he chuckled, "but remind me in the morning and I'll put an advertisement in the Gazette for you." He started to intone in an affected voice, "'Bossy, argumentative and opinionated chatterbox seeks position as valet to a discerning Gentleman. Submissive, deaf applicants will be given preference. References supplied. I'll give you one with pleasure if you behave yourself," and he turned, tweaking her nose before grabbing her hand, throwing the clothes brush on the dresser then pulling her from the room and downstairs for dinner, the pair of them laughing as they ran down the stairs pell-mell like two children.

Dinner was an entertaining affair as Francis and Bella brought Nicky up to date with all the latest gossip and news about friends, relations and what was going on in the Ton, then Cat bored them all for a good fifteen minutes with endless anecdotes about what the baby had done that day, which wasn't much obviously, before Francis pithily told her they'd all fall asleep in their soup if she carried on like that. However, despite his words, Nicky could see his uncle was obviously as infatuated with his new little daughter as he still was with his wife; finally another baby, a daughter, something the pair of them had privately longed for after years of disappointments and heartache, desiring more children after two sets of twin sons who were now almost fully grown.

As dinner drew to a close, Bella wondered how Nicky was going to extricate himself from the bosom of his family without raising eyebrows, never mind what she would do. Fortunately, her aunt made her excuses, saying she needed to go and see to the baby again as she was being difficult with taking her feeds. In the end, her uncle unwittingly provided their escape. Turning to Nicky, Francis said he was going out to his club for a couple of drinks so he could avoid the forthcoming bout of screeching that would start fairly shortly as Elizabeth dealt with her wind after being fed, and he suggested Nicky join him if he too didn't want his nerves reduced to a frazzle. Bella excused herself and said she would go and help her aunt with the baby and the two men strolled away from the house, deep in conversation about the latest style of waistcoats currently in vogue among Gentlemen of the Ton.

Before running upstairs, Bella hastily ordered a footman to

summon her uncle's coach and when she had her cloak on, she raced out of the house and told the astonished coachman to hurry and deliver her round to the back entrance of *Le Lion d'Or*. Once inside, she ordered a bath and hurried up to her apartments to wash and change into her *Lionesse* costume and mask.

Remembering his comments about her perfume the night before, Bella had doused herself in some of her aunt's scent at home earlier in the evening before going to Nicky's room, so now she needed to wash it off in case he recognised it. As she sat in the bath, soaking up to her neck in scented water, she reflected that perhaps it was just as well he was only going to be home for a few days as all this subterfuge would wear her nerves to shreds, trying to remember everything and keep his curiosity at bay. Finally, she was ready and her maid had cleared away the remains of her bath and tidied her dressing and bathing rooms.

Having given instructions to the staff to tell any enquirers she was absent that evening, Bella went through to her sitting room and peered round a drawn curtain to watch for his arrival. She sat patiently, quietly sipping a glass of champagne to relieve the tension and expectation that was racing around her stomach.

At last, she spotted his tall, handsome form lightly run up the entrance steps and she smiled to herself like a satisfied cat. She knew he'd be told she was absent, if he asked, so she thought she'd let him stew for a while. The clock ticked quietly as she added another log to the fire and mindlessly tidied the room again. She wandered through to her bedroom, ensuring nothing there would give her identity away. She'd taken all of her personal items that he would recognise back to Firle House that morning and replaced the bare wall with another painting, so she was just biding her time before sending down to invite him to join her. Eventually, her impatience got the better of her and, as she looked at her clock for the umpteenth time, she summoned a maid to take a short note to Nicky, describing him in detail to her and reminding her to be discreet with its delivery.

Upstairs at midnight, if you want to play again....

• • •

She sat in front of the fire, sipping another glass of champagne and waited. The mantel clock chimed and she watched the door handle turn. Timekeeping had never been his strong point, but tonight it was faultless.

Chapter Six

Nicky had left Francis in deep discussion with a business acquaintance about the current prices of tea and coffee beans and said he was going off to look up some old friends for a drink while he had the chance of a few free evenings. Francis had merely winked at him and told him to ensure whatever gutter he passed out in was relatively clean and with a laugh he'd hurried off and made his way straight round to *Le Lion d'Or*. On enquiring where *La Lionesse* was, he was taken aback to be told she wasn't there.

He'd wandered around the tables for a while, distractedly laying a few random chips here and there, wondering what to do. He was winding himself up into a fine state about her and his necklace when he felt a quiet touch on his elbow and a maid handed over a small, folded piece of paper, curtsied and disappeared. He read the note, breathed a sigh of relief and took out his pocket watch to check the time. Ten minutes to midnight. He smirked to himself and went to get a drink to pass the next ten minutes.

On the stroke of midnight he turned the handle to her sitting room door and strolled in nonchalantly, smiling at her, for all the world looking as if he'd passed the last hour idly gaming at the tables below, instead of contemplating murder if she'd disappeared with his treasured necklace.

"*Bonsoir, Lionesse,*" he greeted her seductively, "did you think about me at all today?" and he took her extended bare hand and kissed it with an exaggerated bow, before turning it over to place a hot kiss in her palm, on her wrist and ran his tongue lightly up the underside of her forearm.

Bella shivered in reaction as she laughed and whispered saucily, "I may have done, but I couldn't possibly tell you, *Milor,*" and he laughed back.

She indicated the seat opposite her at the table and rose to pour him a glass of champagne.

"Did you find my necklace, by the way? It's a family heirloom and has great sentimental value to me so I'd be devastated to lose it," he looked at her anxiously, "more than devastated actually. It's my most precious possession."

"Don't worry, of course I found it and I have it safe." She looked at him, "I gathered this morning it means a lot to you. Did you get it from someone special? Is it an heirloom from your family or a lady friend? Maybe your wife?" she couldn't help it, she was curious to know what he'd say to that query. "You never said if you have one here in England you know, only that there's no one special waiting for you in the Peninsula."

He looked at her oddly for a moment, thinking an heirloom was obviously something personal and it was a strange comment, then laughed and shook his head. "The necklace is a treasured heirloom from my ancestral family and as for my personal life, well, it's a trifle complicated but there's no one special," he paused for a moment as he grappled with an explanation. "In point of fact I do have a wife, but it's just a marriage of convenience. She needed a marriage certificate to claim an inheritance at short notice, and I happened to be convenient," he chuckled. "But she's like my sister truth be told, just a close childhood friend, so it's not a true marriage. I have to see to getting it annulled but I can't sort all that out while I'm buried down in Spain. It's been too long as it is."

"Really?" was all she managed to get out. Bella could have strangled him on the spot. Annulled indeed, a bit late for that now, but she managed to tamp down her anger as he continued.

"Regarding the necklace, it was given me by my father just before he died; it's very old and was traditionally handed down from father to son from what I know. It's the only thing that remains to remind me of my late family and former life in France. That's why it's so precious to me. Literally everything else was lost: my parents, my family home, estates and income. All I had, now have, is my life, which, don't get me wrong, I'm grateful for, but it would all have been very different if circumstances hadn't intervened back then. May I have it back, *Lionesse*? I've felt naked without it all day and I want to get the clasp or chain fixed before I return to Spain," he held his hand out, obviously expecting her to go and get it.

Well, Bella thought, she'd be damned if she would, not after that little gem about annulling his marriage. He could bloody well wait for it a bit longer.

"And what do I get in return for it then?" she purred.

He looked at her. "What would you like?" his lips curled in a slow, seductive smile "Anything to please a lady, or a lioness…"

"Hmmm, I was going to suggest a game of cards, so I could try and win another 'favour' from you, seeing as how I quite enjoyed last night's one."

"Only 'quite' *Lionesse*? That wasn't my impression." Another smile and he licked his lips.

Bella could feel the awareness pulse between them and the air almost crackled; the glasses of champagne had caught up with her as she'd only eaten sparsely at dinner, too wound up at the prospect of what would happen later. She felt quite mischievous. "Well, a man of your talents surely aspires to improve his performance, after all I only climaxed…" She counted the fingers of her hand, "How many times was it?"

Nicky rocked back in his chair and guffawed. "You Wicked Baggage, you made me late back on duty this morning. I'm damn sure it was well into daylight when you woke me up, never mind that 'oh, it's still dark, Nicky, you've got plenty of time'," he mimicked her seductive whisper.

"And have you got to be back on duty early tomorrow morning as well?" she purred.

"Now why would you want to know that *Lionesse*?" he smirked at her.

She held up her fingers and started counting again and another burst of laughter shook his frame.

"You're very presumptuous, y'know," he chuckled, "I really only came back for my necklace."

It was her turn to laugh. "Of course you did. Shall I go and get it and then you can take your leave?"

He held up his fingers and started to count. "I wonder just how many times you can manage in one night?" Bella went hot and cold and felt excitement course through her; this delicious, suggestive Romeo was all hers for now and she wanted him so desperately, once again she could barely think straight. "That's a lot of favours," he said with a smirk. "Last night's extra ones were on the house. Tonight, what do I get in return?"

"Your necklace?" she whispered. "Or do you want to play a game with me for it instead?"

He looked at her consideringly, "Why do I get the feeling it's all one and the same thing?"

"I was only talking about a game of cards," she whispered, the silence crackling between them.

"So was I, but I just have this funny feeling you'll win again and demand another favour, or five or ten – and I'll still be without my necklace." He stared at her impassively but then grinned, "Oh what the hell, I want my necklace *and* I want to make love to you over and over again until you beg me to stop; and what's more, I think you want me as much as I want you, so why are we sitting here pussyfooting around?" He got up abruptly, walked round to her side of the table and pulled her to her feet. He took her in his arms and bent his head to kiss up and down her neck, revelling in her shivered response. He dragged her dress down off her shoulders, his mouth following where her soft skin was revealed, "*Mon Dieu, Lionesse*, I've been dreaming of doing this all day. I couldn't concentrate in those damn meetings I got caught up in this morning, I just want to kiss you and taste your sweet body all over again," and his hands went up to undo the strings of her mask.

"What are you doing?" she cried hoarsely "You can't take my mask off, I told you last night."

"Oh, come on, *Lionesse*, I won't tell anyone. I probably wouldn't recognise you anyway, I've been away from London for so long and I'm going back to Spain in a matter of days anyway."

"No. I can't take it off. I won't let you or anyone see me. No one, but no one, knows my real name either, not even my servants. I am simply *Lionesse* to everyone. You know my terms, just like last night, nothing's changed. My way or no way." She sounded very firm.

"NO!" he bit back angrily. "I won't let you do that to me again. I refuse to make love to someone I can't see, it's completely ridiculous!" he stormed at her, again attempting to reach round her head and undo the strings.

She pulled away from him, backing up towards her bedroom. "If you REALLY want me, you'll do it, otherwise you have to go. NOW."

"*Merde!* What is it with you?" and he swore again, volubly in French, a sure sign, she knew, he was losing his temper. "I WON'T be ordered around by any woman, no matter how much I want her, especially not a fucking tart who runs a gaming hell!"

"HOW DARE YOU?!" Bella shrieked, forgetting to whisper as she too lost her temper. "You know nothing about me, NOTHING! I may run a gaming salon, but this is a respectable establishment, not a whorehouse, you can look at my girls but THAT'S ALL. Most definitely no touching or anything inappropriate, they're merely an amusing decoration to wait on tables or deal – AND I most certainly am NOT a fucking tart!" With that, she stormed up to him and slapped his face.

Nicky's head reared back from the force of her blow and he glared at her, now in a towering rage. "Where's my necklace? I'm leaving…"

"Somewhere you'll never find it!" she yelled back at him.

He grabbed her arm and forced it up behind her back until she screamed with pain. "Where is it? I want it back, THIS MINUTE!"

"I'll never tell you, NEVER! Get out of my apartment," she seethed.

"Oh no, *Lionesse*," he suddenly growled, "not without what I came for," and she whimpered as he forced her arm up further. "Don't make me do this, you won't like it if you make me hurt you," he paused and laughed coldly. "You can count climaxes on your fingers, I simply count the number of men I've killed, and I'm not talking about in a battle situation. I can assure you my count is much, much higher than yours, You Conniving, Thieving Trollop."

Bella was frightened and angry. This was yet another Nicky she didn't know. When did he become such a cold and ruthless individual? She'd never seen him like this.

But then reason kicked in, this wasn't some strange man threatening her, this was her husband, a man she'd known all her life and she knew deep down he wouldn't intentionally hurt someone weaker than himself, especially a woman. She just knew it. She also hadn't grown up with four unruly boys, her Granville cousins, as well as Nicky. As they stood there, panting, as he waited for her answer, she suddenly went limp in his arms and when he let her arm go to catch her, she turned suddenly and kneed him viciously in the crotch.

He instantly doubled over in agony, swearing even more volubly as he collapsed on the floor, groaning in pain. She couldn't help it, the situation was truly ridiculous and she simply collapsed back on her chair laughing her head off, tears streaming down her face under her mask.

Nicky had managed to pull himself back upright and was sitting with his back against the wall, feeling like his testicles were on fire. He stared in utter astonishment as he watched her burst into fits of laughter, tears rolling out from under her mask as she doubled up in mirth. For the life of him he couldn't see what was so funny and it was such a strange reaction.

As her laughter subsided, Bella looked over at him, smiled and got up. She walked over to a beautiful Louis XVI sideboard and found a bottle of brandy inside. Removing the cork, she went back to him and silently handed it over. As he took a long slug of the fiery liquor, shuddering as it burned its way down his throat, she leaned down and kissed his cheek. "Oh Lord, I'm so sorry, but you've only got yourself to blame, you know," and she grinned at him. "I grew up in an extended family as one girl with a lot of really annoying little boys."

She crouched down in front of him and tilted her head to one side in her lion's mask, sighing as she spoke in her hoarse voice, trying to put things right between them and praying he would respond to her simple appeal to his good nature.

"Where the hell did this evening go wrong, Nicky? I was so looking forward to it and you've already said you were too, so can't we start again? We're a fine pair you and I, not wanting to give in to anyone and I'm afraid my temper does run away with itself sometimes. But I promise you I'm not a tart, nor am I in the least promiscuous. I'm extremely fussy in my choice of men and I've turned down more offers than I can remember so am NO trollop. However, I do want YOU, more than anything," she whispered, "but for reasons I truly can't explain, I have to keep my identity a secret," and Bella picked up one of his hands and kissed it gently on the back. "I'd very much like you to stay with me tonight, to make love to me like you did last night. I think you enjoyed it as much as I did despite your objections, hmmmm?" she tilted her head the other way, "But if you really can't face it now, I won't mind and you can have your necklace back with pleasure. I wouldn't dream of keeping something so valuable and precious from you. So what do you say? Come to bed with me, Nicky, my way... please?"

She kissed his hand again as he sat there silently. "If I've wounded you so desperately, we don't have to make love, but I'd get huge pleasure just falling asleep in your arms again, so I give you my word if you have to be up and on duty early, I'll make sure you wake up in good time to get back to your home or barracks to shave and change into your uniform. I might even treat you to breakfast before you go, food that is..." and she laughed at him saucily.

Nicky sat impassively and watched her as she sat in front of him, her head tilting from side to side as she spoke in that fascinating mask. His privates throbbed dreadfully but it was nothing to his horror at how he'd hurt her. How did she manage to make him lose his temper over something so trivial? He'd never laid a hand on a woman in his life. Well, apart from Sooty. A sudden memory popped into his mind of when he'd spanked her really hard her one day when she'd stolen his clothes from the river bank where she'd come across him skinny dipping and he'd had to go back to the house stark naked. He'd been sixteen or seventeen and quite manly even then. He remembered the shrieks of the housemaids when they'd spotted him strolling along the long portrait gallery in Firle Manor, deliberately leaving himself naked instead of finding a towel, sheet or coat in the scullery or back hallway to cover himself. Mrs Collins' face had been a picture and the very upright, proper, elderly housekeeper hadn't known where to look when she'd noticed how aroused he'd got after exchanging teasing banter with the young cleaning maids. He'd never seen anyone go so red.

But this woman had a strange effect on him. She made him laugh, she made him angry, she seemed to sense his moods and know what made him tick. It was uncanny. And she wanted him. She'd come out and admitted it, as well as apologise for something that really wasn't her fault, she'd only been teasing him. And she was right of course. He had enjoyed the previous night and he knew he'd been prepared to do the same thing again when he'd come to meet her tonight, although obviously he'd rather make love to someone he could see. But he'd found the whole episode strangely erotic and arousing and it was a small price to pay for the stunning pleasure he'd experienced. She was right. What the hell were they doing arguing? They should be in bed now, enjoying themselves, playing her games instead of throwing insults at each other.

As she sat and watched, his lips gradually curled into that intoxicating smile and he crooked a finger at her. As she leaned forward, their lips were mere inches apart as he breathed, "I'm so sorry, *Chérie*, I truly hope I haven't hurt you. I'm not like that normally, you just have a strange effect on me. So will you accept my very humble apology? It wasn't your fault at all, it was all mine. I promise I'll make it up to you. You can have as many favours as you can manage, even if I can't manage much for myself at the moment," he grinned wickedly at her, "but maybe you can kiss me better later, hmmmm?" He laughed then, "Oh, by the way, I don't have to be anywhere tomorrow morning, so breakfast in bed at some point would be a delightful treat for this poor wounded soldier, especially if you were the *hors d'oeuvres*, so much more tasty than porridge."

Bella laughed back at him. "Porridge? You're quite impossible, you know that, but I simply can't resist you." She put out a hand to help him to his feet, giggling as he groaned and winced. When he finally stood up straight, she pulled him through to her bedroom.

As they approached her bed, he turned her towards him looking at her seriously. "Are you sure I didn't hurt you?" he gently lifted the arm he'd pulled on earlier.

"No, of course not, we *Lionesses* are tougher than we look," she laughed. "I think you're suffering far more than me, are you sure you're all right?" she tilted her head at him again in query.

"I'll survive," he quipped, then grinned, "annoying little boys eh? I'm glad I wasn't your brother, a baggage like you would undoubtedly have driven me witless."

"Oh, DEFINITELY!" was her enigmatic and laughing reply as she helped him pull off his tight-fitting jacket and went to hang it over the back of a chair.

As she sat down on the side of the bed, he turned to her. "Do you want me to strip for you again?" a naughty smile curving his mouth.

She laughed, "I don't think my heart rate could take it tonight after all that just now," and she waggled a finger at him. "You should have a warning sign round your neck you know, 'Beware all women – I am a very dangerous man!'"

He burst out laughing then pierced her with his eyes, "In which case, *Lionesse,* YOU'LL have to undress me instead," he whispered to her suggestively.

"Now there's an interesting proposition; it'll be just like Christmas or my birthday, except I know what's inside the wrapping," she purred. "Come here," and crooked her finger, mimicking his gesture to her earlier.

He went and stood in front of her and slowly she undid the buttons of his waistcoat, rising to go behind him and pull it off his shoulders. She went and hung it over his jacket. Then she went back to stand in front of him and unknotted the cravat she'd so artistically tied earlier that evening; she threw it carelessly over the end of the bed and started on his shirt, undoing the fastenings over his chest and slowly pulling it out of his waistband. As she tugged, she let her hand caress lower over the growing hardness evident at the front of his skin-tight inexpressibles and, as he caught his breath, she pulled the shirt right out and gradually lifted it up his chest, bending to lick his nipples as she slowly exposed his hot skin. She spotted a faded scar under his ribs she hadn't noticed the previous night, "What's that from?" she queried, bending to kiss it briefly and he chuckled as her mask tickled his skin. "A romantic war wound?"

He laughed lightly, "No, merely the wrong end of a knife from a footpad. I was just being a Good Samaritan and helping out someone he attacked. It's nothing," he shrugged.

"Hmmm, that's a big nothing," she whispered, grimacing and running her finger along the puckered skin. "The Good Samaritan never had anything like this," but he didn't say more, just laughed as her finger tickled where it ran along the scar.

She pulled his shirt right off and simply stood for a moment admiring his muscled torso, his sun-bleached chest hair glinting in the lamplight. Slowly, she ran her fingernail down his chest from the base of his neck to the top of his revealing inexpressibles, taking a detour to circle round and scratch each of his nipples. She waggled her finger in his belly button and then slowly, teasingly, undid the top couple of fastenings of his snug pantaloons. However, as she felt him shudder in expectation, she grinned and instead of undoing the rest, she pushed him down to sit on the bed and bent over to pull off his shoes and stockings.

Putting them over by his jacket and waistcoat, she returned to the bed and clambered up behind him. She reached over and pulled the gold sash out from under a pillow and leaned down to whisper in his ear. "Does the condemned man have any final requests?"

Nicky thought he'd have one final try. "Er...don't do it?" he pleaded.

"Wrong answer," she tutted.

"Take my pantaloons off?" he grinned.

"Aah, right answer," and she ran a stream of butterfly kisses across his shoulders and the back of his neck. "In just a minute," and she wound the sash over his eyes once more, listening to him sigh with frustration.

It took her moments to rip off the mask and wig and let down her hair, then she quickly pulled off her dress, petticoat and underthings and threw them carelessly on the floor. She returned to lean into his back, free now to pull him back against her, wind her arms around him and let her hands rove down over his bare chest as she nuzzled his neck and ran her tongue around his ear, hungry to get her hands on him and feel the warm skin of his body against hers. "Mmmmm, that's better," she muttered, "and the condemned man should stand up now, ready to meet his fate," she purred.

Nicky rose to his feet. Still kneeling on the bed behind him, Bella put her arms around his waist and undid the remaining fastenings on his figure-hugging clothing. Then slowly, she began to peel them downwards, over his hips and down his thighs. As she pushed the material down, her hands caressed his throbbing erection, running her fingers up and down its length before sheathing it fully in one hand, moving it back and forth.

He threw his head back and sighed with pleasure and she moved off the bed to stand behind him and bent down to run a line of wet kisses along his spine. As she bent to push the inexpressibles down the remainder of his legs, she kissed his buttocks and the backs of his thighs.

She kissed the little birthmark she knew was at the top of his left thigh, at the side of his bottom. "Aha, what's this? Why, it looks like a... ah, hmmmmm, a little cat?"

He grinned. "It's not a cat, it's a little lion-shaped birthmark, just like on my necklace. It runs in the family. I can still remember my father showing me his when I was a little boy."

"Well, fancy that," she muttered and ran her finger over it, grinning to herself.

Finally, she pulled off the obscenely tight pantaloons and went to stand in front of him. "Have you finished your inspection?" he queried with a smile, tilting his head to one side as he listened to her quiet breathing, "Or are you going to count my freckles next?"

"Oh, I haven't got time for that now," she sighed, "I've much more important things to do," and finally she snaked her arms around his neck and leaned up to kiss him.

Once again, the simmering passion between them burst into life and he pulled her hard into his embrace to kiss her hungrily. "Aaah, *Lionesse*," he breathed, "I've thought about doing this again all day," and Bella sighed as the kiss deepened and his hands roved urgently up and down her arms and back, caressing her neck and winding her long hair around his fist.

"Your hair feels so long and curly," he lifted a hand to her face and wound a stray long tendril around a finger, "what colour is it? At least tell me that."

"What colour do you think it is?" she teased softly.

He thought then about the colour of her skin, what he'd seen of it: lips, chin, neck, chest, arms and hands. "Hmmmm, why do I not think you're blonde?" he tilted his head as he thought. "Somehow your skin is too creamy, too peachy, ever so slightly olive, to belong to someone with really fair hair; and I don't think you're a redhead or ginger for the same reason, distinct lack of freckles for the latter, so are you a mouse?" he mused to himself, suddenly enjoying the guessing game. "No, definitely not that," he laughed, "a chestnut or a brunette then, or maybe your hair is black, like the night?"

She laughed back at him. "Very perceptive, aren't you? Let's just say I'm definitely not blonde, nor any kind of red or reddish brown, nor ginger and most assuredly, not a mouse. So, simple brunette or ebony, which would you prefer?"

"I have a preference?" he joked.

"Well, it's your fantasy."

"Hmmmm, my fantasy? Well, with that skin, I think... black hair. Mmmmm, yes, long black curls that run all the way down your back." Nicky's hand ran through her hair at that and roved down to her waist. "And your eyes? Let me think," he leaned down, feeling for and kissing both of her closed lids, "what goes with black hair? Black flashing eyes maybe?" he considered, tipping his head to one side. "No, I see enough of those on the senoritas in the Peninsula."

Bella poked him in the chest, "Enough of that, thank you."

He laughed out loud, holding up his hands in mock surrender, "All right, all right, so what's left? Brown? No, too boring and brown doesn't go with black. Shocking colour mismatch, as my tailor would say," another grin as he thought of Benjy. "Blue, then?" a sudden vision of his Uncle Francis and his Great Aunt Elizabeth came to Nicky's mind. "Hmmm, possibly, very arresting on the right people. And then there's green?" Who did he know with green eyes? His stepfather who was fair, his Aunt Cat with her amazing toffee colouring; and Sooty. She had her mother's dark hair and her father's green eyes. Quickly he shut down that thought and shook his head. "Hmmm, I'm not sure... but green I think?" he still said for some unknown reason and put his hands to her face, letting them rove over it caressingly, feeling the high cheekbones under the soft, smooth skin. "So, does my fantasy match the reality, *Lionesse*?" he kissed her again then, tasting, feeling the desire course through him.

Bella was fascinated at his train of thought... and startled. He'd guessed without realising, almost as if he could really see her. Absently, she waved a hand in front of his sightless eyes to reassure herself and shivered. "If that's what you'd like, then that's what I'll be," she purred and lost her train of thought as he bent his head to kiss her again.

He fell backward on to the bed, pulling her with him, unwilling to break the kiss. As they landed, laughing, in a heap of covers and pillows and tangled limbs, Bella inadvertently put her hands on either side of his ribs and, so ticklish as he was, he cringed and laughed. She tickled him, unable once more to resist the temptation.

"Oh no, not again... pleeease," he begged, laughing and wriggling. "Have pity on me, for God's sake, it's not fair when I can't fight back."

"Oh, but I can't resist teasing you," she laughed softly, knowing how ridiculous his plea of weakness was.

They wrestled around on the bed as she tried to tickle him again but he managed to get hold of her hands in his and roll her over, under his strong body. He easily pulled both of her wrists into one strong, vice-like grip and held them over her head. "You really are enjoying having me at your mercy, aren't you, You Wicked Baggage?" he smiled as bent his head and kissed her lightly on the lips. "But I swear to God, one day, I'll pay you back for this and play exactly the same game with you, if it's the last thing I do. Then you'll suffer," he laughed wickedly.

"You'll have to find me first though," she teased. "Just think, you could walk past me one day in Bond Street and never know it was me."

"Oh no, *Lionesse*, I'm sure now I'd recognise you if I saw you. I'd know your scent, your lovely hair. I don't know," he sighed, "I'm just positive I'd know you."

She giggled. "Don't you believe it. You'll never know unless I let you find out."

"I'll just have to kiss and smell all the interesting women in Bond Street with black hair and green eyes that take my fancy, until I do find you," and he bent his head and kissed her again as they both laughed.

"You're so funny when you let yourself go," she said to him reflectively as he released her hands and she lifted them to stroke his shoulders and arms. "You should share your thoughts more often instead of keeping them all bottled up inside you."

"That's an odd thing to say, *Lionesse*. Why do you think I do that?" Nicky was somewhat taken aback she'd seemed to sense his reticence, or self-possession sometimes.

Bella swallowed hard, she hadn't meant to say that; it had just popped out unintentionally. She knew there was always something of a loner about him, a withdrawn self-possession that none of the family, except maybe her late mother, her Great Aunt Elizabeth and sometimes herself as she'd grown a bit older, had been able to penetrate. She thought it was a result of his traumatic early childhood, but seeing him like this, being so close and intimate with him, was like peeling back layers of petals in a flower bud as different aspects of the man he had become were revealed to her.

"Aaah, female intuition," she tapped him on the nose. "We *Lionesse*s can feel these things."

"Hmmm, well, I think it's about time I gave you something else to feel. Now then, are you counting your favours, *Lionesse*?"

"Ready and waiting, *Milor*, how many fingers will I need?"

He loved her all night, responding to her inadvertent challenge, making her climax over and over again until she was limp and exhausted in his arms and she'd fallen asleep, wrapped around him like a human blanket. It was mid-morning when she opened a sleepy eye and looked at the time, shocked to see how late it was. Nicky was still fast asleep beside her, sprawled out in his usual abandonment. She smiled lustfully at the sight of him and the memories of a second scorching night in his arms.

She staggered out of bed, her limbs and brain still lethargic from the intense passion she'd discovered she possessed. He obviously thought she knew herself, but Bella was still coming to terms with the reality of it. Donning a wrapper, she tottered through to her sitting room and rang for her maid and ordered a hot breakfast for two to be served in the sitting room in half an hour. Ignoring her slightly curious look, she dismissed the girl and went back to creep under the covers for a while longer. When she heard the breakfast arrive, a naughty smile curved her lips and she went through to retrieve a plate with a warm croissant and some honey. He'd wanted breakfast in bed, so she would serve it to him, except she intended to be the main course before the reality of the rest of the day intruded.

Nicky woke when he felt his feet being tickled at the end of the bed and rolled around laughing, seeking the comfort of the bedclothes to shelter under. He smelled the tantalising aroma of warm pastry and hot coffee and groaned as his stomach rumbled. "Well, good morning, Lazybones. It's just as well you didn't have to be anywhere important early today," a smiling voice purred in his ear.

"Oh, hell, what on earth is the time?" he muttered as he struggled to sit up and automatically went to pull the sash from his eyes.

"Pardon me, did I say you could take it off? You won't get any breakfast if you do," and she laughed, waving the warm croissant under his nose, "and don't panic, if you truly don't have to be anywhere, just sit back and enjoy your breakfast; you'll never guess what the dish of the day is?"

"Oh lord, how long are you going to keep me a prisoner here and torture me like this?" he grinned.

"As long as you like, You Wicked Man. Here, open wide," and she popped a piece of croissant covered in warm, runny honey in his mouth, kissing him after he'd swallowed it, licking the flaky pastry remnants off his lips. He sighed at the decadent pleasure, trying to remember when he'd last eaten fresh, warm croissants and honey for breakfast. They were his favourite. He'd always had a sweet tooth and had learned quickly as a little boy, with a bit of coaching from his unrepentant Uncle Francis, how to wrap the fierce but gifted cook at Firle Manor round his little finger to get her to make sweets and cakes for him.

Bella knew him well and smiled at his continued sighs of pleasure as she fed him the rest of the fresh pastry and then laughed when he grabbed her hand and licked the sticky honey off her fingers. "The dish of the day will have to be something very special to better that," he challenged, smiling suggestively as he lay back with his arms propped under his head.

Bella crept into the bed next to him, forgetting about the fragrant coffee growing cold on the table, "Oh, it is, it is, I promise," she purred, "even if I say so myself," and she kissed him hungrily, her hand slowly crawling down his body.

Chapter Seven

Nicky was just creeping quietly up the stairs back at Firle House, hoping to avoid anyone who would note he was still in his evening clothes, when he bumped into Francis rounding the corner from the upstairs landing. The Duke smirked at him. "Well, that must have been an interesting and very clean gutter you found last night?" he let the question hang in the air.

"Mmmmm," Nicky replied with a deadpan expression, "it definitely was," and listened to Francis's dirty chuckle as he made his way downstairs. He wasn't sure what the Duke made of his relationship with Bella and whether he thought they would be sleeping together now, but he was going to confront her today, get things straightened out and then seek Francis's assistance to make the arrangements. He went through into his bedroom and summoned a footman to order a bath and some coffee and sandwiches. He smiled to himself as he remembered the cold and congealed food he'd seen in *Lionesse*'s sitting room as he'd left, munching another croissant, after another pleasurable hour in her bed after she'd woken him with that delicious pastry and honey. He realised she must have ordered them in specially for him, presumably assuming that because he was French he must like them, or be used to having them for breakfast. Well, not in the Peninsula, that was for sure. He thought back and realised it was years since he'd had one, specially made for him by Mrs Farthing, the cook at Firle Manor. That female tyrant had always had a soft spot for him, ever since he'd arrived there as an orphaned little boy of nearly five. Him and Fluffy, his Aunt's first big white furry dog, one of Bubbles' forebears. The only other creature to get under the cook's armour. He smiled at the memories.

As he soaked in his bath, munching on his sandwiches, Bella crept in up the back stairs and hurried along to her room. The servants had become used to her comings and goings at all hours so took no notice – just what they thought she was doing she had no idea – but since her aunt and uncle knew the reasons and took no notice, the staff followed suit. They'd concluded she did charity work among the poor and sick, following in the footsteps of her aunt's charitable endeavours, never dreaming of the reality and anyway, she was always far too well turned out to have come from some man's bed.

Bella also ordered a bath and was sitting, drying off her long hair in front of the fire when Nicky knocked on her door. She told him to wait a moment as she hurriedly pinned it up, not wanting him to see how long it now was... fairly sure he wouldn't remember from the previous year, he'd been too preoccupied with shouting at her after her uncle had unexpectedly walked into Nicky's room and discovered them both there, fast asleep in bed.

She went and opened the door and invited him in, walking over to the fire to stand expectantly, knowing full well what he wanted to talk about.

"We have to discuss our marriage, Bella," Nicky came straight out with it and she noted she wasn't Sooty today. "After what happened when I was last at home," he coughed awkwardly, "I'm not sure if we can still get an annulment, it might have to be a divorce now, but I intend to speak to your Uncle Francis about it, unless you have already?" he raised an eyebrow at her.

She watched as he walked back and forth across her carpet, his hands deep in his pockets, face devoid of emotion. "No, I haven't spoken to him," she replied quietly and took a deep breath. "You see, I don't want the marriage annulled, but you know that, and I don't want a divorce now either. You don't want to marry someone else, do you Nicky?" she asked as an afterthought.

"No, of course not, don't be silly," he replied dismissively, "but you know I can't stay married to you, or marry anyone else. I have no money to speak of, no home, no estate to call my own, just a useless, dead title which in a way makes my whole situation even more pathetic," he sounded bitter, "and there's always the chance I'll be killed before this never-ending war is over as well."

"Nicky," Bella cried, "never say that, pleeeease."

"Besides," he looked directly at her, "we've been through all this. You're like a little sister to me and I'm very fond of you, you know that; I just don't love you the right way," he actually looked embarrassed.

Bella stamped her foot in frustration. "I AM NOT YOUR SISTER!" she yelled angrily. "We're NOT related by blood in any way whatsoever. For the last time, get that into your thick, French, ducal head. Nor am I a little girl in pigtails or plaits and a pinafore any more. LOOK AT ME," she poked herself in the chest, "in case you're going blind, I'm all grown up, I'm a woman now." She stormed over to him and poked him in the chest this time, "And, in case you've also forgotten, you didn't have a problem making love to me last year either."

He grabbed her by the shoulders, "I was deadly drunk. I didn't even realise I was at home in my own bed, never mind what I was doing, until it was too late and…you tricked me. I'd never have taken your virginity otherwise. What do you take me for? I'm not that desperate."

"Desperate? You BASTARD!" she yelled again and for the second time in twenty-four hours she slapped him. But Nicky was used to arguing and fighting with the girl he'd always regarded as his annoying but treasured little sister and so, accustomed to her tantrums and how to deal with them, he calmly slapped her back.

"Ooooh, how dare you?!" she shrieked again, stamping her foot and beating him on the chest with her fists.

He pulled them off as if they were irritating flies. "Will. You. Calm. Down. I refuse to let you rile me, You Wretched Girl."

"I'm not a wretched girl," Bella yelled. "I'm a woman, I've just told you. If you took the time to actually look at me for two minutes, you might notice. Plenty of men do."

"Well, good for them," he said coolly. "Even more reason to get our marriage dissolved, then you can go off and marry one of your admirers."

"But I don't want to marry anyone else. I want to stay married to you. I don't give a fig if you haven't a penny, or a home or an estate or that you're a Duke or a soldier; anyway, your home is here with us or with Papa at Arlington. Now I've got my inheritance we can live on that and anyway, you do have your income from those American investments and the ones in the Indies. I know Papa and Uncle Francis keep their eyes on them for you. And I... I... have some other invest-ments now too which will help."

Nicky took a deep breath, "I've told you before, I will NOT live on charity – yours, your father's or Francis's. They've both offered to give me money until I'm sick of it, but I've turned them down flat. Not do I ever want to live off my wife, whoever she might be. I care for you all deeply, you've been more of a family to me than any I would have had in France, I'm sure, but I'm still a penniless orphan. I have nothing else, but I at least have my pride, so I have to make my own way in the world. I might even go to the Americas when the war is over and try and seek my fortune and find a life there. There's quite a large French community in the southern states like Louisiana, espe-cially New Orleans. I've thought about it a lot while I've been away and..."

"WHAAAAT?" Bella interrupted with a horrified cry. "You can't go away and live somewhere else. It's bad enough knowing you're in the Peninsula, but at least that's not so far nor permanent. America is on the other side of the world; it would break Papa's heart and Aunt Cat's too, and Uncle Francis's as well and Great Aunt Elizabeth's... and mine..." she finally whispered.

"Stop being so dramatic; try and be sensible and realistic for once. What else am I going to do? To be honest, it was only an idea, the Americas, though it does sometimes appeal," he spoke almost to himself, "but I presume I'll end up in the Diplomatic Corps since I can speak a few languages. But that still means living abroad and traipsing around from country to country at the whim of some Government bureaucrat here in Whitehall. It's no life for a wife and family."

"I'd follow you anywhere," Bella said quietly, "and I speak French and Spanish almost as well as you. There are plenty of men in the Diplomatic Service who have wives and families, you know that full well. Look at Aunt Cat's godmother. Lady Harriet has a lovely life. She raised her children quite easily and they're all perfectly amiable and happy. Lord Aubrey comes and goes, well not as much as he used to these days, but they've had an extremely contented existence...."

"Lord Aubrey also has a nice private income; that makes quite a difference. Harriet Aubrey has never wanted for anything in her entire life and is surrounded by luxury, so when Lord Aubrey finally gives up flag waving or whatever he does for King and country, they'll both enjoy a very comfortable retirement."

"Nicky, will you stop being so proud and self-reliant. Look here, just supposing I borrowed some money in your name, invested it on your behalf and if it made a nice profit, would you accept that?"

Nicky was a bit taken aback. "I'm... I'm not sure," but then he looked at her suspiciously. "What are you up to, Bella? I know you, you've got that funny expression on your face you get when you've been naughty, or you're doing something you shouldn't and try to look innocent."

"Oh really, I'm not ten any more, You Worm," she glared at him, "and I have not been naughty nor done something I shouldn't. I was just asking. Well, answer me, would you? If the money didn't come from any of us in the family?"

He continued to look at her warily. "I don't know, but, if it wasn't a gift or charity or from anyone here," he waved his hand in the air, "simply just an investment and it was my money, then yes, I suppose so," but he knew her well and pulled her round to face him, looking down into her big green eyes with an intent stare. "Tell me what you're doing, Bella. I know you're up to something but I won't be manipulated, especially by you."

"I'm not up to anything. I was only asking. I've merely had one or two ideas, that's all. I'm also still your wife at the moment, whether you like it or not. You don't think I simply sit here all day sewing samplers or knitting, do you? And I can't paint or draw and I categorically refuse to play the piano." She smiled innocently at him, "Anyway, you don't have to worry, just because you're off fighting the French single-handed in the Peninsula by the sound of it, back here in London, between Papa and Uncle Francis, I'm well-guarded to keep me out of trouble, I promise you."

Nicky rolled his eyes heavenward. He knew it, she was definitely up to her armpits in mischief, he'd stake his life on it. But there wasn't much he could do about it, he'd be off back to Spain in another few days so didn't know what to do. The conversation had gone round in circles and there was no talking to her and she wouldn't sign the papers, she'd made it plain. He decided to leave it for today and go and have a quiet chat with Francis and see what he could sort out on his behalf by way of an annulment or divorce. He sighed in frustration. Bella was the most irritating, intransigent woman he'd ever met, the only one he couldn't persuade, charm or order about to do what he wanted. He wished another man well of her, she could drive him demented instead.

Chapter Eight

When Nicky went downstairs, he discovered both the Duke and the Duchess had gone out to the park for a stroll with his Aunt's dog. He looked at his watch and wondered what to do. He thought about going back to *Le Lion d'Or* and dragging *Lionesse* up to bed for the rest of the day and night and felt his body's instant hot reaction at the prospect. But he resisted the temptation, it would have to wait a few hours. He had to speak to his uncle first. He didn't want another argument with Bella and so wandered around the hall, deciding how to pass an hour or so until Francis returned.

He thought about some of the things Bella had thrown at him during their row upstairs and realised it had been an age since he'd seen the Dowager Duchess of Firle. Like a grandmother to him as well as the Duke, Nicky had always been extremely fond of the old lady whom he'd called Granny Granville when he'd been small. She was now in her nineties, an amazing age. However, he gathered she was finally failing, from the quiet conversation he'd had with Cat before dinner the previous night. They didn't like to mention it in front of Francis as everyone knew how devastated he'd be when she finally passed away.

So, leaving word with the butler that he'd gone round to Hertford Street to visit the Dowager, he set off at a brisk pace to walk the short journey from Berkeley Square to her house.

As a formidable looking nurse showed him into a large, sumptuously decorated bedroom, her instructions to him about not wearing out her charge ringing in his ears, Nicky found Elizabeth Granville sitting up in her magnificent four poster bed, surrounded by mounds of soft lace-frilled pillows. The driving force behind the astounding growth in the Firle fortune, the young woman from an inconspicuous noble family had been renowned in her youth for her beauty and for landing no less a husband than a Duke; into her middle age, she was renowned for her intelligence, terrifying and icy demeanour and lack of humour – rarely seen to smile in public. However, her close family knew a different side to her, especially as she'd grown older, so even though she still had her cranky moments, on seeing Nicky her lined face lit up. "What, come to see me instead of the lions at the Tower, You Rascal?" she whispered, her once cutting voice now hoarse with age and illness. "I'm highly flattered, to be sure. Come here and give your Granny a kiss then," and she held out a pair of wrinkled, withered arms and hands, the hands still bearing rings and there were diamond bracelets on her wrists. Elizabeth Granville never did do anything by halves and was determined to maintain her standards until she was in her coffin.

Nicky strode across the sun-dappled room and pressed a loving kiss on both her knuckles before leaning over to kiss her on both cheeks and hug her gently and very affectionately. "I'm glad to see your brain is still in full working order, even if you're not out dancing," he grinned at her cheekily, "and I think, as ever, you are far more interesting than those mangy lions."

"Ah, such flattery, as bad as Francis," she rapped his hand with the small fan she held in one of hers. "A fine pair the both of you. So, tell me, what have you been up to since we saw you last? Killing lots of Frenchies, I trust?" She looked at him keenly, her blue eyes, so much like her grandson's but not quite the same intense shade of blue, nevertheless still sparkling with life in her lined and wrinkled face. "I'm sorry, My Darling Boy, I know you're French and all that, but they are a vile bunch, really they are, especially that megalomaniac Bonaparte. I hope he gets his bollocks frozen off in Russia; serve him damn well right!"

Nicky hooted with laughter. "Really, Granny, what simply shocking language. I'm quite overcome!" he couldn't help it, the childhood endearment just came naturally as he perched by her on the bed, something in him suddenly wanting to be really close to her as they chatted.

The old lady grinned at him. "Well, Young Man," she looked him up and down through the lorgnette hanging round her neck amongst the lacy froth of her exquisite nightgown, "you're looking tolerably well considering you've been living in a grubby tent or some Spanish hovel for months, and you've caught the sun I see. Frightfully hot down there in summer, dusty too, I remember it well," she mused, looking into the distance for a moment. "But as long as you're keeping out of trouble, that's the main thing." She tapped him on the knuckles again and gave him a speaking look. "The rest of the family, apart from Francis that is, think you're busy soldiering, but I know EXACTLY what you're up to. I've still got friends in the Ministry who pop in to my bedroom for a glass of something and a gossip now and then, even at my age... and regrettably it is just a gossip," she winked at Nicky who grinned back at her joke. First imagining the frightening woman having an affair with anyone, which was too laughable as most of the men he knew quailed in her presence, but then to cover his momentary speechlessness that his top secret activities were known to this forceful elderly lady, his expression sobered. He wondered just how much she knew. He soon found out as she leaned forward and her face became deadly serious.

"There are some very clever people, very nasty people, that Bonaparte is sending down to the Peninsula to cause mischief now Wellington is finally getting somewhere, so you be careful, My Darling Boy, VERY careful – and watch your back," she prodded him with her lorgnette to emphasise her warning. "The powers that be here need resourceful men like you to deal with them, whether it's in Spain, back in France, or even over here in London, and they don't care who gets killed in the process. If you don't deal with these French agents, or kill them when you find them, they'll bear a grudge and catch up with you one day." Nicky stared at her, alarmed she knew what he'd only just been told the previous day. "Trust no-one, Nicky, do you hear me? No-one! Anyone can be bought, EVERYONE has their price, believe me – and it's not necessarily money. They can be got at through loved ones or all sorts of other threats or blackmail," she looked knowing and strangely thoughtful for a moment, as if her mind was elsewhere, but then she shook her head. "That's why I'm worried, My Darling. I know, deep down, you're not cold and ruthless like them, you're too good and kind inside, which makes you vulnerable and, frankly, I don't want you going through what happened to Francis all those years ago." Her face creased in memory of the horror. "He still gets the odd nightmare about it and his back still twinges occasionally when he overdoes things, even now. I know, Cat told me. Idiot man still won't accept he's fifty not thirty," she tutted and Nicky stifled a chuckle.

The Dowager's eyes flashed in anger as she continued her quiet rant, "So, for the love of God, be careful. If you're in any doubt, kill them anyway; don't hesitate, they're just vermin." Nicky had never heard her be so serious or threatening in all the years he'd known her. For several moments they stared each other in the eye and then out of the blue she said, "You listen to me well, My Boy... and remember something else equally important. Bella wants you back in one piece."

"Bella?" What the hell did the Dowager know about him and Bella?

"Yes, Bella. You know, your wife," and off she went again in another lecture. "I'm telling you, Nicky, you'll be the biggest fool in Wellington's army if you let her go," the Dowager grasped his hand, "she's a clever gel, got brains as well as beauty, rather like me," she grinned and tapped her temple with a forefinger. "Gets it from her father of course, infuriating man. You know, I've still not managed to win one chess game after all these years. You'd think he'd take pity on such a poor old lady and at least let me win, just once." Nicky laughed at her. "But she's got spunk as well, not like some of the ninnies I see out and about these days, falling over if someone sneezes. You need a gel like that. I'd wager she doesn't succumb to any of your charm and nonsense, no more than Cat does with Francis. Argued and fought for

England they did when they first married, never saw anything like it. They have their moments even now, she broke a beautiful Sevres vase I gave them a few years ago, throwing it at him," she rolled her eyes, "but they're still obsessed with each other and she doesn't put up with his tantrums and domineering ways. Not for a minute..." she laughed and then paused in this diatribe to cough slightly into a handkerchief and Nicky saw the small spot of blood there. He gripped the hand that held his and choked as he realised what that indicated.

The Dowager smiled back at him sadly as a silent look passed between them, but she pulled her shoulders back and carried on. "So, you pay attention to me, You Rogue. Who cares if you've got no money? She certainly doesn't and neither should you. You could have all mine if I thought you'd take it, just say the word, but quickly mind, I haven't got much longer. Heaven knows, Francis doesn't need it." She leaned forward and looked him in the eye as he leaned closer to her at the tug on his hand. "You're far too self-possessed and proud. Money isn't important and most of the time, neither is pride. Love is, believe me, I know from experience; and Bella loves you. She always did, following you around like some devoted puppy dog all the time when she was a little girl. If you'd asked her to jump into the lion's cage at the Tower she would have. Therefore, when you sail off back to Spain and are sitting in some hole somewhere, waiting to ambush those damn Frenchies, just remember that. Come back and make it a real marriage, have your own family. That's what you need and it will finally give you a focus in your life."

Once again she squeezed his hand tightly to make her point. "I understand you, Nicky, you just need your own family to love. You have so much love to give, but it's bottled up inside you, under that self-possessed suit of armour you wrap yourself in." She sighed and gazed at him lovingly, "You always had so much love to offer when you were a little boy: rabbits, kittens, anything with fur on four legs that looked pathetic or appealing; but you're a man now and you need to let the love out again, to people, not animals. It'll heal your hurt, My Darling, believe me, that deep hurt you carry from your ordeal when you were little."

She lifted a hand and held it lovingly to his face and he put one of his over it. "If you don't believe me, try talking to Francis, he'll understand. Took him a while to grapple with his feelings too when he was your age, but now he's the happiest man I know." Her conversation suddenly veered off on another track. "Have you seen him with my new great granddaughter by the way? Besotted, completely besotted. She's named after me, y'know, and at last, a child with Francis's looks and colouring. I've waited so long to see it – the line WILL continue..." a strange expression crossed the old lady's face as her eyes gazed into the distance once more, re-living a long-ago memory and she coughed again into the handkerchief. Anxiously, Nicky passed her a glass of water from the bedside table and she leaned back into the pillows, closing her eyes. Nicky sat back too, overwhelmed with the outflow of passionate words, warnings and advice that had just streamed out of her like a veritable torrent.

The Dowager rallied herself and sat forward again. "I think I've said enough for now, eh? But do heed me, Darling Boy," she looked deep into his eyes and put the soft, wrinkled hand to his cheek as he leaned towards her again to listen to her hoarse whispers. "You were always very precious to me, like another grandson. Such a brave little thing you were when Carlotta brought you home. What a special woman she was too, so full of love and kindness for everyone. But we had fun, you and I, that spring and summer when they went chasing off to France and after when Francis was recovering, do you remember?" she sighed and smiled.

Nicky squeezed her hand and whispered, "I remember. I was only little, but I've never forgotten it. I'd never had a grandmother in France and you were wonderful, so caring, understanding and loving to me. You're not fierce at all, soft as butter underneath. You understood me even then, didn't you? You understood me all the time I was growing up, how I felt, some of what drove me to be like I am..." a single, lone tear dropped onto his cheek as he burst out softly, unable to help himself, "You're so very special and precious to me too, my Granny Granville; you always have been and I'll miss you when I go away again." He couldn't bring himself to say he'd miss her when she was gone, it was too much.

The old lady wiped his tears away. "Don't cry, My Lovely Nicky.

I've had a long and full life, more than most. I'm tired now, but I've warned Francis I'll come back and haunt you all if you misbehave." He had to smile through the tears that were now falling steadily as emotion gripped him. "Just keep yourself safe and remember me sometimes, hmmm? And think about Bella, have a family. You need her, Nicky; listen to your Granny Granville one last time," the old lady sighed and laid her head back on the pillows again.

Nicky wiped his eyes, choked up with emotion. He never cried, hardened by war and the horrors he'd seen and experienced in his life, way back to his earliest childhood and the terrible, nightmare events at the start of the Revolution that had caused his family to be incarcerated and perish. He sat quietly for a long while, just holding the Dowager's frail hand while she slept and thought about what she'd said, reflecting that this was probably the very last time he would ever see her alive. The thought left him feeling bereft and heartsick. But Bella's words had made him think and he was grateful beyond words he'd come to see the old lady. It had brought home how much his adopted family meant to him and what a caring lot they all were. He promised himself again he would try and write from the Peninsula as and when he could.

A quiet hand on his shoulder made him turn. He glanced up to see Francis, a terribly forlorn look on his face. He gently placed the thin hand he was holding back on the covers and rose quietly to follow his uncle.

Downstairs, they entered a quiet, empty sitting room and Francis poured them both a drink. "Thank you for coming to see her, it will have cheered her up no end," he said quietly. "She was always extremely fond of you, still is of course, you must know that."

Nicky was completely overcome. "How long... how long has she got?" he choked out.

Francis shrugged. "We don't know; it could be days, weeks, even another few months. She's still all there mentally, but her body is failing and she coughs," he winced. "But she has a will of iron, so who knows? She was determined to wait for little Elizabeth's birth despite the doctors giving up on her months ago. It seemed to boost her no end, especially when she first saw her and said she looked just like me.

Funny that, after all her years of ranting at me to have lots of sons," his short laugh sounded desperately bereft.

Francis sighed sadly as he gazed out of the window, "One or other of us try and call in most days – that's why Cat had the baby up here in Town and we haven't gone back to Firle so she could rest and recuperate in the fresh air; not that that woman EVER does what anyone suggests, especially me," he grinned for a moment then sighed again. "Your Papa too. It's ironic, he only went off down to the country for a week with Charlie to deal with some urgent estate business and then you turn up. I wish we'd known you were coming," he shook his head and Nicky's guilt increased even more at another person who would be upset due to his lack of a simple message. He prayed his stepfather would get back to Town before he left again for Spain.

Turning, he spoke softly to Francis. "I saw the blood on her handkerchief. I'm so sorry, Francis, I know how much she means to you." Nicky went over to the older man who'd been his hero and mentor all his life and put an arm round his shoulder. They were both tall, big, strong men and as Nicky saw tears in the other man's eyes as well, his own welled up again. "Dear God, this is what happens when you love someone; the pain when you lose them, it's unbearable. My parents, my old nanny and governess at Valenciennes, then Madre," he took a long gulp of his brandy. "That's why... that's why... I don't want to get involved if I can help it. I need to annul the marriage or get a divorce. Francis, you've got to help me. It's not fair to Bella, to let her worry about me. I never expected all this...this...this...EMOTION with her."

Francis gave him a very strange and intense look, but merely nodded. For a while, they both stood in the silent room, looking out into the small garden beyond, each wrapped up in their own thoughts as they sipped their drinks.

Finally, Francis turned to Nicky, "I think we need to talk about this, about you and Bella, but now isn't the time and I have a meeting this evening with the Foreign Secretary and some other business associates from the City that I can't get out of. Come and see me tomorrow afternoon. I'll clear all my appointments and we can sit somewhere quiet and have it out, once and for all." He patted Nicky on the shoulder.

"It's not that simple, is it? Nothing with Bella ever is though," he reflected and he gave a funny smile.

Nicky shook his head, trying to straighten his thoughts, his argument with Bella going round in his mind, mixed now with the Dowager's words. He was confused and was glad he'd be able to share his confusion with Francis. His experienced, incisive mind usually got to the heart of any problem, but finding a solution was another matter. The two men finished their drinks.

Seemingly unable to tear himself away, Nicky ran up the stairs to stand and stare for one final time at the redoubtable old woman, asleep in the large bed. Francis had to return and gently pull him out of the room once more, but not before Nicky bent over the sleeping form and kissed the beloved face, tears yet again rolling down his cheeks. They finally left the house silently, slowly strolling back towards Berkeley Square. Eventually, they began to speak, talking about mundane matters, then finally laughing quietly and companionably over Francis's comic fears about having a daughter who was going to be a replica of her mother and great grandmother combined, about having to deal with two irrational, argumentative, opinionated and bossy women together in one house.

Nicky then spent a much more cheerful hour over tea with Cat and the demanding baby, grinning as she waved her tiny fists at him, tightly gripping his gently tickling fingers and blowing bubbles when he cooed at her. Cat was hugely amused at his efforts and asked if he wouldn't rather stay and be her nanny than go back to the Peninsula. Nicky chortled with laughter and when a loud yell rent the air once again, said he thought fighting Napoleon would be a far easier job. They chatted idly over their tea and as she rose to go upstairs, Cat told him Bella had gone to bed complaining of a migraine and she herself was going to a charity dinner that evening, so since Francis was going out also, would he like to dine at home alone or would he be going out?

Grateful to have an excuse not to confront Bella again until he'd spoken to Francis, Nicky said he'd take the opportunity to go out and catch up with some friends and secretly smiled to himself at the prospect of his forthcoming evening's entertainment as he made his own way upstairs to bathe and change.

Disgustingly healthy, Bella rarely suffered even a headache and migraines were an unknown quantity to her. However, it was a good excuse to keep the family and Nicky at bay. Having left instructions not to be disturbed until the following day, she'd crept out of the house while he was having tea with her aunt and made her own way to *Le Lion d'Or*. There, she bathed, dressed and settled down to catch up on work before Nicky arrived later. He'd departed that morning without his necklace once again... the carrot left dangling for him to return and gamble with her for it that evening.

Chapter Nine

As Nicky bathed and shaved in the peace of his room at Firle House, his mood turned reflective and then sad again and it was in a pensive frame of mind that he sauntered away from the house later, deciding to walk to *Le Lion d'Or* and take the time to gather his thoughts. He arrived at the unassuming looking establishment not quite an hour later, realising he'd reached it without really noticing anything on the way, so distracted had he been by his meandering reflections and feelings and the disturbing events of the day. He'd slowly strolled along the deserted London streets, too late for shoppers and too early for evening revellers, in complete oblivion. He was directed straight up to *Lionesse's* private apartments where he strolled in and found her sitting at her desk working, when he poked his head round her open door.

"Nicky!" she exclaimed in surprise, hugely relieved she was wearing her disguise already as she rose from her chair. "You're here early. I wasn't expecting you until later."

He bent over her hand and kissed it. "*Lionesse*, I didn't want to go anywhere else. I hope you don't mind? I can always go downstairs and occupy myself at the tables for a few hours if you're busy?"

"No, no," she closed the ledgers she was working on and hastily put them away in the drawers, worried he'd recognise her writing. "It's lovely to see you," and she leaned up to kiss his cheek, the decorative feathers on her mask tickling his nose and she giggled as she watched him rub it to stop a sneeze. "Have you eaten? I can get something sent up quite easily?"

She half expected some joking riposte, filled with innuendo, so was surprised when he sat down in a chair by the low fire, sighing deeply and running a hand across his forehead. "That would be nice. Thank you. I completely forgot I haven't eaten anything other than a sandwich when I got home and a pastry for tea, although my aunt's dog ate half of that."

When he didn't even mention his morning croissant, Bella realised he was distracted and something seemed to have disturbed the humorous mood he'd been in each time he'd visited *Lionesse*. Pouring him a glass of champagne from the ever-ready bottle on her sideboard, she went out to find a footman and order a cold buffet to be sent up, then returned to go and pull up a chair next to him by the fire. She picked up one of his hands and kissed it. "You don't seem your usual charming self, *Mon Cher*, is something the matter?"

Staring into the flames of the fire, Nicky leaned back and sipped his drink. "I'm sorry, it's just been a bit of a day," he turned to her and smiled, "but it's good to be here now; I can forget everything and escape from reality for a few hours." His face looked strained.

"That bad, hmmm?" she said softly. "I'm a good listener, Nicky, if you want to talk about it? Sometimes it's easier to unload to a stranger than those close to you."

"No, no, it's far too complicated, but thank you for the offer." He lifted her hand to his lips and kissed it again.

She looked at him intently, her head to one side. "Your eyes look so sad, what's wrong, Nicky? Come, tell me, I'm happy just to sit quietly and listen," and she clasped his hand between both of hers and squeezed it gently. A log in the fireplace popped as they sat in silence for a while and he drank more champagne. She'd refilled his glass a couple of times before a footman came in to place a large tray of cold cuts, cheese, bread, fruit and more bottles of champagne on her dining table and retired quietly, shutting the door behind him. Nicky continued to work his way down the champagne, staring into the fire and then he spoke quietly. "I had a terrible argument with my wife. Ah, hell, she just won't accept anything I say," he sighed in frustration and paused to drink another glass, "and then, much worse than that, I went to visit someone very dear to me, an elderly relation. She's been like a grandmother to me, but she's dying. I didn't realise and I'm such a fool," he was almost muttering to himself, "and I doubt I'll see her again now." His voice was filled with pain, "She said a lot of things to me this afternoon which made me think: advice, warnings, even a telling off" and he smiled sadly, "I felt like a little boy again at times." He shook his head, "Aah, *Lionesse*, I'm sorry I'm so distracted. I'm bad company tonight I'm afraid, perhaps I shouldn't have come after all, but I just wanted to see you," and he downed another glass, finishing the bottle.

"Oh Nicky, I'm so sorry. I know what it's like when you lose someone close." She pulled his hand to her lips and held it there lovingly, realising he'd been to see her Great Aunt Elizabeth and what a shock it must have been for him to find that formidable woman now so weak and ill. She'd gone downhill quite rapidly in the past year since he'd been away. "I remember what it was like when my mother died, everyone cries, it's a terrible thing," she whispered as she remembered how they'd all cried endlessly at her mother's funeral. Her weeping Aunt Cat hugging her bereft and sobbing father who was her brother; a choked and glassy-eyed Uncle Francis comforting a similarly affected Great Aunt Elizabeth; and Nicky clutching her in his arms as they'd both stood there and cried their hearts out together throughout the service. "But you have your family to support you, they'll understand I'm sure... when it happens."

"They'll be devastated, especially the... my... er... uncle. He's her grandson. Dear God, he was actually in tears this afternoon, I couldn't believe it. He's always been such a strong and forceful man, the rock of our family, and it cut me to the quick to see it." He shook his head at the memory and Bella was stunned at his words. "But I won't be here when it happens, I'll be away," he whispered. Bella got up and opened another bottle. She needed a drink too, to cope with all this, so she poured out two glasses.

He continued to drink for a while and periodically reminisce about his childhood with the Dowager, talking about how she'd first introduced him to the Menagerie and lions in the Tower of London and he made Bella laugh as he explained how they'd become a childhood obsession, driving his entire family mad with his endless demands to continually go and see them. She remembered it well, it had been years before he'd finally grown out of it, around the time, she suspected, he'd discovered the joys of some of the local young farmgirls... and anything pretty in a petticoat.

Over the next couple of hours, Nicky continued to drink and they helped themselves to platefuls of food, sitting back in front of the fire where he continued to part reminisce and part talk about other odd things the Dowager had spoken to him about. He also confessed how guilty he felt at not keeping in closer touch with his family while he was away. "She's right, y'know, the wife. I didn't realise how much they worried about me. Silly really, I was just an orphan they came upon by accident when they were searching for some close relatives to rescue from France at the start of the Revolution." He paused and stared into the fire then continued, "They'd been taken by some bastard after their money, nothing to do with *Liberté, Fraternité et Equalité*, that was just an excuse to haul them off and incarcerate them on some trumped-up charges of treason, or not supporting revolutionary ideals. He'd got my parents as well, but they'd already perished," he swore under his breath, "and all the family fortune disappeared with them, so I'm penniless." He was quiet for a while.

"The old lady thinks I should stay married," he finally muttered into the silence and Bella froze. "But I can't do that, I just can't."

"Why not?" she whispered.

"Well, apart from not having the money to support us in any reasonable fashion, unlike some men I know, I have my pride and absolutely refuse to live off a woman... she's like my little sister," he laughed quietly. "She drives me crazy, such a bossyboots. She was forever tormenting me, playing practical jokes, trying to better me at everything. A complete hoyden and tomboy, covered in freckles in the summer. I used to pull her pigtails and then her plaits as her hair grew longer, box her ears and even spank her, for God's sake, like a big, annoyed brother." He stopped as if remembering something, then he shivered. "I was even responsible for her first proper kiss. She was, probably still is, quite a bookworm for a girl; she was very well educated by her father and she'd read all sorts she found in his library, intellectual and academic stuff, Greek and Latin poetry, not harmless romantic or fairy tale nonsense like her peers, and she was such an insatiably curious brat as well, not surprising given her reading matter, but I couldn't possibly ever do to her what I do with you." He gave Bella a wicked smile and wink and licked his lips suggestively as his eyes roved hotly up and down her body.

Bella swallowed hard. "But you married her? Haven't you ever kissed her since or made love to her? Don't you care for her, even a bit?" she almost reeled at their surreal conversation.

"It's complicated," Nicky sighed, "very complicated," and leaned back, as he reminisced. "She was sixteen and I'd been away at university and then, as luck would have it, travelling abroad all that summer while I tried to decide what to do with my life. I came home and found the house in turmoil. My stepfather, her father, had literally just received a letter from Spain. It had been delayed in delivery, sent by ship via Portugal because of the War in the Peninsula. The ship had run aground in a storm and finally been hauled in for repairs and somehow, some of the mail on board had been overlooked so it had taken almost a year to reach us in England. Her mother, my late stepmother, was Spanish and her father had died and left a not inconsiderable inheritance for his granddaughter. For some reason, some old family disagreement between him and my stepmother, who had run away from home as a young girl, the old aristocrat had stipulated my wife had to be married on or before her seventeenth birthday and then she could inherit. I arrived home and it was just two days before her seventeenth birthday. She needed a husband, I was there, and single. There was no time to arrange anything else. I have an uncle, the brother-in-law of my stepfather and he's very well connected. He quickly obtained a Special Licence and we married secretly and in haste at the local village church near my uncle's estate. It was only ever to be a marriage of convenience, to be annulled as soon as the inheritance came through, but of course because of the War, that took forever, getting correspondence back and forth between lawyers and bankers, papers to be signed, you can imagine.

"Anyway, I wasn't bothered, assuming my stepfather and uncle would sort everything out, including the annulment, so I went off again, travelling further in Europe, doing a bit of a Tour while trying to avoid the War. I gave up in the end, thanks to Bonaparte's shenanigans unsettling everything everywhere and my family were concerned for my safety, so I returned home. After racketing around for a bit, still trying to decide what to do with myself, my family finally bought me a commission in the army after a lot of nagging on my part as they weren't happy with the idea. Inevitably, I was sent overseas and ended up in the Peninsula. I finally came home on leave last year and it was my birthday. I'd been out to celebrate with friends and got very drunk. Very, very drunk. When they delivered me home near dawn, I was falling about all over the place, barely able to stand up. She found me reeling around in the upstairs hallway, completely out of it, so she put me to bed... and, well, one thing led to another and I found her in bed with me in the morning. I don't even remember touching her other than some wispy memories. I obviously didn't realise what I was doing, I'd vaguely thought I was in some cathouse, not in my own home, or I'd never have gone near her. I was horrified after... apart from ruining her, there could have been a child..."

He tailed off after he finished his tale, resorted to more champagne and started to reminisce again. "But of course I care for her, she's become very beautiful now she's grown up. Sooo beautiful, a lot like her Spanish mother; no more pigtails or plaits or freckles, but still a bossyboots," he laughed to himself. "I've always looked after her, she's my little Sooty..." his voice tailed off as he gazed into the fire again and he emptied the remains of the bottle of champagne into his glass. Bella realised he was getting very drunk but the more he drank, the more he opened up and talked. As he moved on from one bottle to another, polishing off glass after glass, the alcohol finally caught up with him.

"An' now I'm goin' 'way again," he slurred, "t'stop th' trubble. Dunno 'ow Granny knew, 's'bloody dangerous," Bella felt the alarm sizzle down her spine at his words.

"Dangerous? I thought you were just a soldier, a cavalry officer, a Hussar regiment isn't it?"

"Mmmmm, I love 'orses, all 'nimals really, like t'breed 'em one day, race'orses, win th' Derby... not tha' that's ever likely to 'appen," he shook his head, "no money, see, but tha's not what I reeeally do," and he tapped his nose. "But there's bad men now, could even foller me t'England an' I can't put 'er in danger, so I've gotta let 'er go. Someone better 'an me, richer 'an me, can look after 'er; she can order 'em around, then I can go an' kill Frenchies like Granny an' th' Min'stry wan' me t'do, top seecrit." He lifted his arm as if he had a pistol in his hand and quietly cried, "BANG!" then he muttered on unintelligibly before finally announcing, "can't let 'em get 'er. I'm 'er big brother an' I gotta look after 'er. Ev'rybody I cared 'bout dies or gets 'urt, or didn't care 'nough for me, 'cept my 'dopted family," and he slumped back in his chair looking into the fire again and downing yet more glasses of the sparkling wine from another rapidly emptying bottle.

Bella was very angry, very upset and very alarmed. Angry both at his continued insistence on being her big brother and not having any money, but even more so that he was obviously involved in some sort of dangerous activity that had nothing to do with the clerical duties he'd inferred he did when they'd argued that morning. She knew he'd been lying then, but nothing like this. She'd merely envisioned him riding into battle, leading his men in a heroic cavalry charge instead of sitting back in a tent writing reports. But this was something else, something terrifying to her already frazzled nerves. She'd bet her Uncle Francis knew more and she was determined to ask him. If not, she was due to visit the Dowager in a couple of days to play chess with her if she was up to it, although of course she let her win from time to time, unlike her father, even though she was every bit as good as he was. She would ask the old lady, beg her on her knees if necessary. She simply had to find out what Nicky was up to. As for his heart-breaking comment about losing his parents, also presumably her mother and now the Dowager, she didn't know how to begin to comfort him, let alone what he meant by whoever hadn't cared enough for him.

He'd finally dropped off into a melancholy, alcoholic stupor in his chair, so she took the opportunity to pull off his boots and tidy up the room, moving the tray of food to leave outside her door for collection. She wandered through to her bedroom and undressed, putting on a simple white voile nightdress and wrap before she returned to the sitting room. She decided to read a book and wait for him to wake up.

A few hours later he finally stirred and sat up, shaking his head and rubbing his face. She put her book down and grinned at him. "You got bubbly brain and fell asleep," she laughed. "I'm amazed you've actually woken up. You've drunk so much champagne, I lost count of the glasses, never mind the bottles."

Nicky groaned. "Hell, I'm sorry *Lionesse,* how can I apologise? I don't know what came over me, feeling so maudlin," he shook his fuzzy head again. "I hope I didn't ramble too much. It was just a bad afternoon, too many memories. I knew I shouldn't have come."

"It's nothing, don't bother yourself," she waved her hand dismissively. "Would you like some coffee?" she offered.

He turned to look at her for several long moments. "I don't want coffee," he said slowly, "I just want you, *Lionesse*. Come to bed with me, I need to feel the comfort of your body, to forget everything. Will you make love to me tonight, *Chérie?* Will you send me to sleep again?

"I thought you'd never ask," she whispered. "Nothing would give me greater pleasure."

He got up and took her hand, leading her through to the bedroom, still slightly unsteady on his feet. She watched in amusement as he pulled off his clothes, throwing them haphazardly all over the place, leaving her to wander round after him, pick them up and hang them on the chair. He then collapsed into the soft bed with a sigh of pleasure as his head fell back into the pile of downy pillows. He pulled one of them into his arms and breathed deeply as he put his nose to it. "Mmmmm, I can smell your delicious scent everywhere, it's more intoxicating than any champagne," he grinned lopsidedly at her, alcohol still making him feel fuzzy, as she walked over towards his side of the bed, picking up his cravat from the floor.

"Untidy wretch, you don't appreciate me," she muttered at him teasingly. He turned to feel under the pillows, pulling out the gold sash and dangled it teasingly in front of her.

"Oh, I wouldn't say that *Chérie,* but perhaps this will make it worth your while?" a wicked smile curved his mouth. "I can't fight you tonight, only fit to surrender my body to do with as you wish. I'm all yours, so help yourself," and he threw out his arms in a show of playful surrender.

"So now you're both drunk and impossible," she laughed. "That's a deadly combination for a poor lioness to cope with, but I suppose I'll have to try."

As she did the previous evening, just before she wound the sash over his eyes she bent to whisper in his ear, "Any last requests from the condemned man?"

"Take your wrap off first, *Lionesse,*" his crooked smile was irresistible and his hot, quiet voice crawled all over her senses.

She hesitated for a few moments, considering the wisdom of her actions, but knowing she was still wearing a nightrail underneath, she put the sash down and slowly complied. His eyes flared with hot desire as he stared at the body showing through the thin voile. She was tall and slender with long shapely legs, but her breasts were luscious and her slim hips rounded just enough as he preferred them in a woman. Her dark curls showed through the thin material but he still couldn't quite tell if they were brown or black and her breasts had nipples that showed pink and full as they pressed against the fine material. His whole body caught fire and he hardened instantly, making her eyes widen as she watched.

As she picked up the sash again and tied it tightly, worried as always he might see her, she whispered, "Anything else?" and she pulled off her mask and wig.

His alcohol-sodden brain was alive with lust now and, wanting to get back at her for this erotic, sightless game she continued to make him play, he thought he'd tease her back. So he pulled her down and growled naughtily in her ear, nibbling it as he spoke, "I want to feel your tongue crawl around and lick me, your lips suck and tease me, so I can climax in your sweet mouth for you to savour and swallow, just like you climax in mine when I taste you – and then after, to pleasure yourself, you can arouse me again so you can ride me. I'm just going to lie here and enjoy it all, as you did last night and the night before," before whispering more erotic requests in her ear, making them redden and burn.

Bella was taken aback, speechless at his shocking language and wicked suggestions. Did he speak like that to all his women, she wondered? Did they enjoy it? Her body went hot and cold at the thought of doing what he wanted, but she realised she was too naïve and ignorant to know exactly the technique of how to please and satisfy him as he so obviously desired, and she desperately wanted to do it for him. As for the rest of his requests, she reddened completely from her chest right up to her hair at the thought of doing them. How depraved had she become in a few days? She laughed to herself in embarrassment as she thought of what he'd done to her and he merely assumed she knew how to do the things he'd requested. She'd have to prevaricate and hoped his drunkenness would cover any of her ignorance tonight. Somehow, she'd sort out her ignorance tomorrow. She reasoned to herself, she was his wife and this was obviously what lovers did in bed, even though her mind boggled at some of it, sure it was far more lurid and naughty than the normality of things between married couples....or was it? As he'd mentioned earlier in the evening, her reading matter had been extensive as she'd grown older, especially some rather lurid Latin and Greek poetry and erotic texts, and other odd tomes she'd come across in her father's extensive library, but none of it had gone into specific detail and somehow the thought of her parents, or aunt and uncle's older friends and relations doing half of what Nicky had suggested to her just didn't bear considering.

So, as she let down her hair, she purred back, "Well, well, well, aren't we greedy? All that, as well as more warm croissants and honey for breakfast," she laughed as he moaned and licked his lips.

She kissed, nibbled and licked up and down his tall, muscled body, revelling in the taste of him, tormenting him as she avoided his erection, until he was writhing in pleasure and moaning for her to satisfy him. Finally, she took him in her hand and caressed him, experimenting and running a fingernail up and down the throbbing hardness and around the sensitive tip, feeling him shudder as he moaned again.

A pearl of white moisture oozed and in fascination she bent down and licked it off, savouring the taste and thinking about his wicked requests. His hips jerked and he groaned and muttered to her softly in French, encouraging, pleading with her to continue as his hands came up to wrap themselves in her long soft hair. She licked him again and dotted a trail of hot, moist kisses down to his balls, feeling his erection swell and pulse as more moisture oozed and she licked that off too. But instead of continuing, she ran her fingers up over his belly and chest to cup his face as she moved herself up to lie across his torso and lean down to kiss his lips teasingly.

"Aaaaaaargh, *Lionesse*, noooooo, don't stop, don't tease and torment me so," he begged. "I can't bear it. You're driving me insane; not being able to see you makes it worse, just feeling your mouth on me, I want more..."

She laughed against his lips as she whispered, "Ah, *Milor*, but if I give you everything you want now, you won't come back to me tomorrow, will you?"

"Tomorrow? Noooooo, I can't wait until tomorrow," he cried softly. "I want you, I need you now."

Bella revelled in the power she seemed to have over him and his desire for her, but as well as the lust roiling around her own body, a great swell of bittersweet heartache and love overcame her as she looked down at him and thought back to his earlier words: *"I couldn't do to her what I do with you..."* She'd got herself into even deeper trouble now, she thought to herself; would he ever forgive her for tricking him again?

Lost for words, she bent down to kiss him once more and felt his hands crawl up her back under her nightrail. She sat back, straddling Nicky's body and peeled off the thin voile garment, up over her head to toss to the floor. His hands curled round to cup her breasts as she lifted her arms and she moaned as he brushed his thumbs back and forth over her swollen nipples. "Ride me then, *Lionesse*, ride me hard," he crooned, "pleeease, now, for I swear if I don't have you soon I'm going to die for the want of it," and his strong hands pulled her down to kiss him, hungry with a desire that was coursing red hot through his veins, overtaking his entire mind and body. Visions of the tantalising body that he'd seen through her thin nightgown racing across his now sightless eyes as he imagined her sitting above him.

He pushed her back up and, lifting her hips slightly, brought her back down to impale her hot and tight wetness onto his throbbing length. He heard her gasp as she absorbed him deep inside and felt her hands claw into his chest as she experienced the waves of intense pleasure that pulsed between them both.

Her hands roving in abandon across his chest, Bella leaned down to kiss and nibble the side of his neck, leaving small bite marks as waves of pure animalistic carnality overtook her. She groaned as she felt him writhe and thrust under her and grasped his hands tightly on either side of his shoulders, their fingers locked, as instinctively she slowly rose up to her knees, experimenting with moving up and off him until he was just poised at her entrance. She stayed there, motionless for a few seconds, watching him, before letting herself sink back down, inch by slow inch and then she squirmed around as she felt him throb deep inside her and without thought she squeezed her pelvic and vaginal muscles eliciting a tormented groan. It was erotic. Tantalising. Realising how much it affected him, she did it all again and again, criminally slowly, the opposite of his earlier demand to be ridden hard, until he was mindless, his head thrown back, swearing and pleading with her in a torrent of French to end his torture. The intense sensual power she felt was intoxicating and Bella threw her head back with a long moan, as she felt the deep spiral of pleasure build inside her.

She leaned down to kiss him once more, her tongue driving into his mouth, coiling around his. As lightning spasms started to explode inside her, she writhed and squirmed as she discovered the ways of pleasuring herself on him and cried out his name as she leaned down and bit his nipples, hard, making him yell in response. Then, as her body rose up and impaled itself down hard on his one final time, he cried out again as his body jerked and his release pumped out as if it would never stop, until he was completely drained and exhausted.

"Oh my God," she panted, as she collapsed onto his chest, feeling his heart thumping madly against her breast, her own body like that of a limp doll.

"*Mon Dieu, Lionesse*," Nicky finally muttered, trying to catch his breath. "Are you trying to kill me?" He pulled her down into his arms, curling them around her comfortingly as they lay together, trying to recover, so overwhelmed were they both by the intensity of what they'd just experienced. Bella leaned down to pull the covers back over them and he kissed her tenderly as she snuggled back down into his arms. Her last coherent thought was he'd been so disturbed by the events of the day, he hadn't bothered to ask about his necklace. In moments, they were both fast asleep.

Chapter Ten

B ella woke as the sun streamed into her bedroom and as she stretched and yawned, she suddenly remembered she'd forgotten to ask if Nicky was supposed to report for duty that morning. Creeping out from the bed away from his still sleeping form, she hurriedly pulled on her nightdress and wrap to go out to the hall, sending a maid downstairs with her instructions to serve breakfast.

She returned to the sitting room and debated going back to bed, but memories of the previous night's events came back to her, especially Nicky's revelations about his secret activities in Spain. She looked through to the bedroom at him sprawled across the bed. Tempted though she was, worry clouded her brain and she realised she'd get no peace until she confronted her uncle and tried to prise some information from him. If not, she was determined to go to Great Aunt Elizabeth and tackle her.

Once she knew what he was up to, she'd be able to confront Nicky and show him she could deal with the knowledge of his dangerous work like an adult, a sensible woman, a wife – and hope he'd stop viewing her as if she was still a freckle-nosed teenager with plaits, to be sheltered from anything and everything serious or unpleasant.

She went quietly through to the bedroom to replace her mask and wig, then went over to the bed and undid the sash round his eyes. Once loosened, he subconsciously pushed it off with a sigh and rolled over, burying himself under the covers once more. She laughed, remembering what a lazybones he'd always been in the morning before he joined the army. Memories of dropping cold wet sponges on him or tickling him with one of the maid's feather dusters popped into her mind and she shook her head in amusement. She heard the breakfast tray come in and went back through to get him some strong coffee. With all the champagne he'd drunk, he was bound to have the most horrendous hangover.

She put the cup of coffee on the nightstand and tickled his nose. He swatted her hand away as if it were an annoying fly so she moved her tickling fingers to his ear, then back to his nose, then round to the back of his neck, running them up into his thick, wavy hair. He groaned and pulled a pillow over his head. "Come along, Lazybones, I've brought you some coffee." She shook his shoulder, "Do you need to be on duty today? It's past eight o'clock if you do?" She got a groan in response. "If you ask me nicely, you can have a warm and tasty croissant." Another groan and she laughed. "So that's the thanks I get for my trouble. Well, I'll just send them back downstairs then; I'm sure the footmen will appreciate the treat."

A bleary eye appeared over the sheet. "Noooooo," he whispered, "they're mine," and she forgot herself and giggled.

"Better get up then before they go cold. There's some strong coffee too, plus ham and eggs and cheese, if you can manage that." She crooned at him in mock sympathy, "Do we have a headache by any chance?"

He pulled the sheet back over his head and swore at her.

"Tut, tut, shocking language, *Milor*. Right, cold wet flannel, I think," she spoke to the sheet.

The sheet moved down a fraction and a voice emerged from underneath, "Don't you dare."

"I'll tickle you instead."

"Noooooo."

She went to the bottom of the bed and put her hand under the covers, searching until she located a foot to tickle. When that one moved she found the other. In his effort to escape her tormenting fingers, his head and shoulders gradually emerged from under the covers as he wriggled away up to the top of the mattress.

"You are a veritable pain in the neck," he enunciated each word slowly and she giggled again. "I don't have to be anywhere until later this morning," he groaned and put a hand to his temple. "Why couldn't you let me sleep?"

She handed him a cup of coffee as he sat up with another groan and leaned back against the headboard. "Nice warm croissant?" she asked him.

He sipped the fragrant hot coffee with a relieved sigh, "Are you going to feed me again?" he managed the glimpse of a wicked smile.

"No, you don't deserve it. You can serve yourself today after those shocking suggestions you made to me last night. I was quite overcome," she fanned herself with her fingers and pretended to be shocked, which of course she had been, if he but knew.

"No you weren't," he grinned at her. "I can't wait until tonight. Wild horses won't keep me away," and he winked, "though after last night's performance I'm not sure I'll survive. Talk about *hors d'oeuvres* and *entrée* prior to the main course and dessert." A wicked grin suffused his face, "And I'll get my revenge for your teasing, you'll see."

Bella merely smiled, glad of the mask covering her blushing face.

He held out his empty cup of coffee, looking pleadingly at her, a charmingly boyish smile creasing his features and his eyes twinkled. She recognised the look well. The entire female household staff at both Firle residences and their home in Arlington had fallen under its spell at some point or other. Grinning, she merely stood back and pointed towards the sitting room, "The coffee pot is that way and so are your croissants."

She walked through to the sitting room and left him to get up. As she served herself some coffee and munched a croissant, she heard him get out of bed and wander through into her bathing room. Some ten minutes later he finally appeared wearing just his tight inexpressibles, random water droplets still sparkling on his face, chest and tousled hair where he'd obviously splashed himself with cold water in an effort to dissipate his hangover. He looked impossibly attractive and her belly lurched.

She poured him some more coffee and watched as he savoured first one, before ploughing his way through the remains of the croissants before attacking the eggs and ham, still warm under their covers. Obviously his hangover hadn't affected his appetite; he was disgracefully robust and she chuckled.

"What's so funny?" he queried, his mouth still full of soft, fluffy, scrambled eggs.

"You are," she grinned. "I can't believe you drank all those bottles of champagne last night and can still manage to eat all this food."

"But I'm hungry. I didn't eat much yesterday," he spoke as if it was a frequent occurrence to drink so much without any serious after-effects. "Fine champagne never affects me in the same way as drinking too much brandy or port or cheap red wine. They're the killers in the headache stakes," and he shook his head and shivered.

"I'll try and remember that and I'd best buy in extra for my champagne bar for your next visit," she joked, "you drink it like lemonade."

"I won't be drinking that much tonight, I can promise you. Not with what you've got in mind for me," and he laughed seductively. "I'll be counting the hours all day. What time would you like me to come this evening?" He gave her the most lecherous wink even though his expression had been completely deadpan.

"Will you behave yourself," she couldn't help but laugh. "You're outrageous, whatever am I going to do with you?"

"Well, last night you said you would su...." but she cut him off with a finger to his lips.

"All right, I know, I know," she laughed, "but perhaps I should make you earn your main course. I think we should play cards first."

"Whaaat?!" he cried. "But you promised!"

"I did no such thing, I merely intimated you couldn't have everything you wanted at once," she said airily.

"I don't remember that," he pouted.

"Well that's what happens when you drink endless glasses of my best bubbles."

"But what'll happen if you win?" he looked crestfallen and Bella creased up with mirth.

"Nothing," she taunted, still laughing. His face was a picture. "Unless I take pity on you."

He looked at her and she could see his mind turning. "Hmmm, I think we should try something different. I somehow got the impression the other evening you're very clever with cards; you certainly wiped the floor with me," he looked pensive, "but then you run two gaming houses so it's not to be surprised you're something of an expert." Another thoughtful look, then, "Tell me, do you play chess or draughts by any chance?"

Bella nearly exploded with mirth again. The rascal, she well knew what he was playing at.

"Oh, both a bit, I learned years ago in my youth," she replied vaguely. "Why?"

"Hmmm, if you do, then we might be more evenly matched. Just you against me, with no luck involved if the cards don't run the right way for either of us."

Bella tilted her head to one side. "I take it you're no expert either then?" she queried innocently.

"No, not really. I just play chess now and again. It passes the time in the Officers' Mess sometimes when we're off duty and get bored with cards."

"Mmmmm," she replied. "That's seems fair then. Shall I find a board and some pieces for this evening? I'm not even sure we've got one here or at my other club, but I might as well buy one. Some guests might want to play one evening," she made it sound very vague and mundane.

"Good idea. So that's agreed?"

Bella nodded.

She sat back and sipped the rest of her cooling coffee as she watched him finish off his breakfast. He was a complete villain. He was actually a very good chess player, well he should be, he'd been taught as a little boy by a master: her father. He hadn't got the memory or ability to think endless moves ahead and strategise as his stepfather had, but he was still a formidable player. He and the Dowager were a good match and when he'd been at home they'd often battled royally, to her intense pleasure and his. However, Bella had also been taught by her father and she did have his brain. The pair of them were the only ones capable of beating either Nicky or the Dowager. Even the Duke invariably lost to those two. Nicky had never beaten Bella however, much to his endless annoyance, even when she was still a young girl. Oho! Would he get his comeuppance tonight, she decided. She'd have to be very careful as he knew her style of play – but of course he wouldn't suspect anything so she'd let him think he'd got her on the run, then turn the tables on him. It would be a treat to watch him wriggle, it would serve him right for trying to cheat. 'No expert' indeed!

"So, *Lionesse*, this is very domestic," he broke into her reverie, "what are you up to today then?"

"Oh, the usual," she waved her hand airily. "Doing the books, organising the staff, going over the menus and entertainment for the next few weeks, nothing very exciting."

"No shopping? What about our game tonight?"

"Oh, I'll send a footman out to find a chess board. I've got a lot of paperwork to catch up on."

Nicky was frustrated. It had occurred to him to lie in wait, hidden from sight, until she went out one day and then he'd catch up with her and discover her identity that way. After all, he was well trained in watching and following people unobserved. But she was obviously going to be busy today. He'd seen her engrossed in her ledgers when he'd arrived the previous evening and realised she was deeply involved in the running of her clubs and she wasn't merely a front for someone else.

Bella was amused. It wasn't hard to realise the only way he thought he'd find out who she was would be to watch and wait for her to go out without her disguise. Well, he'd have a long wait. There was more than one exit from the building, whether the front, the back or the side, and he couldn't watch them all. She'd find out what he was doing today and be extremely careful to ensure he wasn't around when she left to return home.

"What about you?" she made her query a joke. "Military manoeuvres in the Park? Marching up and down in front of the Palace?"

He laughed, "Not quite, *Chérie*. I have to report in to my superiors later this morning, then hopefully I'll have the rest of the day to myself. I need to spend some time with my family – actually I'm hoping my stepfather comes to Town today. He didn't know I was on my way to London and has been down in the country. I haven't seen him since last year so hopefully, he'll get here quickly so we can spend some time together before I have to depart again."

"How long are you actually going to be here for?" Bella queried. "You only arrived the other day, surely you're entitled to some proper leave?"

"There's a war going on, *Chérie*, and matters are critical in the Peninsula. I'm not actually home on leave, I was only sent to deliver some dispatches and collect more to take back with me along with some verbal situation briefings. I'm just a simple messenger really." That wasn't what he'd inferred last night, thought Bella. "I have to return as soon as some urgent papers I'm taking back are ready. I'm just grateful I've been able to have some time off here, a few days at home, while I wait for them to be prepared."

"I won't see you for much longer then?" her voice was sad. "How many days do you think you have left before you have to go, Nicky?"

He sat silently for a while, then shrugged his shoulders as he leaned towards her and picked up one of her hands, turning it over in both of his. "I don't know, one or two maybe?" He paused, "I'm so sorry, *Lionesse*. I would really have liked to spend much longer with you. The last few days, or should I say nights," he smiled at her, a certain look in his golden eyes, "have been... fascinating," a pause as he thought, "entertaining, quite unusual, rather erotic, special," he finally whispered, "sublimely special." He raised her hand to his lips and kissed it lingeringly. "I won't forget you, you know. How could I? I've had an extraordinary *affaire* with you and I don't even know what you look like. Only a glimpse of your luscious body," he paused again, "it's all been quite surreal."

She was silent, just sitting, watching him. He shook his head,

"You've no intention of letting me know who you are, letting me look at you before I go, have you?"

She shook her head in response, "It's best we keep it that way," she whispered, "then I can be just a pleasant memory and there'll never be a chance of any repercussions."

"You'll be more than a pleasant memory, *Lionesse*, surely you know that? What we've shared has been extraordinary. I can't remember when I've met a woman who's had such an effect on me as you, even without the strange game you've made me play. We just seem to have a, I don't know, a connection. I feel it every time I kiss you and I think you've felt it too, hmmm?"

Bella was stunned and merely nodded. She didn't know what to say, only glad he too had felt the lightning that fizzed between them whenever they touched or came together. Her dilemma was whether to tell him, reveal herself, but when? Before he left? When he returned...or never? She needed to think.

Still at a loss for words, she broke the spell of their intimate conversation and rose to her feet, muttering about her paperwork, shooing him into the bedroom to get dressed while she cleared away the remnants of their meal.

He came out, ready to take his leave of her, but as he went to take her in his arms, he smiled wickedly and pulled undone the belt of her wrapper and let the robe fall open, revealing the thin white voile nightrail. Silently she stood still as he pushed the wrap off her shoulders and arms and it slowly dropped away to the floor. He stepped back, hands at his sides, his gaze roaming over her body.

As his golden eyes slowly moved downwards, Bella watched as they flared and sparkled with desire and a telling bulge grew in the front of his tight pantaloons. One of his hands lifted and he touched her breast through the thin material of the otherwise modest, high-necked and long-sleeved gown. Her nipples swelled and she gasped softly as he lowered his head and gently nibbled and sucked first one then the other through the thin, almost transparent, silky fabric. Her eyes closed and her head dropped back as heat sizzled through her. She felt his hands on the fine cloth. Though she knew she should stop him, she was lost to the haze of lust that had shot through her quivering body and she simply hadn't the will as, bit by bit, he raised the hem and lifted her nightrail up above her waist.

They stood still in the silent room as he stared at her lower body then he whispered, "Black," and lifted his triumphant eyes and smiled at her again. He let the material drop and raised her limp hand to place a hot kiss in the palm. "Ten o'clock tonight then, *Chérie?*" he whispered in query. She nodded dazedly and watched as he quietly walked out through the door.

Chapter Eleven

Nicky made his way home, grinning like a schoolboy. It had been quite a night and now he knew she had black hair. It wouldn't take much more pushing and he was determined to get her mask off. As he walked briskly, the fresh morning air cleared away the last of his hangover and when he got back to Berkeley Square he hurriedly bathed, shaved and changed into his uniform and was just making his way over to the front door when the butler coughed behind him. "Excuse me, Your Grace," Browning was punctilious to the nth degree and had always insisted on addressing Nicky by his title, even as a child. To him, a Duke was a Duke, no matter what his age or circumstances, even if the child had been a mischievous little rascal at times. "I thought you should be aware we are told to expect the Baron and Master Charles some time mid to late afternoon. May I therefore assume you will be returning in time to dine at home this evening?"

"Yes, of course, Browning, thank you." Then Nicky had a sudden thought, "I need to send a message, can you find a footman for me? I'll be just a moment," he hurried back up to his room and the small escritoire there and scribbled a hasty note to *Lionesse* explaining his stepfather was arriving in Town and he would therefore have to spend some time with him that evening, therefore he might be delayed in getting to *Le Lion d'Or*. He apologised and said it would be eleven o'clock or maybe even midnight before he would be able to join her. Sealing his note and writing the direction on the front, he ran back down and handed it over to the waiting footman, asking for it to be delivered as quickly as possible. Then, turning his mind to more serious matters, he put all thoughts of his family and *Lionesse* to one side and hurried off to hail a hackney to take him to the Ministry of War.

Expecting merely to sit in on another round of meetings to be briefed on confidential messages to take back to Wellington, then handed documents to carry to Spain, Nicky was instead shown into the office of a retired Colonel of his Regiment whom he'd met previously at a couple of army dinners.

"Ah, de Bresancourt, good to see you again, M'Boy. Do take a seat... want a bit of a quiet chat, don't y'know." The elderly, upright and aristocratic, white haired man waved Nicky to sit and then sat back in his own chair, steepled his fingers and studied the young officer across from him for several silent minutes. Finally he spoke, slowly and consideringly.

"As y'know, we think we finally have the French on the back foot down in Spain, especially after Wellington took Badajoz and then Ciudad Rodrigo a month or two back. Read the more detailed reports and situation summaries you brought with you. Wellington will have Marmont shortly, no contest, man's no Masséna, so then it's on to Madrid, hopefully. Bonaparte's a fool to have got rid of one of his most capable Marshals just because of a little setback; they happen, fact of military life, look at Wellington as an example, but there you are; he'll come to grief himself soon, megalomaniacs always do, you mark m'words. But never mind that, to other matters that concern y'self," and he took a deep breath as he rocked back in his chair and gazed at Nicky again, making that man slightly uncomfortable.

"We've come across a slight problem, y'see; call it a little local difficulty, local as in Spain, which requires someone with local language skills and contacts, plus other...ah...abilities." He paused yet again and watched Nicky's impassive face intently. "I know you've been working undercover there for a while, doing reconnaissance, liaising with the rebels and guerrillas, helping with some other useful little jobs, blowing up or disrupting French communication or supply lines and so forth." Nicky merely nodded. "But this, how shall I put it, our little problem, requires a bit more finesse, cunning and complete ruthlessness." He hesitated, "Tell me, M'Boy, how much did you get involved when any guerrilla groups you were with got hold of any French troops out foraging, or separated from their main camp? Nasty tales we've heard here about what they do to them; ah... how can I put it? Not very British?" and a distasteful eyebrow quirked.

Nicky grimaced slightly. He knew what the man was referring to. "I know what you mean, Sir, but fortunately I've never had to witness anything really unpleasant or gruesome. If I had come across it, I'd try to prevent it, naturally; I don't hold with that sort of activity, it's not necessary in my personal opinion; just shoot the bastards or cut their throats, quickly and cleanly, if you need to dispense with them, but don't think me squeamish or incapable of being ruthless because of that. I've seen my fair share of blood and guts and killed when I've had to, however, I doubt any guerrillas would take much notice of me as I'm British; they may appreciate our military capability but think we're a trifle fastidious. I just happen to think for the most part we're a trifle more civilised, though we're by no means perfect and there's bad eggs everywhere, as I hope you will agree?"

"I do as a matter of fact, but was just curious and you've answered my question. Right, I digressed, now back to our little problem. I won't lie to you, M'Boy, the task is very dangerous. We've lost four men already trying to deal with it and we need to try another tack. Based on information I've had about you, I think you may be the right man to help us. I know you've not had much experience in this field but, quite frankly, we're running out of options and your name was suggested to me." Nicky continued to look at him impassively and the elderly colonel continued, "To be frank with you, you're still quite young and inexperienced and I'm not entirely convinced you have that streak of ruthlessness this type of work requires, despite your assertions just now, but time is of the essence and you're on your way back to Spain, so we might as well give it a try. We have absolutely nothing to lose but," and then he leaned forward and looked Nicky straight in the eye, "possibly your life, as the risks are great, not just of being killed... but more, far worse, if you're caught."

Nicky drew in a sharp breath at this and his brows rose. "I'm only telling you this as I'm not ordering you to take on this mission. If you do want to help, King and country and all that, we would make it worth your while. But you have to understand and consider the risks very carefully. You'll be dealing with some extremely clever and vicious individuals, Bonaparte's best. There's absolutely no guarantee you'll survive." Nicky looked back at the old man, his eyes narrowing.

"How much worth my while?" he asked slowly.

The colonel's eyes widened. Normally, the regimental officers had paid large sums to buy their commissions and came from reasonably wealthy or noble families. They were fighting for glory and their country, money was not usually an issue for them and if they wanted promotion, they often purchased that as well. He knew this young man was a Duke, albeit a displaced French one, and he was a bit taken aback by his apparent greater concern about money than the danger he faced. However, he did his best to answer. "Well, promotion, naturally, a better salary, a better pension... and I think possibly we may be able to offer assistance and a word in the right ears, if we get rid of Bonaparte and the Bourbons eventually get back their throne of course, with an appeal to get your family estates restored."

Colonel Melrose might have been slightly surprised at Nicky's first answer, but the elderly colonel had done his homework on his man.

Nicky's body language didn't show how he'd almost jerked at that carrot and he didn't hesitate. "I'll do it," he said succinctly.

The Colonel still hesitated. "Are you sure you don't want to discuss it with your family first? I know you don't have a wife or children, we wouldn't have suggested it to you otherwise, but still, the Dowager would be livid if she thought we'd forced you into this; she'd have my liver for a start."

Nicky's was momentarily stunned, but then it all fell into place. No wonder his Granny Granville knew so much about what he'd been doing. But how did she know these people? "How do you know the Dowager and what has she said about me?" he asked curiously.

"Oh, known her for years," replied the Colonel thoughtfully. "Remarkable woman, knew m'father, y'know, gather he was one of her suitors back in the day and they stayed friends after she married the Duke. Brain like a machine, especially for a female. Most unusual and quite frightening really, woman with a brain. Knows all sorts of people all over the place though. Been a very useful contact for the Foreign Office and us. She's very highly thought of in one or two quarters where they've sense enough to ignore the fact she's a female, though she terrifies the life out of me sometimes. Often think she'd frighten old Boney to death," and he laughed at his own joke. He leaned back again and smiled at Nicky, "She told me a lot about you, y'know, recommended you in fact, but I had to promise her it wasn't too dangerous. Afraid I was a trifle economical with the truth there. She was the one who said you weren't ruthless enough, I hope she's wrong in this instance, for once?" He left the question hanging.

Nicky absorbed all this information as he sat back and considered again what the colonel had just said. He wasn't afraid of danger and realistically he wondered what life would have had in store for him if it weren't for the interminable war with Bonaparte. Although the British were still fighting in India and the new United States, with a military presence across many parts of the world, he merely supposed his army career would simply have taken him further afield than the Peninsula. He didn't have the finances to socialise among the higher, wealthy reaches of the Ton like other young men of his ilk, no matter how much money his stepfather and uncle offered to give him, so the army was his career and a means to an end. He certainly wasn't looking to die any time soon, but fatalistically he believed he was as much at risk from being a regular soldier and going into battle with all the carnage that resulted in, as working undercover where at least he was more responsible for his own decisions and destiny. He was amazed his Uncle Francis had managed to keep his marriage to Bella a secret, but he was sorting that out and there was no one else in his life to worry about. Nicky sighed and realised he'd been caught on a hook, good and proper, with the promise of restitution of his lost family home and lands in France, not that he had the means to do anything with them, but it would be a start.

Side-lining his thoughts, he looked up at the Colonel again. "I've told you, I can be and have been as ruthless as necessary. I've been well-trained and have no close family to worry about. It's my decision, my life. I'm your man, Colonel Melrose."

"Good, good. Capital!" The colonel rose to his feet, "Hoped you'd accept, M'Boy, thank you," and he came round the desk and intimated Nicky to follow him. "I'm going to introduce you to someone now, he's in charge of these, ah, other matters and little problems. We're straying out of normal military territory here, y'see, although of course it's all connected in the larger landscape. He'll be your main point of contact going forward, but if ever you need anything, de Bresancourt, just let me know, what? Oh, and please do give my regards to the Dowager, when you next see her," he clapped Nicky round the shoulder and gave him a speaking look. "How is she by the way? Not looking quite the thing when I last saw her," and he tutted sadly and shook his head.

Nicky followed the older man out of his office and they walked down interminable corridors of the warren-like building in Whitehall. "No, Colonel, she's not too good. I saw her yesterday as a matter of fact, but she's got a will of iron so who knows how much longer she'll last?"

"Mmmmm, quite, quite," remarked the colonel shaking his head sympathetically and they walked on.

"Do you know her grandson, the Duke, by any chance?" Nicky enquired.

"Aaah, now there's an interesting man," the colonel replied enigmatically. "Yes, of course, known him for years too and catch up with him now and again; another mine of useful information and interesting and pithy opinions, rather like the old lady in Hertford Street. Talked to him about you too, y'know. He knows the score of course, but seems to think you've got hidden depths and would come good when up against it." Any further revelations were halted as they'd apparently arrived at their destination and the colonel knocked on a plain door which carried the simple designation: 'Department of Information'. Walking through a large outer office where a lone, nondescript man in plain clothes was reading through some documents, Colonel Melrose merely nodded at him and walked past his desk to knock on a further door.

"Come," sounded from within and the colonel ushered Nicky through in front of him.

"Morning, Melrose." The man intently studying papers in a file on his desk lifted his head.

"Morning, Ashcroft. I've brought your latest potential recruit. May I introduce Nicholas de Bresancourt, the Duke of Valenciennes. He's on secondment from the Hussars."

Nicky bowed briefly as another middle-aged, nondescript, rather aesthetic-looking man rose to his feet and offered his hand to shake. "Miles Ashcroft. Pleased to meet you."

"I'll leave you to it then," said the colonel as the two shook hands. "I've given him an overview but will leave you to brief him properly and confirm his appointment." He turned and nodded his head at Nicky, "Good luck, M'Boy, and take care. Remember, regards to the Dowager if you see her again before you leave," and with that and a nod to Ashcroft, he walked out of the office, closing the door quietly behind him.

Nicky looked around another spacious room filled with cupboards, bookcases and shelves stuffed with books, files and piles of papers and documents. Various maps of European countries hung on the walls and apart from Ashcroft's vast desk, there a large table surrounded by several chairs and over in front of a fireplace sat two comfortable chairs with a small table in between.

Picking up a file of papers, the nondescript looking man indicated Nicky should join him in front of the fireplace and so the pair went and sat down in the armchairs. Nicky looked at the other man curiously. Miles Ashcroft was tall and spare with receding greyish hair, simply but neatly styled. He was dressed very plainly, almost austerely, nothing special about his restrained tailoring to make him stand out, although his jacket and waistcoat obviously came from a good tailor. Nicky knew expensive tailoring when he saw it. His cravat was immaculately but not fancifully tied and neither too high nor too low on his neck. There was a gold pocket-watch barely visible on his simple waistcoat and the man sported a small gold signet ring one of his little fingers, all of the rest long and elegantly aristocratic with beautifully manicured nails. However, he was in no way effete. He was one of those nondescript people you would never notice or remark on when passing in the street or at any event, but could also fit in anywhere. However, when Nicky looked up into Ashcroft's face he was struck by the man's eyes. Above sharp, pale cheekbones, they were piercing grey, almost silver. As they appraised Nicky, they appeared to miss nothing. Nicky felt himself inspected minutely, from the top of his head to the tips of his boots and got an impression of fearsome intelligence behind the high forehead and impassive expression as Miles Ashcroft surveyed the man in front of him.

Ashcroft prided himself on learning a lot from his consideration of how people presented and conducted themselves and he'd already read a small dossier on the man he was now studying intently. The tawny hair was immaculately styled in the latest fashion and had obviously been recently trimmed as there was a suntan mark around his neck, across his forehead and down the sides of his face, suggesting he'd let it grow long and unkempt most of the time while he was in Spain. His closely shaven skin was clear of any blemish and a light golden brown, obviously no stranger to the sunshine and obviously not bothered by it. He obviously took care of himself and ate properly, since he radiated good health. Unusual, large, golden coloured eyes with black flecks surrounded by thick black lashes stood out on an unbelievably handsome face which Ashcroft surmised had to be inordinately attractive to the female of the species, with a well-shaped nose and sculpted cheekbones and he'd noted the man's teeth were white, straight and even. Wide, expressive lips were curling slightly upwards and Ashcroft got the impression he was being privately laughed at in some way.

Unlike a lot of men of his age and social standing, the man didn't sport long sideboards and looked immaculately groomed, right down to his nails, although the callouses on his hand were apparent when he'd shaken it; he noted the small signet ring on his little finger. Those hands, with their long, elegant fingers, were now loosely draped over the arms of his chair as he relaxed back in it, apparently unconcerned he was being studied, as he was obviously studying the man in front of him, in return. It was noticeable to anyone he had a muscular physique; it had struck Ashcroft from the moment he'd strolled into his office behind Melrose. The man was well over six foot and well-proportioned and carried his uniform with a languid, easy grace. That uniform was immaculately tailored to fit him perfectly, so he seemed to be someone who cared for his appearance as well as denoting a degree of wealth. If his uniform didn't give him away, his beautiful boots did, to those who knew what they were looking at. Ashcroft recognised handmade boots when he saw them and even though they were worn in, these ones fit perfectly and were expensively made by an expert.

The general impression Ashcroft had was of a wealthy, fit and extremely handsome young man in his middle to late twenties who would stand out in a crowd. Yet there was no sign of the languid, bored indolence common among his peers in the Ton. In fact, quite the opposite. There was an aura of... leashed power, he decided, about the man. As if he was ready to spring into action if anything untoward suddenly happened, despite his relaxed manner. Ashcroft just knew he was alert and reaching his own conclusions about him. He wondered what sort of a brain there was behind those unusual eyes and he now understood the man's nickname, related to his title: The Lion of Valenciennes. He did indeed appear to have a leonine look about him, a trait apparently carried by former members of his ducal family down the centuries. Indeed, if his hair had been longer, the resemblance would be even more pronounced. Ashcroft wondered if he was as proud and brave – and intelligent – as a lion, or as patient, stealthy and ruthless as a hunting cat after its prey; for the role under consideration, he would certainly need to be most, if not all of those things.

Ashcroft opened the file of papers on his knee and reconsidered their contents for a while as Nicky sat in silence. Without preamble or any small talk, Ashcroft looked up at him and asked, "How come you learned to speak so many languages? I gather you are completely tri-lingual in English, French and Spanish?"

"And I also speak some German and a smattering of Portuguese and Italian, as well as a bit of Greek, I suppose," Nicky sighed as he prepared himself for some interrogation of his career and character, obviously going further than Colonel Melrose. "I was born in France, though I escaped when I was about four and a half, in 1790, soon after the start of the Revolution. I was one of the lucky aristocrats, so French is my mother tongue. I was fortunate to be adopted by a French family who were also fleeing to England and I grew up here and was schooled at Eton. However, although my step-father is French, my step-mother was originally Spanish, so we spoke all three languages at home and with extended family. I went to stay with an elderly relation from time to time in my youth and when she discovered I had a flair for languages, she arranged for me to have German lessons. She took them with me so we could converse together and practise what we learned."

For a moment Nicky smiled at the memories of him and the Dowager laughing as they grappled with lengthy German verbs while they sat in front of the fire in her sitting room in Hertford Street, that now silent and cold room where he and Francis had stood only the day before. "Then, while I was studying at Oxford and just after, I went to Italy for a couple of extended summers and picked up Italian while I was touring around there. It wasn't that hard as I'd studied Classics, Latin and Greek, at Eton and my step-father is quite an academic, so had also encouraged and tutored me over the years... and the Portuguese merely comes from my time in the Peninsula."

"Hmmm, fascinating. A useful talent. Tell me, what language do you think in?"

Nicky considered for a second or two, it was an interesting ques-tion and no one had ever asked him that, nor had he ever thought about it himself. "Well, mainly English when I'm here, but when I've been in France, which hasn't been for many years obviously, or spent time with my adopted French relations speaking French all the time, I tend to think more in French although lately, while I've been in the Peninsula and living among Spaniards, in Spanish. But I suppose it's mainly English." He hesitated, "I'm sorry, it's not that straightforward," he shrugged.

"Hmmm, fascinating," Ashcroft repeated, "and, when in critical situations," he raised those piercing eyes to Nicky, "if, for instance, you were captured and tortured, or *in extremis* when you're very drunk or fornicating with a woman, what language do you think in then? Or what language do you speak?"

Nicky's eyes widened at another, even stranger question. "Well," he pondered, "I've never been captured or tortured so I wouldn't know; I suppose it would depend what country I was in and who my captors were. When we were doing our training and were put through some interrogation practice, I always answered in the language I was supposed to, no matter how hard they pushed me," and he reflected back on the beatings and rather unpleasant treatment he'd received at the time, the training had been extremely thorough. "But then, I suppose, deep in my subconscious I knew it wasn't genuine, so I don't know what I'd do in reality."

"And women, what language do you think in when you climax?" Ashcroft pushed. "Our reports say you're quite one for the ladies, quite the rake. Aristocratic ones, common ones, working ones, single ones, married ones, you don't appear to be fussy." He tutted but got no response from the impassive face across from him. "Though not men, nor any particular perversions." He tutted again. "I'm told you don't gamble rashly, nor use noxious substances I trust, opium for instance?" Nicky now looked slightly aghast at the intrusively personal questions; he'd expected to be asked about his former undercover work, liaising with the rebels in Spain, etc... and just how much did the man know about his love life? Not too much, he trusted, given some of what he'd been up to before joining the army and going overseas.

"Well, I... why do you need to know that?"

"Agents can be blackmailed if they have secrets or perversions they don't want people to know about, or nasty habits which are an addiction. There's many who've been caught out by a clever woman, believe me."

"I don't use opium or other concoctions, never felt inclined though I have tried them," he shrugged. "They didn't do anything particular for me except make me either hallucinate unpleasant visions or drowsy and fall asleep and I could do without all that. A nice French brandy is more my poison and I can't gamble with money I don't have. But I like women as much as the next man," Nicky answered with a grin, now just bemused by this line of questioning from someone he'd literally only just met. "I enjoy fornicating with them every which way, but what's perverted?" He quirked a roguish eyebrow and thought he'd play the man at his own game. "Some people think anything other than the missionary position is perverted," smirking as he shrugged.

"This is a serious conversation, de Bresancourt, don't be facetious. If I ask a question, I expect a serious answer. I have to make decisions here, a judgement as to your suitability. If you work for me, I'll expect you to go to any length, carry out any task, in order to achieve your objective."

"Yes, Sir. Sorry, Sir." Nicky apologised and then smiled at the older man in his best, irresistible fashion.

However, he discovered Ashcroft was immune to any sort of charm or humour as the man merely looked at him, waiting, his grey eyes sharp. "I am not your parent, your teacher, nor in the military. I will remind you for a second time about your facetiousness. Answer the question," he said, in a cutting tone.

Nicky had lost the thread of the original question so merely responded, "I'll do whatever a woman wants. As you seem to know, I'm not inexperienced in these matters but I'm not a selfish man, nor an animal. I actually prefer it if the lady is pleasured then so am I as it makes for a better experience in my considered opinion, but I draw the line at anything really strange. I'm not a follower of the dear Marquis de Sade, if that's what you mean?"

"Would you go with a man if you had to? Oh I know it's frowned upon and not discussed, but I'm quite sure you're aware of that side of life, being the man you are."

Nicky wondered what sort of man Miles Ashcroft thought he was but kept that to himself. "I'd rather not," and shuddered slightly.

"And, as I asked, what language do you think in and speak when you climax?"

"Damn me, for God's sake!" exclaimed Nicky but then looked at Ashcroft's impassive face and continued. "It depends on the woman. Some women like me to speak to them in French, especially English women," he smiled wickedly, "even if they haven't a clue what I'm saying. It could be a market list for all they know, but generally I suppose I tend to think in French when I'm in bed, it just seems to be the more expressive language, but if I'm enjoying myself I tend not to think at all...!" Nicky sat back and smiled. He recalled the jaded and brainless young matron to whom he'd whispered a list of menu items and cooking ingredients as he'd made love to her one night while her husband was away at his hunting box. She'd declared him to be the most romantic man she'd ever met and he'd laughed to himself at her foolishness. She was very attractive but had bored him senseless. Looking at Ashcroft again, he added more seriously, "When I'm on duty, I wouldn't let myself go to the extent I'd give my cover away if that's what you're getting at, so I try to keep away from beautiful, tempting women," he added with an impassive expression but Ashcroft had seen the humour in his eyes.

Ashcroft gave him a hard look and shook his head in frustration. "I see." he merely said. Then in a complete change of tack, "You're in the Hussars, a competent rider then?" Nicky nodded. Ashcroft read down a list of his accomplishments, "Regimental fencing champion, rifle and pistol champion, cross country running champion. You did well at school too, I see; no mean feat at Eton for a French *émigré*. You got to be Deputy Head Boy, hmmm..." he mused to no one in particular then read on, "Aha, your superiors think you're a bit of a charmer," he looked at Nicky with a raised eyebrow, "more than 'a bit' I'd say, handsome fellow like you," and Nicky shifted uncomfortably in his chair. "I'm not complaining. Useful attributes, charm and good looks, in our line of work. Many a wife or mistress has given someone away just through a bit of charm in the right places from the right man." His smile was like a frightening Cheshire cat, except it wasn't really a smile, just a facial expression with no emotion behind it and he went back to his papers again, reading through endless reports he'd acquired about the man seated opposite him.

Then he looked up and smiled properly, "Aaah, now this is more like it. Regimental chess champion, well at least you have a brain as well as good looks, brawn and good dress sense. Always appreciate a man competent at chess. Demonstrates an ability to strategise in my opinion, consider options, review previous moves, forward think, evaluate an opponent. Are you that good?" he suddenly asked.

"Tolerably," replied Nicky, not wishing to boast, "but most of my fellow officers are more into their horses and card games than intellectual, thoughtful board games that can take hours sometimes, so I wouldn't put too much importance to that accomplishment, as well as some of my others, like running," and he chuckled. "My stepfather actually taught me chess when I was a boy, said it would train my brain, if I could locate it," he chuckled again, "I've never managed to beat him, but then neither has anyone else except his daughter on rare occasions. He taught her as well and I think he might have let her win. He's got an amazing brain. Quite a scholar too, but not just dusty tomes or ancient Greek and Latin; he knows so much about everything." Suddenly a picture of Bella with long plaits popped into his mind, her and her father battling over a chessboard at home in Arlington while she chewed the end of one. She'd beaten Eddie a few times, but only a few and when she'd crowed, Nicky had seen the smile on Eddie's face and had his suspicions, but she really had inherited a brain like her father's. They were well matched now and he smiled to himself. He was looking forward to seeing his Papa again that afternoon. It had been far too long.

"Really?" Ashcroft scribbled in his file. He was always interested to hear about clever people, endless coded missives, stolen or retrieved from various enemies, were always appearing in his offices and he needed people with superior intellect to help try and decode them. If they were foreign as well as British patriots, so much the better for his purposes. He made a mental note to effect an introduction with Baron Edouard de Mornay.

"And you've been working undercover in Spain, I see. I gather from Colonel Melrose you've done the various training courses?" he raised an eyebrow.

"Yes, Sir. Ah, Lord Ashcroft is it? Or Mr Ashcroft?" replied Nicky, unsure of the man's situation, but this line of questioning was straightforward to deal with. "I can blow up most things with a bit of gunpowder, load a rifle or musket or pistol in the dark, forage for food, live rough, survive interrogation, the usual useless things," he grinned until he saw Ashcroft's face and then his voice went serious again, "and I know how to kill. With any sword or knives and daggers, poison, all sorts of methods, or with my bare hands. We had a strange oriental fellow on one of the courses I did. He could break bricks with his bare hand. Extraordinary. He showed us all sorts of tricks, how to fight with our feet as well as our hands for instance, also to kill silently. Most damn useful thing I got to experience. Wish I could have learned more from him, but not enough time...." he mused as an afterthought.

Ashcroft ignored Nicky's query about his name and title. "Have you killed many men in cold blood? Premeditated, as opposed to battle, or a fight or a duel?"

"Some."

"Any women? Children?"

"No." Nicky's voice was quiet.

"Would you have a problem doing so?"

"Premeditated? If it was necessary? Women? Then yes, certainly. I'm not a fool, I don't think they're the weaker sex most people believe they are, physically or mentally. They're certainly cunning and devious at times," he thought of the Dowager and smiled to himself, "and as capable of killing as men, even if most are not physically as strong as them." Nicky thought of the Duchess of Firle. He knew how many men she'd killed in her efforts to rescue the Duke, when he'd been captured while trying to save his uncle and family from the same people who'd killed Nicky's own parents.

"Good. Sensible man." Ashcroft nodded "But would you kill a child if you were told to?"

"I hope I never have to face that." Nicky looked up at Ashcroft, horror in his eyes. "I don't enjoy killing anyone or anything, even an animal." He paused and Ashcroft raised an eyebrow. "I told Colonel Melrose when he talked to me, I've killed plenty, it happens in war and when you have enemies, or to right a wrong; and make no mistake, I do it if I have to. But a child? Accidentally would be bad enough but premeditated? I'm sorry, I don't think I could, but I hope to God I never have to find out." He looked at Ashcroft, thinking the man would probably now consider him unfit for the task at hand but Ashcroft looked at him and actually smiled briefly.

"Good. I need hard, ruthless, clever and resourceful men working for me, but not callous killers and animals. They need some basic moral compass. As long as you remember some children can be brainwashed to become very dangerous; just look at some of the vermin that inhabit the Dials, the Rookery or the Stews. They have the same, or worse, in some of the big cities in Europe, India and the Far East, take it from me. Those 'children'," Ashcroft accentuated the words with his fingers in the air, "would kill their own mothers for a guinea." He left the comment in the air and Nicky nodded as Ashcroft looked at his papers, contemplated, then asked, "So, as a French Duke, what are you doing in the British army then?"

Nicky laughed sharply but he was glad to be back on more straightforward territory. "A Duke, yes, but Duke of nothing these days," he spread his hands and shrugged. "No home, no estates, no money, no family, except my adopted one. My title is empty, no more than a joke. Therefore, what else is there for a man like me?"

"But you've had an exceptional education and upbringing. You live at one of the best addresses in Town with access to two country homes in Sussex. You've travelled, you have impeccable social connections and you 'appear' a man of wealth and means and, of course, you have your Commission. You just need a rich wife. You're an attractive man, surely it's a simple solution to find one? Plenty of wealthy men in trade or commerce want to buy a title for their daughters, enough of our aristocratic families over the years have colluded in that when their fortunes have waned or been lost for one reason or another. And what about your adopted family, they obviously support you?"

Nicky looked angry. "I don't want to live on charity all my life and I don't expect my adopted family to support me *ad infinitum*. Nor do I wish to be bought like a piece of meat or live off a woman. Some men might be happy with that state of affairs but not this one. I'm not that desperate. When all this mess with Bonaparte is over, if I'm still alive, I intend to think about my options. I had considered going to the Americas; I hear there are many opportunities there if you have enough ambition and determination."

"I see. A proud man with principles, eh?"

"If you like, yes." Nicky said forcefully.

"Fine. Let's discuss Bonaparte then." Ashcroft suddenly changed the subject yet again. "I take it you know he's going into Russia now? The Grand Army is on its way and massing on the Neman River as we speak, ready to cross. Big mistake that, in my considered opinion. He's going to come a cropper."

Nicky nodded. "Does seem a step too far, even to me, and most people I've talked to with an understanding of military matters and geography. Big country, vast. Wild, ruthless men those Cossacks. Damn cold in winter too, but the man's a megalomaniac. Lost the plot." Nicky shrugged. "No idea why he needs to expand his empire, isn't Europe big enough? He's having enough trouble keeping all of that in order, why add to his problems?

"Quite so," nodded Ashcroft, "well put. But it's to our advantage that he's not put in a personal appearance in the Peninsula again. Nevertheless, Wellington still has a way to go in Spain and it's critical there at the moment. Even if he's not there himself and has foolishly dispensed with Masséna, Bonaparte still has some very competent Marshals. However, if the man keeps pulling his troops out of the Peninsula to support his actions further east in Europe, that may give us the edge we need to push the French right out of Spain. And if he does come a cropper in Russia, then maybe the rest of Europe might be persuaded the man's not infallible and help us be rid of him. The Prussians for a start."

"So what do you need me for?" asked Nicky curiously, glad they now seemed to have gone past a discussion of his personal character traits.

"Well," mused Ashcroft, sitting back and putting his file on the small table between them, "Bonaparte has finally realised Wellington is no pushover and that his Marshals need some support if they are to resist him with fewer men. While he's been focussed on central and eastern Europe and keeping his wretched Continental System in place, he's had his agents busy undermining or crushing any fermenting resistance and mostly been very successful. So, now he's preoccupied with Russia, we think he's sending some of his troublemakers and assassins down into the Peninsula to cause problems for Wellington, the Portuguese and the Spanish rebels and guerrillas... and deal with their ringleaders."

"Interesting," Nicky merely nodded his head.

"There are a very select handful of these individuals dotted across Europe. We don't know who they all are of course, as they keep themselves well under cover, but a couple have surfaced in Spain. One of them is particularly venal and a rather nasty piece of work. We think he's been after some of the gold Rothschilds are now sending to Wellington to keep the army and rebels paid and fed, as well as doing Bonaparte's dirty work undermining or disposing of key elements of the rebel leadership and anyone with any sense or capability in the Spanish Government or military."

"Reeeally?" it was a soft, interested comment, not a facetious one.

"We've been on this man's trail for the past year and we're sure he's in Spain now. He's a bad egg; extremely clever and quite vicious, a cold-blooded killer. He took out three of our men on his case in central Europe. We never discovered the final whereabouts of two of them, but he left the third for us to find, as a sort of message, I presume. Shocking sight," Ashcroft actually shuddered. "I won't go into details, but our target is on the loose in Spain, we're convinced of it. We had a fourth man looking, but then he went missing too. We found him a month or so ago. He'd been captured, tortured and left for dead, but we managed to get to him before he died, that's how we know who the perpetrator was. Should have seen what they did to him, don't know how he survived as long as he did. Appalling. Terrible..." another shudder. Nicky shivered.

"We're sure now that he's planning to disrupt the movement of gold to Wellington and ambush a delivery soon. If it doesn't get through to the Allies in the Peninsula that will cause us major problems, therefore keeping Bonaparte happy. I'm sure you know, Wellington isn't like the French; he insists on buying food and supplies for his troops, not scavenging off the local communities and taking all they have. The Spanish rebels need financing as well, to keep them going and on side. But we understand this man, this agent, actually wants the gold for himself as well as causing disruption." Ashcroft leaned forward and put his hand on the arm of Nicky's chair, looking him directly in the eye, "We need a man to find him and you've been recommended. You would need to stop the ambush, or at least warn us of his plans in time, then kill him and any associates he may have. We're not sure if he works alone or has men helping him, either French or Spanish."

Nicky swallowed hard. "Is that all?" he joked. "Sounds like a picnic."

"I assure you, de Bresancourt, this is no laughing matter," Ashcroft rasped at him coldly. "Four good and competent men have died trying to put a stop to his murderous activities. MY men and I'm beginning to take it personally. If we don't get rid of him now, he's going to be a thorn in our side, causing no end of trouble as the British move through Spain - providing Wellington keeps lucky and continues his successful push - and the last thing we need are the Spanish rebels and guerrillas losing their nerve at this critical juncture. What there are of the Spanish military are useless, too busy arguing amongst themselves and proving totally unreliable when you need them, not that I need to tell you that as you've no doubt seen for yourself, but the guerrillas and rebels have done wonders in harassing the enemy and providing intelligence, so we need to keep them enthused and demonstrate our appreciation."

"I apologise," said Nicky, "I didn't mean to jest, but that's no mean task. He could be anywhere in Spain. How do I even start to find him? Do you know what he looks like? And what's the fellow's name, by the way? I take it you know now?"

"He has various aliases and calls himself assorted names, depending on where he's operating, but we believe his real name is Bernheim, Frederick Bernheim," said Ashcroft.

Chapter Twelve

Nicky's body stiffened in shock and his face blanched at the mention of a name he hadn't heard in years. Ashcroft looked at him curiously, "You know of this man?"

Trying to get a grip of himself, Nicky shook his head. "No, not at all. I'm sorry. It's just that name... Bernheim," he spat it out in a whisper. "It was a man of that name who was responsible for the murder of my parents and their retainers and the subsequent loss of my estate and fortune. The *sans-culottes* didn't get them, he and his associates massacred everyone at Valenciennes except my parents and myself, but they died at his hand soon after. My father was tortured to death, my mother was expecting another child and miscarried and died after being raped and badly beaten. He tried to do the same to my step-father's family, except they were rescued in time and by a fortunate quirk of fate, took me with them; that's how I survived, but they had to leave everything behind as well, in order to escape from France. As it was, we only just got out by the skin of our teeth."

Nicky took a deep breath and continued, "I don't know if you've ever met the Duke of Firle, but the Duchess is my step-father's sister. We're a very close family, that's why I've been so lucky with my upbringing. The old lady I referred to earlier, about my German lessons, is the Duke's grandmother, Lady Elizabeth Granville, the Dowager Duchess of Firle. Anyway, the Duke also had a run-in with this Bernheim and his men, and very nearly lost his life as a result. It was the Duchess who killed Bernheim eventually and saved the Duke. It's an old story in our family, not many people know. It happened, oh it must be over twenty years or so ago now." Nicky shivered. "I'm sorry, but it's that name. The man destroyed a lot of lives, including mine," he ran a hand over his face and pulled himself together. "I apologise, of course it's not the same man, the Duchess killed him. There must be hundreds of men in France with that name, it just took me by surprise; please excuse me," he apologised hastily and politely, slightly embarrassed by his outburst.

Ashcroft looked at him even more curiously and intently. "That's a very interesting story. Tell me, where did all this drama happen? It wouldn't have been in Normandy, by any chance?"

Looking at him in dawning horror, Nicky nodded. "How did you know that?" he whispered.

"Oh, I know a lot of things," Ashcroft replied softly, tapping the side of his nose, "including the fact that you are in fact married to the Baron de Mornay's daughter." Nicky gasped and blanched again.

Ashcroft smiled mirthlessly. "Oh, don't worry, de Bresancourt, old Melrose doesn't know, or your superiors in the military. But before ANYONE gets introduced to me personally, let alone comes to work for me, I look into their background, connections and character extremely carefully, no stone unturned as it were. One cannot afford to be too careful and you ARE French after all, with French step-relations."

Nicky stared at him, aghast. "I know why you married her, don't worry and yes, I am acquainted with the Duke. Tolerably well actually, also his old battle-axe of a grandmother. I asked him about your marriage and he confirmed you're getting it annulled since it's served its purpose now. It's been kept very quiet for obvious reasons for the young lady's sake, so rest assured your little family secret is safe with me. But Melrose is right on one point, I don't take on anyone with a wife and family or serious responsibilities. It's not fair on them, particularly in these troubled times, as unfortunately our attrition rate has been quite high lately."

Nicky was still speechless at how much this seemingly nondescript man knew.

"Anyway, that story about Bernheim is most interesting and I intend to look into it a bit deeper. Don't be concerned though, what's spoken within these four walls stays within these four walls. No one will know about your marriage, your family, or the Duke's connection with Normandy or any other Bernheim. In fact, no one knows we exist here at all, except for a very select group and Melrose is my connection, a conduit to the military when I need it. He knows everyone who's anyone in the army and I have another associate who is in the same situation with the navy. As far as the rest of the Ministry here," he waved a hand around vaguely, "they think we're just an Information Department shifting paper about all day on bureaucratic nonsense, and as far as most people are concerned, I don't exist."

Ashcroft looked at his watch fob and stood up abruptly so naturally Nicky did the same. "I'm afraid we'll have to call it a day for now, de Bresancourt, our conversation has taken longer than I anticipated and I have to go and brief the Prime Minister on some new intelligence we've just received from eastern Europe. We're all keeping a very close eye on what's happening in Russia, the repercussions of what Bonaparte does could be critical, also that of the Tsar. However, I'll look into that Bernheim business, see if it's just a coincidence or not and let you know, but I think there may well be a connection. Interesting. Most interesting," he looked thoughtful. "Also, we'll pull together some background papers for you to read on your way back to the Peninsula so you'll know as much as we do about OUR Bernheim and his network, such as it is. I assume you know to burn them when you've finished, even if you're on board ship, as with everything else you ever get from this Department?" Nicky nodded. "Good. We'll give you some funds and I'll get someone to brief you on how to communicate with us before you go, plus I'll make arrangements for you to draw whatever further monies you may need when you get to Spain. Come back here tomorrow morning. Ten o'clock sharp. There'll also be some confidential papers I'll want you to take to Wellington, up to date intelligence. They'll be ready by tomorrow too."

Nicky bowed briefly and they shook hands. "Welcome to my little organisation, de Bresancourt – you may address me simply as Ashcroft. I hope you're as good as everyone tells me you are," he looked Nicky in the eye, then up and down, as if in final assessment. "You're a bit young and frivolous for my taste, too much the joker, but hopefully you've got the message. This is no picnic outing we're organising here," his voice was cutting and sarcastic, "Oh, by the way, whatever you do, don't play cards with anyone you get involved with. Your emotions are far too obvious, even if you think they aren't. Stick to chess, or the ladies. That's obviously where your strengths and talents lie," and with that he walked over to his door and waited for Nicky to precede him out. Nicky realised the bizarre interview was over and despite the sarcastic comments, he'd obviously passed muster.

He left the building and walked into the summer sunshine, his head spinning from the events of the morning. He wondered what he'd let himself in for. He sauntered along, across Green Park, heading in the general direction of Bond Street, intending to do some shopping and purchase some more simple shirts to take back with him to Spain, his mind now on his forthcoming meeting with his uncle. They would certainly have some interesting matters to discuss.

Chapter Thirteen

"**B**OO!" A pair of hands came down over her eyes and a deep voice whispered in her ear, "I'd recognise you anywhere." He often played the trick on Sooty, it was one of his favourites.

"NICKYYYYY!" Bella let out a horrified screech, dropping her parcels and causing a stir amongst the sedate shoppers in Bond Street as she turned, thinking he'd somehow uncovered *Lionesse's* disguise.

"Damn, you don't have to look so shocked, Sooty, it's only me," Nicky laughed, straightening the elaborate bonnet he'd knocked slightly askew. "Been shopping I see. Come on, show me what you've bought, anything nice for me?" He playfully pulled at her packages as he helped her pick them up from the pavement.

"Oi, get off, You Nuisance," she complained with a light laugh, "no, there's nothing for you here, you don't deserve anything." She clung fast to some large parcels she definitely did NOT want him to peer into: a new chess set and some other items for that evening. "Unless you want a new rattle that is, or some mittens?" She fished out a little pink and silver rattle she'd bought for Elizabeth and a minute pair of silk mittens, threaded through with pink ribbon, "Though I think these are a trifle on the small side for an oaf like you!"

He grinned as he waved the rattle in the air before handing it back to her. "Have you got Francis's carriage waiting somewhere? Can I cadge a lift back to the house? If you've finished your shopping that is? Why do you always buy so much? The shop assistants must see you coming," he teased, shaking his head. "Where's your maid by the way? You know what Francis is like about you ladies being out by yourselves."

"Oh, fiddle faddle, don't you start lecturing me," Bella ordered bossily and laughed, then snapped her fingers in the air as she spoke. "Anyway, I don't take any notice of Uncle Francis, any more than Aunt Cat does," she grinned back and set off along the street pointing to the Ducal carriage with a footman waiting alongside.

"I did come in the carriage though, it's just along here." With a huge sigh of relief that he hadn't recognised her alter ego, Bella gave Nicky a pert smile and piled all her packages into his arms on top of his own shopping, beckoning him to follow. "Come along, Slave. This way. Hurry up, don't dawdle, or I'll take a stick to you, You Feeble Halfwit!" She set off down the street with him trailing in her wake, in full Bossy Sister mode.

"Oh yes, Mistress, anything you say, Mistress, I can't help it if I'm feeble… bloody hell, Sooty, what have you got here? It feels like you've bought half the street. Never knew rattles were so heavy," he muttered, laughing as he made his way after her back to the carriage.

Bella had had quite a morning. As soon as Nicky had disappeared off, she'd hurriedly bathed and dressed and made her way back to Firle House where she presented herself in her uncle's study. Knocking and peering round the door, she'd found him already deeply ensconced with one of his secretaries. "I'm sorry to trouble you, Uncle, but could you spare me just a few minutes?" Francis looked up. "I know you're busy, but it really is important."

Francis raised an eyebrow and sighed. The family knew to leave him undisturbed to work, especially in the mornings, unless it was either urgent or very important, but Bella looked serious so he nodded at his secretary, who diplomatically got up and left the room as Bella hurried over to sit in the now vacant chair by her uncle's desk.

"What is it, Poppet? I'm a trifle busy this morning as I promised Nicky I'd spend some time with him this afternoon. I need to speak to him about Valenciennes business," he added, not wanting his niece to know the real subject matter of their discussions.

"Oh, it won't take long, I promise," she smiled at him winningly.

Francis rolled his eyes at her. "No woman EVER says something won't take long and means it," he chuckled. "So what is it, Sweetheart? Have you overspent your allowance? Or do you need some more investment capital?" they both laughed.

"No, nothing like that, which reminds me," said Bella with a superior and satisfied smile, "did you see the banker's draft I left for you, repaying the remainder of the loan you gave me for the two properties?"

"Yes, I did, thank you very much," Francis grinned. "You must be turning over a tidy profit in those two little establishments to have paid it all back so quickly. How long have they been open? Five, or is it six months?"

"I told you they were a good idea," she smirked back at him saucily. "I do know what I'm doing."

Francis looked across at Bella smirking at him. He was amazed at what she'd achieved in such a short time. She was an extremely clever and astute young woman, just like his grandmother had been, except with a much sunnier nature and he smiled sadly to himself. "Obviously," he replied, "though I never really doubted it with Eddie for your father. Are you sure you don't want to come and work for me?" he raised an eyebrow at her.

Bella threw back her head and shouted with laughter. "I don't think your managers and staff would appreciate a twenty-one year old girl, a FEMALE, telling them what to do, do you? It would be unheard of, the world would think you'd run mad and clap you in Bedlam."

"Oh, I don't know," chuckled her uncle, "it would certainly put the wind up them, that's for sure; as for the world, they can go hang as far as I'm concerned, as you well know," and the pair of them laughed companionably.

"So, Bella, what did you really come to ask me?" Francis looked at his pocket watch pointedly.

"It's about Nicky, Uncle Francis."

The Duke sighed. "Now why does that not surprise me?"

She came straight out with it. "I want you to tell me what he's really doing down in the Peninsula."

Francis sat back in his chair. "Do you now. What makes you think I know anything about his doings there, apart from being a soldier, that is?"

"Uncle, don't start that with me, I had enough of it with Nicky yesterday, and the day before that. I thought you at least would acknowledge I'm adult enough to be told the truth." Bella banged her fist on his desk and Francis looked slightly taken aback at her vehemence. "He told me all he does all day is read and write reports and carry messages. Then he had the gall to say he was too busy, or out in the field, to write to us all and the post was bad. However, whatever the reality, that doesn't seem to stop all the other families from getting the odd letter now and again, so if he's got time to write reports, surely he can take five minutes to send something to us to say he's still in one piece and not dead in some Spanish ditch!" She let out a frustrated sigh, "He acts like I'm still ten, running around in a pinafore with my hair in plaits and playing with dolls. He drives me completely mad." She leaned forward and looked her uncle in the eye, "But I'm a big girl now, apart from being his wife. I'm not a fool as YOU well know. I just KNOW he's involved in something far more dangerous than being a simple soldier and I know," she poked herself in the chest to emphasise her words, "that YOU know what it is," and the accusing forefinger turned in Francis's direction.

"Oh Lord!" sighed Francis, "Heaven save me from clever women," and he smiled before looking at her more seriously. "Look Bella, I certainly don't take you for a fool, far from it, as you well know." He paused and his face looked sympathetic, "Yes, I do have some idea of what Nicky has been and is still up to, but I've given my word in certain places that I won't discuss it, with ANYONE, so I can't discuss it with you. I'm sorry, Sweetheart."

Bella looked frustrated and angry and Francis had immense

sympathy with her, so he took a deep breath and continued. "However, I will tell you this, but consider it very carefully." He sat forward to speak quietly and forcefully to her. "You know neither your Papa, Aunt Cat, my grandmother, as well as myself, were happy with Nicky's decision to join the army and we all did our best to dissuade him. We did that for various reasons, but at the end of the day he is his own man so we couldn't stop him and could only support him as best we could. The main and obvious reason we objected was because we care for and love him a great deal and know that being an ordinary soldier is extremely dangerous. You charge into battle and it's in God's or Fate's hands if your time is up, whether from a stray musket, mortar or cannonball, or some enemy soldier cutting you down with a sabre. You can be as big and brave as Achilles or Hector, or as strong as Hercules, but it's a hell of a job and if you happen to be in the wrong place at the wrong time, even a messenger..." Francis made a cutting motion across his throat and Bella shuddered, "and Generals get killed as well, you know, also Kings and Princes. Remember your history books, Bella; think of King Harold at the Battle of Hastings with that arrow in his eye, or Richard the Lionheart fighting in France a century or so later, then there was Richard the Third at Bosworth in the Wars of the Roses, the three Scottish Kings, James the Second, Third and Fourth, all killed in battle... and there are many more examples. No one, absolutely NO ONE, is safe on a battlefield. Nicky is a soldier and soldiers fight, but all I will say is that he IS doing some, ah... extracurricular work for Wellington." Francis paused momentarily to consider his words before continuing and Bella sat silently, hanging on his every word.

"It's like this, Bella: Nicky speaks Spanish and French like a native, even better than you or me, and most people think we're good, especially our French – so it stands to reason the Army wants to make use of someone with his skills. However, it's a different sort of danger that he faces. I happen to think he's possibly at LESS risk doing this than on the battlefield where his fate rests with others and is out of his control. At least working on his own, or with a small group of others, he controls where he goes and what he does to a certain extent. If he goes into something risky or life threatening, it's on his terms, so hopefully he's considered the best way to go about it, not because he's blindly following someone else's orders which may be right or wrong. Either way, he's still fighting the French, just in a different way." He sat back and let his words sink in.

"I see," said Bella thoughtfully. "You mean he's some sort of agent or military spy?"

"I never said that," responded her uncle enigmatically, "but I do believe it's difficult for him to send us letters like other officers do to their families, so go easy on him, hmmm?"

Bella looked at her uncle and nodded. "Very well," she said reluctantly.

"Good," sighed Francis with relief. "I promise if I do get word about him from any of my contacts, merely to know he is still safe, I WILL let you know; but, you have to promise me you won't tell ANYONE else; not your father, nor your aunt. Do you give me your word?"

Bella picked up Francis's hand and kissed it fondly. "Yes, Uncle, I promise. You know I'm very good at keeping secrets." A speaking look passed between them and she grinned. "Thank you for telling me and explaining. I'm not sure if it's made things easier, but at least I under-stand a bit better. You know how I feel about him," she sighed.

Francis patted her cheek, "Yes, I do know, Poppet. It's a damned mess, but you're both grown up now and I don't like to interfere. You really have to sort out your own problems," he sighed again, "but you know I'm always here to try and help and give advice, so is your aunt, deranged though she may be at times." Francis smiled then, "She sometimes sees things differently to me, well she's a woman, but talk to her, Bella, unburden yourself; nothing will shock her I can assure you." He winked, "She's a good listener, not that old that she can't remember what it's like to be young and foolish and in love."

Bella smiled and leaned over to kiss him on the cheek. "Thank you, Uncle, thank you so much for talking to me as an adult. You're such a sweetie pie you know. I'm sorry to have disturbed you."

She got up to leave and gazed at him somewhat sadly. He grinned back at her and sighed theatrically, "Aaah, Bella, Bella, there was a time when ladies used to swoon at my feet and tell me I was dashing, heroic, a terrible charmer and heartbreaker; but now look at me, reduced to being a mere sweetie pie. How can I cope with it?"

She laughed then as she walked out and Francis watched her go, the smile immediately leaving his face when the door closed behind her. His thoughts turned to Ashcroft and the interview he was having with Nicky that very morning about the 'problem' in Spain. It was a damned serious business and hugely dangerous. He only hoped he was right in believing Nicky could handle it. Otherwise, he'd never forgive himself for recommending him to Ashcroft.

Having left her uncle to his work, Bella pondered her next problem and was still wondering nervously what to do about it as she went through to the sunny morning room and somewhat fortuitously found her aunt sitting there, playing with the baby. Thinking fate was on her side, she took a deep breath. "Aaah, the very person," she smiled. "I need some advice, Auntie, if you have the time?"

Cat looked up, smiling, "Bella, My Love, of course; come and sit down. Shall we have some tea before Madam here has another tantrum?" Bella rang the bell and when a maid appeared, sent her off to bring up a tea tray before sitting down next to her aunt.

"So, what can I do for you?" Cat looked at Bella expectantly, thinking they were going to have a conversation about fashions or what invitations Bella should accept from the piles stacked on the mantelpiece in the family sitting room, despite the lateness of the Season.

A footman appeared then with a tray of tea and Bella poured out two cups and sat back, nervously sipping hers as she wondered how to broach the subject of her problem. As with her uncle, she decided to jump in at the deep end. "Well, Auntie, you see, I need some information about... er... about men; well about fornicating, you know, intercourse, actually."

Cat choked and just managed to avoid spluttering hot tea over the baby in her lap. "Heavens, Bella, I... er... of course, Darling." She pulled herself together and smiled, "What do you want to know,

Poppet?" She rushed on, "I'm so sorry, after last year, you know, with Nicky, I assumed it was a bit late for you and me to have a little chat. It was all a bit unexpected. I didn't realise you were... erm... you know... going to consummate the marriage." Cat took another large gulp of tea and continued curiously, "Er, anyway, I didn't think you were sharing a bedroom with Nicky now, not since last year or since he's been back this week, or am I wrong? He, um… hasn't been here most evenings." Cat felt she was treading on eggshells, but she and Francis well knew he'd not been home at night. Neither of them was sure exactly what was going on between Bella and Nicky. She was also desperately sorry for Bella as everyone in the family knew how she felt about the man and had never made a secret of it amongst her close relations.

Evading her aunt's direct questions, Bella merely said vaguely, "Well, we are married and we have spent some time together," then she took a deep breath, "and that's my problem, Auntie. I know about the theory and basics of making love," she waved her hand airily as if this was a topic she discussed all the time, "but I'm a bit lacking on the reality, the technique front as it were, and thought you could give me some advice... and, er... instruction."

Cat coughed again. "Instruction?" she whispered, her eyes widening and half her brain wondered what this 'some time' was and when it had happened, but she had no time to ponder that before Bella continued.

"Yes," said Bella, matter-of-factly, now getting into her stride in this rather delicate conversation. "You see, I've searched the library here, but I can't find any books on the subject and I need to know... need to know how to... er..."

There was a pregnant pause as the two women gazed at each other. Cat looked at Bella with a slightly glazed expression as Bella leaned over and whispered in her ear, "Take him in my mouth..."

"*Mon Dieu!*" Cat gasped. She only lapsed into French when she was really surprised about something, or lost her temper, the latter usually with her husband. She looked at Bella in complete shock and amazement, her cup rattling in its saucer.

Bella was beyond upset when she saw the shocked expression on her aunt's face and thought she'd made a terrible mistake but, as she watched, wondering what to do next, Cat silently put the baby back down in her little cradle, got up and went over to the sideboard and returned with a decanter of brandy and two glasses which she then proceeded to fill. Handing one to Bella, she sat back and looked at her, taking a long gulp from her glass, then burst out laughing, much to Bella's consternation.

"You are the absolute limit, Bella, that's hysterical!" She doubled up with mirth and by the time she'd managed to stop laughing, Bella was looking at HER in amazement. Cat grinned at her slyly and asked, "So, why do you think I would know how to do that, My Girl? I'm the very upstanding and proper Duchess of Firle, I'll have you know," and she giggled like a schoolgirl, despite being in her middle forties.

Bella grinned back at her and shocked Cat for the second time that morning. "Well, you see, Auntie, I know you know... because... I once saw you start to do it to Uncle Francis in the stables."

"WHAAAAT?!" Cat screeched and brandy slopped all over her lap.

"Oh, it was years ago, down at Firle. You'd gone off on one of the horses looking for Fluffy, who was on the missing list as he was quite old and forgetful by then and, of course, you hadn't taken a groom. Uncle Francis was having one of his grumpy days and when he discovered you'd gone out unaccompanied, he completely lost the plot, you know what he's like about that." Cat grinned at her and Bella giggled. "Anyway, all the household disappeared into their corners while he stomped about having a hissy fit and I went down to the stables. I wanted to look at the new litter of kittens the stable cat had just had anyway, so it was a good excuse to keep out of his way," she laughed. "He must have seen you come back as he came storming down to the stables to meet you. All the grooms and stable lads saw him coming and made themselves scarce. When you came in, you and Uncle had the most almighty row; shocking language, Auntie, by the way," Bella waggled her finger and tutted at Cat who merely laughed. "Both of you were completely mad and Uncle said something to you and you slapped him. It was very funny, then all of a sudden he just looked at you and changed," Bella snapped her fingers, "just like that, then he started to kiss you. I'd never seen anything like it. I had no idea he was so... um... passionate. I was only about twelve or thirteen and I was boggle-eyed. It was nothing like I'd seen Mama and Papa do and they were bad enough." Cat blanched and gulped down some more brandy. "Anyway, when he came up for some air, he apologised for losing his temper and you apologised for slapping him and for going out without a groom. I remember he was mumbling something about fishermen. I didn't understand but it must have meant something to you as you giggled, gave him a very suggestive look and then said you'd better apologise properly or else you really would be in trouble, then you went down on your knees in front of him and started to undo his breeches."

Cat cringed, looking completely shocked and embarrassed and actually went pink. "*OH.MON.DIEU,*" she muttered, gulping down her entire glass of brandy, pouring herself another as Bella continued. "I wasn't sure what you were going to do and thought I ought to go away, but I was so embarrassed to be caught there, that I kept quiet and stayed where I was, up in the hayloft where I'd been looking for the kittens. Anyway, you'd undone his breeches and he was... er, quite... er... you know, erm... ready... and you were just starting to... er..." Bella coughed and Cat gulped down more brandy before choking, "when he bent down, he chuckled and said if you wanted to apologise that much, you'd better go back to the house and upstairs, then he could punish you more appropriately for your recent misdemeanours, which were apparently many and varied, not just going out unaccompanied; so fortunately he did up his breeches and the pair of you disappeared and we never saw either of you for dinner or the rest of the evening..."

Cat looked at Bella for a moment and then the pair of them both burst out laughing again. They toasted each other's drinks and, as Bella said she couldn't face looking at her uncle for weeks afterwards as she was so embarrassed by the visions she kept getting, they both doubled up with mirth, shrieking with hysterical laughter. At that point, the baby decided to howl and into the middle of this chaos burst the source of their mirth, demanding to know what the devil was going on as he was trying to work. At the sight of an irate Francis, both women collapsed with laughter again and he looked from one to the other in confusion. Having seen them both clutching a glass of brandy as well, with the decanter in front of them, at barely eleven in the morning, he was even more irritated, amazed and nonplussed. Cat merely waved at him, "Oh go away, Francis; read a report or buy a ship or factory or something and send Mary to take your impossible noisy daughter away, unless you want her of course?" she grinned at his horrified expression, while the baby was screaming for England by now.

"Oh, for God's sake, this place gets more like an asylum every day. Go to Scotland? I should go to bloody China and that's not far enough away." Francis muttered and turned to stomp out of the room as both women fell into further fits of giggles.

When their laughter had finally subsided and a harassed nanny had come to collect the red-faced baby, Cat looked at Bella and smiled. "You know, Darling, what's so funny, why I laughed so much when you first asked me? It's that I was in much the same position as you when I first married your Uncle Francis. In fact, I went to your mother for advice." Cat sighed, "She was SUCH a good friend to me and now here WE are, how ironic is that?" She put her hand on Bella's and grinned at her, "I have to say, some very useful and interesting information she gave me too."

Bella looked back at her aunt with astonishment. "Really?"

Cat nodded. "I was a bit embarrassed at first, but your dear Mama thought it was beyond funny so I soon got over that," she laughed. "Therefore, Sweetheart, what exactly is it you want to know? I will do my best to help you," and she winked at Bella, "after all, I've managed to keep your wicked uncle entertained and out of the clutches of anyone else for the past twenty years, so I must have been doing something right..!"

Over the next couple of hours, amid much laughter, Cat did her best to relax Bella and broaden her education. "It's absolutely no good being embarrassed, My Girl," she advised, "or imagining people you know doing things like this, as I'm sure some of them would faint at the thought, but then of course, one never knows what goes on behind closed doors," she mused. "But never mind other people, this is about you – and you'll never get anywhere if you don't lose your inhibitions, especially with a man like Nicky." Cat rolled her eyes, "He reminds me so much of Francis when I first met him," she looked dreamy as she thought back to when she was in her twenties. "I'd never met such an attractive man. Women just fell at his feet and as for charm? It simply oozed out of him. I was lost from the first time he looked at me with those big blue eyes of his," she sighed. "Even though I've paddled Nicky's backside when he was a naughty little boy, he's grown into one of the most good looking and charming rakes, er, rogues," she quickly corrected herself, "I've known and he only has to crook his little finger for women to go running to him in droves as well; much as I know you must hate that."

She looked curiously at Bella, who had thought back to Nicky's salacious striptease for her the first night he'd met *La Lionesse*. HE certainly had no inhibitions she thought, blushing. "I know, Auntie, that's my problem. He still sees me as fourteen with plaits and dolls or my nose stuck in some book, even though I'm grown up now and I think I'm reasonably attractive."

Cat laughed. "The man's a fool, but then so are most men. As for "reasonably attractive"? Bella, you know you're beautiful, quite stunning now in fact, especially when you make an effort," she chuckled. "But with what I've just taught you and a little shopping expedition for some far more interesting or alluring undergarments, corsets, garters and frivolous whatnots, you should have something to amuse him over the next couple of days. There's so much more I can tell you, I promise," she waggled her finger at the younger woman, "just let go, Darling, and follow your instincts; you're your mother's daughter and you're such a passionate little thing at times. I'm sure you've hidden depths and Nicky will come round, or I'm not a Frenchwoman. If you put your mind to it, he won't know what's hit him," she giggled but then patted Bella's hand. "I know he cares for you, you've just got to persevere if you want him," she sighed. "Men can be so dense at times, that's what your Mama always said and she was so right. But whatever you do, don't be a doormat and fall all over him; men like Nicky need a challenge to keep them interested, don't be like the rest and just succumb because he rolls those lovely golden eyes at you and smiles. You know what makes him tick, what he likes, so use that knowledge to your benefit and you'll keep his interest, even if he doesn't realise what you're up to." She leaned over and kissed her niece, "I know you love him, Darling, so go and get him. Please come and talk to me any time. In fact, I look forward to hearing how it goes... in as much detail as you care to share!" She grinned wickedly, making Bella giggle as she got up to leave. "Now then, I suppose I'd better go and see what my dreadful daughter is up to and pacify my dear husband to stop him emigrating. You, My Sweet, have to go shopping," and with that, the smiling Duchess sashayed from the room.

That was why Bella had bumped into Nicky in Bond Street, having purchased not only a chess set but some quite tittilating ladies' underclothes from a rather insalubrious establishment certain 'ladies' obviously frequented. How her aunt had known about that little emporium Bella hadn't asked, but giggled at the thought of Auntie Cat wearing some of the items she'd seen on sale and wondered what her Uncle Francis would have made of them. What a pair the two of them were; if only people knew! She realised Nicky wouldn't be seeing much of her purchases, but the tightly fitting, smooth satin and lace, what there was of it, would cling to her curves and hopefully excite him as much as her aunt suggested it might. Bella giggled to herself again, if only her aunt knew the half of it. It was going to be an interesting night.

Chapter Fourteen

W hile Bella spent the afternoon washing and curling her long black hair and generally pampering herself, Nicky spent the afternoon ensconced in the Duke's study.

When he sauntered in and greeted Francis, the older man smirked at him. "Rats in last night's gutter then, I see?" Nicky ran an embarrassed hand up to lift his collar over the tell-tale bite marks *Lionesse* had left on his neck and merely winked back.

They did indeed briefly discuss matters connected to the Valenciennes holdings, but Nicky was too preoccupied to be overly concerned at the predicted rise or fall in the prices of sugar, tobacco or cotton and its impact on his income for the forthcoming year, or diversifying some monies into some newer investments and sources of income. So, with a sigh, Francis abandoned trying to discuss business with him, not Nicky's favourite topic at the best of times, reluctantly turning the conversation to the Peninsular War.

"So, you've seen Ashcroft I take it?" he sat back in an armchair and lit himself a cigar, his hand toying with the stem of a beautiful cut glass snifter of brandy.

Nicky was seated opposite, hunched forward and with a sigh he looked across at Francis. "You know all about it, don't you? Was that how Ashcroft found me, through you? Although Colonel Melrose insinuated it was the Dowager?"

Francis's face was completely impassive as he merely nodded. "A bit of both, actually, two ends coming together. I thought about it for weeks, I wasn't sure, but I think they would have approached you anyway. Ashcroft has a way of keeping an eye out for potentially useful operatives and with your skills, you're exactly the type of man he needs. He and Melrose are thick as thieves and he probably got the old boy to go fishing in Hertford Street and report back, especially once he discovered how long he'd known Grandmother." He looked Nicky in the eye, "I wouldn't have recommended you if I didn't think you could do it, Nicky, but they're desperate, they need you," he sighed as he rubbed his forehead in concern. "But you have to promise me you'll take care of yourself. Try and harness your 'act first and think later' tendencies, hmmmm? We all want you to come back to us in one piece, you know how we felt about you joining up and nothing's changed." He looked desperately serious, "I know how dangerous this mission is. These agents of Bonaparte's are completely ruthless." His composure finally broke, "Dear God, I hope I don't regret it," he muttered as he downed a large gulp of his brandy.

"I'll be careful, I promise," Nicky tried to reassure Francis. "I've been in enough hairy situations already not to know when to keep my head down. But I've made some useful contacts here and there with people who want to rid Spain of the French, so hopefully someone will give me a lead to the particular bastard Ashcroft is looking for." He looked up at Francis curiously, "Did you know he apparently wants to steal one of Wellington's gold shipments? They're nothing more than glorified criminals, most of them, always looking to feather their own nests," he rasped. "In my book that makes them easier to deal with than those fanatical zealots with only politics on their mind."

"Yes, I had heard a rumour to that effect," muttered Francis. "But don't make the mistake of thinking any of them are a pushover and, if you come up against one who is both greedy and fanatical, be on your guard." He shook his head worriedly, muttering to himself under his breath, obviously concerned. "Oh, by the way, Reynard is back in Spain again so if you need anything, anything at all, go and find him.

He's one person you know you can both trust and rely on. I'll get you his latest direction and send a message to let him know you're in Spain, probably in French-held territory and might be in touch." He looked intently at Nicky then and finally leaned forward to touch his arm. "Are you all right, Nicky? You're very quiet. Look, for heaven's sake if you don't want to do this, you only have to say." Nicky gazed at him silently and Francis said persuasively, "Talk to me, it might help," he laughed briefly, "I'm the only one you can talk to – after all, I do have a little experience of leading a double life, as you well know," he grinned. "I can tell you there were times I thought my number was up." His expression went serious again, "I know what it is to be frightened, Nicky," he said very quietly, "so talk to me, it's no disgrace to feel like that."

Nicky took a deep breath, reached a decision and lifted his glass to drain back the entire contents. "The man I'm after, his name is Bernheim. He has a connection to Normandy..." he left the sentence hanging in the air as he looked over at Francis and watched the blood bleach from his face. Just as his own had when Ashcroft had mentioned the dreaded name.

"No... NO! Nicky, the man is dead. Cat killed him. I watched it happen right in front of me. Oh my God..." Francis was horrified.

"Francis, it's definitely not THAT Bernheim, but it must be a relation; the coincidence is too much, as are his crimes. Did the bastard have any family? Do you know?"

Francis shook his head. "I have absolutely no idea and we don't know what happened to his body afterwards, not that it was our main concern at the time and I was out of it, as you know. I never bothered to find out, never needed to." He was still white-faced with shock.

Nicky shook his head. "When Ashcroft saw my reaction to the name, he asked me why. I... I told him a bit about what happened, Francis, my parents, the de Mornays, you... though nothing about The Shadow of course, I was very vague about it all." He tried to look reassuring when he saw Francis's alarmed expression. "I'm sorry, but I thought Ashcroft should know something, in the circumstances." He paused to reflect for a moment, "However, I'm sure Ashcroft knows more than he's letting on about this Bernheim he... I'm... searching for.

Anyway, he said he would have more information for me tomorrow morning, so I'll update you as soon as I've seen him." Nicky sat back, glad to have shared his unknown fears with the one man who would understand. Francis would now also realise why there was no way he would turn down this mission.

They continued to converse quietly for a while and Francis gradually encouraged Nicky to unburden himself about his fear of what he'd let himself in for and what working for Ashcroft would really involve, whilst trying to reassure him as best he could. Finally, they both sat back with a sigh and remained silent, each contemplating the situation. Francis finished his cigar and got up to replenish their glasses. Nicky looked at him then and said quietly, "You won't tell anyone about this Bernheim business, will you? Papa couldn't cope with it and I don't think Cat could either and... well, Bella doesn't know anything at all, so she doesn't matter."

Francis looked at the younger man as he sat down again. "Of course not, I wouldn't dream of it, you have my word. But don't dismiss Bella as some brainless ninny, Nicky, she's far more perceptive than you give her credit for. She worries about you incessantly, even more than the rest of us if that's possible." His voice changed as he spoke, "That's what happens when you love someone as she does," he said meaningfully.

Nicky looked belligerent. "Well, she'll have to get over it. I'm telling you, Francis, I'm not for her. She deserves someone better, someone who can care for her, provide for her. That someone is obviously not me." He laughed harshly. "Anyway, given Ashcroft's attrition rate, she'll probably be a widow by the end of the year, so that will solve the problem."

Francis looked seriously alarmed and then cross. "That's nonsense, Nicky, and you well know it! For heaven's sake don't tempt fate either. Unlike you, do you think Bella cares a fig about being a Duchess and having an estate and a fortune? She's got more sense than you, that's for sure. She understands what's important in life," Francis got up and started stalking back and forth across the carpet as he spoke. "No, you can't live on fresh air, I understand that and I also understand and empathise with your pride in your title and heritage, no matter that you joke about being the Duke of nothing. But – you do have a small income and you're part of our family. Blood relation or not, you're as good as, so you'll never want for a home as you'll always have one with us, or a roof over your head to live somewhere separate if you'd rather that; heaven knows I own enough property. You're Eddie's eldest son as far as he's concerned, me too, also Cat, and another grandson to my grandmother; you've given her such joy over the years, God bless her, surely you know that too. I don't have to tell you how precious you were to Carlotta, which is also very important to Eddie, as if the man didn't care for you enough as it is. We all LOVE you, why can't you accept that? I know I've asked you before, but come and work for me if you like, earn a living that way, anything you want to do, but stop trying to ruin your life and Bella's. She's quite a woman if you'd only open your eyes to see it; just what you need, in my opinion."

He turned and glared at Nicky, finally giving vent to his feelings as the words exploded out of him, "You're a fool to give her up, a complete fool!" Francis swore under his breath. "There, I've said it. I'm sorry, I've tried to keep out of what goes on between the pair of you but I can't stand aside and let you throw something valuable away because you're too bloody proud to accept you really are a part of our family." He stopped his pacing to look down at Nicky who was sitting impassively now, "Oh, I'll sort out your annulment or divorce if you REALLY want me to, money in the right places will see to that. Plus, I'll get her to sign the papers, but I wish you'd reconsider. Please, Nicky," he paused for breath after his outburst. "You DO care for her don't you?" he finally asked.

"Yes, of course I bloody care for her, she's like my baby sister, which is part of the problem. Why can't you all accept I don't love her the same way she loves me?" he exclaimed. "Would you want to fuck one of YOUR sisters, Francis?"

Francis looked at Nicky with a shudder and then he burst out laughing. "Have you SEEN my youngest sister lately? Or any of them? Urrrrrrgh! I can't believe we come from the same family or that I'm related to anything so obviously bovine, both body and brain," he made a vomiting motion and Nicky choked on a laugh. "Seriously,

Nicky, believe me, I do understand how you feel, but Bella is beautiful, unlike my sisters and mother's family. Then there's the fact, of course," he smiled strangely, "that she's NOT your sister." He held up his hand as Nicky went to interrupt, "Oh I know, we've been here before, endlessly, round in circles, but I still don't quite understand you," he sighed. "However, if you say you don't love her, if you're sure, then I can't make you," he said sensibly but then followed that with a thoughtful comment. "Though there are plenty of happy marriages based on far less than your friendship... and you could always close your eyes when you go to bed if it's THAT bad," he grinned wickedly, chuckling.

Francis returned to his seat and gazed seriously at the younger man who was again sitting impassively, finally giving a defeated sigh. "I'll tell you what. I'll get the papers drawn up, ready for you both to sign when you return from the Peninsula." He gave Nicky a meaningful look. "Believe me, you WILL return. But I want you to think seriously about it all while you're away this time and I promise I'll talk to Bella, try and make her understand how you feel. I'll also get Cat to drag her out to every party, ball, rout and soiree she can, to see if we can't find her some other man to catch her interest. Then, when you're back, we'll sort this matter out once and for all. But I'm telling you, I won't interfere. You and Bella BOTH have to agree, either way, what you BOTH want and I'll fall in with your decision."

He held out his hand to Nicky. "Give me your word you'll think about all I've said, about Bella. It's not as if there's anyone else is there? I give you my word I'll talk to her, try to explain your point of view. She won't argue with me, like she does with you."

They shook on it and Francis smiled at Nicky. "Right, enough seriousness for one afternoon. Damn, I hate all this family drama, it wears me out," he rolled his eyes. "I think I heard Eddie and Charlie arrive a while ago, if I'm not mistaken, so let's go and join them and the ladies and forget about everything for a while, hmmm?" The two tall men rose to their feet and strolled companionably over to the study door and, as they passed through it, Francis remarked, "Have you got some ear muffs ready? My little Lizzie has been quiet for all of three hours," making Nicky laugh.

After Nicky had hugged his step-father and little step-brother and they'd caught up on their mutual news, the whole family sat down for tea and pastries and Cat dumped Elizabeth in Nicky's wary arms while she presided over it all. After he'd been violently hit on the face several times by her new rattle, courtesy of Bella, Nicky declared her to be even more bloodthirsty than her mother and recommended she enlist forthwith to go and fight Bonaparte. The whole group collapsed with laughter, whereupon the belligerent little girl let out a piercing wail and the party broke up as everyone sought to escape the dreadful commotion that followed and to get ready for dinner.

Bella was relying on Nicky to find some excuse to escape the house after they'd all dined and, sure enough, he suggested he, Eddie and Francis should adjourn to Brooks's for a few drinks and a game or two of cards. Bella said she had a piano and violin recital she'd been invited to anyway, at one of her friends, so she would enjoy that. She looked at Nicky's face and smiled serenely, knowing the thought of an evening listening to the violin was a sure way of ensuring she wouldn't see him for dust, just in case he'd vaguely thought of accompanying her. She also knew her aunt wasn't particularly interested in the music either, so once the men had happily sauntered off towards St James, walking slowly to allow for her father's limp and after her aunt had retired upstairs to catch up on her correspondence, Bella summoned a carriage from the stables. Clutching her various parcels, she quietly set off to *Le Lion d'Or*.

Chapter Fifteen

It was nearly eleven by the time Nicky managed to escape and he hurried off to *Le Lion d'Or*, leaving his Papa and Francis deep in a card game with several of their friends. Francis fractionally raised an eyebrow when he made his farewells, merely commenting quietly for his ears only, "Mind the rats..." and resumed his concentration on his hand of cards.

As he entered *Lionesse*'s apartment, he found her quietly working at her desk again. She turned at his entrance. "Did you get my note? I'm sorry to be delayed, but my step-father arrived this afternoon and I had to spend some time with him this evening." He went over to her and bowed over her hand, kissing it lingeringly.

She smiled up at him. "I would have been disappointed if you hadn't been late; family are important, especially when you're away fighting in a war and don't get home often. Men who fight in the Americas or India are probably away for years and that must be terrible for their loved ones left behind." She closed her ledgers and put them away then rose and went over towards the small fire and the low table that had been set up there between two comfortable armchairs. A chess board sat ready on it and on a nearby occasional table sat some dishes containing an assortment of sweetmeats and candied fruits and a bottle of champagne chilling in a large ice bucket. A decanter of brandy and more wine bottles were also arrayed out and a selection of cigars and cheroots sat next to them. Candelabra and lamps flickered around the room and the fire gently crackled.

Nicky watched *Lionesse* as she walked. Instead of her usual bronze or golden-coloured dress and her saucy tail, she was wearing a golden satin peignoir that clung tightly to her curves and as she moved, sparkling gold thread caught the candlelight and gleamed in the material. The long wide sleeves covered her arms and although it had a high neck with a fastening at her throat, the front was narrowly slashed open to the fastening that kept the robe closed under her breasts, allowing a tantalising view of her cleavage. It looked sensual and alluring on her slenderly curvaceous body. He wondered what she was wearing underneath and felt his body harden and respond to her provocative outfit and the perfume he was now used to smelling all over her delicious torso.

"Come, sit down. Help yourself to a drink," she purred. "Would you pour me some champagne?" She sighed, "Adding columns of figures is thirsty work," and she smiled at him blandly.

Nicky opened the bottle and poured them both out a glass of the sparkling liquid. As he stood in front of her with his back to the fire, he raised his glass in a toast. "May the best man," his lips curved wickedly, "or lioness, win," and he took a long mouthful. Before he sat down, he pulled off his tight-fitting evening jacket, loosened a couple of buttons on his waistcoat and then spotting the cigars on the sideboard, picked one up and after smelling its evocative aroma, cut the top and lit it with a taper from the fire. A whiff of spicy tobacco permeated the room as he took a couple of puffs and leisurely sat down opposite her.

She sipped her drink slowly and smiled. "Did you have a good day?" she enquired mildly. "Busy with military manoeuvres, I presume?"

"Oh, tolerable," he drawled. "I had a run-in with a regiment of French cavalry around the Tower of London, then an elephant escaped and I had to round it up… but other than that, it was fairly mundane." He sipped more of his drink. "And you?"

She laughed, then curled her fingers into claws and growled, "Grrrrrrr, busy hunting, looking out for some unsuspecting prey to toy with," she licked her lips, "you know, the usual lioness chores."

"I didn't realise lionesses could add up," he grinned at her looking through the alcove and over at her desk.

"Aah, you should never underestimate a lioness, she has all sorts of skills."

"Really?" he smirked, "I had no idea. I should really appreciate finding out about those in more detail."

"Well, there are plenty to see and research at the Tower of London, if you can find them among the marauding French and rampant elephant, obviously."

"Tsk, tsk, how inconvenient, I'd better investigate closer to home, then," and he leaned over to try and lift up the hem of her gown, his golden eyes sparkling with humour.

Bella swatted his hand away. "Better beware disturbing a sleepy lioness," she yawned, "it could be an extremely risky game."

"Oh, I think I'll gamble; after all, I'm a brave soldier. I have to submit to whatever game the enemy wants to play and hope I survive."

They sat and looked at each other across the low table and the air crackled between them as they flirted, their banter laced with amusing innuendo. Nicky sat back and took a long draw of his cigar, blowing a series of rings up into the air. Bella watched in fascination, her heart beating nervously under her robe as she purred, "Shall we start?" She picked up a black and white pawn and momentarily put her hands in her lap before holding out two fists in front of him. "Your choice," she whispered as he pulled one towards him and kissed the knuckles. She turned her hand over and revealed the white pawn. As she replaced them both on the board and turned it so the white men were in front of him, Nicky winked at her and Bella waited for him to make his first move.

They skirted round each other for a good half an hour, getting the measure of the other's play. She hadn't played him for several years and Bella soon realised he was now seriously good. He'd obviously been practising and she told herself to pay closer attention. This wasn't going to be as easy as she'd expected. She and her Papa had always known Nicky was no fool, indeed he did have a deal of wit and intelligence which he tried to hide most of the time, only stirring himself to use his brain when something really interested or concerned him... but they both knew he was more than intelligent; she decided he was stirring himself now.

Nicky sat back indolently, thoughtfully enjoying his cigar, watching the woman opposite him. For someone who claimed only to play occasionally, she was quite good. He smiled to himself, the game was evidently going to take slightly longer than he'd anticipated, but they had plenty of time and he would enjoy baiting her while they played. He continued to wonder what she was wearing under her robe, noticing teasing glimpses of fine golden lace when the folds of satin slipped open as she moved forward to make her moves. But he wasn't going to let her distract him, he was determined to win and get the mask off her face once and for all.

Another hour passed and he'd finally realised he had a battle on his hands. While he was pondering his next move, Bella rose and strolled over to the sideboard. She picked up a very thin cheroot and put it between her lips. As she bent to light a taper in the fire, Nicky watched lustfully as the outline of her pert buttocks showed clearly through the tight satin and he shifted uncomfortably in his chair, losing his train of thought as she returned to her seat and contemplated the board.

As she sat there, elbow on the arm of her chair, holding the cheroot between two long, elegant fingers, Nicky watched in fascination as she stared at the board, deep in concentration and occasionally inhaled the tobacco. "I didn't know you smoked those things. It's unusual for a woman," he commented softly.

"Mmmmm, only very occasionally, when I'm in a difficult card game, or when I need to concentrate. It helps me think," she answered quietly, not looking at him, her mind obviously elsewhere as she leaned down to pick up her glass and slowly sip her champagne.

Another half hour passed and Nicky rose from his chair to wander back and forth across the room, contemplating the board, deep in thought. He'd lit another cigar and he puffed as he walked, his strange golden eyes narrowed behind their thick curtain of dark lashes, his mind now totally focussed on the battle in which he was engaged. The mantel clock ticked in the silent room and there was the odd pop from the last of a still burning log in the fireplace. Miles Ashcroft would have approved mightily if he'd seen his new agent reviewing his situation and opponent and all potential moves so thoughtfully. The facetious joker was obviously taking a temporary respite.

Another hour passed and Bella finally knew she had him. She stole a glance at his face, seeing the deep anger seething there as he realised he had nowhere to go. "Check," she whispered, moving her bishop.

Slowly, Nicky raised his eyes to the masked woman opposite him, his golden orbs now glittering with fury and resentment as he saw no way out for his king. He couldn't believe she'd bettered him yet again and rage roiled around inside his belly.

"You fucking, lying, BITCH," he bit out and Bella recoiled at his sudden, unexpected venom. "You told me you were no expert."

Bella was angry he was so cross. After all, he'd tried exactly the same trick on her and after all, it was only a game. But then Nicky took all challenges seriously. "You can talk," she replied sarcastically. "You said you weren't an expert either and you only played now and again. You're just as guilty of trying to trick ME."

They stared at each other. "I don't like being manipulated by any woman," he said slowly in a cold, cutting voice, "and that's exactly what you are; a conniving, manipulative, lying bitch." He paused, "What I can't make out is why you're bothering with me? It's not as if I have any money for you to win, I'm just a soldier, or have you taken so many other poor bastards' fortunes you're bored with it now and you need some other form of entertainment?"

"How dare you!" she whispered slowly and icily.

"I should have guessed you were playing with me, yet again. After all, you run two of these places, so you must be good. Tell me, *Lionesse*," he rasped, "have you enjoyed making a fool of me, making me play your games?"

Bella was incensed at his insults. "You're tolerably amusing I suppose, but you've passed the time for me this week, so you can go off home now if you like. You lost, after all."

Nicky's head reared back as furious rage overwhelmed him. "THE HELL I WILL!" he shouted at her. "I'm not your toy to be picked up and used when you feel like it, then tossed away. Besides, you've still got my necklace, You Bitch!" With that, he reared up from his chair, knocking the table and chess pieces flying and grabbed her by the arms. "You've been sitting there taunting me with that bloody outfit you're wearing all night, trying to distract me. But I'll be damned if I'm going home without something of what I came for," and he dragged her across the room, through the alcove and forced her face down across her desk, pulling her arms behind her back and holding them in an iron grip. Bella screamed and swore at him, wriggling to break free but to no avail. To her shock, she felt him lean down and pull up the hem of her robe and the nightgown underneath and raise them up to her waist, tucking the cloth under her captured hands, leaving her legs and buttocks exposed and naked.

"GET OFF ME, YOU BASTARD!" she shrieked. "I've had my fill of you, you don't amuse me anymore. GET OUT. Go on... GET OUT!"

"Not until I've taught you a lesson, You Bitch," Nicky grated and smacked her hard across her bottom.

"NOOOOO!" Bella screamed and writhed more furiously to try and escape. "Get off me, I hate you, I hate you!"

"Oh, so you don't like playing MY games then?" His voice was like shards of ice. "That's a pity as I find them quite entertaining," and he smacked her again. "Perhaps this will teach you a lesson not to practise your wiles on poor unsuspecting fools like me in the future. No wonder your husband doesn't want you if this is how you behave. At least I know MY wife loves and cares for me, she'd never dream of treating me like you have."

Beside herself with humiliation, enraged beyond belief and appalled at his words, Bella yelled at him without thinking, "I don't know what I ever saw in you, why I ever wanted you, I must have been insane. You're not the man I thought you were!"

Nicky was incensed with the woman, out of his mind with fury at both her and himself. She defied him at every turn, had tricked, humiliated and manipulated him, had stolen his most precious possession, yet still he wanted her. The sight of her naked beneath his hands aroused him beyond all reason and he ripped open the fastenings to his pantaloons, overwhelmed with such powerful lust that he simply forced her legs apart and drove himself into her, unable to control himself any longer.

She wasn't dry and unready. She was very wet, tight and hot – more than ready for him, which infuriated him even more as he listened to her screams as he entered her. He leaned down over her and pulled a hand into each of his, forcing them forward, on to the top of her desk. As he thrust deep inside her, she bucked against him and moaned, the feel of her soft buttocks against his skin inflaming his lust to even greater levels, if that were possible. He whispered in her ear, "More lies, *Lionesse*? You said you hated me, you didn't want me, I didn't amuse you anymore, but it doesn't feel like that to me... you feel like the trollop you undoubtedly are," and he slapped her bottom again as he pulled back slowly to thrust hard and deep inside her once more, making her cry out, again and again, finally unable to stop himself pounding wildly into her, rendering her mindless, sobbing with need, until she was begging him to give her the climax she craved.

They were both totally lost in the passion that had overwhelmed them and as Nicky felt his spine tingle and release rising, he instinctively lowered one of his hands down to caress between her parted thighs and rub his thumb across the sensitive wet flesh. At his touch, she screamed once more and jerked back against him and as he felt the powerful spasms roil through her in wave after wave, engulfing and contracting around his hardness deep inside, they caused him to erupt volcanically and blackness momentarily overwhelmed him.

He collapsed on top of her and they lay panting together on the desk. Bella could feel his heart thumping against her back in the silent room as she shifted uncomfortably against the edge of the blotter, his heavy weight pinning her down.

"*Mon Dieu*," Nicky muttered, gasping for breath, shaking his head to try and clear the mists of passion from his brain. He's couldn't remember when he'd last experienced a violent climax like that. He felt shattered. But as he lay over *Lionesse*'s prone body, waiting for his heartbeat to calm, his eyes moved over her, registering where he was and where she was and, as his brain slowly clicked back into reality, almost of their own volition his fingers moved to the strings of her mask, now mere inches from his face and they started to grapple with the ties.

"Don't do it." A halting, breathless voice came from underneath him. "Or you'll never see me or your necklace again." His hands froze, then gradually, reluctantly, dropped back down on top of hers on the desktop.

Nick slowly pulled himself off *Lionesse*, straightened his clothes and silently, he went to stand over by the fire, leaning a shoulder against the mantel, trying to get his befuddled mind around what had just happened. He watched as she slowly pulled herself upright and the satin robe slithered back down to cover her body and legs again. She turned and leaned against the desk, looking across at him, seeming as stunned as he at the explosive and passionate interlude they'd just shared.

Recalling what he'd done, his head bent momentarily as he spoke quietly, "I'm so sorry, that was unforgiveable. I don't know what came over me." He looked up again, "Are you all right?"

Bella nodded her head shakily, not quite knowing what to say, her legs still feeling like jelly from the stunning climax she'd just experienced, not to mention how it had happened.

"I lost control," he muttered. "I behaved like an animal." He ran a hand over his face, "I'm a Gentleman, I never..."

"I'm fine, I'm... it's all right," she interrupted raggedly.

"No," he bit back, "it's not all right. I'm a Gentleman and not in the habit of treating a woman like that. I... I apologise. I lost my temper, I beg your most humble pardon," he bowed, back to the polite and well-mannered aristocratic man he was, not the wild, impassioned, uncontrolled individual he'd suddenly turned into for a few brief minutes. "I'll remove myself forthwith." He pulled away from the mantel, picked up his jacket and was halfway across the room when Bella spoke again.

"No," she whispered, "it's not all your fault. Don't go..." and she held out her hand.

He stood still, turned and looked at her, unsure.

"Pour me a drink and one for yourself," Bella laughed shakily. "I think we need it after that. I'm... er... that was..." she couldn't finish her sentence.

Nicky poured brandy into two glasses and came over to hand her one with an impassive face, then retreated back to lean against the mantel, drinking deeply from his and taking several deep breaths to try to restore his equilibrium.

Bella took a gulp from hers and coughed as the raw spirit coursed down her throat, but at least it sparked some life into her temporarily shattered brain.

They looked at each other across the silent room. "You're a very proud man. You certainly don't like being beaten, do you?" she said quietly. It was rather a statement of the obvious.

"Yes, I am, but that's irrelevant. And no, I don't like being bested by anyone, but that's no excuse for my behaviour." He ran his fingers through his hair distractedly. "I don't hit or smack women, well not like I did to you, unless we're playing those sorts of games, but that's not what went on here."

Bella ignored that reference, something else she needed to inform herself about, no doubt. "But it WAS just a game, Nicky, it wasn't serious," she merely said.

"You lied to me," he said harshly.

"You lied to me too," she accused.

"I wanted to win," he stated baldly.

"Was it that important? It was only a game of chess," she said more softly.

"Yes, it was important to me. It was more than a game and you know it."

"Nicky, this is Mayfair, we WERE just playing. It's not Madrid or besting the French, for Heaven's sake."

"I know that, but as I said, I don't like being beaten, ESPECIALLY by a woman," he grated.

"I don't like being spanked, so there you are," she huffed in exasperation. "Oh, you and your insufferable manly pride."

They continued to glare at each other.

"You're absolutely impossible," he declared frustratedly.

"So are you," and she grinned at him. "Let's call it quits, Nicky, hmmmm?"

She stood and stared at him, watching his emotions at war with each other and then finally, a wicked smile started to curl his lips and his eyes glittered at her. "Ah, *Chérie*, but there's just one little point not quite right there."

Bella eyed him warily. "Oh? And what might that be?"

"I rather think you did like being spanked," and he gave her a look that would have earned him a slap from most respectable women.

"Ooooooh, you, you..." she stamped her foot and felt herself go red under her mask and he burst out laughing.

"Come, *Chérie*," he coaxed, "come and sit down. Stop standing over there looking like a cornered lioness," and he pulled round her chair, inviting her to sit as he bent to pick up the overturned table and glasses, the chess board and scattered pieces. He threw another log on the fire and refilled her glass with more brandy and did the same with his, helping himself to a piece of candied fruit along the way, smiling and licking his lips as he savoured the sugary treat. He then wandered over to the sideboard and picked up a small cheroot which he lit from the dying fire and finally sat opposite her with a deep sigh. "So, *Chérie*, where do we go from here?"

Bella sat back with her drink and watched him, lounging indolently in the chair opposite, now completely relaxed and calmly sipping his own drink. One long booted leg was crossed over his knee and the cheroot drooped from a couple of long, tanned fingers as they idly toyed with the tassels decorating the soft leather. Whatever he'd been doing in Spain, his nails were now clean and manicured even if the skin of his hands was slightly roughened. She thought about how they'd felt caressing her skin and shivered. Altogether, he looked immaculate, Bella concluded, eminently desirable too and was a hugely tempting sight, in spite of what he'd done to her just a short while before.

"I'm not sure," she replied, tilting her head on one side as she regarded him. "You seem like a great big pussy cat sitting there, all happy and relaxed, looking like you want nothing more than to be stroked and petted," she smiled as he leered at her playfully. "But, as I've recently discovered," she paused to lean forward and make her point, "in a mere second," she clicked her fingers in the air, "you change into a snake in the grass and strike unexpectedly," and she hissed at him. "Hsssssssss."

He threw his head back and roared with laughter. As he uncrossed his legs, she leaned even further forward and poked him in the chest with her forefinger. "You, *Milor* de Bresancourt, are a very dangerous man," her fingers moved to one side of his chest. "What's more, I wouldn't now trust you from here," another poke, "to here," and her fingers moved a bare few inches sideways across his chest for a second dig. "Therefore, I'm not really sure what to do with you," as she lowered her voice almost to a whisper, "especially as you've already taken your pleasure, DESPITE being beaten," and she tutted at him, shaking her head as she leaned back in her chair again.

"Well, I wanted my revenge," he said, laughing wickedly. "But dangerous?" he shook his head, "I really am just a pussycat – and of course you can trust me."

"That's what the foolish and very dead mouse thought," another shake of her head as she smiled.

He laughed. "Oh no, I really am harmless." He held up his hands. "Look, no claws at all," however he spoiled the effect when he grinned naughtily at her, "but my revenge hasn't nearly been satisfied yet, *Chérie*, and I seem to remember you made me a promise last night; in fact I've been thinking about it all day."

"That's regrettable. You should have considered it before you pounced on me," she teased, "and I did beat you, fair and square, so you can't complain. I just need to work out how to make you pay the penalty."

"I WILL go home if you want me to," he offered, but it was a very half-hearted offer and he smiled at her hopefully.

"Now why on earth would I want you to do that?" she laughed. "Unlike some people, I'm not in the habit of cutting off my nose to spite my face." She got up then and sauntered over to get herself another cigarillo and stood in front of the fire, staring at him through her mask as she smoked, deliberately teasing him and keeping him waiting for her next move. Although her plans had almost gone awry, they were back on an even keel now and all she had to do was draw him in. She grinned, "So, you've been thinking about me all day have you?" she purred, turning to throw the half smoked cigarillo in the fire. "Ah well, everything comes to he who waits... eventually." With that, she crooked her finger at him and turned to walk into the bedroom, the satin gown whispering around her legs.

Nicky knew she was up to something, he knew women well and even without seeing the rest of her face, her self-satisfied smirk gave her away. Excitement coursed down his body as he followed her, wondering what she had in store for him now. The mind-shattering sex he'd shared with her after their chess game had taken the edge off the raging lust that had pounded insidiously through his veins all day, despite the distractions of his meetings with Ashcroft and Francis. He suspected she was planning on making him pay for that spanking, but the thought of those luscious lips and her hot mouth caressing him, everywhere, was all he could think about as he tossed back the last of his brandy and followed her, his eyes riveted on her swaying hips and the outline of her rounded buttocks under the thin golden satin.

As she turned back the covers on the bed, he strolled through to her bathing room to use the closet and when he returned she was sitting idly on a chair in front of the small fire, watching the flames that had now burned low. He leaned down over her shoulders, his hands caressing her breasts through the soft clinging satin, a lone finger running up and down her cleavage. He whispered in her ear, "Please, *Chérie*, I'd do anything to see your face, to make love to you and watch you reach your pleasure. I have to leave for Spain in the next day or two, have pity on a poor soldier, hmmmm?"

He was almost impossible to resist and the temptation to reveal herself to him now was enormous. But as he uttered the fatal words about leaving for Spain so soon, she knew she wanted at least one more night with him before the enormous fight she feared would take place once she told him the truth. She was just a coward who loved him too much she concluded, so, hardening her heart, once again she turned to him and whispered, "I can't do that, Nicky, no matter how much you want it, as you might not like what you see." She tapped him on his nose, "Consider it PART penalty for losing," and she made herself smile saucily as she rose from the chair and turned to run her hand slowly down his chest from his neck to the fastenings of his form-hugging pantaloons and then lower. "You're about to find out that being beaten, by a woman, isn't such a terrible thing."

She started to undo the remaining buttons of his waistcoat and, unresisting, he let her pull it off and hang it over the back of the chair. She then pulled undone his artfully arranged cravat, draping the long, narrow length of linen around her neck. Slowly, she raised her hands and undid the lacings of his shirt and he bent to allow her to pull it off over his head. She stood for a moment, admiring his torso yet again. It was always the same, this fascination with the hard, rippling muscles in his arms, chest and abdomen and slowly she ran a fingernail across the taut flat nipples of his chest, watching in self-satisfaction as he gasped softly and the muscles of his abdomen contracted. Pushing him down into the chair, she then bent to pull off both of his boots and stockings and as she removed the second and stood back up, she cocked her head to one side and said naughtily, "I think that'll do for now, come over here," and she pulled him up and over towards the bed where she pushed him down once again.

As she stood and watched him, he lolled back on his elbows and grinned at her curiously. "What now, *Lionesse*? I'm only half undressed, aren't you going to finish the job?"

"All in good time," she purred. "Move yourself up a bit, up to the headboard," and she moved forward as if she was going to join him on the bed. He pulled himself up and scooted backward to loll back again, relaxing against the pile of soft feather pillows, looking at her expectantly.

She gazed at him. "So, my fine pussycat, you assure me you're not a dangerous beast, even without any claws, hmmmm?"

"Harmless, completely harmless," he held up his hands in surrender, looking innocently at her. "Your mice are all completely safe from me," he grinned.

"Foolish mice if they believe that," she leaned down over him. "I know better and I've told you, I don't trust you. You're far too dangerous for your own good." She picked up one of his hands, pulled the cravat from around her neck and wrapped it around his wrist, pulling his arm back to fasten it securely to one of the bedposts. She stood back silently, looking at him, waiting for him to object.

As he lay there, watching her tie up his wrist, Nicky realised what she was going to do and groaned. He didn't know whether to be angry, or just give in and enjoy the torment he knew he now had in store, all night he presumed, given the episode over her desk for which she'd no doubt want vengeance. He knew it would be torment: unmerciful, delicious, erotic and eventually, shattering. He groaned again and simply surrendered to La Lionesse's revenge.

"No objection?" she queried, hearing him groan.

"Do I have any choice?" he looked amused. "Hobson's choice I assume?" and he laughed.

"Oh no, nothing to do with Mr Hobson, you always have a choice, you always HAVE had," she smiled at him knowingly. "You've just chosen to give in to me, to enjoy yourself, instead of going home. A bit like being happy for me to win at cards or LETTING me win at chess, if you wanted me to, if it suited you," she let the thought sink in to his mind. "I've never stopped you from leaving if you really wanted to go, if you didn't want to play my games; until now." She walked round to the other side of the bed, pulling the thin belt off the wrap she usually wore which was draped over a chair. She didn't touch him, merely held out her hand and waited for his decision to surrender to her or not. They both knew he could simply lean across and release his tethered wrist if he wanted to, but he didn't. Another theatrical groan and he lifted his arm and put his hand in hers. She tied his wrist to the other bedpost and she crawled up onto the bed and sat and looked at him, her hot gaze under the mask roving over his torso, resting pointedly on the bulge at the front of his pantaloons. "You see, I somehow think you're protesting too much," she smiled salaciously at him. "I believe, deep down, you rather like being bested, by a woman," and her fingers slowly wandered up his leg and teasingly caressed him through the fabric of his tight clothes. As he moaned and ineffectively pulled against the ties that held his wrists, her hand continued upwards and teased across his chest, her nails scratching at his nipples again before creeping up his neck and a finger circled his lips. His golden eyes burned into her.

She sat back and sighed. "It's just you and me now, Nicky, all alone. I feel like I'm in the Garden of Eden having you here, simply for my pleasure, all night. My personal piece of paradise."

He laughed at her, eyes sparkling. "And what does that make me?" he asked humorously. "Adam, the only man available? Or the snake you accused me of being earlier?"

She grinned back at him wickedly, saying slowly, "Oh, neither of those, *Mon Cher*. You're the apple... temptation itself," and as her fingers caressed his hardness again, she bent her head to run her tongue around his navel, making him draw in a quick breath and writhe slightly before laughing again as the whiskers on her mask tickled his abdomen.

"You know, *Lionesse*, you've missed your calling," a sensual smile curled his lips, "you should have been a courtesan. You'd make a fortune, why bother with all this?" and he lifted his head and eyebrows slightly to make his point.

She put her head on one side. "I couldn't do that," she whispered, "I have a husband, remember? Actually, all this is his and I have to run it for him."

"His? Really? But you said he doesn't want you, fool that he is. So why bother?" he shook his head in wonder, not understanding.

"Because I want to. If... no, when he comes back, he can decide what to do with it all, including me," Bella replied quietly.

"But why waste your life on an idiot like that? You're young and attractive, I think, unless there really is something terrible under that mask, which I somehow doubt, no matter what you say," he thought back to her earlier comment about how horrified he'd be to see what was underneath. "You should find a man who appreciates you." He looked at her musingly, "How old are you, *Lionesse*?" he asked, tilting his head on one side as he perused her assessingly.

She smiled saucily at him, "How old do you think I am?"

He chortled. "That's a terrible question to ask a man. You think I want my face slapped again? Perhaps I'd better retract that query. So tell me how old you think I am instead? That's much safer, I can't slap you if I get offended," he joked and playfully tugged on his bindings.

Grinning at him, she playfully poked and prodded his torso and felt the muscles of his biceps, then crawled up nearer his face and pulled his mouth open to peer in and run a finger over his sparkling white teeth. She sat back, appearing to ponder. "Ooh, about fifty at least," she giggled as he grimaced at her. "No, actually I'd say half that, such a wonderful specimen that you are," another grinning poke at his hard biceps, "hmmm, twenty-five? No, twenty-six... twenty-seven maybe?" Of course she knew exactly, he was just over five and a half years her elder and she smirked at him. "Is that a good guess?"

Nicky merely laughed and looked at HER. He'd bedded women of all ages and he was an expert on the species. Although he couldn't see her face, her body and skin were firm, fresh and smooth; she was still very young, he decided. Early twenties he estimated. He wondered, again, what on earth she was doing at that age running two successful gaming establishments? She was very intelligent, he'd come to realise, as well as being beautiful under that mask, he'd convinced himself. He was somehow certain about it, it was becoming an obsession to see – he knew he'd not felt any scars or marks, but maybe she had a birth-mark, or a port wine stain? He wouldn't be able to feel that; they were disfiguring to look at but wouldn't affect the feel of her skin... but everything else about her was so lovely he couldn't imagine her face wasn't. He asked himself what on earth her fool of a husband was doing abandoning a woman like that? But perhaps the man found her independence, intelligence, assertiveness and capability intimidating or off-putting? A lot of men would. He'd grown up surrounded by women much the same, to a greater or lesser degree, women like his Granny, Cat Granville, his Madre and also Bella, so it didn't bother him, nor the other men in his family who also appreciated women like it and he and they generally found silly, vacuous or submissive women such a bore, which was why he found *Lionesse* so attractive. He suspected if he discovered she really was beautiful under her mask she would be almost his ideal, his perfect woman... but in the meantime she remained such a compelling mystery.

Nicky continued to look at *Lionesse* and wonder. She was definitely a Lady. Her accent under that strange hoarse voice was like cut glass at times and even when she was raging at, or loving him, she never completely lost it. Her general demeanour, the way she carried herself and behaved, all spoke of an aristocratic or wealthy upbringing. Her elegant hands were soft too, so she obviously never did menial work. He thought then about the banter they'd exchanged - she was very witty, clever and knowledgeable on a whole host of subjects – so she'd been extremely well educated, which was also surprising for a woman... and he'd been stunned when he'd seen her doing her books. Accounting was no job for any Lady, let alone a woman normally; in fact, a large number of men, including him, wouldn't know where to start on something like that either. It was all quite extraordinary. She was such a challenge to him too, he was completely fascinated with her. She'd never bored him for a minute since he'd first met her several nights' previously, which was very unusual. He normally found most women palled after a few days, especially the younger ones who had little or no conversation, let alone an individual thought in their pretty heads. Even just sitting quietly playing cards, or chess, for hours with her had captivated him. She was a complete enigma and he was totally in thrall to her. Indeed, almost his ideal as he'd already concluded, so the desire to see her face was becoming more than an obsession.

They sat looking at each other and *Lionesse* idly tickled her fingers across her captive's abdomen again. "Oh no, that's definitely not fair," he gasped, "so not fair; it's positively cruel."

"Well, what else am I supposed to do with a prisoner except torture him?" she grinned.

"I could make plenty of suggestions," he suggested with a lecherous look.

"Hmmmm, I'd wager they're bound to be much too pleasurable, knowing you. So, if I can't tickle you, I suppose I could just leave you here and go and finish my bookwork and then just go to sleep. It is rather late after all," she got up off the bed and turned to start to leave the bedroom, waving at him as she went.

"Whaaat!" he exclaimed, looking worried. "You can't be serious? You wouldn't?"

She turned to look at him from the doorway, "Sleep well, my poor soldier," and she blew him a kiss as she walked slowly out of the room.

Nicky lay and fumed. He couldn't believe she really intended to leave him tied to the bed by himself all night. No, surely not? He swore under his breath but refused to call after her. He tugged on his wrists but they were tied tight. He swore again and cursed himself for being a fool. He cursed her for being the most annoying woman he'd ever met.

It was silent in the bedroom and silence emanated from the sitting room. The minutes passed and all he could hear was the mantel clock ticking. But just as his temper was about to reach volcanic proportions, his captor sauntered back in as if she hadn't a care in the world. She carried a small glass dish.

"Nice and grumpy now, are we?" she chuckled as she saw his angry face. "Oh Nicky, you are sooo easy to tease," and she wandered over to the side of the bed, putting down the dish on the nightstand. It was full of chocolate delicacies.

Heaving an enormous sigh, he shook his head and swore again. "You are more than impossible, You Wretched Baggage," and he laughed ruefully. "Whatever are you doing to me?"

"In this prison, inmates sometimes get a treat for being particularly good, so here's yours, not that I'm one hundred percent convinced you deserve it, mind," and she grinned as she popped one of her delicacies in his mouth. She'd bought them that morning from a small shop just off Bond Street where a chef had set up a little business and developed the art of making sweets and candies for his well-off clientele with a new chocolate concoction. Bella knew they were a particular treat and these ones his favourites. Wonderful dark chocolate with a soft creamy interior flavoured with brandy. Savouring the sweet concoction, Nicky licked his lips and looked longingly at the dish and then back at her with an amused, pleading expression. "I promise I'll be good," he grinned at her as she popped one and then another in his mouth and watched as he lay his head back, obviously enjoying them.

"Mmmmm, I haven't had some of those in years," he sighed, "and the brandy ones are my favourites. May I have another? How good do I have to be? I can be the most model prisoner you've ever seen."

She watched, extremely amused as he gobbled up another two,

then she prodded his hard, muscled stomach. "Tut, tut, *Milor*, you'll get fat and then all your women won't want you anymore."

He burst out laughing. "Who cares if I can have more of those chocolate trifles."

Bella sat down on the side of the bed and fed him the remaining chocolates one by one, a huge smile on her face as he ate the last one and gave an enormous sigh of pleasure.

"Ahhhh, they were wonderful, who needs women?" he chuckled.

"Oh, so I really should go and do some work then?" she teased. "You obviously have no need of me now after all that lot."

He rolled his eyes at her. "I wouldn't say that but I'm still waiting for you to keep your promise."

"Are you now? Since when do prisoners get to make so many demands? I thought you were supposed to be a model one?"

"After all those lovely chocolate bon-bons, I got the impression I was the jailer's pet."

"Hmmmm, yes, I did say you were like a big pussycat. I suppose you think I'm going to stroke you now?"

Nicky lay there and had to laugh. She was winding him up a treat and he would just have to be patient while she had her fun. He thought back over the evening and what a see-saw it had been already and it was far from over. He reflected he'd miss her terribly when he went back to Spain and was determined to come and find her again when he returned. She was too perfect to lose from his life, even if she *was* married.

Bella watched him laugh and ran her hands over his lightly furred chest, stroking the sun-bleached hair there. "Aren't you supposed to purr if I do that?" she enquired, smiling naughtily.

"Oh, you have to do a bit more than that to get me to purr," he quipped softly.

"Really? Do I?" she teased and started to stroke downwards, over his belly and the waistband of his pantaloons and then back and forth over his constrained erection, feeling it grow even larger as she stroked. Nicky's head fell back and he closed his eyes as the pleasure coursed through him and then he opened them again and sighed as slowly, she let her hand go over to where the fastenings were and she undid them, one by one, deliberately taking her time to tease him. Then, as his eyes glittered at her, she gradually peeled the tight garment down his legs, pulling it off to toss on the floor.

He watched as her hands ran slowly up his legs and, after drawing tantalising circles round his belly and thighs with her forefinger, she finally started to stroke the hard, throbbing length of him, from his balls right up to the tip. A pearl of moisture leached from the end and slowly, she wiped it with a finger which she then lifted to her lips, tasting and savouring the flavour of him as her tongue came out to lick her fingertip.

"Aren't you purring yet?" she whispered.

"Aaah, *Lionesse*," he crooned back, "you have to do a bit more than that. You promised."

"Still making demands, hmmmm?" she chuckled hoarsely and stroked him again, letting her hand slowly close around his length and move up and down a couple of times. She watched him as he lay there, watching her caress him, desire and pleasure evident in his golden eyes as he enjoyed the spectacle. Grinning evilly, she slowly pulled her hand away and moved up the bed, over to his side and snaked her hand under the pillows to pull out the golden sash.

When he saw it, Nicky groaned. "Oh no, *Lionesse*, no. I wanted to watch, pleeease?" his deep voice begged in frustration. "I can't stand it, the pleasure I'd get, you can leave your mask on surely? You can ride me after too, then I can see you when you climax. Oh please, noooooo..." and he shook his head, pleadingly.

But she ignored him and dangled the sash wickedly in front of his face as she purred, "You can't have everything; you lost, after all, remember?"

He swore at her, his frustration evident. "Any last requests from the condemned man?" Bella teased, as she had the previous evenings, before sitting back and waiting.

"Take off that damned wrap," he bit out. "At least let me have one look at what I'm missing," and he pulled on his bonds angrily.

She smiled as she slowly got off the bed. She'd gambled he would ask that so unhurriedly, she started to undo the catches on the golden robe, watching him watching her. The fastenings undone, bit by bit she slid the satin off first one shoulder, then the other, letting the garment slither to the floor as she gazed at him speculatively. As his eyes took in what she was wearing underneath, she saw his gasped, indrawn breath and his eyes widened and glittered. Not that she was wearing very much. The thin, gold coloured lace barely covered anything worth mentioning, held up by two wisps of golden silk ribbon. The whole concoction, supposed to be a shift, only fell to her thighs, fitting tightly where it touched her skin and leaving her knees and long shapely legs bare. Artfully designed and threaded here and there with more sparkling gold ribbon, it still managed to push her curvaceous breasts upward and they spilled out over the top of the lace, the pink of her areolas evident, the nipples now engorged, taut and hard. The small triangle of black curls at the apex of her legs clearly showed through the fine lace as did her slender torso.

"Checkmate, again, Nicky," she whispered.

He stared at her as she prowled towards the bed and his lips curved in a hungry smile. She had woken the sleeping lion although she had him temporarily caged. *"Mon Dieu,"* he muttered, "if I'd known you were wearing that under your robe, I'd have surrendered our game after three minutes, not three hours!"

"Ah, but then I wouldn't have had the pleasure of beating you properly," she teased, "and now I'm having MY revenge on you, for lying to me."

She slowly climbed up onto the bed and straddled his lap, sitting slightly above him and then leaned forward slowly to caress his abdomen and chest, then his shoulders and arms. He had a full view of her breasts, tantalisingly close, the nipples almost asking to be sucked and nibbled. He groaned and squirmed under her, the frustration starting.

She leaned up to check his wrists were still bound tightly and purred as she did so. "This is for lying to me, as I can't trust you now not to pull off my mask," then she bent forward to wrap the sash round his frustrated eyes, "and this is for what you did to me on my desk." After she'd checked the silk was effectively bound and tied tight, she whispered in his ear, "How am I ever going to be able to concentrate and add up columns of figures when all I'll be able to think about is you, rutting behind me and how you felt when you released inside me, right there, where I work, never mind spank me…"

As Bella sat back up and pulled off her wig and mask with a sigh of relief and then let down her hair, Nicky bit out, part sadly and part angrily because he was so frustrated, not only at not being able to see her, but also not now to touch her in that teasing piece of fluff she was wearing, or to slowly undo the ribbons and pull it off. "Are you satisfied, *Lionesse*, to have me helpless like this? Is this how you truly get your pleasure?"

"Not really, *Mon Cher*," she whispered and leaned down to finally kiss him gently. "Though I have to admit I love playing with you, love teasing you, you're so easy to wind up like a clock," she kissed him again on the end of his nose, "but you're about to discover that people who lose in MY games, usually end up feeling like they've won, and captives in MY prison never want to escape." She kissed him then, deeply and hungrily, as she'd been desperate to do since he'd arrived hours before, her hands stroking down his captive body, to caress his erection, teasing and tantalising until he was moaning under her and then she muttered, "You've had your chocolate treats, I want my apple."

As he felt her long hair tickle and caress his body, Nicky's bound hands opened then fisted with the aggravation of not being able to touch or see it. "Are you sure the condemned man has no final, final request?" she breathed.

He was on fire. "Have mercy," he groaned. "I think your torture is probably going to kill me tonight," and she laughed saucily.

As she'd done the previous evening, Bella once again licked, nibbled, sucked and kissed him all over his body until he was a seething mass of want, writhing, jerking, begging her to touch him. His wrists were already almost rubbed raw with his desperate efforts to escape the restraints and his head was thrown back into the pillows as he was lost in the disorienting blindfolded blackness of sensuous pleasure. His alternative senses were alight, burning hotly as, for a while, she teased and played with him, bringing him almost to a climax several times as she began to get more experienced with what she was doing, before easing off and leaving him hanging on the edge and swearing at her venomously. The instructions of what Bella's outrageous aunt had euphemistically called 'tantalising bedroom activities' were paying dividends!

Then, when Nicky thought he could truly take no more of her torture, she finally bent over him and took him in her warm, soft mouth. The sensation was overwhelming and he bucked and cried out as she sucked and licked, doing things to him that made his body feel like it was being consumed in a vortex of tortured pleasure.

As she pulled her mouth off him yet again, on the verge of exploding down her throat, he swore endlessly in voluble French and Bella slowly got off the bed and sauntered through into her sitting room. Pouring herself a cup of coffee from the pot she'd set to simmer over the fire while she'd first left him tied to the bed, she also picked up a couple of cubes of ice from the bucket on the sideboard and popped them into a glass. Then, taking both cup and glass she made her way back. Silently she put the glass on the nightstand but sipped slowly from the cup of boiling hot coffee before climbing back on the bed. When he felt the burning and heated sensation of her mouth on him, his body went rigid with shock, but when she then popped an ice cube in her mouth and bent to him again, he shrieked as the sensation nearly took off the top of his head and spasms of tormented ecstasy roiled up through him. Nicky truly thought she would kill him at the rate she was going. Marie-Catherine Granville had taught her niece well. She'd originally learned her technique from Bella's mother, Carlotta, and a couple of very amused and close friends of hers, as well, obviously, from Francis; but where he'd experienced those tricks and many others was a whole other story.

Bella thought of the lessons her aunt had given her and smirked to herself as she teased Nicky mercilessly. She finally took sympathy on his tormented plight and bent down to whisper in his ear, words of suggestive, sensuous, tantalising French, also given her by her Gallic-born aunt with much giggling that morning, which told him, amongst other much more erotic and rather perverted things, to let go and climax deep down her throat. She bent her head once more and as her lips closed around him and sucked hard, her hands caressing his balls, he literally screamed with the delayed ecstasy exploding through his body and she felt the hot essence of him burst deep into the back of her throat.

Bella sat back, gasping and coughing slightly and wiping her mouth, a hugely satisfied smile curling her lips as she watched her captive lion recover from the experience she'd just given him. His body was covered in a damp sheen of sweat and she could see his heart thumping erratically in his chest. As she leaned over to gently kiss his mouth, letting him taste his flavour still on her lips, she heard a low mutter and what sounded like, "Purr, purr, purr."

Her head fell back and she cracked with laughter. "Impossible man, but losing isn't so bad is it, hmmm?"

"I wouldn't know," he whispered, "I think I'm dead."

"You'd better not be," she leaned down to kiss him again, "I'm far from finished with you yet."

She left him for a few moments to go into the sitting room and returned with a freshly opened bottle of chilled champagne and a glass. "Are you thirsty?" she enquired and he nodded.

Bella poured some out and took a deep mouthful; she then bent over him and let the cold, bubbly liquid stream into his mouth from hers. "Shame you ate all the bon-bons, you'll just have to put up with this... more?" she queried as he swallowed and sighed.

"Much, much more," he whispered and between them they emptied another couple of glasses, interspersed with passionate kisses.

As she kissed him, Bella herself was so seized up with desire, she could barely restrain herself from climbing on top of him and finding her own release, but she was determined to continue with his torment before she did so and repressed her own longing to concentrate on his body once again.

As she recommenced her torturous progress down his torso once more he moaned, "Aaah no, *Lionesse*, not again, I can't stand it, you'll kill me... ahhh!"

She laughed naughtily up at him, "But you just told me you were dead. You can't die twice, but wait," he heard her fingers snap, "of course, you're a pussycat so you've obviously got a few lives left to use up," and she took him in her mouth once more as he writhed under her, lost to the tormenting pleasure he could feel building in himself again.

Once more she brought him to the brink several times, only to pull back, until she could stand it no longer. Her lips left him and she moved sinuously to lay down across his body, twisting on top of him so he could feel the friction of the fine layer of lace that lay between his skin and hers. As her hands caressed up and down his bound arms, she kissed and bit his neck, leaving a large flowering red mark to indicate her progress, then moved up to kiss all over his face before covering his lips with hers in another kiss of such carnal longing, he moaned, pulled and strained against his bonds in the want to take her in his arms and make love to her properly instead of being forced into submission again.

"Nicky, oh Nicky, I want you so much," she moaned. "I can't bear the thought of losing you." Bella was lost and mindless and her unthinking words just came out of their own volition. As she pulled herself up to plunge - hot, wet and needy - down on top of him, tears of love and unfettered emotion coursed down her face and she sobbed as all the roiling feelings inside her coalesced together: fear and worry for his safety, deep intense love and passionate, lustful desire as the spasms and waves rolled outwards from her belly.

"Release me, let me go, *Lionesse*," Nicky begged and pleaded, pulling hard again on the ties on his sore wrists as he felt her writhe around him and heard her sobs and the emotion overwhelming her, wanting only to pull her into his arms and hold her tightly and protectively as they found their release together. But she was too engrossed in her own heart-wrenching feelings; she bent forward, kissing him again in a torrent of need and gripped his bound hands frenziedly in hers, knowing the whole tenor of her relationship with him had now changed irrevocably because of the past few days. "NO... NEVER! I'll never let you go now," she screamed and was lost as her senses were overwhelmed.

The power of her climax sent Nicky over the top with her and, as another mind-shattering release overwhelmed his own senses, he felt her go limp on his chest as she collapsed in a torrent of feeling, intermittent quiet sobs still choking her and as she lay panting, with her face buried in his neck, her hot tears scalded down to his chest.

Nicky cursed long and hard to himself, still unable to escape his bonds, his sore wrists a testament to his frustrated efforts. He swore that this was the last time he'd allow her, or anyone, to put him in that position. No matter what she said, how much she prevaricated, this was the last time she'd play games with him. What had passed between them that night had moved their relationship beyond that. He'd given a lot of women extraordinary pleasure over the years, but none had reacted with the depth of emotion he knew *Lionesse* had felt for him and that he felt for her. That she had given him a night of unbelievable passion was also in no doubt and he knew now there was both a mental and physical connection between them that had taken things to a different level, even after so short a time.

He cursed again, against fate for taking him back to Spain so soon before he could get to know her better, her absent husband for putting her in the situation she was in - running gaming saloons was no occupation for a Lady - and for the sorrow the wretched man obviously caused her. He would happily kill him, if he knew who he was, if he knew who she was. And that was the nub of his problem; he now wanted her for himself, but that wasn't to be, given his imminent departure.

Bella roused herself and wiped her face, horrified at how she'd let herself go, how she'd nearly given herself away. Again she wondered if she should reveal herself to him now, but once again she took the coward's way out. She lifted her head to peer at the windows between the gap in the drapes. The candles had long since sputtered out and although it was still dark, the glow of dawn was just starting to shed a glimmer of light in the black sky and a couple of birds were twittering. It had been a long night and she was too tired, too emotionally shattered to face the enormous argument she knew would ensue. She would tell him tomorrow, she decided. Surely after all they had shared he would now see her in a different light and accept her as his wife.

She heard him curse. "Are you all right, *Lionesse*?" he asked, his voice rough with concern.

"Yes," she whispered, "of course. I'm sorry, just a bit emotional," she gave a shaky laugh.

"Untie me, *Lionesse*, release me, it's enough now," he pulled on his wrist yet again and winced. "I'm not doing it anymore. Games are all very well; as you know, I like nothing more than to play, but this has gone beyond a joke now. You can feel it too, this connection between us," he said softly.

Bella drew in a breath as she heard the frustration and the seriousness in his tone and his words. Torn, she didn't know what to do. "Yes," she whispered, "just a moment." She sat up and dithered, considering one more time what to do.

"Are you on duty early tomorrow?" she queried as she moved over on the bed.

"What's that got to do with anything?" he asked. "Are you going to untie me?" She could sense his anger now.

"Only that I wondered, if you needed to sleep for a few hours, or wanted breakfast?"

"I'm a soldier. I'm used to being without sleep and I'm not interested in breakfast. Untie me, *Lionesse*," he ordered brusquely.

She clambered off the bed. "Yes, yes," she prevaricated, "what time are you leaving?"

"I have matters to attend to and I have to report in. I must be away reasonably early."

That decided her, Bella couldn't face an argument now and then have Nicky walk out in the middle of it. She got up and drew the heavy drapes over the window, cutting out the now brightening dawn light, so the bedroom was again in almost blackness barring a solitary candle burning low on the nightstand. She went and found her mask and put it down on the bed, looking at it with serial hatred now; she'd had enough of her games too. Then she clambered back up on the bed and started to undo the ties round one of his wrists. As she did so, she gasped in shock as she felt the soreness where he'd rubbed the skin raw in his efforts to break free. She peered down and saw the redness and broken skin, "Oh my God, Nicky, oh no. I never meant for this to hurt. What have you done?" she whispered, kissing his tender, sore wrist.

Nicky laughed sadly. "You Silly Puss, what did you expect? I'm not a man to just lie here patiently or submissively. You drove me near insane you know, with what you did," and he shook his head in despair and some amusement. Hurriedly, she moved over to release his other hand and kissed that wrist as well. But as he went to undo the sash round his eyes she took hold of his hands. "Wait, just a moment before you do that," and she bent to kiss him, gently and softly. As her lips met his, his arms stole around her and he sighed. "Ah, *Lionesse*, this is what I want, just to hold you," but as he pulled her round under him, revelling once more in the feel of her skin as his hands roved over her body, his mouth opened over hers and the kiss changed. The powerful charge that had simmered between them all night took over again and passion ignited. They kissed each other hungrily until their immediate need was temporarily sated and the tenor of the kiss changed again into one that was gentle, tender and sweet.

Bella was nearly overcome with it and all the love and concern she felt for him poured out of her into that tender kiss as she succumbed to the wonderful feel of his strong arms around her, revelling in the protectiveness she always experienced when he held her.

A great wash of tenderness overcame Nicky as he felt her soft, yielding body in his arms again. The passion she seemed to always ignite in him took over as soon as his lips met hers, but as the passion eased and the kiss changed, the emotional and caring feelings he experienced almost overwhelmed him. She clung to him and whimpered as if he was the most precious thing in the world and, his emotions overwrought, he knew he would have to come back and find her. He NEEDED to come back and find her... when he'd got through his mission in Spain.

She pulled away from him with a sigh and leaned back to pick up her mask off the bed. Sensing and hearing what she was going to do he simply said, "Leave it off, *Lionesse*; surely we've gone beyond secrets now, this isn't a game anymore."

Bella paused one more time. "Tomorrow," she whispered brokenly. "I promise I'll leave it off tomorrow and... and then you'll find out what I look like, who I am," and she picked up the now hateful mask and tied it round her face for the last time. But she left her wig off. He knew she had black hair and she reckoned in the dim and shadowy room he still wouldn't recognise her. He hadn't seen her with her hair down loose for years... that eventful night last year it had been in the usual thick plait she slept in. Anyway, what did it matter? She sighed. "You can take the blindfold off now," and she blew out the candle.

Nicky pulled and fiddled impatiently at the tight knots behind his head and eventually, the sash unwound and came away. He took one look at her masked face and grimaced but then he realised she'd left her wig off and an abundance of long, thick black waves was drifting over her shoulders and down her back to her waist. "*Lionesse*," he whispered, "your hair..." He put out a hand and wrapped some long soft curls around it, gazing, almost transfixed at the luxuriant profusion of it, seeing it for the first time, even in the darkness. "It's beautiful, just like you."

He tugged on her hair very gently, pulling her until she was enfolded back in his arms again and he leaned back against the pillows, releasing a deep, contented sigh. "Sleep now, *Chérie*, hmmm?" he whispered, his fingers absently playing with the gold ribbons of her flimsy undergarment, but he seemed happy to merely leave them in place, an amused smile on his face. He settled himself more comfortably, cuddling her back against his chest, his chin resting in her soft hair. "*Mon Dieu*, what a night," he muttered and let his eyes slowly close. "No more secrets after tomorrow, you hear me?" and he leaned down to plant a soft, tender kiss on the side of her neck. But just as sleep was about to claim him he whispered naughtily in her ear, "And that includes telling me where you picked up that disgraceful language and those suggestions. I was quite shocked," he teased. "Maybe we can explore them next time, hmmm? Now those are MY type of games..."

Blissfully snuggled up against his chest with his strong arms around her, like a pair of spoons nesting together, Bella merely giggled softly as she drifted off to sleep.

Nicky woke early, now that he had no blindfold to disorientate him. He looked towards the window and saw sunlight around the edges of the heavy drapes. He stretched lazily, trying not to disturb the slumbering woman next to him. He was tired and could have done with sleeping for hours more, but his mind was racing; not only with thoughts of *Lionesse* and the expectation of finally discovering her identity, but also with questions for his next meeting with Ashcroft with, hopefully, more news of the mysterious Bernheim. He knew he wouldn't be able to sleep with all those thoughts now clamouring for attention in his mind, so with a quiet groan, he got up and padded over to the window to pull back the curtains and see what the time was.

As sunshine streamed into the room he turned back to the bed and a smile curled his lips as he looked at the body lying there. She was splayed out on her stomach, one hand reaching out towards where he'd been lying. Her excuse of a nightrail, or was it a shift, or half a chemise, and he smiled as he contemplated it, had ridden up to her waist, leaving her bottom and long shapely legs bare to view. He couldn't resist leaning down to place a warm, moist kiss on each buttock, hearing her quietly sigh with pleasure at the touch of his lips on her skin and the rasp of his morning stubble. Long coils of thick, silky black hair meandered down her back and across her pillow, obscuring her face. He reached out to touch it and, as if it were almost alive, a wavy lock curled around his fingers. Hot tongues of desire ran rampant through him but he tamped them down regretfully and pulled the sheet up over her. She murmured contentedly in her sleep at the feel of his gentle hands on her shoulders as he tucked the sheet round them. He checked the clock on the mantel and, with his own sigh, silently padded through to her bathing room. He washed and dressed and rubbed some salve on his sore wrists that he'd found among a host of bottles and pots on her dressing table; as the clock chimed the hour at eight o'clock, he heard movement in her sitting room as a footman quietly brought in a tray with warm croissants and coffee and left it sitting on *Lionesse*'s dining table.

Lured by the smell, Nicky wandered through and sat down to help himself to a cup of the hot fragrant brew, happily munching his way through several croissants, liberally doused with both honey and preserves as the fancy took him. He had a second cup of coffee and, feeling replete and more like his usual self, he rose to saunter back into the bedroom. *Lionesse* was still sound asleep and much as he wanted to wake her, he smiled ruefully and let her be. He turned to leave but as he was just at the door, the urge to kiss her once again overwhelmed him. He returned to the bed and pulled the sheet down and once more he planted a kiss on each pert buttock. He grinned as she sighed at his touch and watched in amusement as she rolled over to his side of the bed, pulling his pillow to her, whispering his name and cuddling it. Silently he pulled the sheet back up and leaned down to whisper in her ear, "Sleep well, *Ma Chérie;* I WILL see you later."

Chapter Sixteen

But the day turned into a disaster.

Nicky walked back to Berkeley Square and went up to his room to change into his uniform, ready for his meeting with Ashcroft, but actually wondering if he needed it. He still wasn't sure if Ashcroft's little department was 'military' or not, despite his connections with Colonel Melrose and his opposite number from the Navy. But he decided to err on the side of caution just in case he ended up in another meeting in the War Ministry or Foreign Office.

Glad he'd escaped the notice of anyone in the house, he was just making his way across the hall to go out when Francis came out of his study and called him back. "On your way to see Ashcroft?" he enquired quietly as the two men came together in the hall. "You will let me know what he's found out about Bernheim, won't you?"

"Of course," Nicky replied. "I'll be coming straight back here after I've seen him. Are you here all day?"

"Yes," replied Francis. "I'll be in my study. Just come and find me, you're my priority over everything."

As Nicky nodded and turned to go, straightening his uniform, Francis quietly added, "Give my regards to Ashcroft... oh and Nicky..." Nicky turned his head at the amused tone in the Duke's voice, "tut, tut, that rat must have been hungrier than ever last night; did it tie you to its plate before it had its dinner?" and with Francis's lecherous laughter ringing in his ears, Nicky pulled his shirt collar and cravat and uniform jacket collar as far up his neck as they would go and his sleeves down over his wrists. He marched from the house, muttering under his breath about bewitching women.

With plenty of time on his hands, Nicky made his way over to the Ministry at a leisurely pace and on presenting himself to the 'Department of Information' was escorted off by another unmemorable employee to receive a variety of confidential documents to take back to the Peninsula, mostly for Wellington's attention, but he noted some were addressed to Scovell. He was also given a thin file of papers which he was told contained all the information the Department currently had on Bernheim's movements, previous activities and current presumed location. There was also a vague description of the man, but on a quick scan Nicky decided tall, slim, slightly olive complexion and dark haired could apply to a large number of the male population in Spain and Portugal. Finally, he was handed a bank draft for a not inconsiderable sum of money which he was told to draw on before he left for Spain. Returning to the outer office by Ashcroft's sanctum, the unmemorable employee bade him sit down and went to retrieve a large box from a locked cupboard, silently handing it over to Nicky. "Tell me if they're comfortable," was all he said. Nicky opened the box to discover an identical pair of boots to the ones he was wearing. "Look at the heels," the other man advised tonelessly. Turning the boots upside down, Nicky did as he was told and discovered after a fiddle that both heels swivelled round to reveal a hollow compartment in each that extended under the slightly raised sole. Without a word he was handed over a couple of sheets of folded paper which, on inspection, contained ciphers and codes. "Keep the papers in the boots. You'll need them to send messages through to us here until you're sure you've memorised them, if you can. On no account send anything unless it's in code. If you get any messages from us, they'll need to be transcribed in the same way."

Nicky was fascinated. "Unless you've memorised everything exactly, if you lose your boots, you're stuck, so I suggest you keep them on whatever you're doing, even sleep in them if necessary. The only way to get another set of codes is to send us a confidential message via Wellington himself, but Lord Ashcroft would rather you didn't do that unless the situation is absolutely critical. He would prefer you come back to London personally to collect another set. He doesn't trust ANYONE. Kindly remember that and try not to lose the boots. You have very expensive taste," he tutted, "especially to get them made up so quickly. They've only just arrived here as it is."

Nicky grinned at the man. His boots were a personal indulgence – he didn't have many – but they were comfortable and hard-wearing and being handmade specially for him, they fitted perfectly. He pulled off his own and put on the new pair. They were a perfect fit also – obviously from the same bootmaker in St James's. The craftsmen there must have worked non-stop through the day and night to make them up from the personal pattern they kept for him and he smirked at the thought. This was a very strange organisation, to be sure, to be able to facilitate that. He pulled off each one and placed the small sheets of folded paper into the cavity inside each heel. He pulled the new boots back on and sat back and waited to be summoned by Ashcroft, taking the opportunity to start to read the information they had gleaned on Bernheim.

"...And so you must depart within the hour," concluded Ashcroft. "If the man IS still in Madrid, the quicker you get there and pick up his trail, find out what he's up to and deal with him, the better. As it is this last information we've had, such as it is, is at least two weeks old by the time it travelled up here from Spain. There's a fast Navy sloop *en route* to Portugal which can drop you off at a quiet spot on the coast somewhere between Santander and Gijón. It's on its way from London and is currently waiting for you now off Portsmouth. If you make haste, you can be there to catch the morning tide tomorrow," he looked meaningfully at Nicky. "After that it's up to you." He paused, looking at his new man. "You know how to keep in touch?" Nicky nodded. "Good, good, we're relying on you, de Bresancourt. Just be very careful. I really don't want to lose any more agents, if I can help it."

"I'll do my best not to extend your ex-agents list then, less paper to file," Nicky quipped, earning him a glare from Ashcroft. "In any case, I want to get back to London as quickly as I can. I hadn't expected to be leaving quite so abruptly, I'd thought to be here for another day or so." A reflective look crossed Nicky's face as he momentarily gazed into the distance out of one of the office windows.

"Really?" Ashcroft raised an eyebrow in the direction of the mark he'd noted on Nicky's neck. *"Une femme intéressante?"* he queried. He didn't often make any suggestive or even light-hearted remarks.

"Something like that," Nicky grinned, his mind racing as he thought about how he could go home to collect his belongings and then stop off to cash in the draft and finally call in to see *Lionesse* before setting off for Portsmouth, wondering if he could do without a visit to his barracks as well, trying to recall what he'd left there, otherwise he'd ask Benjy to sort that errand out.

"Hmmm," Ashcroft looked at him piercingly, his grey eyes boring into Nicky's. "Just make sure you keep your thoughts on the job in hand. London and its dubious attractions can wait until Bernheim isn't a problem to us any longer."

"Yes, Sir. Sorry, Ashcroft," Nicky stood up to leave.

"By the way, we've arranged for a fast carriage to collect you from here, go to your barracks for whatever belongings you need that you keep there, stop at the bank and then take you back to Berkeley Square. As soon as you've packed up there and made your farewells, it will take you straight to Portsmouth."

Nicky's stomach lurched but he kept his face impassive. That would make a visit to *Le Lion d'Or* extremely difficult. He'd intended to borrow one of Francis's fast horses and ride down himself, or perhaps borrow his racing curricle, if his baggage was too much for the horse, which would give him more precious hours in London. But he was determined to visit *Lionesse* before he left - to finally see her face so at least he could have something to remember while he was away. And then, when he returned, he would pick up where they had left off early that morning. Part of his mind and body was still reeling from the events of the previous night. And of course he had to retrieve his necklace.

He bowed briefly to Ashcroft as he turned to leave his office. The tall, nondescript-looking man rose from his chair and took his hand in a cool and surprisingly firm grip. "Good luck, My Boy. Remember, be extremely careful at all times, use the brain people tell me does exist inside your head – even if I have my doubts – and try not to do anything TOO rash." Facetious to the last, he turned to go silently back to his desk as Nicky left the room.

As he sat in the carriage on his way to his barracks, Nicky's mind went back over the conversation he'd had with Ashcroft. "So you see," that individual had spoken thoughtfully, "we have reason to believe the man who caused so many... ah... problems for your family and the Duke of Firle as well as the de Mornay family, plus many others from what we've been able to find out, given it all occurred over twenty years ago, one Edgar Bernheim, was none other than the father of the man we now seek."

Nicky's eyes had widened as Ashcroft spoke. "It's been difficult to find out exactly what happened to him, but whilst researching the background of the son, one of our contacts managed to locate an old mercenary in Normandy who worked for the father on and off around that time. He'd been in the army originally, left, we're not exactly sure why, possibly booted out as he was a rather unsavoury individual according to the report, before he signed up with the local militia who worked for the Governor of Normandy at the time; that man was Edgar Bernheim. We also gather Bernheim's so-called 'militia' were a most unpleasant unit of men, more like a small private regiment, greatly feared in the region for their brutality and venality, so he no doubt fitted in well. When this militia were disbanded, after Bernheim Senior was removed from office and a new Governor was appointed, our informant re-enlisted in the army when the French Revolutionary Wars began and they needed experienced soldiers and weren't too fussy about their background. He was wounded out and finally retired

back to his home village. According to the old soldier, the elder Bernheim was an extremely nasty piece of work, like father like son obviously, but he had an obsession with some smuggler called The Shadow
who'd apparently been a thorn in his side during most of his time as
Governor."

Ashcroft lifted his head to look at Nicky as he paused, but Nicky's
face was immobile. So he continued, "The last information our contact
discovered about Bernheim Senior was that he'd finally captured the
fellow, even though he'd been relieved of his Governorship. He was
apparently after the tidy little fortune the smuggler was rumoured to
have made from his activities right along the coast, over on that as well
as this side of the Channel, involving a bit of pirating as well, apparently. Fellow had quite a reputation it seems. But something went
wrong and Bernheim Senior was found dead in the ruins of the old
Rouen Fortress with some of his men and no one has heard anything of
The Shadow since. This old soldier we questioned told us he'd been
involved in the capture of The Shadow but he'd gone off duty after
they'd killed the rest of his accomplices. Bernheim, along with his lieu-
tenant and right-hand man, were planning to torture and extract the
information about his ill-gotten gains, but exactly what happened, he
had no idea." Ashcroft shrugged his shoulders, "We couldn't find out
any more about that event, no matter how far we trawled and dug.
However, we did learn that his son, Frederick, OUR Bernheim, came to
Rouen to visit and pay his respects a while after he got news of his
father's death. No one knew of his existence apparently, and he'd been
away at school out of France, and someone else had seen to the
funerals of the dead men, we don't know who that was, but then then
the son simply disappeared again. The ruins of the Fortress mysteriously blew up several months after so there's nothing left to investigate there either, records and so on. Whether any of the men are still in
Bonaparte's army somewhere, we don't know, but they'd be impossible to find, obviously."

He'd sat back looking curiously at Nicky again. "I was interested in
your remark that the Duke had had a run-in with the man and the
Duchess had killed him? This must have been after the business with
the smuggler then. Do you know the details by any chance?"

Nicky hadn't known what to say, so merely remarked, "Not a lot of the details. I was only a young child at the time, just about turned five. I was still getting over the trauma of escaping from France and losing my parents and everyone I knew. Why don't you ask the Duke? I'm sure he'll tell you about it..." How was that for wriggling out of awkward questions with the perfect excuse? Francis could sort that little problem for himself, he thought. If the situation hadn't been so serious, Nicky would have chuckled, but this was no laughing matter.

"Yes, yes, of course," Ashcroft had said, "quite understandable. However, even though they were related, I don't think it can have any bearing on our current problem since it was so long ago and our target was still at school when his father was occupied with maintaining law and order in Normandy. However, I'll call on the Duke shortly and see if he can fill any gaps. I don't like loose ends."

Nicky had released a sigh of relief at that and made a mental note to warn Francis about his impending visit... and Ashcroft's 'gaps' and 'loose ends'.

A shout broke into his reverie about how curious coincidences came around. He jumped from the carriage and hurried into the regimental barracks to collect or sort out the few personal military items he always kept there in a private trunk, when he'd first arrived a few days before. As he climbed back in, he called up to the driver to make a stop at the bank and then, on the way to Firle House, gave him directions to *Le Lion d'Or*. A gold coin thrown up in the air to the man elicited a nod and a wink and ensured the stop would not be reported, so Nicky hoped. The longer he talked to Ashcroft, the more wary he became of the perceptive and prescient man.

At *Le Lion d'Or*, Nicky rushed in and went straight upstairs. The doorman and footmen were now used to seeing him come and go to the owner's apartments so no one tried to stop him. However, as he burst into *Lionesse's* deserted sitting room, he bumped into a grubby young cleaning girl on her way out.

"Ooooh, yer pardon, Sir," she smirked cheekily, bobbing a curtsey and nearly dropping her bucket full of dusters, rags and brushes. She couldn't help but stare at Nicky, seeing him up close. The handsome army officer had been the source of much gossip below stairs, being the first and only man the owner had ever entertained in her private apartments, so the young maids had goggled at his good looks and fine form as he'd come and gone with regularity over the past few days. "I didn't sees yer comin'. Madam ain't 'ere by th' way, if yous woz lookin' fer 'er?" and she blushed as she realised she'd been gawping at him, so turned tail and fled.

It hadn't occurred to Nicky that *Lionesse* might be out and he was beside himself. He called back to the servant, now disappearing down the corridor, "Hey... just a moment. Where is she? When are you expecting her back?"

The young girl turned curiously. "I dunno, Sir," she shrugged. "Madam's offen not 'ere fer days, see, an' Mister Gardner's in charge then; mebbe 'e can 'elp yer... but acshully..." she scratched her head for a moment with soot-blackened fingers as a thought occurred, "don't bovver yerself wiv 'im as I dids 'ear 'er say this mornin' when she left, she wudn't be back til ternight... if'n that 'elps?"

"Tonight?!" Nicky exclaimed, aghast, but the maid nodded and turned to make her way back down the stairs to the kitchens.

Nicky returned to the sitting room and sat at *Lionesse's* desk. He put his head in his hands and swore long and hard. There was no way he could wait until tonight to see her. Ashcroft would have his head if he didn't get to Portsmouth and the waiting ship, not to mention Colonel Melrose, his superiors or even Wellington; he'd be charged with gross misconduct or who knew what else... and what was even worse for him personally, he had no idea what she'd done with his precious necklace.

Frantically, he started to pull open the drawers of her desk, tugging out ledgers and papers, piling them chaotically everywhere in his haste to search. He broke open a central locked drawer, uncaring of the damage and not interested in whatever was secured there, but only found lengthy documents and papers about the two gaming saloons. Being a curious man, on any other occasion Nicky would have poked his nose into *Lionesse's* private papers, so obsessed was he with her and her secrets, but on this occasion he had no time. Despite tipping the drawer upside down, of the necklace there was no sign.

Rising to his feet, he turned out every cupboard and cabinet in the sitting and dining area as well as *Lionesse's* study and then did the same in her bedroom and dressing room. As he fruitlessly searched, his frustration grew. Finally, he realised his hunt was pointless. His treasured chain and little golden lion were nowhere to be found and neither was the woman who knew where they were. He returned to her desk, banging his fist down in anger and frustration, once more burying his head in his hands. There was nothing he could do, there was simply no time left. Eventually, admitting he had no alternative but to leave, with a furious sigh he retrieved a blank sheet of paper from the litter on the floor, found a quill and ink and scribbled a hasty note for the elusive woman.

Lionesse…

My Orders came through to leave, Much Earlier than I had Expected.

I came to see you, to Find Out who you are and to say Au Revoir, not Goodbye, but you are Not Here, and I am Unable To Wait.

I simply cannot Disobey my Superiors or my Orders. These are Serious War Matters and Extremely Urgent.

He paused to think what to say, suddenly taking in the havoc he'd created in her apartment.

I apologise for the Mess, but I ~~wanted~~ needed my Necklace. It means Everything to me, as I told you, and actually Far More, but now You Have It.

Please, please, I Beg You - Keep it Safe as I WILL return - for it, and for you.

N de B

Nicky was about to fold the note, but had a final thought.

. . .

P.S: If you have to Leave This Place, or Go Away, or any other Eventuality strikes before

I can come back for it, or if you simply want it to Disappear, would you take it to the

Duke of Firle at Firle House in Berkeley Square and leave it with him or for him.

PLEASE Lionesse. If you need Money and think to Sell it, the Duke will give you Far

More than anyone will offer as he knows its Value To Me. Thank You.

P.P.S: I will Never Forget the past few days. I will come back and Find You. I Promise.

He had no time to write further, so merely folded the note, quickly sealed it with some wax to keep nosy domestic staff out of his and *Lionesse's* affairs, wrote her name on the front and took it into her bedroom to leave it on her pillow. Then, his emotions in turmoil, Nicky slowly walked out of the apartment, down the stairs and outside to the waiting carriage.

When he arrived at Firle House, the coachman told him to hurry or they wouldn't reach Portsmouth in time and he didn't like driving on deserted roads in the dark if he could help it. Footpads and highwaymen, he muttered direly.

Hurrying inside, Nicky headed straight for the Duke's study and burst in without bothering to knock. Seeing his fraught expression, Francis looked alarmed and immediately dismissed his secretary, asking him the close the door on leaving.

"Damn, damn, DAMN! Francis, it's the very devil. Ashcroft has ordered me to Portsmouth and on a fast ship to Spain that is apparently now awaiting my arrival in order to catch the tide early tomorrow. I have a carriage waiting outside and I have to leave, NOW," he bit out in frustration. "I wasn't expecting this, I'd thought to have at least one if not two more days in London, but then I wasn't expecting to be caught up in Ashcroft's activities. Hell, I didn't even know the man existed 'til yesterday. I'm so sorry, I had matters to deal with before I left and I wanted to talk to you again."

Francis looked at the extremely agitated young man and bade him sit, striding over to his sideboard to pour him a drink. "Calm down, calm down," he soothed, "surely the coach can wait another thirty minutes, for God's sake? Now, what else has got you in such a state, Nicky, apart from your unexpected departure?"

So Nicky told him all that Ashcroft had said about Edgar Bernheim and that the man he was now going after was his mysterious son. Francis looked stunned. In fact, he went ashen for a brief moment, then looked even more shocked when Nicky told him to expect a visit from Ashcroft, who was planning to ask him about what he knew of The Shadow's connection with Bernheim Senior, how the Duke himself had been involved and especially, how the Duchess had come to kill him.

"I'm so sorry, Francis, that was all my fault. I'd no idea at the time it would create such problems for you to explain. The coincidence of the family connection is beyond belief. I told Ashcroft this morning I didn't know much as I'd been a child at the time and still traumatised by my escape from France and losing my parents. It seemed a good excuse and I thought it best for you to think up a suitably discreet story in the meantime and deal with him your way. I'm sure you can fob him off. He can't possibly ever suspect you and The Shadow were one and the same man."

Francis patted him on the shoulder, "Don't worry, Nicky," he smiled, waving a long, elegant hand in the air and drawing attention to his immaculate waistcoat, still with its trademark priceless jewels for buttons. "I'll deal with Ashcroft. Now really, do I look remotely like a dirty, uncouth smuggler who disappeared, presumed dead, over twenty years ago?" He grinned down at the worried younger man. "What's more, given how rich I am and have been since my youth, why on earth would I need or want to take up such a nefarious and dangerous occupation in the first place? The idea is beyond absurd and doesn't make the slightest sense... as I shall tell Ashcroft, if he enquires too deeply!"

Nicky breathed a sigh of relief and then updated Francis on all the other information he'd been given about Bernheim and matters in Spain. "That's all, Francis. I'm sure you'll hear more in due course, but now I have to go," he muttered reluctantly.

"Of course. Thank you for the intelligence and the warning. I've got some information for you too. You go and get your things and I'll scribble it down, then I'll go and find Eddie, Charlie, Cat and Bella. They'll all want to see you before you leave and fortunately, I'm sure they're all somewhere around the house." He sighed, "It's a damn shame you have to run off like this. Bloody Ashcroft! You've only been here for a few days. It's not long enough, not damn near long enough!" He shook his head as he muttered and swore under his breath. "You've hardly had any leave to speak of since you joined up and were sent down to the Peninsula almost straight away. Fucking Bonaparte. Fucking war..." and he continued to swear and stomp around as Nicky rose to go and pack.

Nicky hurried out and ran up the stairs to his room. Francis followed in his wake, shouting loudly to the butler and footmen to find the Baron, his son, the Duchess and Miss Arabella and summon them down to the family sitting room as quickly as possible as the Duke was leaving imminently to return to Spain unexpectedly. As an afterthought he also ordered some bread and cheese and anything else the cook could rustle up in a few minutes to be placed in the carriage for Nicky to eat and drink on the way, suspecting he'd not had a chance to eat so far that day, having no idea where the man had spent the night or what time he'd left wherever he'd been... and it was a long journey to Portsmouth. Browning hurried off towards the kitchens, calling out on the way to footmen and hovering maids to rush and find the family members as quickly as they could and everyone scurried off in different directions.

In his room, Nicky hurriedly changed out of his uniform and ran around looking for his portmanteau, sorting out the few items of clothing he intended to take. Given his mission, he needed to travel light and he already had a large satchel of documents and money to carry.

While he was sorting through his shirts, jackets, buckskins, breeches and pantaloons, Bella entered the room behind him. "You're leaving so soon?" She looked completely distraught. "Can't you stay a little longer?" Her voice sounded broken and tearful.

"I've been ordered to go today, now. There's a navy ship waiting for me at Portsmouth and I must catch the tide early tomorrow as I have urgent dispatches for Wellington." He tried to explain while taking in her distressed expression. He put down the small pile of clothes he was sorting through and pulled her into his arms to give her a big, comforting, brotherly hug. "Now, now, Sooty," he crooned, rubbing his hands down her arms, "I'll be back before you know it, and I promise I WILL try to write this time." He looked down into her tearful face, "I don't want another of your set downs, now do I? You're such a bossyboots," he smiled gently at her as he tweaked her nose and wiped a tear away with his thumb.

"Oh, Nicky, please be careful," Bella cried as she started to sob. "I know you're off to do something dangerous and I simply can't bear it!" She threw her arms around his neck and wept into his shirt front.

He kept his arms around her and let her cry, nuzzling his face in her freshly washed hair, piled up on top of her head in an artful concoction of curls. She felt so familiar, he thought, just like when they were children and he'd comforted her when she'd fallen off her pony or out of a tree she'd been trying to climb. As her sobs eased off, she raised tearful eyes to his, "Kiss me goodbye, Nicky," she pleaded. "Pleeease. Properly, just for once."

"Sooty, I ca..." Nicky looked down at her worried and sad face but didn't have the heart to say no, so never finished his denial. He told himself he'd kissed all sorts of women he had no feelings for, so merely closed his eyes and took a deep breath and placed a light, gentle kiss on her lips.

"Nicky, oh Nicky," Bella breathed, opening her mouth over his to kiss him back, sweetly and longingly, all the love in her heart pouring out to him.

Nicky stiffened slightly as he felt her kiss him back, not a sisterly kiss at all, but strangely he didn't want to pull away and continued to stand still, letting the kiss deepen. She felt so warm and loving in his arms, familiar even; slowly he let his senses take over and pulled her closer. Of its own volition his tongue ran into her mouth and as it met hers, he felt a jolt run through him. She moaned, a deeply sensual sound, as he kissed her with growing ardour, his hands now running up and down her back and round her buttocks to pull her hard against him.

Outside in the hallway, Francis was just about to walk through Nicky's open door when he saw the pair of them kissing passionately. He looked on in silent amazement. This was no sibling kiss, it looked like a lovers' kiss, deep and intense. Nicky's vehement denial about not being able to bring himself to kiss Bella appeared to be hollow words. Somewhat bemused, he turned silently to leave them to it and made his thoughtful way back downstairs to wait with the rest of his family.

Nicky pulled his head back slowly and opened his eyes, looking down into Bella's passion-drugged green ones, the remnants of her earlier tears still visible on her cheeks. Gently, he raised a finger to wipe them away again. "Christ, Sooty, where did that come from?" he whispered, totally stunned at what had just happened.

"Nicky... I... I have something to te... I need to... to confe..." Bella was on the verge of telling him she was *Lionesse* when Benjy, the Duke's still occasional valet, bustled into the room, not realising Nicky wasn't alone.

"Here you are, Your Grace, half a dozen of my special shirts, fresh from the shop; I brought them for the Duke but never mind; good job I was still here, I was just going to leave and go back there for the afternoon. Is there..." he came to an abrupt halt when he saw Bella still in Nicky's arms. "Oh, pardon me, Sir, er... Miss Arabella," and he turned, embarrassed, to hurry out.

"It's all right, Benjy," Nicky called after him, somewhat relieved by the interruption. He looked down at Bella, saying quietly, "Go and wait downstairs, Sooty. I'll be there in a few minutes." He spun her round and gave her a light push in the direction of the door.

The spell broken and the opportunity to tell him missed, Bella sighed and slowly went downstairs to join her family and wait for Nicky to say goodbye to them all.

They were gathered in the cosy, informal family sitting room with its worn, comfortable armchairs and sofas that had been the hub of Granville family life for two decades. The Duchess had decided they needed somewhere private they could all relax, put their feet up on the furniture, to read or gossip or entertain boisterous children without worrying about being untidy, spilling or breaking things. Cat was already weeping, Eddie looked worried and unhappy; the Duke merely stood impassively, an arm around his wife's shoulders, trying to comfort her. Charlie, Bella's studious, introverted, timid little brother, was unfortunately out somewhere in St James's Park with his governess, gone to feed the ducks and get some fresh air apparently, with a handful of footmen frantically trying to find them. Bella came in and went straight into her father's arms, needing to feel his reassuring presence as she grappled with the prospect of the love of her life going off again to an uncertain and very dangerous future, far away.

Finally, having handed his bag and satchel over to Browning to put in the waiting carriage and asking him to pacify the impatient driver, Nicky went into the family room to make his farewells.

Cat went straight up to him and pulled him into a tight, loving, motherly hug, kissing him fervently on both cheeks as tears coursed down her own. He'd always been like another son to her and she'd done her best to mother him after Carlotta, his beloved step-mother, his Madre, had died giving birth to Charlie. "I'll pray for you every day, My Darling," she sobbed. "Please, please be careful and come home to us safe. You're so precious to us all and we love and care for you so much," and she wiped her eyes with an already soaked handkerchief. Nicky hugged and kissed her back and swallowed hard as she turned away, her tears now a veritable river down her face. The Duke came forward.

Francis handed Nicky a folded sheet of paper. "This is a list of places where Reynard is planning to camp over the next few months, certainly until Christmas, I gather. Well, as much as he knows how long he's going to stay in one place, you know what he's like. Remember, he can help you if you need it, or can get an urgent message to me.

You know our methods," Francis then leaned down to whisper in Nicky's ear, "Remember, My Dearest Boy, if you get into trouble, money solves a lot of problems. Most, if you throw enough at them. You MUST believe me when I told you I'd give my entire fortune away, if necessary, to get you home safe. So forget your damn pride. If you need my help, contact Reynard, or just give people my name and direction, whatever it takes if your life is at stake. You're more important to us, all of us, than anything and everything. I have bottomless pockets which mean nothing to me. Money can be replaced, but people, very precious people cannot..."

Nicky looked up at him, tears shimmering in his eyes. "Thank you, Francis," he croaked. "I'll remember. I... I don't know what to say. I never do with you."

"Nothing. No words are necessary. Just come back to us safely because we ARE your family, always have been, always will be." With that, Francis pulled him into a long and emotional hug and kissed his cheeks, French-style. He went then to cuddle a bereft and weeping Cat as Nicky turned to his step-father, also with tears in his eyes.

"Goodbye, Papa," he whispered. "I'm so glad you made it here last night." Nicky hugged the older man tightly with enormous love and affection, the man who'd been the most loving and caring father any son could wish for. The complete antithesis of his real, remote and cold father whom he could barely remember. Eddie kissed Nicky and hugged him back. "Take the greatest care, *Mon Cher Fils*, and I know your Madre's looking out for you from heaven. I feel as if she is watching us sometimes, I really do, her love for us was so strong." The reference to his late step-mother choking them both, as it always did. Her untimely and tragic death had left a deep hole in everyone's lives in the family.

Finally, Nicky turned to Bella, his little Sooty.

They'd been cleaning the chimneys in the former de Mornay family house in Chelsea on the day she'd been born and the five-year-old Nicky had been fascinated by the brushes and black dirt that cascaded down into the fireplaces. 'Chimney-sweep' and 'soot' were new words in his rapidly expanding English vocabulary, so after one look at the new baby with her amazing mop of black hair, inherited from her

Spanish mother, even before she'd been officially named, he'd called her his 'little Sooty' – and it had stuck.

Bella walked straight into Nicky's arms and hugged him like she never wanted to let him go. Once again, heartbroken tears ran down her cheeks in a torrent and she buried her face in his shirt as she sobbed brokenly. "Oh, Sooty," he joked, "look what you've done to my shirt, AGAIN. Can't you use a handkerchief?" The other three laughed quietly, despite their sadness, but Bella just sobbed harder. Nicky put a finger under her chin to lift her face and looked down at her. "I'll be fine, BossyBoots, you'll see. It'll take more than Boney's men to get rid of me. I'll be back and pulling your hair before you know it."

As they stood and looked at each other, a frisson seemed to pass between them and slowly, Nicky bent his head and kissed her. Once again, desire flared unexpectedly and he suddenly pulled her hard into his arms to kiss her deeply and passionately. After a few moments he eased back and the kiss turned tender, gentle and loving. It all seemed so familiar to Nicky that he felt peculiarly uneasy. It was as though he'd kissed her before, even recently. He put it down to this strange feeling that he was kissing his sister, who he knew so well, but who wasn't really his sister after all – and that he'd just kissed her upstairs. Three pairs of curious eyes watched them in rapt fascination, but once again they were interrupted as the butler knocked and came into the room.

Browning coughed. "Excuse me, Your Graces, Baron," he looked at Francis, Cat and Eddie before turning to Nicky. "Your Grace, the coachman is getting rather agitated. I have tried to pacify him but he says you MUST leave."

Nicky looked over at the austere, punctilious man who had run the Duke's London household like an efficient machine for nearly three decades. "Thank you, Browning, tell him I'm just coming." The butler nodded and quietly left the room and Nicky gazed into Bella's tear-filled eyes one final time. "Look after yourself, Sooty, and tell my Granny Granville goodbye for me. Please explain what has happened, hmmm? I was going to see her again before I left, but…" he looked over at Francis as he said that and an already emotional Francis nodded sadly.

"Whatever am I going to do with you?" Nicky whispered to Bella finally and gently tweaked her nose. "I'm sure I simply don't know," and with that enigmatic statement, he bent and kissed her briefly once more, blew a kiss at the other three, then turned and strode purposefully from the room, his heart lurching and bursting with emotion for his family and holding tears back with great difficulty.

They all hurried after him and stood on the drive, waving and crying, as the carriage swept around, through the gates into Berkeley Square and disappeared.

Chapter Seventeen

NEAR SALAMANCE, SPAIN : MID-JULY 1812

Nicky continued to unwind in the quiet spot he'd found by the river bank; he hadn't had a chance to take any sort of proper break from the undercover or liaison missions which had occupied his time previously in Spain, nor the frantic few days in London when he'd only slept for a few hours each night he'd been there. He didn't sleep well on the ships he'd journeyed on to and from England, always being woken by bells, or the tramp of feet on deck, or simply the rolling of the boat in the choppy waters of Biscay or the Channel. Now, he wanted – needed – to be rested and sharp ahead of the dangerous mission he'd been tasked with, knowing his life often depended on his alertness. So he dozed, gradually tanned the whole of his body and, while he lay and relaxed, with time to focus, his mind once more roved over and took stock of the current state of his personal life and in particular, the events of his few days in London.

His main concern was that he'd lost his precious necklace with its little golden lion charm, the only tangible reminder of his former aristocratic life in France and his dead father, whose necklace it had originally been, as well as his father's, grandfather's and great-grandfather's before that... and Nicky missed it. Frequently, he found himself subconsciously reaching for the chain that was no longer there.

It was funny how when he'd worn it, he'd never given the heirloom a moment's thought from one week to the next. But now, it felt like a piece of him was missing. Again, he cursed fate for taking him away from London so unexpectedly quickly, but he also cursed himself for his own carelessness in losing it in the first place.

Now he had the time, space and distance to look at things more dispassionately and analytically, he thought about the necklace. He would actually have bet what money he had there was nothing the matter with the clasp. He never took the thing off, couldn't even remember when he last had, if ever, so was amazed the fastening wasn't permanently tarnished and corroded closed. The chain had been pulled, tugged and caught on clothes over the years and had never given way. That first night he'd spent in *Lionesse's* bed when he'd lost it had been erotic, but not energetic, so why should the catch suddenly come undone or break?

Ergo, *Lionesse* must have released it and taken the chain off him while he was asleep. But why?

He now presumed she had meant to ensure he came back to see her again, but surely after the night they'd spent it was pretty obvious he wouldn't be difficult to persuade, even if he had been cross when he'd left due to being late. And why hide it? Anyone, especially a woman meaning to tease and appropriate it in jest, would surely have just dangled it round their own neck? But she had hidden it, instead of flaunting it at him as he would have expected, given the joke it had become between them. She'd been on the missing list when he'd arrived in a panic on his way out of London at such short notice, so he'd turned her apartment upside down trying to find it. Surely she would simply have left it in a drawer as she'd promised to return it to him before he returned to Spain? He was sure she'd meant it. She certainly didn't need to steal it, she was obviously quite a wealthy woman: her clothes were the finest and followed the latest fashion... and then it suddenly occurred to him she never wore any jewellery of her own, other than a plain wedding ring, which was certainly strange in a woman. Another puzzle. Then he thought about her *Lionesse* outfit and the all-encompassing face mask. They were cleverly and exquisitely designed and made by someone very creative and accomplished.

Her apartment was beautifully, tastefully and expensively decorated with antique French furniture, ornaments and paintings. Everything was the most luxurious, comfortable and best quality. Those little gaming establishments of hers were turning a nice profit, he was sure. He hadn't visited her other one, but had made a few enquiries.

Also, the necklace wasn't really valuable. It was mainly gold, but something else in it tended to make it tarnish when he wasn't at home and kept it clean and polished. However, that had its uses as it passed for a small metal trinket to anyone who looked at it, like other people wore a cross or St Christopher or other religious charm. No one but his family knew or understood the sentimental value it had to him, his one and only link with his roots. Surely, if *Lionesse* wanted to take something more obviously personal or valuable, she would have taken his ring? He looked down on the small circlet on his little finger. That was solid gold and deliberately now tarnished, like he kept the necklace when he was on military duty. It had been a gift from Francis on his seventeenth birthday and carried the crest of Valenciennes: snarling, rampant lions.

As he retreated to a semi-shaded area for a while to have a drink and munch on some bread and local sausage, Nicky's mind wandered off the mystery of *Lionesse* and his missing necklace and thought back to his youth and the Duke. The man had been his hero, from when he, his step-mother and the Duchess had first rescued him as a little boy from the grim Rouen fortress. He'd been as much of a father to him as his step-father at times, especially after his step-mother had died and his Papa turned into a veritable recluse, buried away in grief down on their small country estate. Where Eddie had encouraged the more artistic, practical and academic side of his education, Francis had overseen the more physical and recreational side. From buying and teaching him how to ride his first pony and how to fight, with fists, swords and knives, to lessons in charming people generally, but especially the ladies.

It had been Francis who took him up to London on his seventeenth birthday. They had gone to his tailors for a complete new wardrobe as befitting a Young Man About Town, thence to a little jewellers in Bond Street where he had overseen the design and production of Nicky's little signet ring, so like the one the Duke himself wore all the time. And then finally to the discreet and exclusive little establishment between the fringes of Mayfair and St James, run by the charming Marguerite Beaumont. She had given him over to her bevy of girls, ostensibly for one night's entertainment and education, not that he thought he needed much at the time until he discovered what he didn't know. But with the Duke's encouragement and permission to stay on, Nicky had eventually returned to Firle House, his home, a full week later, much to Francis's mirth and the Duchess's amused disapproval.

After the untimely death of Carlotta, his Madre and step-mother, Nicky's totally distraught and shattered father couldn't face living in the former family home in Chelsea with all its memories of the woman he'd loved so much, so had sold it and retreated to their country home in Arlington, with a nanny for his new baby son. The son his mother had been determined to give her beloved husband, even though she knew another pregnancy would be a risk. Carlotta had been Eddie's world and he was lost without her. She had been the one and only woman who had seen beyond the cripple with the frightening and disfiguring facial scars that the world saw, and fallen in love with the man he really was underneath. Eddie had hibernated and hidden himself away in Arlington to mourn, leaving his sister, Cat, and Francis, to care for the orphaned Bella and Nicky, themselves bereft and lost without their beloved mother. That was why Firle House in Berkeley Square was now their home, along with the rambling Firle Manor, rather than the cosy country house in the depths of the Sussex countryside that their father loved for its peace and seclusion – but it was far too isolated and quiet for his two older children. They wanted and needed lively company, to socialise and enjoy themselves as they grew up and Edouard de Mornay used Firle House as a base when he did make the effort to come to London for business or to visit with his children. It had seemed an unfeeling arrangement, but it had worked. The family were very close, Nicky had been away at Eton a lot, then at Oxford or travelling and Bella needed mothering. They both loved their father and understood how the loss of their mother had affected him and he loved his children, all of them, but was sensible enough to realise Cat and Francis, also the Dowager, Francis's grandmother, could offer Bella and Nicky all the things they needed as they matured and grew older, that he was unable to give them alone.

Nicky admired Francis so much. Again, he bitterly regretted that his unintentional revelation about what had happened in Rouen all those years before, when he was a small boy, had now resulted in Ashcroft poking his nose into Granville affairs. But, as he thought of Ashcroft trying to get to the bottom of the story of French smugglers and gypsies, plus the destruction of the grim Fortress, he smiled to himself. He wished he could be a fly on the wall when Ashcroft tried to get the better of Francis as he sought his information. Perhaps he shouldn't worry after all.

Then, replete, Nicky returned to the sun and as he rolled over like a spit-roast, his mind roved back yet again to Bella, his Sooty. Those last kisses they'd shared had affected him strangely. In one way, they'd made him feel very uncomfortable, as he'd expect from kissing a woman he thought of as a sister. Yet he'd found them strangely arousing and, as everyone kept pointing out, she WASN'T his sister. She was his WIFE if he'd but admit it, an unwanted wife, one he'd actually made love to once, not that he could remember that event, he'd been so drunk and it was so long ago. But that wasn't all. When he'd kissed her she'd felt different, yet so familiar. No longer his little shadow who traipsed round after him constantly, teasing him endlessly and being a perpetual nuisance. She'd turned into a woman, a beautiful woman like her late mother, his beloved step-mother with her Spanish looks. Bella had felt warm, loving, caring and familiar, like a well-worn pair of slippers, but she'd stirred his blood and made him aroused when he'd kissed her goodbye in his bedroom. He shivered.

Thinking of his reaction to Bella, his mind turned yet again to *Lionesse...* and the necklace. She didn't need the money selling it would bring and couldn't possibly have known its sentimental value. So why had she hidden it somewhere so secure? He surmised that being a gaming house, she must have some secure hiding place some- where to keep money, so the obvious conclusion was she'd put it away in there. But why? To anyone it looked just a cheap necklace although he'd given it a quick polish once he'd arrived back in London and had washed and cleaned himself up at the barracks before going out. However, there was absolutely no way she could have appreciated how much it meant to him although he had told her it had some sentimental value. The whole thing was a mystery.

As he lay there, thinking through the puzzle slowly and rationally, Nicky's mind wandered to the woman in the midst of it. Unbidden, images of her luscious body and beguiling smile on that last torrid night together, in that golden lace bit of fluff, yet again tantalised his mind. He lay back on the hot, soft sand and closed his eyes, remembering the look and feel of her as he'd taken her over her desk and then later, the touch of her hands and mouth as they'd roamed over his body, her soft lips and tongue as they'd licked and teased him almost beyond endurance. Memories of how she'd ridden him, carried away on a surging wave of torrid ecstasy and emotion, tormented his brain and he felt himself harden with an overwhelming pulse of hot desire. He threw one arm over his eyes and groaned, but of its own volition his hand strayed down his body to caress and fist his throbbing erection. Once again he remembered the feel of her hands and mouth on him and he continued to pleasure himself until he was lost on a moaning tide of lust and need and, with a sharp cry, he erupted over his sun-baked belly, his heart pounding and his mind on fire.

He lay there, disgusted with himself. It had been years since he'd done something like that. For a woman to take over his emotions and mind to such an extent to make him self-indulge, was both horrifying and demeaning. Whenever he'd felt the need, he'd always managed to find a willing woman, so having to pleasure himself had never really been a necessity and he'd grown up with a tight hold over both his emotions and senses. He controlled his body, certainly not the other way round. He rose and shook himself, throwing his sweating body into the cooling river waters, determined to leave the encampment and find a real woman, one with a face, with whom he could enjoy fornicating properly and normally, to push those tantalising memories of the woman in a mask out of his mind.

The following morning, Nicky inspected himself in the small, tarnished mirror he shared with a host of other officers in the tent where they did their best to wash and shave. He himself hadn't shaved or trimmed his hair since leaving London, knowing what was now in front of him, and his stubbly, bearded face and unkempt, tousled head were now matched by a darkly tanned skin, all over. He'd let his nails grow long and, deliberately, there was some dirt under them. He smiled into the glass – flashing white teeth sparkled in his swarthy face and his golden eyes gleamed under bleached flecked brows, their surrounding lashes still obstinately dark though now with golden tips. He was wearing a simple, half open, bleached cotton peasant shirt, somewhat creased, with tight grubby breeches; as for his boots, his beautiful, new, hand-stitched boots, they had now lost their tassels and the shine was buried under a layer of dried mud and grime.

He didn't look English. He didn't look like an officer or a Gentleman of any nationality. He certainly didn't look like a Duke. He grinned at himself in the mirror. He looked perfect.

Picking up an old, worn leather jacket, a peasant cap, some saddle-bags and a Spanish guitar, he was all you would expect to see in an itinerant musician or casual labourer, working in *tabernas*, markets and fairs – indeed anywhere to earn a few coins to feed himself and provide an occasional roof over his head. He collected an innocuous-looking nag from the quartermaster and quietly rode out of Wellington's camp.

Chapter Eighteen

LONDON: SEPTEMBER 1812

Three months after Nicky's departure, Bella discovered she was indeed expecting a child. Mornings of queasiness and an expanding waistline had finally sent her to the doctor, privately and quietly. As her carriage slowly made its way back to Berkeley Square, she recalled the first night she'd let Nicky make love to *La Lionesse* and vague memories of him asking heatedly if she wanted him to withdraw came back to her. Of course, in her ignorance and passionate abandon, she had neither understood nor cared, no more than she'd thought about it the first time she'd crawled into his bed, but now she had reaped the consequences. Not that she was particularly angry or regretful, indeed quite the contrary... but she was still apprehensive as she realised it would make matters even more difficult between them when Nicky returned. She sighed. She would have to tell her family soon and face the barrage of questions such an announcement would create. She decided she might as well get it over with and resolved to do the deed over dinner that night, as her Papa was currently staying in London on one of his periodic visits.

Three soupspoons stopped in mid-air as she calmly made her news public. Her father was first to react, rising from his chair to limp round and pull her into his arms for an emotional hug, his formerly handsome, now scarred face alight with both astonishment and joy. "Bella, *Ma Petite*, My Darling Girl, I'd absolutely no idea! You and Nicky? By all that's wonderful…"

Bella looked up into his beloved face. "You're going to be a *Grand-père*, Papa," she said softly, watching as his eyes lit up with pleasure. It was so good to see him smile. He hadn't done it a lot, nor laugh much, since her mother had died and she hoped this would be a turning point for him.

Her aunt merely grinned at her at first, knowingly and wickedly, then followed her brother round to hug Bella too and only she noticed the sly wink Cat gave her before she returned to her seat and her soup. "Oh my God, that means I'll be a Great Aunt," she then declared in horror. "I can't deal with that. It sounds like I'm some old grey matron, like Mama or Aunt Harriet," causing everyone to chuckle and Francis to declare he'd now have to go out in the morning and buy her a walking stick, diamond encrusted of course, which made them all laugh again, his predilection for extravagant gifting to his family was well known.

The Duke then merely looked at Bella, an enigmatic expression on his face. "I'm delighted for you both, Bella, though obviously some-what surprised…but there you are." He paused to give her a mean-ingful look and surreptitious tilt of his head, knowing she would get the message and come and see him privately after dinner, "For sure, that'll be a nice surprise for Nicky when he comes home…"

The conversation moved on and Bella told them she thought the birth would be before Easter the following year. Before dinner broke up and she and her aunt left her father and uncle to their port, Bella asked everyone to keep the news to themselves, inasmuch as she didn't want anyone to write it to Nicky. Not that they knew if he received their letters as he never, ever, wrote back. She merely said he would have enough to concern himself with in the Peninsula and she didn't want to worry him. It would be a wonderful surprise when he arrived home. Looking across at her uncle, she told him she was going to visit the ailing Dowager the following day and would give her the good news then. The old lady was now fading rapidly and the family visited daily, always expecting the worst.

In Francis's study later that evening, he came straight to the point. "You're a woman now, Bella, with more sense and knowledge of the real world than a lot of your peers and this is a serious matter, so I'm not going to beat around the bush and be delicate. The child IS Nicky's, isn't it?" He raised an eyebrow at her. This was the ruthless, business-like Duke who ran his affairs including the vast Firle estates and trading empire with a rod of iron and intimidated far more powerful people than she, from Government ministers to City and foreign bankers. The family rarely saw this side of him but now on the receiving end of his penetrating gaze and cutting voice, Bella felt like she was on trial.

Nevertheless, she sat up straight and looked him in the eye. "Yes, Uncle, it IS Nicky's. It could never be anyone else's," she said forcefully.

"Reeeally. Well, I'm not going to say I not completely amazed," Francis said sarcastically and sat back in his chair, his hands steepled under his chin and regarded the young woman seated opposite him. "Nicky sat in that very chair just before he left and vehemently told me he couldn't possibly kiss you, never mind make love to you," Francis leaned forward to make his point, "because you were too much like a sister to him. And now this..." his hand indicated her midriff. "Oh, I saw the pair of you kissing goodbye, AND in his room also by the way, which was a surprise to me, but a child?" His cutting voice turned sarcastic again. "Can you explain it to me, Bella? You see, I happen to know he didn't spend one single night under this roof while he was here in London."

Bella paled, wrung her hands in her lap, then blushed. "Well, you see, Uncle, neither did I," she whispered and tried to explain without going into too much detail. "We were...we were in my apartment at *Le Lion d'Or*."

"Reeeally?" said Francis witheringly again. He sounded so much like his formidable grandmother in her prime, he would have laughed if he wasn't so curious as to what had happened.

"Er...yes. You see, he came there with some regimental friends as soon as he arrived in London, before he came home to see us here, me, the family," she hesitated a moment. "Oh, I don't think it was intentional, he just got caught up having a few drinks out on the Town with some old military friends on the spur of the moment, they were home on sick leave, and he found himself at the *Le Lion d'Or* with them... and, well, one thing led to another."

"I see," Francis said quietly, "and...?"

"Well...well...we played cards... and..."

"Yes, Bella...and?"

"Oh, I can't tell you, Uncle, it's much too embarrassing. But you have to believe me, the child, it IS Nicky's."

"I'm sure it is, Puss," Francis said dispassionately. "You may be a crafty and clever little minx, but you're no liar, nor a trollop. I also find it hard to believe you'd have an affair with anyone else when you're moving heaven and earth to keep your marriage to Nicky intact. I know, we all do, how much you care, how much you love him. You do, don't you?" it was really more a statement than a question.

"Yes, Uncle, very much," she muttered. "I can't bear the thought of losing him." Her big green eyes shone with tears as they looked into her uncle's narrowed sky-blue ones.

"What did you do, Bella? He was dead drunk the last time, was it the same this time? You got away with it once, second time not so lucky, eh?"

Bella looked at the Duke and blushed even more, then hung her head and shook it.

"Oh for heaven's sake, I don't want the details. I just need to understand what's going on. He's going to be furious when he comes home, isn't he?"

"Yes," she whispered.

"So what happened? Are you sure he wasn't drunk? How did you manage it?"

"I... I... " she dithered.

"Come on, out with it, Bella, for heaven's sake. You're no milk-and-water Miss and you and I have always been straight and forthright with each other, even if the subject matter of our conversations hasn't stretched quite as far as fornicating," Francis tutted.

"I had my lion mask on, with the wig... you've seen them," she stuttered. "You know, we agreed I should keep my identity secret at the Clubs, so... he... he... he didn't recognise me. He didn't know who I was..." she whispered in a strangled voice Francis could barely hear.

"OH. MY. GOD!" stuttered Francis, sitting back in his chair, more than somewhat stunned.

"It's been almost a year since he was last home, which wasn't for long, and before that, it was years, so he doesn't know me very well now I've grown up a bit more and matured. I think he still pictures me with pigtails and freckles half the time."

"I'll be damned," Francis swore as he realised what she was trying to say. "He doesn't even know he's been to bed with you, does he? He thinks it was someone else?"

Bella nodded, shamefaced, but then looked at Francis pleadingly, "Oh, Uncle," she cried softly, "I didn't mean for it to happen, truly I didn't. He just turned up that night and I couldn't believe it was him. I hadn't seen him for a year... and there he was... and..."

"And...?" Francis prompted softly.

"We played cards, we flirted. I... I... don't know what came over me, but he was so funny, so charming, we got on so well... and... and... I wanted him so much," she finally whispered as she hung her head. "Then we went up to my apartment... and... and... and I... we..."

Francis held up a hand, "Spare me the rest, Bella," he shook his head. "So, how many times did this happen?" He paused as he looked at her guilty red face. "Oh, dear God!" his eyes widened as he realised, asking slowly, "Every night? He was with YOU? And you never said anything? You never told him?" Francis was staggered. "But I don't understand, he's not a fool. He's grown up with you for God's sake – and you were in bed together, well I assume you must have gone to bed at some point? How didn't he recognise you?"

Bella nodded and reddened even more, her hand now twisting the skirt of her dress. "I had my mask and wig on," she whispered. "I was going to tell him... but..."

"You kept that fancy dress on all the time? All night?" Francis was bemused now. He'd seen her outfit and tried to imagine making love to a woman with that wig and fancy mask on, complete with whiskers and all the other furry lion's face decorations. It was meant to be eye-catching and amusing and it didn't lend itself to a very intimate form of lovemaking... which left far more creative options. Nicky was a womaniser, a ladies' man *par excellence*, but Bella? He looked at her sitting, blushing, opposite him. Apart from that one night, the debacle with Nicky the previous year, she hadn't any other experience, she'd just admitted it. And every night? Surely Nicky would want to kiss her? Francis thought for a moment about the outfit Bella had created with the help of Benjy, his sometime valet, now tailor to the discerning of the Ton and occasional modiste to select aristocratic or wealthy ladies who knew about and coveted his skills in producing beautiful and striking gowns. The mask covered virtually all of her face as they wanted to be sure no one from the Ton would recognise her. Francis smiled to himself. He'd stake his life the Nicky he knew would definitely NOT spend four nights with a woman without kissing her. There had to be more to this, he decided.

Francis was intrigued and getting very amused now, so curiously he asked again, "Why didn't he recognise you, Bella? He surely kissed you?" he kept his face serious and his expression completely deadpan, not without difficulty.

"I... er... we... er... yes," she whispered. "Of course he kissed me."

"How did he manage that with your mask, Bella?" Francis pushed.

It was like being a fish caught on a hook, not being able to wriggle off. Bella turned an even darker shade of beetroot and finally blurted out, "I took it off, my wig also, but only after I'd blindfolded him. That's why he doesn't know it was me." It burst out in a strangled whisper.

Francis looked at the hideously embarrassed young woman opposite him and burst out into a shout of disbelieving laughter. "WHAAAAT?!" he guffawed, "You absolute witch. How the hell did you manage to persuade him to allow that? Every night?" He literally doubled up in mirth, completely beside himself with laughter at the visions in his head. "Bella, My Darling, I always knew you were an extremely clever girl, but you obviously have hidden depths even I never suspected!" He continued to laugh, now holding his side where a stitch had formed. "Oh my God, poor Nicky, he's going to want to kill you, Bella, that's for sure."

"I know, Uncle. I was going to tell him, really I was. I thought that perhaps once he realised it was me and that I wasn't some little freckle-faced hoyden any more – and that I am definitely NOT his sister, he might... well he might accept me as his wife," she finally stated sadly. "But then he had to leave again so suddenly and I was here, not at *Le Lion d'Or*, so I never had the opportunity. I was going to tell him the day he left, when you saw us in his bedroom, but Benjy came in and... and... then the moment was lost and off he went in such a rush." She sighed, "I've got his necklace too," she whispered, pulling it out of the front of her dress where she now wore it.

"GOOD. GOD. ALMIGHTY!" Francis was really stunned now. "How the HELL did you manage to get that off him? I've never known him to remove it since he was five," he said slowly, "and even then, only when your father replaced his temporary short chain with the original long one for when he got bigger. It was like it was forged closed around his neck." He was almost in disbelief.

"I took it off him that first night while he was still asleep; he thought the catch broke in bed," she blushed again. "I thought if I had it, it would ensure he'd come and see me again the following night as I knew he'd want it back. It became something of a joke between us, but now he's gone off without it and I know what it means to him," she choked. "Oh, Uncle Francis, he went to my apartment before he left. He tore the place apart looking for it because I wasn't there to give it back to him. It was in the safe in the fireplace mantel." Tears started to roll down her face, "I feel so guilty and it's such a mess. I never meant this to happen." Then she threw herself on to his lap, into his arms and wept copiously, just like she had at times when she was a little girl.

"Oh, Bella, Sweetheart, don't cry, Puss. What's done is done," Francis hugged her comfortingly. "People do silly things when they're in love. I know, I remember, I did my fair share," and he smiled at her as he patted her cheek. "At least his necklace is safe. But you're right, it is a mess," he sighed as he pulled a handkerchief out of his pocket and dabbed her eyes before handing it over for her to blow her nose, nois-ily. He couldn't repress a grin though, "If that isn't the funniest story

I've heard in a long time," he chuckled again. "I can't wait to see Nicky's face when he comes back and finds out he's going to be a father, or he might well be one by then. He's going to be fit to be tied. I think we'd best evacuate the house as he's going to explode when he realises what you've done, what you did, let alone that the woman who made him play those games is you."

Bella gave a shaky laugh. "I know. Ah, um, could you tell him first, Uncle? He won't get so angry with you…" she looked at him pleadingly.

"Oh no I won't," Francis grinned at her again. "You got yourself into this pickle, you deal with the consequences."

"Oh Lord," she sighed. "I suppose I'd better tell Aunt Cat too. She'll have to know something about it or she won't understand what on earth is going on."

"I tell you what," chuckled Francis, "I'll tell her."

"You won't tell her EVERYTHING, will you? Please, I don't know how I'll face her."

Francis was beside himself with amusement. He knew he'd have to tell every detail to his wife who would no doubt find the whole story as hilarious and outrageous as he had. "You'll get over it, Puss. If I don't tell her, she won't understand. I certainly couldn't make it out until you explained EVERYTHING to me." He gave her a wicked look. "Come now, Sweetheart," he pushed her off his knee and stood up next to her, putting a comforting arm around her shoulders, "we won't have to worry about all this for a while anyway. Nicky's only been gone a few weeks and it's going to be quite a long time before we see him again, I'm afraid."

"Have you heard anything yet, Uncle?" Bella looked up into his now serious face.

Francis shook his head. "No, Puss, but it's too soon for news. You know I'll tell you as soon as I hear anything. I promise. Anyway," he sighed, "at least I can consign all those wretched annulment and divorce papers into the fire. That's one less job I'll have to sort out."

"Oh, Uncle," Bella leaned up to kiss his cheek, "I've told you before, I don't know what we'd do without you." She put her hand through his arm as they made their way out of his study, back to join her father and aunt in the sitting room. As they went out through the doorway, Bella looked up at Francis. "I'm going round to see Great Aunt Elizabeth tomorrow afternoon, she's getting frailer every day I see her," Bella paused as she knew how upset everyone was about the old lady, especially her uncle. She knew it was only a matter of time now before his grandmother passed away, perhaps just days. "I'm sure she'll be over the moon when I tell her Nicky is going to be a father, it will cheer her no end. You know how she dotes on him."

Francis patted her cheek, "Thank you, Sweetheart, you've been so good, going to see her so frequently, especially now you have your... ah... 'little business' to run," he winked at her and smiled sadly. "But yes, she'll be delighted to see you and to hear your news." He sighed, "She's always been quite adamant you and Nicky are a perfect match and she'd do anything to keep you together. So, your little, er, affaire, three months ago, has played right into her scheming hands." Bella giggled. "Actually, she'll be thrilled. She'll be giving you lists of baby names and all sorts of instructions if I know her, it'll make her day." Bella was glad to see her uncle smile at the thought as they walked into the sitting room together.

Chapter Nineteen

Bella sat by the ornate bed, holding a weak, wrinkled hand in hers. "So, he's going to be a father, Auntie," she said softly, watching as the fading blue eyes momentarily lit up with pleasure. "What do you think he'll make of that?" Bella grinned at the old lady, propped up on piles of white lace frilled pillows in her sunny bedroom the following afternoon.

The frail old woman coughed, delicately spewing small droplets of blood into the white handkerchief she held to her thin, bloodless lips. "It'll be the making of him," she whispered hoarsely. "It's the most wonderful news, just what he needs, to have his own family at last. He'll be ecstatic, when he comes to terms with what he's created," but she gave Bella a meaningful look as she answered her in throaty gasps.

Bella smiled sadly at the Dowager, realising she was weaker than ever. "That's the problem, Auntie, it's going to be a shock to him. He won't be expecting it and I don't know how he'll react; probably strangle me, if I know Nicky."

The Dowager was well aware of the strange relationship between Nicky and Bella, although, as with all the family, she knew Bella loved the young rogue to distraction, she always had; a young girl's crush had developed and matured into something much stronger as the years had passed. Bella had often confided in the old woman, finding her an easy and wise outlet for the worries and concerns that she couldn't talk about elsewhere, even to her outrageous Aunt Cat. The Dowager knew Nicky well and she loved him, Bella knew, so she seemed to understand the angst and confusion Bella had so often felt about her relationship with him.

"Reeeeally? What have you done now, You Little Minx," she asked softly, smiling at the young girl. "Come along, tell Auntie 'Lizbeth. I just know by the look on your face it's something truly dreadful this time."

So, with a bit of encouragement from the older woman, the whole sorry story finally came out for a second time. The Dowager had not known about *Le Lion d'Or*, nor its sister club, as she'd been so ill and Bella hadn't wanted to distress her in case she didn't approve. But, as she should have known, the old lady cackled and coughed with laughter when she heard her grandson had put up the money to get them started. Her amusement grew further when Bella told her both establishments were in Nicky's name as a means to generate some income which he would accept, even if, at the moment, he knew nothing about it. When she heard the two gaming houses were generating quite some profit, the business-minded Dowager laughed even more. But when, haltingly, Bella finally told her about how she'd seduced Nicky, dressed as *La Lionesse*, the old lady had such a fit of hysterical mirth, just like Francis when Bella had told him, she couldn't stop coughing and Bella had to support her in her arms as she violently spewed blood into her handkerchief. "Oh Auntie, I knew I shouldn't have told you, I never meant for you to get so exercised," Bella muttered, horrified.

"Nonsense," the old lady whispered as she caught her breath, "it's the best tonic I could have had, far better than those vile medicines the doctors make me swallow. Gaming saloons and lions? Fancy dressed staff? What a marvellous idea! Oh, you wicked girl! Oh, my poor Nicky! Whatever next? Blindfolded? It's too funny for words, I had no idea you had it in you. How disgraceful is that and how tantalising and naughty... and now a baby! You've got him! Hah! CAPITAL!" She slapped the coverlet weakly, she was so entertained. "I couldn't have devised a better plot m'self!" Her dull eyes lit up with irrepressible humour as she grinned from ear to ear. Then she continued, quite energised, "When I discovered my wretched grandson had spent most of his disreputable youth leading a double life as a smuggler and sometime pirate, I thought I'd heard it all, but now to find out YOU, a girl of barely twenty-two, runs two of London's newest gaming clubs, and he... he's put up the money and it's all in Nicky's name... oh that's too rich." She looked artfully at Bella, "What's more, you're making a nice little profit, My Gel... and I'd expect nothing less! Gambling houses are a licence to print money, but of course I don't need to tell YOU that!"

Bella grinned and nodded her head. "Of course, Auntie, I'm not my father's daughter for nothing, nor the niece of the ruthless Duke of Firle and great niece of the simply amazing Dowager Duchess of Firle. What would you have me do, open a couple of hat shops?" The pair of them giggled companionably. Bella was relieved and happy that notwithstanding her personal concerns about Nicky's reaction, she'd regally entertained the old lady and made her laugh so much, despite the coughing.

But as they calmed down and Bella went back to holding the frail hand, a sad and concerned expression took over her face again. "Oh Auntie, he's going to be so angry. I'm worried he'll just up and run away and never come back; you know how stupid he can be when he gets into a real strop about something. He threatened to go to the Americas, you know. I don't know what to do!" Finally, two frightened tears plopped down on her cheek, followed by another and another. This was something she hadn't revealed to her uncle the previous evening.

"Now you listen to me, My Gel, you must never give up on him," the old lady whispered, "NEVER! You hear me?!" She gripped Bella's hand, "I'm sure deep down he loves you, he just needs to come round to seeing you the right way," she tutted. "These demnable wars, taking good men away for years at a time. First in the Americas, now here in Europe and God knows what's going on in India. It's interminable. Nicky hasn't spent enough time at home, that's why he still sees you as a little sister." She shook her head, "But he cares for you deeply, I know he does, so you MUST persevere. You've got the baby now," she pulled

Bella towards her and looked deep into her eyes, "so don't give up. If you truly love him, wherever he goes, go after him. He's quite single-minded but needs you, Bella, he just doesn't realise it. You must follow your heart or you'll never forgive yourself if you let him get away, you'll regret it for the rest of your life and never be truly happy…" she leaned back on her pillows, breathing shallowly, a faraway look in her eyes. Bella just sat patiently and let her rest.

After a while, the old woman stirred and tried to sit up, a determined light seeming to appear in her faded blue eyes. "Now then, Bella, I've decided. I want to tell you a story. My time is nearly up, we all know that, so it's about time. I had thought to tell Cat, but you're the right one to say this to, especially now with your worries about Nicky, so just sit and listen to me." Then, in a halting, whispery voice Elizabeth Granville began to speak…

"Once upon a time, in the reign of the previous King George, there lived a bright young gel. She was tall and striking with dark hair and blue eyes and she was considered the beauty of her family as none of the rest looked like her, nor had her intelligence; she took after a distant grandmother and her line, apparently. They were a well-connected family, but just minor nobility themselves, a simple baronetcy. Unfortunately, the father was something of a wastrel and reckless gambler and not a very competent manager of his lands, so it wasn't long before the family coffers were empty and he found himself with his estates to let and a wife, son and four daughters to look after. His and the family's great hope, was that the eldest daughter should go to London and make a brilliant match. A wealthy husband with a good title to boot, so she could save the family and launch her sisters so they, too, could find good husbands. Therefore, with the last of the family money which they'd begged and borrowed, at the age of just seventeen she was sent to London and launched into Society. She made quite a stir in the Ton and soon had several eligible bachelors chasing after her, as well as plenty of suitors who weren't either rich or noble enough for consideration. That all of them bored her to tears and weren't in the least attractive to her was unfortunate, but she knew her duty and would have to make up her mind by the end of the Season when she turned eighteen.

"Then, one day, she was walking down Bond Street, gazing into shop windows and literally bumped into A Man. He simply took her breath away. He was the most handsome devil she'd ever seen. Very tall, taller than most men, broad-shouldered, thick, black, wavy hair and a wicked smile that made her heart beat faster just to look at him. But it was his eyes that were his most compelling feature. They were big, startling sky-blue eyes surrounded by thick black lashes. Any woman would die to have eyes like that..."

Bella gasped, it sounded just like a description of her Uncle Francis.

"Well, that was it, smitten, love at first sight," sighed the Dowager. "A complete *coup de foudre* – and it seemed like the feeling was mutual. However, there was, not surprisingly, A Problem. The handsome young man was the younger son of a Scottish Earl who had lost virtually everything except his life in the first Jacobite uprising in 1715. The vast majority of his extended lands and holdings had been confiscated and he was lucky to come out of the mess alive. The family lived in some mouldering old castle on the banks of a loch in the distant Highlands, surrounded by a tiny estate with a remote hamlet at its centre and a handful of tenants. With no prospect of any future there, the enterprising younger son had come south to seek his fortune, leaving his older brother at home to look after their ailing father and inherit what was left when the old man died, to make what he could of it. The young man's name was Alexander. Lord Alexander Kinross, the son of the Earl of Invermory."

"The pair were infatuated with each other and met wherever and whenever they could, if the young gel could sneak away from her mother, who fortunately was not a very good chaperone; certainly no match for a clever young girl in love who wanted to be anywhere but boring recitals, soirées or dinners where her ardent young lover was not present."

Bella rolled her eyes, completely riveted by the tale. "Auntie? Ooooh, you mean you and him? You... you were lovers? Proper lovers?" she whispered, taken aback.

The Dowager smiled and sighed, "Of course, I couldn't resist him. I was completely overwhelmed and in love and he, naturally, made everyone else I met pale by comparison; as if they weren't already dull and boring enough," she sighed as she paused to reflect. "He was so handsome, so charming, so funny, everything was a joke to him. He could charm the birds off the trees with his Scottish accent, no lady was immune, certainly not me, and when he kissed me I was lost... every time," she sighed again. "One look and my heart used to thump; when he touched me, my skin burned; I simply couldn't resist him, it was love and lust combined, intense and passionate. He was quite some lover, even in my innocence I realised that, so I was over-whelmed every time we escaped to be together, especially as he seemed insatiable and as desirous of me as I was of him."

"So what happened?" asked Bella, almost speechless and completely fascinated as she tried to imagine the indomitable and sometimes terrifying old lady as a young woman in love and in the throes of a torrid, passionate and illicit *affaire*. Her mind almost boggled. The Dowager paused to cough again and when she'd recov-ered, after a few sips of water which Bella help her to drink with diffi-culty, she continued with her story.

"Well, the Season was coming to a close and the young gel had to make a decision about one of her suitors as there was no more money for another Season and the situation was getting critical. She had, by this time, been introduced to the Duke of Firle. Being middle-aged, he was a somewhat older man than most of her admirers and a long-time bachelor; he was reasonably wealthy, not as wealthy as some of the other comparable titled peers, but he was still much sought after by matchmaking mamas due to his ducal title which went back for centuries. Unfortunately, he was also rather pompous and extremely dull and boring, not terribly attractive and far too fond of the bottle. However, after years of avoiding matrimony, he'd taken a fancy to the striking young debutante and knew he needed to take a wife soon to get an heir to his title as he only had a younger brother who wasn't married yet either. The gel's mother was extremely hopeful he would make her an offer, despite her lack of a dowry, another problem not in her favour.

In the meantime, away from the social whirl of the Ton, Alexander had decided there was nothing for him here in England and had decided to go to the Americas and seek his fortune there. He'd introduced the young gel to a group of his Scottish friends; all like him, penniless, but full of ideas and ambition. They, too, had left Scotland and come to London to make their way in the world, some just needing money to invest to set up businesses, others to buy or develop property as London was growing apace; or some, like Alexander, deciding to go abroad to seek their fortunes there, either east or west. He and some of these friends announced they were going to sail west, to the Carolinas shortly, in a mere few weeks, it being far better and safer to sail across the Atlantic in the summer than the winter. The young gel was devastated and completely torn. Alex, as she called him, begged her to go with him. He was a good man, even if he was something of a rogue with an eye for the ladies, but he wanted to marry and make an honest woman of her because he loved her and wanted to take her away to make a new life with him in the New World. He said it wasn't fair she should have to sacrifice herself for the benefit of her family, especially her wastrel father and useless siblings. Alex was a strong, determined, single-minded man and was frustrated with her dithering; regrettably, he had little sympathy with her situation even though it was the way of things, so he told her to stand up for herself or she'd regret it. He said she only had one life and she should make the best of it. That was why he'd left Scotland; there was nothing there for him and he wasn't going to waste his life in the back of beyond, impoverished and listening to his father and others ramble on about the Stuarts and what might have been, The future looked potentially worse for the clans if young Charles Edward Stuart this time had another go at rebelling against the English and claiming the throne from George – and of course, he was proved right, as you know that's what eventually happened in 1745, but that's another story. In the meantime, the young gel realised she was going to have his child..."

Bella gasped, her mouth opening in a big O. "She was in a terrible state and simply didn't know what to do. She was only just turned eighteen and had led a relatively quiet existence in the country so was a bit naïve in some ways and had no one to give her any advice in her predicament, so she was completely devastated. Although she was quite headstrong personally and far more intelligent than her siblings and female peers, she had always been very dutiful and her family meant a great deal to her. She couldn't contemplate going away rather than marry one of her suitors. That would mean her father would lose everything, their house and what was left of the estate, with also the probability he would end up in Debtors' Prison, leaving her mother and younger siblings destitute. BUT, on the other hand, she loved Alex desperately and was going to have his child. When she told him, he went mad and threatened to go and see her father and demand she marry him straight away. They had the most terrible argument. She told him she simply couldn't go away with him as her family's predicament would always be on her conscience and she didn't think she could be happy and live with the knowledge that they would very probably be in trouble without her.

The Dowager coughed again and managed to sip some more water. Bella was fascinated. "The pair argued endlessly and finally, Alex ran out of patience as his ship was due to sail and he couldn't wait any longer. So, he left by himself and the young gel promised she would consider running away to join him once she had married and saved her family situation, which was very silly as that would have caused a terrible scandal, but she simply wasn't thinking straight, she was so much in love and being pulled two ways, virtually torn in half. However, apart from all that trauma, she was still pregnant. Finally, she woke up to reality and applied her brain to her problem with the result seeing her set out to seduce the boring Duke of Firle. He didn't know what had hit him as the innocent young gel had learned a lot from her experienced Scottish lover, and ensured the man was so drunk when they first did the deed he never realised she wasn't still a virgin; so they married shortly after at the end of the Season because she told him he had got her with child. She became the Duchess of Firle and with the settlement he received from the Duke on the occasion, her father was able to pay off most of his pressing debts and the family was saved."

"Oh my Lord," whispered Bella, totally gripped by the tale.

"Once Alex had left, as I said, the young gel got her head in order and grew up very quickly, well she simply had to. Being quite clever and conniving, as well as desperate, she pretended to be sick and delicate during most of her pregnancy, so it was no surprise when she gave birth much earlier than expected, and she had a son. The Duke was delighted and, thankfully for the new Duchess, the babe appeared to take after her family, so no one was any the wiser as he hadn't inherited his real father's dark colouring and looks. But he was still her and Alex's son and the prospect of running away and abandoning him was unthinkable to her. Also, for some perverse reason she couldn't quite explain to herself, she didn't want to deny him the ducal inheritance he now stood to gain, albeit untruthfully and illegitimately, so taking him with her was also out of the question. It was A Mess and she was such a misguided fool. Meanwhile, the Duke had continued with his drinking and found it more and more difficult to service his young wife in bed to get a spare to the heir and she soon realised she'd only really been a passing fancy to him. He was more in love with the bottle than his wife or any woman. They'd only been married a couple of years but now he'd done his duty, the Duke became less and less bothered about a 'spare' and returned to his bachelor existence and his indulgence in port and brandy with his cronies at his club; it therefore seemed there would be no further children to inherit. If there'd been a second son, the girl had thought she and Alex's son could disappear together, which was one of the fairy-tale plans she dreamed about and concocted as she slept alone and yearned for her lost lover over in the Americas."

Bella sat there, completely stunned. The Dowager had paused to rest for a few minutes and Bella tried to take in the enormity of the story that was unravelling. Stirring herself again, the old lady continued:

"And then, one day, not long after, probably due to the alcohol, the Duke had a seizure. It didn't kill him, but he lost a lot of his faculties and he became an invalid. The Duchess, meanwhile, gradually took over much of the running of the estates. Having now matured somewhat and become quite hard-hearted from losing the love of her life, let alone married to a man who was a boor and totally uninterested in her or their child, she found herself fascinated by their management. The Duke's younger brother was not much different to his older sibling and had little interest in estate management. He was also no match for his young, intelligent sister-in-law who considered him an idiot of the first water.

So, other than the care of her young son, since she was not of a frivolous disposition and never had been interested in sewing, sketching or music, and all the usual things young women apparently should do, the young Duchess found herself bored, frustrated and lonely. She therefore became increasingly involved in the running of the Firle lands and holdings. Just like the Duke's brother, the bailiffs and managers employed by the Duke were a fairly useless and lazy bunch of individuals and they also were no match for a clever and now quite assertive and bitter young woman. So they took their orders and did as they were told and were gradually replaced by more efficient individuals she appointed personally. Over time, the estates were reinvigorated and had never been so well managed. Having found she had a real interest in business matters, the young woman now looked at ways to improve the family income. Everyone had assumed the Duke was wealthy – up to a point he was, or had been – but with lack of interest except in too much alcohol and gambling, matters had been allowed to slide until she'd taken control. She kept a low profile – well, she was a woman and, of course, trade was frowned upon in the aristocracy.

However, she remembered the young men she'd been introduced to a few years previously by Alex. Now, having monies at her disposal, she got in touch with some of them and quietly invested in their enterprises. And more. When they went overseas, they represented her interests and she invested further. Some went to the West Indies where she bought sugar plantations and cotton and tobacco plantations in the southern American states. Some went east and she bought a small fleet of ships to trade in the spices and goods imported from and exported overseas by England's growing empire in India and the tropics. She invested in property in London and in the growing industries in the north where factories and mills were springing up. She bought shares in mines to provide the fuel needed to run them and heat the homes of the population across the country, or if she could, she eventually took over the mines altogether. Wherever she saw the chance of a profit, she invested and frequently put in more efficient management. The more she did, the more successful she became. It was as if everything she touched was a triumph and she was completely obsessed with it; well, she had nothing else in her life apart from her son.

Through her title and connections, she made it her business to be introduced to the rich, the powerful and the influential in the land. Government advisors and ministers; City merchants and bankers; successful men in trade and newspaper or gossip sheet publishers. Although it was frowned upon for the aristocracy to go into anything commercial, she didn't care. In any case, no one thought a mere woman, a Duchess even, would do such an odd thing. Most thought she was simply a pleasant and charming titled lady to talk to and she was still something of a beauty, so quite a few men chased after her for an *affaire*; she used them quite ruthlessly if they had any value to her, as her heart was dead and buried somewhere in the southern states of the Americas and no man made her feel what she'd had with her lost Scottish love. But apart from that, she listened and heard business deals being discussed over dinner parties and at receptions. Many men wondered how they suddenly lost contracts by being undercut, or properties because they were outbid. The Duke became more and more incapacitated and finally passed away from another seizure, leaving his young son to inherit the title. The boy was still being tutored, so his mother continued to run matters until he reached his majority and after that he went off on the Grand Tour. However, and much to her regret and disappointment, the boy wasn't like his mother, nor his real father, more like his maternal grandfather. He had no interest in or head for business, so even when he came of age, he simply left matters to his mother to run and did exactly as he was told. He was sent on the Grand Tour simply because his mother was worried he'd fall in with the wrong crowd and start to gamble like his maternal grandfather or drink like his supposed father."

"Oh my God, Auntie," Bella was now sitting with her mouth half open, listening to the history of her Granville relations.

"Over the years, the Duchess became something of a fearsome and remote individual. She'd subsumed all her feelings and energies into building up the Firle title and estate for the benefit of her son, Alex's son, but he was a sore disappointment to her. Ironically, which of course had made her even more bitter, Alex had, as he predicted, made a fortune for himself in the Americas. She'd watched him from afar, unable to help herself. His father had died and so, eventually, had his elder brother who had never got round to getting married, so, even more ironically, he was now the Earl of Invermory and a very rich, self-made man. He'd given up waiting for her years before and had married, now with a family of his own. She continued to follow his endeavours and the bitterness had eaten inside her like a canker, making her seem cold and distant and hard. But it was the only way she knew how to deal with the deep-rooted sadness, anger and remorse over the situation she had made for herself. Her son cared little for the estates or business and spent most of his time at his club, so the Duchess found him a complaisant, vacuous wife from a good family, who eventually did her wifely duty and, after several daughters, finally bore him a son."

"Uncle Francis…" Bella whispered to herself.

"The Duchess took one look at the baby and knew he was going to be the spit of his real grandfather. Black hair and big sky-blue eyes. He was called Francis – many Dukes of Firle had been called Francis apparently – but she insisted his second name be Alexander and everyone assumed he inherited his colouring from her. As he grew, only she could see he was a complete replica of his real grandfather, not only in stature and outrageous good looks, but in temperament and personality too. The wicked smile, the charm, the sense of humour and adventurous, determined spirit. From her, he had inherited a strong-minded and resolute disposition and a serious head for business, not that his grandfather hadn't also obviously had one, having made his own entrepreneurial fortune. The boy's mother had no further children. The little gels looked and acted just like their mother's side of the family, so she was more interested in them and female fripperies, not to mention endless imagined ailments, than dealing with a wild, disobedient and roguish little boy who was at times completely uncontrollable, except by the Dowager Duchess as she now was. His mother also became consumptive and frail, even though her health problems were imagined most of the time, which meant as the boy and his sisters grew older, she took to spending a few months overseas in warmer climes in winter, to suit her health. Her silly daughters were a harmless, brainless lot and quite well looked after by a set of governesses and tutors, in her absence, overseen by the Dowager. The mischievous and headstrong boy was sent off to school to get him out of everyone's hair and instil some discipline in him, a major failure for the most part. The Duchess therefore got into the habit of spending the spring and summer in England and the rest of the year abroad and, as her children grew, the longer time she spent away. She returned periodically for some winters to launch her daughters in a Season as soon as they were decently old enough and managed to find them suitable titled, wealthy husbands as quickly as possible. Then, having fulfilled her duty, she retired abroad more or less permanently to live in the relaxing ex-patriate community in southern Italy, until she passed away a few years ago.

"While the Duke spent his life in his club, drinking and gambling to his heart's content and the girls were looked after by governesses and their mother when she was at home, or not apparently suffering from some mysterious ailment or another, the Dowager became both mother and father to the growing boy and a strong bond was forged between them. He resolutely refused to bow to her commands and frequently did exactly as he wanted or the exact opposite of what she'd ordered, but she loved him for it and every time she looked at him he reminded her of the man she'd lost, especially once he'd grown into manhood and inherited the title from his father. That man had a seizure in his club one day, too much port and brandy, just like his father, except his heart attack killed him on the spot, so the new Duke inherited when he was only in his mid-twenties."

Tired by her long narrative, the Dowager gripped Bella's hand, "However, that's all a bit irrelevant. More important – in fact, the moral of my tale – is that there wasn't a day went by when that woman didn't bitterly regret the decision she'd made not to go with the man she loved. He'd warned her she'd regret it and he was absolutely right. In the end, it had all been for nothing. Her father gambled away his estate eventually and did everyone a favour and shot himself; her brother joined the army and settled permanently in India to work for some maharajah when he finished his service and retired with a nice pension and an Indian mistress, but died soon after of some tropical disease; the remaining daughters had all married before their father's death with little assistance needed from the new Duchess of Firle, so her mother went to live with one of them when she was widowed and eventually passed away after a few years.

"In the meantime, Alex had made his fortune and inherited a title. The terrible irony of it all never left her. Her life had been cold and empty and although she'd had the odd *affaire* now and then to try and escape her loneliness, her heart had never been in it and as she'd suspected, no man could compare to her first love and lover. She'd made the Firle fortune what it was, but had realised money was nothing without the love of a husband or family with whom to share it. They were what was important in life, and when one does finds true love, one should never throw it away. Her one delight had been that her beloved grandson had done the right thing and married for love, a deep and all-consuming, passionate love, to a beautiful, headstrong, intelligent woman who made a wonderful Duchess and he now had a happy and close family. Finally, she herself had come to love her grandson's extended family of in-laws, especially the little boy they had rescued and adopted from France at the start of the Revolution. She identified with and understood his self-possession and struggle to make something of his life, despite its terrible beginnings and the effect it had had upon him as he grew up; just like the young girl had done – very similar, in some ways, after she made the wrong decision in hers...and the man she'd really loved had also done the same..."

The old lady lay back on her pillows, eyes closed, still gripping Bella's hand. Bella simply sat immobile and speechless, completely aghast at what she'd heard as its implications sunk in.

"Does Uncle Francis know?" she finally whispered.

"No, My Sweet," the old lady whispered back, "you're the first living soul I've told." Bella gasped. "I was going to tell him, but he's so proud of the Firle name, his title and position now, despite all his moaning and groaning to the contrary, I was terrified if I told him he'd just up and walk away from it, go back to being a smuggler or sail to the Americas and abandon everything I worked so hard to achieve for the family, everything I'd sacrificed my life for. Despite his rather disgraceful youth, he's a very upstanding man now, a respected pillar of the Establishment, even though he does have his moments now and again…"

"Good God!" Bella muttered, still aghast.

"As I said, I had thought to tell Cat, a few months ago, as I suspect she'd understand why I did what I did, but I never got round to it somehow, the moment was never right. But the Granville family is strong now, new blood, Alex and Rennie, Gerard and Philip, they're strong boys, like their father and a bit wild like their mother who I think they take after, so the Firle Dukedom will go from strength to strength. And now there is Elizabeth…" with a big effort she pulled herself up again and leaned towards Bella waving a frail hand in front of her, waggling her little finger and pulling at the ring on it.

"You see this," she twirled the small gold ring on her finger and, as Bella leaned down to look at it more closely, seeing a worn and faded coat of arms, the hoarse voice whispered, "I've never taken it off from the day he gave it me, other than to have it made smaller to fit my finger. That was the day he sailed away and kissed me for the last time and told me he loved me, the day my heart broke. I'll never forget it. I so nearly changed my mind and ran on to the ship after him… what a fool I was that I didn't. Nor get on one that was leaving the following week to catch up with him that way. But when I'm gone, promise me, Bella, you'll take it and keep it for Elizabeth. She's going to be strong and determined like me and her father and great grandfather, finally a child from their stock. I can see by her looks already every time Cat or Francis brings her to visit; she has their eyes, not mine – and that mop of thick black hair – so I just know she'll be a dreadful trial to my Francis." The ghost of a grin lit her face. Bella nodded, grasping the hand with the ring, "When she's old enough, old enough to understand what it's like to be in love, and what love really means, tell her the story and tell her…" the Dowager coughed, "tell her whatever she does, whatever her family says, she's to follow her heart. She's NEVER to do what I did," another cough, "and neither must YOU, Bella, My Love," and with another fierce paroxysm of coughing the exhausted old lady collapsed back on the bed, blood spattering the sheet where it escaped the handkerchief she put to her mouth.

"I promise, Auntie, I give you my word. But, but, what about Uncle Francis?" Bella whispered hollowly. "Surely he should know? He's not going to run away now..."

The Dowager opened her eyes briefly and smiled with an effort, "No, My Sweet, I suppose not. I hope not, but one never knows with him. His rivers run very deep and he's such an enigmatic man at times, one never knows what he's contemplating. But I just can't face it, not now, so you'll have to tell him for me; do it in your own good time, you'll know when the time is right." With her last strength, she fished under her nightgown and pulled a fine, long gold chain with a gold key on it from around her neck. She dropped it weakly on the coverlet from a now shaking hand, "Upstairs, the room, my special room... his portrait... my Alex..."

And with that, the once indomitable Elizabeth Granville fell back into the pillows, completely drained and exhausted, her eyes closed, her breath coming in rasps and yet more blood now visible on her thin lips.

Bella leaned forward and wiped the lips gently, but it seemed to leach out now in an unstoppable, slow flow. She was completely overcome with emotion at what she'd been told and she leaned down, clutching the Dowager's hand, her fingers twirling the ring, now so loose on the old lady's thin little finger. She put the chain with the key over her own head and tucked it inside her dress where it sat next to the little golden lion, a second treasure of other people she was now the custodian of. Sad tears rolled down her face and she finally gave in to quiet sobs as she lay there, her head on the coverlet.

It was as she lay there that Francis found them, when he walked quietly into the room a short while later. Bella raised tearful eyes to him, not knowing what on earth to say. She merely shook her head and watched as her uncle softly wiped the thin lips with his own handkerchief and then sat down on the opposite side of the bed, taking the old lady's other hand in his own and lifting it to his lips to kiss gently.

Bella could see tears in his eyes and one by one, fat drops rolled down his face. It was as if he sensed the end was near.

Bella never knew how long they sat there, watching the dying woman, listening to her rasping, shallow, now uneven breathing and the rattle in her chest. The nurse came in and silently looked at her charge, dabbed the bloodied lips with a damp cloth and lightly shook her head with a very sad expression when Bella and Francis looked up at her. She quietly left the room, pulling the door to behind her. About five minutes later, Bella looked up and saw Carstairs, the Dowager's devoted butler for as long as she could remember, standing forlornly just inside the now open doorway, other members of the household staff lined up behind him, looking sad and a couple of the maids and the housekeeper were weeping softly. Carstairs himself looked completely devastated and bereft, on the verge of tears himself.

Finally, the Dowager opened her eyes and looked across at her beloved grandson. Her eyes were misty and glazed, "Alex, my special, my one and only and forever love...forgive me for not coming..." she whispered. "I've always loved you, only you, and it's taken me so long... but I'm coming to join you now... at last," and with those whispered words, Elizabeth Granville closed her eyes and fell asleep for the last time.

Francis was momentarily puzzled at his grandmother's words, but when he realised she'd finally passed away, he forgot them as his emotions got the better of him and he lay his head on the covers and wept, still gripping a lifeless hand in his own, his shoulders heaving with sobs. Bella was crying too and slowly, she reached down to pull the ring off the old lady's finger and put it on her own. Then she got up and went round to the other side of the bed to do her best to comfort the weeping man. He'd always been the central, towering strength of his family, all of them, their rock, the one everybody went to with their problems, expecting and knowing he would somehow solve them. She suspected his endless jokes and self-deprecating humour were merely a cover to a deeply caring and much more serious nature, and to watch him like this, overcome with grief, was more heart-wrenching somehow than almost anything she'd seen, even when her own mother had died.

Having just heard Elizabeth Granville's devastating story, she now understood the deep bond that had existed between her and Uncle Francis and Bella knew it would take him a long time to get over his grandmother's death, no matter that it had been expected. Just as he was everyone else's strength, she suspected the formidable old woman had been his, in many ways.

She leaned down behind him, putting her arms over his shoulders and pulled him gently back into his chair, silently handing him a clean handkerchief from her pocket; then, just as she had when she'd been a little girl and needed a hug, or even as a grown woman the evening before, she went round and sat in his lap and gave him a big loving kiss on his cheeks, trying for once to comfort him as he'd often comforted and reassured her. So they sat there, deeply forlorn and sad, weeping gently together, their arms around each other: the big, strong, still handsome man and the young, beautiful woman... as the sun went down and shadows filled the room.

They never noticed Carstairs come over and reverently kiss the Dowager's hand for the last time and then her cheek, as tears ran down his own lined face and he gently folded both hands carefully on the coverlet, fussing over her to the last. Nor did they see the rest of the household staff come in and pay their last respects, standing with heads bowed at the back of the room. She'd terrorised the lot of them, for years, but somehow, underneath it all, they'd seen past the crustiness and all her old retainers cared for her deeply, just as she had cared for them.

Chapter Twenty

T he funeral was an immense affair and reported in all the papers and gossip sheets. Bella had never seen so many important people from all walks of life, from the Government, the Royal Family, the Military, the City and many charities, together with the cream of the Ton, all gathered together to mourn the Dowager's passing. For an ordinary and little-known woman, Elizabeth Granville had made her mark, not only in the Ton, but in many parts of the outside, real world in which she'd participated.

The Duke looked pale, remote, aloof and impassive, as he stood, clad in black from head to foot. Bella knew he was holding himself together with a great effort as, during the service, he read out a tribute he'd written to his grandmother. It was so heartfelt, Bella choked with emotion as he spoke. Her aunt wept constantly and her father too. Both French and both very emotional at times, now more than ever. Clad in black like their father, Francis's four tall sons stood sombre-faced and quiet for once, and looked impossibly sad. As a last mark of respect to their great grandmother, the four had insisted on carrying her coffin into the big church in Mayfair, along with their father and a close friend of his, Richard Ambrose, the Earl of Keswick, who had also known the Dowager well since his childhood and stood in as the last pallbearer for the one other family member who couldn't be there. Nicky was noticeable by his absence to those who were familiar with the family, but they also understood he was away in the Peninsula with the army fighting Bonaparte and would bitterly regret his unavoidable absence. The Dowager's fondness for him and his for her, was well known. For the six pallbearers, it had been their final tribute to the woman who had forged the Firle family into what it was now from the moment she'd become a Granville. All Bella could do was leave a small posy of flowers on his Granny Granville's coffin with words from Nicky that she thought he would have written himself, if he could have been there. The flowers were a golden colour and there was no name on the bottom of the message, just a drawing of a lion, not very dissimilar to the pendant he wore constantly on the chain round his neck.

Black-clad like her aunt, Bella stood in the church, weeping silently into her handkerchief, her father's arm around her shoulders. She longed to feel the comfort of Nicky's arms hugging her, just as they had at her own mother's funeral. She'd written to him a few days previously to tell him the sad news and that one of her last thoughts had been of him. She had no idea if, or when, he'd get the letter, but she'd felt better for having sent it. She was determined to write again, to tell him about the funeral and how many of the great and the good had come out to pay tribute, knowing how much he would regret not being there so say his own farewell.

The family then gathered for the Reading of the Will. Not expecting to be invited to the event, especially as they'd been summoned to the lawyer's office instead of the man coming to Firle House or Hertford Street as would have been expected, Bella sat with her father, aunt and uncle, just the four of them, as the solicitor droned on through a lengthy list of bequests to charities and retainers, past and present, which constituted the first part of the lengthy testament, before he apparently got to the second and pertinent part of the document. He told them this element was highly confidential and the reason they were in his deserted, quiet office and not anywhere servants could eavesdrop. It was all very mysterious. As they listened, seated on hard and uncomfortable chairs, none of Elizabeth Granville's loyal servants had been forgotten, including the devoted Carstairs, who would now have a lovely cottage of his own to retire to, along with a housekeeper to look after him and a quite sizeable pension; he would no doubt be overwhelmed when informed of his employer's generosity which would see him enjoy a very comfortable old age.

At last, the lawyer raised his eyes to the four fidgeting and bored family members and coughed. "As you know, Your Graces, Your Lordship," he addressed them punctiliously, "the late Dowager Duchess had, ah, a rather eccentric turn of mind at times, especially in these last few years. She in fact changed her Will some three months ago; however, I should tell you this was not some sudden aberration of a sick woman or an elderly individual who had lost their wits. She had been considering some of the amendments for quite a while as I had drawn up a couple of drafts and she simply tinkered with the last one, according to current circumstances, before signing the final version. Before giving you the finer details of the bequests, she requested that I read this private and confidential letter to you all, which she also wrote at the time of instructing me, the day after I went to her home in Hertford Street. I gather from Mr Carstairs it was the last time she managed to go downstairs to her private sitting room and the footmen had to carry her. This is the last letter she ever wrote herself in its entirety, although I gather she carried on dictating notes on business matters to her secretary for two or three weeks after, until she found everything simply too much. She insisted on writing this missive in her own hand, due to the personal comments in it and Carstairs said it took her all day, sitting at her escritoire. Apparently, she was exhausted when she was done, but you know what a formidable, determined woman she was, so…" he shook his head and sighed as he paused, looking at them all, "anyway, I thought you might like to know that."

He coughed delicately again and straightened his wire rimmed spectacles before breaking the seal over a pack of several folded sheets of paper and as he opened them, his audience could see they were covered in an uneven scrawl of spidery writing with ink blotches here and there. "Unfortunately," he intoned, "His Grace, the Duke of Valenciennes, cannot be present today, but I trust you can commend the details I am about to impart on to him when he returns from the Peninsula and he can then read the letter for himself. I will, of course, be writing to apprise him officially of the Will contents, as he is Mentioned, so he may visit me on his return to comprehend the bequest." The elderly man then took a deep breath, "However, this is Her Grace's own explanation for the bequests that she wanted me to read to you at this sad time: the final words of Elizabeth Theodora Granville, Her Grace, The Dowager Duchess of Firle, written on the eighteenth day of June in this year of our Lord, eighteen twelve…"

The four family members looked curiously at each other, then turned their eyes as one to the solicitor as he started reading from the long, handwritten letter.

My Beloved Family,

I sincerely trust you have not shed too many tears at my Funeral, for really, I am not worth it, Old Battle-axe that I have been or "Er Indoors' as I believe I am referred to in Certain Quarters in Berkeley Square, or down at Firle."

Francis and Cat looked at each other and couldn't help but smile softly at Benjy's original nickname for the old lady that many of the servants had also unofficially adopted. Cat squeezed her husband's hand as she could see his eyes start to water again.

I suppose the Great and the Good and plenty of the Not So Good or Great, all turned out. I trust they did not bore you all too much. Notwithstanding the late Mr Pitt, who in my Opinion did seem to have some Interesting Ideas and something of a Grip of matters in these Challenging Times of Revolution and War, in Europe and on the other side of the Atlantic Ocean, who sadly passed before his time. What a Useless Collection of Individuals most of the rest of them are, so it is little wonder we are still at War. I often wonder what would have happened if I had been able to enter Politics. A Forceful and Practical Woman would soon have sorted out what to Tax and what to leave Well Alone, we see things so differently and far more sensibly than men... as well as deal with that Corsican brigand, Bonaparte, instead of letting matters drift on for as long as they have. We have been At War for too many years, and the consequent Damage to the Nation's Finances has been appalling. Maybe one day, people will See Sense and put a Woman In Charge.

There was a collective laugh at her last comments and her prescience over the recent funeral and attendees; the solicitor tutted, obviously disagreeing with the Dowager's opinions and continued to read.

As I sit writing this letter, My Beloved Nicky is on his way back to Spain and I trust and hope with all my heart he is still Safe and will soon come home again to Bella, HIS WIFE! I have told him in No Uncertain Terms that I think this State of Affairs should continue and I trust that Someone will beat some Sense into him if he starts muttering again about a Divorce. Perhaps my dear Granddaughter-in-Law should go and find her old Rapier and Stiletto and threaten him. That appears to do The Trick with most men, I gather, so to this end, in case she has Misplaced or Lost them, or they have rusted away from non-use, I am bequeathing some Replacements for her...

The solicitor put the letter down on his desk and went over to a large, long wooden box lying on the floor under the window of his office. He lifted the lid and drew out the most magnificent, jewel-encrusted rapier and dagger, with respective scabbards for them, which he carried over and laid in the Duchess's lap. The jewels were large and fine and the items were worth a small fortune. Attached to the hilt of the rapier was a label: *"Just in case Francis forgets himself one day, and you have to Remind him again who Really is In Charge."*

Cat, who until that moment had been sitting black-clad, pale and sombre, struggling to smile and laugh, actually did burst out laughing as she shared the label with her husband. He too had been looking forlorn for days, but he genuinely chuckled at last when he read the message in the familiar scrawl and he picked up his wife's hand and kissed it lovingly, nodding his head to her in submissive obeisance. The pair of them laughed sadly, with their heads together. The solicitor sat down at his desk again, cleared his throat and picked up the letter.

To my Very Dear Friend, the Baron de Mornay. Regretful and Frustrated as I am, My Clever Eddie, that I never did manage to Beat You at any game we played, and we certainly Tried Most, I am eternally grateful you never, ever Let Me Win. There is no other man, well perhaps Francis sometimes, who has done that apart from You. Most men are such fools, they thought they could Get Round Me by letting me win at cards or indeed anything else, but of course You Knew Better and you knew me well enough to understand the Inspiration it gave me to Battle On to the Last. To this end, and to remind you of the Fascinating Pleasure and Frustration I have had over the last twenty years or so of pitting My Brain against Yours, to no avail, here is a Little Something for you.

As everyone smiled and Eddie laughed, again the solicitor put down the letter and rose to go over to the sideboard that graced the back wall of the room. Four heads turned as, somewhat theatrically, he pulled off a large cloth which was covering a beautiful chess set. It gleamed in the candle and lamplight and Eddie gasped as he realised the board and pieces were all solid gold and silver, the kings and queens with jewel-encrusted crowns, the other men also decorated with jewels. It was a work of art and obviously extremely valuable. The secondary reason for the Will reading at his office was becoming clear. Back at his desk, the solicitor then continued:

A final thought, My Dear, Sweet Eddie. I know how much you loved your Carlotta, as did we all. I know she will never be replaced in Your Heart. But you are such a Lovely Man in so many ways and I hate the thought of you Mouldering Away down in Sussex by yourself, with just your books, even if you think that is What You Want to Do. Although she will always be there to care for you, Bella is a woman now with her own life to live and Charlie will be Grown and Away before you know it. And so what of Your Life? You are NOT old and still have So Much to offer the World, as you ALWAYS have. I will no longer be around for you to Visit and Challenge, so I have resolved to Interfere. Well, what else would you Expect of me? I have Interfered in everyone else's business my Whole Life, so I am certainly not going to stop now.

There is a Charming, Delightful, Young-ish Widow with whom I have become Friendly over the past few years. She lives a bit further down Hertford Street in fact. We play Cards and the occasional Game of Chess to pass the time, as well as discuss Current Affairs and Events and, My Dear Eddie, she has a Brain! Now, would I tolerate her if she didn't have one?! She, too, is Lonely, having been married off when young to a very elderly man who died several years past and there are no children, much to her Sadness. As well as having a considerable degree of Intelligence, she is also a Kind, Caring and Witty woman and Quite Presentable. I know she is not Carlotta, but I thought she might occasionally Keep You Company and play a Game of Chess from time to time. Although her disposition tends to be quiet, she has a Very Lively and Enquiring Mind and plenty of Opinions on all manner of subjects so you will certainly not be bored. She may even make you Smile and Laugh a bit more as those features on your lovely face have been Visibly Lacking for some time now and we all Miss Them; I certainly have. With regard to the Chessboard, I am not saying this lady will ever hope to beat you, but she has managed to beat me on occasions so I know she will at least give you a Run for your Money! Who knows, you may even come to care for her a little too - stranger things have happened. I have left her direction for Cat to call on her and Hopefully, she will introduce you both and I will leave it for you to Take Matters from there.

Be happy, My Dear Man, and smile again. You have Hidden Depths, trust an old woman to know there is Far More to you than most people see or ever realise, and it would be such a Waste if no one else got to appreciate them!!

. . .

Eddie coughed and went slightly red at this, but the other three looked at him fondly and Cat resolved to go and find this paragon of a widow the following day to effect an introduction forthwith. She, too, thought her brother should find some companionship, indeed had been surreptitiously nagging and encouraging him to go out socially for the past few years, but with little success. She smiled to herself. Trust the Dowager to throw down the gauntlet and actually do something about it for him. The lawyer coughed politely again and Cat turned her attention back to him as he continued reading.

Bella, My Sweet Girl, you remind me so much of your Dear Mother. So Loving and Caring, So Passionate, and So Much Missed by us all. But she was a Strong Woman underneath, as your Papa, Uncle and Aunt well know. You, too, have that Strength. My Darling Nicky needs this. He is The Lion of Valenciennes and he needs a Lioness by his side, Strong and Determined as well as being Loving and Caring of her Family and Offspring. So, Bella, you are a Duchess too – remember that. And as I told your Aunt many years ago, take No Nonsense from anyone (and that includes Nicky and your Uncle Francis!).

Duchesses need Jewels and Ornamentation, if not for their Own Pleasure, simply to remind people of who they are. I know you have the Beautiful Rubies from your Mama, and they of course have Great Sentimental Value, but, My Dear Girl, Duchesses should have so much more! Therefore, I am leaving you My Collection, My Personal Jewellery Box. I simply could not be bothered to trot round to Firle House every time I wanted a Bracelet or a Pair of Earrings to wear – so Fatiguing and Irritating. Heaven knows your Aunt does not need them, given what is in The Firle Collection and I know she will agree. Wear them with Pleasure and think of Me sometimes when you do. You will be a Beautiful Duchess, here in England and hopefully once more in France, if they ever manage to be Civilised in that country again and Stop Chopping People's Heads Off.

. . .

Oh, and by the way, I know you sometimes Let Me Win when we played Chess, you Lovely, Soft Hearted Girl, but don't ever let Nicky win; he needs and Thrives on the Endless Challenge, as did I with Your Father!

Bella gasped when she heard this last comment, it was as if the old lady knew what had happened between her and Nicky. She laughed to herself. She would miss her dreadfully and as the solicitor got up yet again, she looked down in her lap and twirled the inconspicuous gold ring that now rested temporarily on her little finger. The solicitor beckoned Bella over to the sideboard and indicated a large chest containing many drawers, inviting her to open them. Inside each drawer, on velvet trays, was layer upon layer of fabulous jewels: necklaces, ropes of pearls, earrings, bracelets, brooches, rings and even a couple of tiaras. The most extraordinary collection glittered up at her.

As her eyes opened in astonishment and she gasped, her aunt rose to go and peer over Bella's shoulder. "I think there's a lot more than this as well, Sweetheart," she said quietly to her niece. "The Dowager was an immensely wealthy woman in her own right, never mind Francis and the Firle fortune. I know she bought jewellery for herself like you and I buy gowns or hats. She told me once it intimidated people when she faced them, dripping with such obvious wealth. I've no idea if that's so, maybe it was, fifty or sixty years ago. Personally, I find it all too ostentatious and that's why I don't wear many of the Firle jewels when I'm out on the Town, except when I have to go to big or important events, or we have to go to Court and State functions, or Francis wants to impress someone. But these are all yours now, so you can please yourself. Enjoy them, Poppet, you are a Duchess after all, so go and intimidate who you like!" She laughed and then leaned down very close to whisper in Bella's ear, "There's so much of it all, you could decorate yourself completely, without any clothes on. Think about that and a Certain Person. Lesson number fourteen and counting…" She winked and grinned as Bella looked round at her, blushing crimson.

They returned to their seats, smiling conspiratorially at each other and waited for the solicitor to move on.

And so to my Grandchildren and Great Grandchildren. The latter are the Delight I knew they would be, given how Special their parents are. Here, I am talking specifically about Francis and Marie-Catherine and their children, not those ninnies who are so much like their mother along with their boring and very worthy husbands and offspring. They were never Remotely Interested in me, even as children, kept as far away as possible from me in fact, and never visited Hertford Street from one year to the next, as if I was invisible... so I wish them Well and that is all!

I could leave Bequests to my Four Favourite Boys, my Hooligans, but quite frankly they will have more than enough from Francis and the Firle fortune so they certainly won't need anything from me – and knowing how Impossibly Wealthy and Generous my Grandson is, they will want for Nothing. So I bequeath them My Love and Encouragement to find their own way in the Real World as much as it is possible for them to, given their status already. Hopefully, they may learn to Appreciate what they Have and, like other members of this family, be Generous with it to those Not So Fortunate as they are, until such time as they Inherit, by which event I hope they are more Sensible than they appear to be now!

Francis and Cat laughed and rolled their eyes at each other, but turned to listen to the solicitor as he spoke on.

My new little Granville Great Granddaughter is another matter, however. Scream and squall for England as she currently does, and the way she waves her little fists around and generally Demands Attention from everyone, only then to Disdainfully Ignore it, seems to indicate she has inherited some of My Traits, as well as her Father's Looks, her Mother's Temperament (please, My Dear Cat, don't ever let her near a Sword or anything Sharp, or with a Trigger) and the more Determined and Enterprising Characteristics of her Forebears.

. . .

To this end, and mainly to Annoy her Father, I am bequeathing her One Third of my remaining Estate. Having been a Dreadful Womaniser in his youth, I am quite sure Francis is now going to be even more Overbearing and Protective than he currently is to the women of the family, so when Elizabeth gets older, and wants Her Own Way, this will Irritate the Hell out of him! I only wish I could have lived to Watch and Enjoy it! This money will give her some Independence, encourage her to Live her Own Life and follow her Heart, without Interference and I am Instructing her Cousin, my dear Arabella de Bresancourt, Duchess of Valenciennes, to be her Trustee until she is Seventeen. After that, she must merely Guide her to manage the money until she is Twenty-one, and then Elizabeth can do Exactly as she Wishes. Bella is her Father's Daughter and I have complete faith in her Ability to Oversee Elizabeth's Fortune (with some Guidance from her Father and my Grandson if she wishes it).

Ha! My Darling Francis, just you wait! I would Poke My Tongue Out at you, if I was there, just as all your boys used to when you Tried to keep them in order. I do believe I never Poked My Tongue Out at anyone in my Entire Life, but please Imagine it, as I finally wish to do it, in absentia!

Bella was somewhat astonished but then joined in the cracks of laughter as she, her father and aunt observed the Duke's grimacing face. He shook his head, smiling, however, as he accepted his grandmother's comments in good grace. Bella thought about the Dowager's words concerning Elizabeth's 'forebears' and what they really meant and she knew she would soon have to talk to the Duke and tell him the Dowager's story. But she would wait until the worst of his grief had passed and he could deal with the stupefying information she had to impart.

The solicitor coughed and the four of them turned back to listen.

. . .

And so, Francis Alexander, my Dearest, Darling Boy, for that is what you have always been to me, more Son than Grandson in an odd way. There is Nothing I can leave the Man who has Everything – Wealth, Health and, most importantly, Happiness, except the knowledge that, if it is possible and I find myself there, I will be watching over you from Heaven, and Haunting You if you do something of which I Disapprove! You have been the Joy of my Life, in ways of which you have No Conception, and if I can in any way Inspire You to continue to be half the Wonderful and Amazing Man you have become, that will be My Reward and, I hope, Yours.

Bella felt her tears rising yet again and looked over to her aunt who was already wiping her eyes with a handkerchief. She was leaning over to hold her husband's hand as he too swept a stray tear from his cheek.

However, I could not let this moment pass without having Something to Say to you from my little seat in Heaven; as I said, I hope that is where I will be, rather than 'Downstairs', so I do have a little Bequest for you too:

To think you were a Nefarious Criminal for all those years and I never knew! Trust you to be the only one to get Something Past Me, you Wretched, Irrepressible Man, and I never did find out what you did with your Ill-Gotten Gains either......

Bella giggled quietly as she looked at the solicitor's horrified face as he read the words. He might have been aware of the bequests but obviously the letter contents were another matter. She tried not to look at her uncle, privately hoping the shocked man could keep his mouth firmly closed. Now, apart from the physical presence of the bequests mentioned, she understood the need to read this missive out in the seclusion and privacy of his office. Obviously something the Dowager had instructed. She couldn't imagine what the very upstanding solicitor must make of her remarks, his firm having been lawyers to the Granville family for years. The man must be completely astonished and disbelieving. She wondered what else was going to be forthcoming.

Therefore, since you seem to have been so Fascinated with Cross Channel 'Activities', I am leaving you the Controlling Interest in a number of little Enterprises I have started, in France and here in England, with their own Native Management and which operate Transport Services between England and France, sparse as they are at present. A couple of these even go down to the Peninsula and across to the Netherlands, both for People and Goods. Oh, and My Dear, they are all LEGITIMATE! One day, soon I hope, Wellington will hopefully Get Rid of that megalomaniac Bonaparte, not to mention his wretched 'Continental System', and then we will all be able to Resume our Visits and our Business with the Continent in a Civilised and Profitable Fashion. These little Enterprises will therefore be well placed to Take Advantage of that situation as and when it happens. I do believe there is also a Small Fishing Fleet in amongst the companies, in case you need to have another of your little 'Holidays'.

Having pulled himself together after the touching words she'd written, Francis burst out laughing on hearing his grandmother's bequest. Only she and his wife knew of his little escapes, totally incognito, on an ordinary, random fishing boat, from the fleet that operated out of the little harbour of Newhaven near the Firle estate. As for the cross-channel fleets, he himself had already been considering the opportunities that would open up once the War was over and had been discussing them with Eddie. Trust his canny grandmother to be streets ahead of him. He laughed again and shook his head. He would miss her dreadfully.

The solicitor had arrived at the final few pages of the letter and they all turned to hear the end of this fascinating, touching and amusing missive.

. . .

And so to My Little Lion, well not so little now. You have grown into a Striking and Wonderful Young Man, as I always knew you would. Endlessly Brave and Proud, just like you were when you were a Little Boy. I had thought of getting you your own Menagerie of Lions, better than that mangy lot in the Tower, since the species still seems to have some Strange Fascination for you, but since you have Resolutely Refused all our offers to provide you with a Home of your Own, you would have nowhere to keep them. I really do not think my neighbours in Hertford Street, or those of Francis in Berkeley Square, would quite like it if we looked after one or two in our back gardens for you!

Everyone except the solicitor laughed at this, each having traipsed round the Tower of London on countless visits to see the lions in the menagerie kept there throughout Nicky's youth, his fascination with the big beasts a constant joke in the family. Of course it was the Dowager who had taken him to the Tower in the first place and she herself had come in for her fair share of family teasing over the years as being the cause of his obsession. All because of his necklace and the French nickname for his Ducal title, *Les Lions de Valenciennes*, the Lions of Valenciennes.

However, I simply will NOT Allow you to continue to be Homeless, no matter how much you Prevaricate and Refuse us all. Now you have a Wife to consider and hopefully, Children before too long; or will you procreate Cubs? Meeeeeow or should that be Rawwwwwr?!

The lawyer's audience chuckled as the man gainfully tried to make the appropriate animal noises and three pairs of amused eyes turned to look at Bella as she blushed, her hand subconsciously hovering over her expanding waistline.

. . .

So, My Lion, My Darling Boy, for like my Grandson, I am afraid you have always been my other Precious Little Boy too, I will not let you Get Away with Refusing Me any longer. I am Interfering, again, and therefore bequeathing you My House on the corner of Hertford Street with Adjacent Mews, Stable properties and all the Contents, as well as the Carriages, Horses, Retainers and everything else connected with it.

Bella took a deep breath; although on the corner of a quiet little street, mid-way between Hyde Park and Green Park in the heart of Mayfair, the apparently unostentatious double fronted house, was actually in a prime location between the fashionable Park and the large mansions of the Ton in and around Mayfair, like the Firle London home in Berkeley Square; it was in fact quite spacious inside, having been extended by the Dowager through the addition of the larger house next door at some point and contained a vast collection of valuable furniture, antiques and paintings. The several outbuildings and stables, in the mews behind, housed a selection of beautiful carriages and horseflesh. The Dowager never went anywhere that was not in extreme luxury or comfort. Bella wondered what Nicky would do with it all and giggled again. He'd be livid!

For a woman who was always covered in jewels and insisted on the finest of everything, it had puzzled people why she chose to live in such an unostentatious house, in a quieter part of Mayfair, even if it was magnificent inside. Not even the Duke understood. She had always laughed dismissively and merely said she liked the location. However, no one knew it had been outside that very house, in a carriage that had been waiting to take her back to her temporary London home for the Season, that Alexander Kinross had kissed the seventeen-year-old Elizabeth Marchmont for the first time, on their way back from a secret rendezvous in Hyde Park, as he'd been unable to resist her any longer. Nor she him. And what they'd done together in that closed carriage had swept her away like a hurricane and been the prelude to their passionate, intense *affaire*. She had never forgotten the incident, or the kiss and everything else that went with it, nor the man who'd given it to her and had swept her off her feet in the process. When the house had come on the market, she had bought it immediately and moved out of Firle House on some pretext, to make Hertford Street her new home. Over the years she had only to look down on the street corner from her bedroom window, or out from her ground floor personal sitting room and study, for it all to return to her as if it had been yesterday – even though EACH TIME, her heart cracked a fraction more with regret, bitterness and thoughts of what might have been. It was a secret she'd taken to her grave.

I know Nicky may well still be in the Peninsula when you read this Letter as I know I have not long left of my life. However, I Steadfastly Refuse to Believe he will not come home Safe and I, like the rest of you all, My Family and His Family which are one and the same, pray every day that this is so. Bella, My Sweet, I therefore want you to move into the house whenever you like and Do As You Wish with it. Redecorate, refurbish - my taste is old-fashioned and elaborate for today's more restrained style, so I will leave it to you to make a Home for yourself and Nicky and fill it with Love, Laughter and Happiness.

In addition, I have also purchased a small Country Estate, near to both Firle and Arlington, which I also bequeath to Nicky. This will keep all the family near each other in Sussex when they feel like Rusticating, as they often do, from the exigencies of life in London. Nicky can go over to France easily from there when the War ends and oversee his Affairs at Valenciennes, as I am Convinced he will get his Old Home Back one day.

To run these Establishments and lands, I am therefore leaving Nicholas de Bresancourt, the Duke of Valenciennes, the remaining Two Thirds of my Estate.

Bella gasped, Eddie and Cat grinned at each other and the Duke looked enormously amused and pleased in equal measure.

. . .

Nicky, My Love, whether you like it or not, you now have a Fortune to go with your Ducal title. There should be More Than Enough to buy back many times over, all the Lands and Properties that used to belong to the Valenciennes Estate in France, such as they were, if that is what it Takes and that is what you wish. I have been there already and seen for myself the ruins of the beautiful Chateau that now needs Rebuilding and Restoring to its Former Glory. I tried on your behalf to get all or some of the Estate back for you, but even I have so far failed. The situation in France being as it is, I am afraid no one will do Anything, despite threats, coercion or enormous bribes; nothing works there at the moment. It is a Typical French Mess.

Incidentally, Nicky, I would just like to add here, for the benefit of Everyone Else party to this Missive, so therefore NOT General and Public Consumption, that whilst Poking My Nose into what was going on in Valenciennes, I had the opportunity to speak to some people who lived in the vicinity and remembered your Father, Antoine, the previous Duke. Although they were mainly former tenants, old Estate workers and some Riff Raff, they knew him and of him. Nicky, I can promise you, you are NOTHING like him and should never aspire to be so. Other than the Pride you have in your Title, which of course is very Proper and Appropriate at the Right Level, except he was apparently Full Of It and his own Self-Importance, you are a Good and Caring Man and not at all like your Father who appears to me to have been Universally Despised, Disliked, even Hated. I regret to say he seems to have represented the Very Worst Traits of the French aristocracy - unemotional, disdainful, hard and totally Unfeeling or Concerned for the welfare of the poor people who lived and toiled on his Estates for his Benefit and were his Responsibility.

Fate is so strange sometimes, is it not? Your parents met with a Grim Fate at the hands of Bernheim, but I think they would have been Easy Targets for the Revolutionaries and sent to the Guillotine in any case. Fortunately, YOU were spared. I have never been a Religious Woman, as you well know, but it does make me believe there is a God in Heaven sometimes, with Angels who interfere in Strange Ways. You may find this a Tasteless and Cruel

Comment, but I have always Spoken My Mind. Nicky, I know what you experienced in Rouen Fortress had a Terrible Impact on you, something I still believe Haunts You. However, you must NOT regret losing Your Parents when, instead, you were adopted and brought up by two of the Most Caring and Loving People I ever had the fortune to know, and the Man you are today is a Reflection of their Wonderful Parenting, as, of course, is My Dear Bella. I doubt you would have grown to be like your Father, I simply cannot believe that, but the way he was would have had an Effect on you, if you had all survived The Revolution. So there, I've said it, even from Beyond The Grave. You know I never Minced My Words but that is my Heartfelt Opinion and I trust you will not think any the less of me for it. I also felt you should know what I discovered so you understand about your Family Roots. Regrettably, of your family's Fortune, I, like Francis and Eddie, could find no trace. But, WHO CARES? You have mine now and it isn't Tainted by hatred or gained through the suffering of the poor Estate workers of Valenciennes.

Francis and the rest of the room looked stunned for a moment as the vehemence of the old woman's words reached out from the letter once again. Suddenly, Francis burst out laughing as he reflected on what his scheming grandmother had been up to. My God, he thought, she certainly had been a secretive, interfering, outspoken, if well-meaning old baggage, but if SHE hadn't managed to get far with Valenciennes, there was no point in him or Nicky pursuing matters until the War was over and a new French government was in place. Maybe there'd be a restoration of the monarchy and some rights returned to the old aristocratic families still surviving. Her opinion of Nicky's parentage was fascinating and probably accurate. He remembered back to the little boy he'd rescued from the Fortress and the harrowing tale he'd learned about the fate of the Duke and Duchess of Valenciennes and Nicky's retelling of his own experiences after they'd all been captured by Bernheim. He thought his grandmother was probably very right in her opinions and knew Eddie and Carlotta had been exceptional parents to the orphaned, bewildered and traumatised little boy. Not to mention his grandmother's loving input as well. As the solicitor coughed, he hurriedly turned his thoughts back to the lawyer who had noticed his faraway expression.

But finally, I want you to hear One Further Thought, Nicky, and Hear Me Well, even from Beyond The Grave. Much as I understand your deep-rooted Need to feel your Title is not an Empty One, nor a Joke, and your Bitterness at losing your Parents, your Fortune and Estates, (but do reflect on what I have just written) and your Pride which has made you Refuse all our offers of financial help… believe me when I tell you, and I know this from Personal Experience, all the Wealth, Prestige, Possessions and Money are for NOTHING *if you have no one to share it with, no one to love or love you back, because True Love is a wonderful thing if you're lucky enough to find it. Just ask Cat, Francis or your Papa.*

Now you need to let yourself go and let us in because WE love you, all of us, in your close, loving family. Not the romantic or passionate love of husband and wife which is special and precious and can be a once in a lifetime thing, but family love is just as strong, only in a different way. When you have your own children you will understand that better. However, Bella loves you a lot, quite passionately now, we all know that, even you, deep down, I am certain of it. So do NOT let her slip through your fingers; as I've just said, Love is Everything, *you have to Believe Me.*

And so, My Dearest Family and Friends mentioned herein, there we are, My Bequests and a few Thoughts and Reflections. I hope they will bring you a little Laughter and Happiness, as well as Food for Thought, and I will finish with a few final words from my Heart.

I want you all to know that I love Every One of You very dearly, even those wretched hairy dogs of yours, My Dear Cat! Except for My Darling Francis, my existence had been cold and empty for many years, so when he found and married his Marie-Catherine and introduced her and her family and little

Nicky to me, it reminded me again of what life should be like - Happy, Loving and Caring. We are an Eccentric Lot, but we are Aristocrats, so people are Not Surprised and, quite frankly, as I have often said over the past few years, Who The Hell Cares! And I won't apologise for my Shocking Language in this Missive either, there are others in this family who Blaspheme Far Worse than I - is that not so, My Dear Cat?! You have all given me a Wonderful Family to be part of for the past twenty years and for me, that was Completely and Utterly Priceless.

Be safe, be well, all of you, and continue to Look After each other as you have done over the years. That is your Strength and no one will better Our Family if you continue to Love and Support Each Other. Even if you fight some of the time, the love is always there, and teach your children to do the same.

Thank you for Everything, and God Bless You All.

Elizabeth Granville

As the solicitor tidied the many pages of the letter and handed them across to Francis, the room was silent and four people wiped their eyes, each lost in their own thoughts and memories of the woman whose final words they had just heard.

Francis gazed through the window of the lawyer's office and tried to pull himself together, the contents of the letter going round in his head. She had been manipulative to the end, determined in her own way to try and make things right for Nicky, especially his relationship with Bella. Apart from the amusing bequests, that was at the heart of her letter. She obviously believed Nicky cared for Bella in a carnal way, as well as a brotherly, familial one, despite his personal assertions to the contrary. Up to now, he himself had tended to side with the younger man, but maybe he was wrong? His grandmother's letter had been written three months previously, so she hadn't known then about what had happened between the pair of them and the advent of a child. It sounded to him as though it was written shortly after Nicky had visited her for the last time. Bella had told him she'd revealed her story to the Dowager just before Francis had arrived the afternoon the old lady died, how she'd laughed her head off and was pleased as punch at the news of the baby. He was so glad she'd known about that and had been laughing just before she'd passed away.

It had been a terrible couple of weeks but the initial torrent of grief had now eased somewhat and, though Francis knew he would miss his grandmother greatly, her letter had eased some of the sadness. He smiled as he thought of how she was reaching out, even in death, to interfere in their lives; her intentions only for the good, as, deep down, he knew they had always been.

However, it remained to be seen what Nicky would do, now he had homes and a fortune to boot. Bella didn't give a fig about that, Francis knew. But Nicky? He wasn't sure how he'd react to all the momentous news he was going to receive when he next came home.

In amongst all the trauma of the Dowager's passing, Francis, Eddie and Cat had realised they would have to announce to the Ton about a marriage to explain Bella's pregnancy, so they used the opportunity of the Dowager's death to concoct and let slip the story that Bella and Nicky had been quietly married while he was home on leave, over the Dowager's deathbed, as she had pronounced him to be her heir. The servants at Firle House would know nothing had gone on there so it was the perfect cover story since the house at Hertford Street was maintained with only Carstairs and a skeleton staff, plus nurses and doctors who came and went. The devoted Carstairs would say nothing, they all knew. Francis quietly explained to people that Nicky had been unexpectedly called back early to the Peninsula before any announcement or quiet celebration could be organised, then of course the Dowager had died, so it was all quite inappropriate. So that was how they explained the marriage and Bella's pregnancy. What certain people in the Ministry of War and Department of Information thought about it all when the tale reached their ears, was never known and Francis didn't care.

As the four of them quietly made their way back to Berkeley Square in the big, luxurious Firle carriage, Francis decided he wasn't going to interfere between Nicky and Bella. They would have to sort out their problems themselves and he smiled to himself as he remembered he still hadn't told Cat what had really gone on with Bella at *Le Lion d'Or* while Nicky had been home those few short months before. The Dowager's death the day after Bella had told him had put all such amusing thoughts from his mind. He resolved to relate the whole story to his wife that evening. They needed cheering up and he smirked to himself as he thought how much she would laugh, just as he and his grandmother had.

Cat and Francis were sitting in front of the fire in his suite of rooms later that autumnal evening. Francis, as ever, reading through his interminable reports and paperwork, she glancing desultorily at a novel in her lap, but her concentration was elsewhere.

Staring into the flames of the fire as she drank the last of her cup of cocoa, Cat turned to Francis, "She was such a well-meaning old lady, wasn't she?" she reflected softly.

"Hmmm, sorry, My Love?" Francis put aside his papers and looked up at her; he'd been miles away.

"Your grandmother, she was so well-meaning," Cat repeated. "Trying to sort out everyone's lives, trying to help them." She paused, "I never realised it at first, but as I got to know her better, I saw beneath that hard shell she put on for the world."

"Yes, she had a heart of gold really. Look at what she did this afternoon," he sighed, but then laughed softly. "You ARE going to find the Widow of Hertford Street and introduce her to Eddie, aren't you?"

"Of course," Cat laughed, "I have her direction already and I will call on her first thing tomorrow." Then she looked thoughtfully at Francis, "That's the easy part, but dealing with Bella and Nicky is a whole other problem. I'm not sure how he's going to take it, his inheritance, that is, never mind the baby," and she grinned. "Which reminds me, what were you and Bella gossiping and whispering about in your study the other week? I saw that look you gave her when she made her announcement at dinner." Cat waggled a finger at her husband, "I meant to ask but what with everything else, the funeral and now today, it completely slipped my mind," she chuckled. "I hope she hasn't got another mad idea in her brain and wants to open more gaming establishments?"

"Oh no, nothing like that, thank heaven, though dammit, I wouldn't put it past her at some point," he sighed with a smile. "Actually, I merely wanted to check that the baby was Nicky's." Francis tried to look deadpan but had to laugh as he saw the shocked expression on his wife's face.

"WHAAAT?! *Mon Dieu*, Francis, really, don't be so idiotic; of course it's Nicky's!" Cat exclaimed in exasperation.

"Well, I happen to know he spent every night he was home, not at home, so I did wonder, and me being me, I asked her."

"Good lord. If that had been me, I would have punched you on the nose," said Cat sternly.

"Hmmm, yes, well, it's a good job Bella isn't you," he grinned. "But it definitely is Nicky's, I can assure you of that. However, getting HIM to believe it, is going to be a SLIGHT problem…"

Cat looked at Francis curiously, wondering at the suddenly deadpan, pretend-innocent look on his face and his suggestive comment. "Whatever do you mean?" she laughed. "Immaculate conceptions only happen in The Bible, not Mayfair, and Bella is increasing in size nicely, so we won't find the heir to Valenciennes has been delivered onto her doorstep in Hertford Street by a visiting stork. Nicky did have some contribution to the process so why wouldn't he believe it?" Again she laughed as Francis tried to look mysterious. "Come on, out with it, You Bumpkin. I know you know something and are just teasing me. What on earth is it?"

Francis smiled wickedly, pulled his chair round nearer to her and proceeded to relate the entire tale, bursting into guffaws of laughter when his wife sat and stared at him, stunned in disbelief, mouth gaping open like a fish at several points.

"WHAAAAT?!" she finally exclaimed. "Francis Granville, are you seriously trying to tell me Nicky spent four entire nights making love to Bella without knowing who she was? That's completely preposterous. You have to be joking, surely? Oh come on, you're telling me a fairy tale."

When he shook his head at her, still laughing, she giggled girlishly. "I've heard of being kept in the dark, but really..." and she threw her head back and shrieked with laughter.

"There was me, thinking Bella was still quite innocent. You should have seen the state of him a couple of mornings I caught him on his way in or out," Francis rolled his eyes at his wife. "I knew she was a clever puss, but had no idea she had such hidden erotic depths, or knowledge, come to that," Francis chuckled. "Everything from bites on his neck to marks round his wrists. Un-believable. I thought he'd been to play at Marguerite's, or some other cathouse with friends and the girls got a bit carried away. It just goes to show you can't trust any woman. Good God, I thought I'd die laughing when she first told me. I could hardly believe it of her. How on earth did she persuade him to do all that? And what the hell has she been reading to know about that sort of thing in the first place... or who has she been talking to, more like?"

Cat's mind went back to the very informative, slightly tipsy and amusing conversation she'd had with Bella that one, long-ago morning while Nicky was at home and, as she remembered it, another gale of laughter overcame her. She had a very good idea of how persuasive her niece had become and from where she'd acquired her knowledge. However, she had no intention of sharing that little gem with her husband, so merely said, "Well, that young man seems to have spent a good deal of the last few years when he's been at home, charming and pleasing an inordinately large number of women, if rumour is to be believed, no doubt encouraged by you," she poked her forefinger into her grinning husband's chest, "so obviously, we should put NOTHING past him if he REALLY wanted to please *La Lionesse*. He must have been very taken with her to do it though, I have to say," she giggled as an afterthought.

"I still can't believe she persuaded Nicky to do it, not to mention all the other antics they obviously indulged in." Francis shook his head in disbelief, "One night yes, but for four nights? It's quite surreal and bizarre."

"Perhaps he enjoyed it?" suggested Cat blandly as she got up to put her cup back on the tray near the door, then disappeared for a few moments into her bedroom and dressing room. She came back out holding a long black sash she'd worn with the mourning dress she'd had on that afternoon for the visit to the lawyer and walked slowly over towards her husband.

"And what, pray, are you intending to do with that?" Francis looked dubiously at his wife, amused suspicion on his features.

"Oh, I thought I might conduct an experiment, find out if such a silly thing is possible. In fact, I've just volunteered you as a specimen for my experiment."

"Have you now? And how are you going to persuade ME, Your Grace?" a seductive, curling smile creased his handsome features.

"Oh, I don't know, Your Grace, but I'm sure I'll think of something." She licked her lips suggestively and took hold of his hand, pulling him over towards the vast four poster bed before pushing him down into the soft mattress.

Cat clambered up next to her husband as he lay sprawled against the pillows and straddled his lap. Now just past fifty, but still incredibly handsome and youthful, Francis was a very energetic and fit man despite the hours spent sitting at his desk. His firm and beautifully muscled torso glimmered in the soft lamplight as his wife undid his velvet dressing robe and his stunning blue eyes sparkled up into hers. He smiled at her as she looked back at him, an evilly playful expression on her laughing features. "Why do I feel like I'm facing an execution?" he chuckled as she leaned forward to wrap the sash around his eyes.

"Because you've always been an evil villain, haven't you, My Shadow" she giggled back at him and unwittingly parroted her niece's words. "Now then, does the condemned man have any last requests?" she whispered with a saucy smirk on her lips.

"How did I allow myself to get into this situation?" he murmured humorously. "I never should have told you. I might have known it would give you disgraceful ideas."

She laughed naughtily as she finished tying the sash and pushed him back down into the pillows, her hands caressing his already aroused body. "I asked for a last request, not a commentary, Your Grace. You can tell me what you think in the morning, when, or maybe if, I let you see again, depending on how my experiment goes."

Francis groaned as he now realised he was in for a night of erotic torment at her hands, but he submitted willingly, as Nicky had done had he but known, overwhelmed with desire for the tantalising Frenchwoman he still loved passionately and who had never ceased to keep him fascinated and entertained... in and out of his bedroom.

"Have mercy on me, pleeeese, I beg of you," he pleaded theatrically as she merely laughed and bent her head to start his erotic, teasing torture.

"Now then, Your Grace, where shall I start to be disgraceful? For of course you have no idea who I am and I could do some shocking things to you and get away with it." Francis merely sighed in pleasure and gave himself up to her playful wiles, the pair of them softly laughing together; the despair and sadness that had been hanging over them since the Dowager's death, finally easing as their love, desire and closeness gave them comfort and an escape for a while from the realities of life and death.

Francis's tall, strong torso rolled over on top of Cat's and his sightless hands peeled off her nightrail as his mouth started to roam over her voluptuous curves, still attractive and firm despite three pregnancies, thanks to her active life, whether riding, walking her dogs or practising fencing several days a week, much to her husband's amusement. He knew what she liked and how to make her pant with desire. "Hmmm, who is this strange woman I wonder?" his tongue laved her nipples and he gently bit and pulled on them causing her to wail and jerk. "Do I know her?" His mouth moved up and down her body, his tongue eventually licking and savouring between her legs as he tasted, teased and aroused and then mused, his deep voice crawling over her seductively, "Aha!" he muttered, rising back up her body again, finally giving in and kissing her deeply and then entering her tormentingly slowly before stilling deep within, ignoring her pleading moans in French and the nails digging into his buttocks as she tried to force him to move and give her the climax she was now clamouring for. "I'd know her anywhere, the perfume, it's that deranged Duchess who kills evil villains. Are you going to kill me tonight, now you have me at your mercy? I'm completely innocent of all charges, I give you my word, I'm only a boring English aristocrat, so I don't deserve to be executed..."

"Innocent? Hah! Francis Granville, I know your alter ego personally and intimately and the day either of you are at anyone's mercy, I'll eat the dog's dinner. Not even Bernheim could break you, so why did I EVER think you'd be a willing experimental specimen for me to practise my wiles on?" she moaned and sighed, waiting on him to decide to put her out of her misery, as totally under his sensual thrall as ever. Her plan to torment him, like Bella had obviously tormented Nicky as per her lessons, had gone awry, as always. She'd been the toast of London in her youth, the stunning, unknown, eccentric French *émigrée* with a penchant for enormous hairy dogs who had captured the heart of the reclusive, elusive Duke of Firle, but no other man had ever come near to affecting her as he did, in bed or out.

"Because I am your slave, My Love, I always have been, from the day I dropped down from the old apple tree by the wall in your orchard; but only yours," he kissed her leisurely, listening to her panting and feeling how wound up she was, "and one day, I think Nicky might realise he's in the self-same boat with Bella. I can't wait to watch it all; another poor fool trapped under the spell of a captivating witch... this time a woman with her beautiful mother's Spanish looks and her French father's brains. What a nightmare combination for any man to deal with..." and he chuckled, "even a lion," and Cat giggled at his joke. "Now then, Your Grace, never mind lions, back to your little experiment, is this what I'm supposed to do...?"

Chapter Twenty-One

SPAIN: AUTUMN 1812

While Wellington took his chance and fought his next battle with the French at Salamanca on 22nd July, Nicky was making his circuitous way towards Madrid. He meandered through villages and small towns, picking up odd bits of work in stables, anywhere or anything he could find. He'd always had an empathy, an affinity with animals, ever since he'd been a small boy of five and had been allowed to adopt a kitten, then a baby rabbit he'd found under a bush in the garden. This affinity had become more focussed as he'd grown older and discovered a real talent for dealing with and training horses. He'd always had a daydream of owning his own stables one day and breeding horses, but that was a pastime for wealthy men. He had to make his own living and way in life, so that indulgence was just a fantasy. But in the meantime, his knowledge of and ability to deal with horses had proven useful when seeking itinerant employment as a screen for his real undercover missions for the British army in Spain.

Where there was no casual work in livery or other stables, he would pitch up in the local bar or marketplace with his guitar to play for his supper, entertaining customers with his light, crooning tenor voice. His good looks, inviting smile and sparkling eyes enticed the women who sat, watched and listened with rapt attention. When he'd finished for the night, he'd find one to take to bed. These were mostly women who worked in the bars or hostelries themselves, or at some of the larger local whorehouses. Given with whom he was dealing, and from Eddie's practical encouragement when he'd joined the army and got posted overseas, he tried to use one of the new-fangled 'skins' when he could, to stop him picking up the pox or any other nasty disease, much to the fascination of the women who'd rarely seen any men use them, certainly not their usual customers. He merely said it was the latest thing in Madrid and much as he disliked them, they served their purpose and stopped him worrying.

Overwhelmed for once in their hard lives by the charms of a handsome and attentive man, the women, usually paid for their services, were rapturous with the pleasure he gave them in bed and became easy prey for his apparently idle questions about their other customers, lovers or employers. In the stables, at horse fairs and in markets, with his obvious flair for managing even difficult animals, he soon got talking to other men – owners, buyers, grooms, coachmen and stable hands - anyone who was likely and inadvertently to mention other strangers, particularly French ones, or unusual work being offered. The slightest clue was noted and stored away for future consideration and investigation. But Nicky heard and found out nothing unusual. He caught up with old contacts in and around the area, among the guerrilla groups and other men happy to exchange information for a few gold coins, but they, too, knew of nothing out of the ordinary.

Following his victory at Salamanca, Wellington moved eastward and entered Madrid in early August. Nicky kept out of the city centre and patrolled the ring of towns and villages further afield, keeping an eye out for French vermin fleeing the English dogs who had liberated the city and were now in charge.

The French retreated south-east to Valencia and Marshal Soult evacuated the southern region of Andalucía and withdrew north-east with his men to Valencia to join up and combine forces with them. This new combined army soon posed a serious challenge to Wellington's hold on Madrid. In the meantime, the recently defeated other French force was regrouping and rebuilding its strength again. While Wellington made plans to counter the threat from the south-east and retain his hold on the Spanish capital, he also looked to the north and the strategically important city of Burgos, an important French supply base. He moved there to lay siege to it towards the end of September, but the French strongly resisted his efforts.

With Wellington heading north, Nicky focussed his attention on the eastern and southern regions where the French had retreated to reorganise themselves, but his search remained fruitless.

Then, a gold shipment arrived in Madrid. A frustrated Nicky went to visit Wellington near Burgos.

"I feel I'm on a fool's errand," he sighed as he sat in Wellington's tent late one evening in mid-October, having arrived in the English camp under cover of darkness. "I've not been able to find out anything about Bernheim, or any other French agents for that matter – and your gold has arrived intact. It's as if Bernheim doesn't exist." He looked over at Wellington directly, "So what do you wish me to do now, Sir?"

Wellington looked over at the scruffy man. His hair was long, unkempt and curling around his face and well down over his grubby shirt collar; he hadn't shaved for weeks and his swarthy face was dirty, as were his clothes. He'd even acquired what looked like a small metal ring in one ear. He was almost unrecognisable as the man he'd spoken to a few months before. If it wasn't for his cut glass English aristocratic accent and impeccable manners, he looked for all the world like a disreputable, dirty gypsy brigand, albeit a fair one. Wellington's impassive face curled into a slight smile.

"Keep looking," he said simply. "The French are regrouping and will come back at me from all directions, make no mistake. Bonaparte's marshals won't give up that easily and I hope they aren't thinking straight or it could get difficult for us again. This damned war is proving a monumental challenge for us. Unfortunately, the Spanish Government and Spanish Establishment in general also seem to be falling to pieces; therefore, if I and our Allies have to fall back over the winter and prepare ourselves for another big push forward in the spring, that will be an ideal time for your man, or the French in general, to strike, thinking they can destabilise our whole effort. More fools they!" he said forcefully and sarcastically, not deterred by the way his luck seemed to be changing, yet again.

Arthur Wellesley, his title now upgraded further to Marquess of Wellington, leaned back and considered his man thoughtfully. "Make no mistake, de Bresancourt, Bernheim's out there, biding his time. The fact you can find no trace of him is why he's so dangerous. This shipment we've just received is only a small one. The big delivery will come before the end of the year, ready to tide the Spanish and us over the winter. I suspect that's the one he's after. If he gets his hands on that, it will cause me, us, great problems – especially with our Allies in such chaos. You HAVE to find him and stop anything he may be planning. We are relying on you."

"Very well, My Lord. I'll go and talk to Scovell and see if he's picked up any nuggets of information, then I'll be on my way. I might as well go back to Madrid and start from there again." Nicky rose to take his leave and bowed.

As he was about to go through the tent flap, Wellington's parting words caught him. "He's out there somewhere, de Bresancourt, hiding under a stone like a scorpion waiting to strike. Be VERY careful and trust no one, the whole country is in chaos."

Nicky turned and nodded his head. "I'll watch my back, Sir. Thank you. I certainly don't want to get bitten, but if you're certain he's there, then I WILL find him." He turned and disappeared into the night.

He made his way to Scovell's temporary quarters and spoke quietly to the men on duty. They'd picked up nothing of interest and he sighed in frustration. As he was about to leave, however, a sudden thought crossed his mind and going to sit at an empty table, he picked up a piece of paper and a quill and started to scribble.

Mid October.

Greetings from Sunny Spain - or should I say Buenos Días!

· · ·

Hopefully, you will all be glad to hear I am still in one piece. Life is interminably boring and I have done nothing much but sit in the sun and drink wine for weeks, apart from the odd foray to inspect a few bars in Madrid, which 'Nosey' liberated in early August.

We are now laying siege at Burgos and by the time you receive this you will no doubt have heard the outcome. Again, laying siege is such a tedious business, just dawdling around all day, waiting for someone to come out and wave a white flag. You see, I have even found the time to write you a letter!

However, duty calls, so I must away. My love to you all. I trust you aren't missing me too much and Elizabeth has taken over the house now, with Bubbles as her second in command! Is Francis still there, or has he decamped to Scotland?

Thinking of you all,

N

He grinned to himself as he read it. That should keep them all quiet for a while and at least some of it was true. He knew that underneath the humour, it would put their minds at rest; albeit temporarily.

He folded the note, sealed it and wrote its direction on the front. Then he left it with one of the English officers in the tent, safe in the knowledge he would ensure it went in a courier's bag to the Ministry in London, then on to the Duke, in two or three weeks rather than wait for the usual post to be shipped back with the rest of the soldiers' mail home, which could take months. Another grin; knowing the right people did have its uses sometimes.

He slipped away from the camp and the besieging British forces as inconspicuously as he had arrived, and set off back in the direction of Madrid.

As he made his way south again, his mind wandering down odd paths as his horse plodded along, the irony of his situation didn't escape

Nicky. Here in Spain, he was seeking a faceless, mysterious Frenchman who was undoubtedly extremely clever; a tall, slender man with dark hair and dark eyes who was bent on making mischief for the British army. Back in London, he'd left behind a faceless, mysterious English woman, but one with a French name, *Lionesse*, who came from a French family and spoke French fluently. She, too, was tall and slender and had dark hair, though her eyes were still unknown and could well be dark as well. She was also extremely clever. For reasons best known to her, she was clearly intent on making mischief for him - an officer of the British army - having made off with his necklace.

The situation was bizarre, the coincidence odd, but the similarity between the two ended there.

The woman wasn't dangerous, well only to his libido and senses, he chuckled to himself, just a mysterious nuisance and challenge, but she'd be easy to run to earth when he got back to London, he was sure. Images of her constantly filled his mind at night, even when he was with other women, unable to stop himself making comparisons... remembering the feel of *Lionesse's* body, making love to it, the stunning passion that had exploded between them, especially the last night before he'd left London and what she'd done to him. The other women all fell far short and were NO comparison to her.

Frederick Bernheim, however, was another matter. He was proving elusive and impossible to track down, even so much as a tiny snippet of information. He WAS dangerous, extremely so if he believed Ashcroft and Wellington. Although he didn't know the former very well, his opinion of the commander of the British army was high; the man was far from stupid and didn't frighten easily, but he'd gone out of his way to warn Nicky to take care and watch his back. Nicky wasn't going to ignore that. If Wellington was concerned about the plans of one solitary Frenchman when he had the whole French army to deal with, that told him a lot.

Bernheim also played on his mind constantly and gave him the shivers. He didn't understand why, never having even met the man, but Nicky simply had a bad feeling about him. He put it down to the man's father and once Ashcroft had mentioned the hated name, that had opened up a stream of nightmares and terrible memories he'd kept locked away for years, buried deep at the back of his mind and which rarely escaped, certainly not like they had when he was a child. They were his personal and private cross to bear, the extent of which he had never, ever, shared with anyone; not his Papa and Madre, not even Francis. But now, they'd returned with a vengeance and plagued his dreams. They often started as an erotic, pleasurable fantasy about *Lionesse*, what they'd shared and what he'd like to do to and with her when he found her again, but then frequently became distorted and morphed into a horrifying or sickening nightmare with both Bernheims at its centre, father and son, either or both egging on the father's second-in-command, Pierre Dupont, a man who had been so depraved, cruel and evil, Nicky still couldn't think about him without feeling physically sick.

And so Nicky returned back to Madrid and his dangerous mission, his thoughts tormenting him, his intuition making his stomach churn as he contemplated finding and confronting a man with a face like his father, wondering incessantly how much alike they would be...

To Be Continued...

Read on to Part 2 in the series, Undercover Lion, as Nicky, now operating alone and cut off from the British forces, continues his search for the ruthless French agent, Bernheim, and any of his associates. How will he find him when he doesn't even know what the man looks like? And if he does track him down, will he be able to stop any plot to steal the gold shipments? How will he manage to do that when he has no help?

To give you a little taste of what is coming up next, keep reading…

UNDERCOVER LION

Preview

Chapter One

Nicky was sitting at the bar in a scruffy *taberna* in a dirty back street of Madrid, desultorily sipping his glass of wine and smoking a cheroot while he contemplated his next move. December was approaching and Wellington's prediction about the French had been proved right. They had regrouped and fought back. Confronted with forces attacking him from two sides, Wellington had been forced to abandon his siege at Burgos and retreat westwards yet again, nearer to the border with Portugal; the allied British and Portuguese army was in disarray and it was their good fortune that Marshal Soult, who was chasing them, on the back foot and outnumbered, rather strangely declined to attack on the old Salamanca battlefield. Such are the fortunes of war and it was undoubtedly Wellington's lucky day.

Madrid was now re-occupied by the French though they had not left a garrison there, instead choosing to chase the Allied forces with all men available. The city was therefore in turmoil and things were not looking good for the British. However, Nicky had faith in their commander and was certain Wellington would sort himself out, regroup his forces and fight his way forward again after the winter.

However meanwhile, he himself was isolated, with still no sign of Bernheim or any of his associates.

As he leaned on the deserted bar, waiting for the evening's clientele to drift in, a young girl entered and perched on the stool next to him, eyeing him to assess his worth as a potential customer. He turned and smiled down at her, his lips curling in a charming smile. She couldn't have been more than fifteen, sixteen at most, he decided, her dark hair waving down her back and black eyes flashing. The epitome of the type of women he'd teased Wellington about, if a tad younger, making him grin to himself. However, despite what she obviously was, this girl looked young and still unspoiled and in a flash of memory, reminded him in a vague way of Sooty as she'd been at the same age - all bravado and innocence, very slender and still developing her figure, on the cusp of womanhood. Except, this girl knew exactly what she was doing. He sighed; she was too young to be selling herself to any man who would pay a few coins.

The young girl grumbled at him, "You're only the singer, aren't you?" realising who he was when she spotted a guitar on the floor leaning against his stool. Like her, he was there to earn a few *escudos* if he was lucky, she thought, so was unlikely to spend even a few *reales* on her, when he no doubt needed to buy himself some dinner.

"Afraid so, *Señorita*, just a poor singer," but Nicky's eyes sparkled as he grinned at her, the smile lighting up his handsome features. "And you are…?"

"I'm Rosita," she announced grandly, tossing her head and thrusting out her chest in an effort to make her small, pert breasts seem more prominent.

"Are you indeed," his soft voice whispered, amusement obvious in his tone.

She grinned saucily back at him and winked. "I certainly am." Tilting her head to one side, she then asked thoughtfully, "I ain't seen you 'ere afore. Is this the first time you've sung in *Las Miraflores*?"

"Nah, I've been 'ere a coupla times, but I've been workin' around the city centre recently; more punters," he shrugged. "I've played an' sung at most of the *tabernas* and cafés there now, so I thought I'd come back 'ere an' see what was on offer. Are you expectin' it to get busy later?" Nicky's accent was choice and common. His beloved late step-mother would have cringed to hear it.

"Dunno, mebbe," she shrugged also. "With all the comin's an' goin's, first *los soldados Franceses*, then *los soldados Ingleses*, no one knows from one night to the next 'ow busy it's gonna be. Not good news for a poor workin' girl like me," she grumbled again and sighed.

"Mmmmm," Nicky nodded vaguely, wondering to himself if he should wander off and find a busier hostelry. But as he looked down at the young girl again, she smiled at him and he decided he might just as well stay there. At least she was pretty and amusing, certainly better fare than some of the other women he'd been forced to spend nights with recently in his search for information.

As he drank some more of his cheap wine, Rosita eyed him more closely. "Did you ever work at *El Toro Negro*?" she asked curiously.

"Yeeeees, for a few nights," he answered slowly. "Why?"

Her eyes lit up. "I bet it was you!" she exclaimed, narrowing her eyes as she looked him up and down in an assessing, womanly way, a professional way, especially at the front of his disreputable breeches, smiling wickedly.

"Me? What am I supposed to 'ave done?" he laughed. "Not guilty, whatever it was," as he held up his hands.

"Do you 'member a girl there called Madalena?" Rosita asked. "She worked the bar most nights."

Nicky thought back. Endless *tabernas*, names and faces drifted across his memory; how many bar workers and serving girls called Madalena had he met? He hadn't a clue. "Hmmm, I'm not sure, why?"

Rosita giggled naughtily. "I share a room with 'er sometimes, an' you fit the description she gave me of a man she met." She looked him up and down again, taking in the tousled, long tawny hair, wide shoulders and muscled chest, flat stomach and firm thighs in the tight, almost indecent breeches. "She said there was an itinerant singer there for a few days, a coupla months back, who gave 'er the best night of 'er life. She can't stop talkin' 'bout it."

Nicky burst out laughing. "It's probably someone else," he demurred. "Spain is full of itinerant musicians an' dancers tryin' to earn a livin' while this fuckin' war drags on."

"Oh, I don't think so," Rosita said slowly, leaning forward to run her fingers through his still bleached hair, down his neck and into the opening of his scruffy shirt. "What's your name?" she asked softly.

He looked back at her. "Most people call me León," his lips curled in a lecherous smile and he leaned towards her to bend down and growl in her ear. "Rawrrrrrr... do you want me to scratch your itch too, then?" and he ran his fingernails, grown longer to play the guitar he carried, round her neck and down her back.

Rosita felt a shiver run right down her spine and her belly spasmed with a coil of lust as she stared into his golden irises. "*Diiii-osss!*" she muttered, rolling her eyes and fanning herself with a hand, "NOW I understand Madalena," as Nicky merely sat back and grinned wickedly at her, his perfect white teeth standing out against his still swarthy features.

"*Tal vez, más tarde, Querida?*" "Perhaps later, Sweetheart?" he whispered and Rosita's heart thumped in her chest.

The bar gradually filled up. Rosita waited at the tables, actually turning down a couple of offers for her favours from paying customers in hopeful expectation of a night with the attractive man who was now sitting strumming his guitar, occasionally singing a traditional melody to entertain the punters.

Nicky had originally only learned to play the guitar as a small boy to please his Madre, as he called his late Spanish step-mother, to keep her entertained with a small reminder of her homeland. As he sat and played that evening, memories of her dancing around the drawing room in their house in Chelsea or their country home at Arlington, as he'd sat and practised a flamenco tune, made him smile sadly. It was she who had taught him some of the traditional Spanish songs he was singing now. As he played, Nicky's eyes lifted towards the ceiling, wondering if she was truly looking down on him. He rather hoped she was.

In the early hours, once the last of the customers wandered off and after Rosita had helped the landlord clear the tables and tidy the bar, Nicky begged the use of one of the two unused rooms upstairs in lieu of payment for his services and held out his hand to the young girl in invitation to join him.

He peeled off her cheap peasant clothes gradually as they lay on the thin mattress in the small attic room, making her cry with pleasure, literally shedding a few emotional tears, as he slowly kissed and caressed down the length of her body. Totally unused to such gentle and loving consideration from any man, Rosita writhed and gave herself up to the passion that was overwhelming her senses, experiencing a depth of feeling deep inside that she'd never known before. As he turned her over and started to kiss down her spine towards her soft, rounded buttocks, Nicky couldn't help but notice the remains of weals across her back. Rising to look more closely at the barely healed scars in the dim moonlight coming in the window, he whispered in shock, "Who's done this to you, *Querida?*"

Rosita rolled over onto her back again, looking up at him in embarrassment. "Oh, 'tis nothin'. I'm sorry... please..." she hesitated, "please don't stop, just ignore them."

Nicky looked back at her seriously. "Nothin'? How can you call that nothin'?" he asked angrily and pushed her over to inspect the nasty weals again. "You've not been beaten, you've been whipped, hard," he bit out. "D'you 'ave a pimp who did this, or was it a customer?" His eyes flashed. "Tell me, *Querida*. I swear if it was your pimp I'll go an' do the same to 'im! *Christos*, you're just a young girl!" He looked at her assessingly, "'Ow old are you anyway, Rosita? Don't you 'ave any family? If you don't mind me sayin', you speak much better than most of the other girls, 'ow the 'ell did you get into this life?" Nicky always tried to match his common accent to the other person, mainly to make them feel more at ease, so had been relieved to speak much more normally with Rosita, merely dropping a few consonants here and there. Ashcroft would undoubtedly have been fascinated and impressed by his communication strategy!

"I'm fifteen," she whispered, frightened she'd angered or put him off and he would throw her out. "My parents were killed a few years back; the war..." she shrugged sadly. "They 'ad a small bookshop 'ere in Madrid, but I've no relations an' I was left to fend for meself after they died or I'd 'ave starved. I... I've been by meself since I was eleven, nearly twelve." Nicky's shocked expression made her even more apologetic. "I'm sorry, I'm sorry, it wasn't a pimp. I don't 'ave one... it was... it was just a customer. Please don't make me go; please, León, I'll do anything, whatever you want... I'm sorry," and she leaned up to grasp his hand and kiss it pleadingly.

Nicky pulled the trembling young girl into his arms and gently soothed her, softly rubbing his hands up and down her back and bending to kiss her face, down her neck and shoulders to her small, rounded breasts. "'Ush now, *Querida,* stop apologisin'. You don't 'ave to go anywhere. I just can't stand the thought of anyone abusin' you like this, the man must be an animal. Did you know he was like that when you went with 'im? Whatever 'e paid you, it wasn't worth it."

Rosita sighed and relaxed back into Nicky's arms, waves of pleasure once again roiling through her body as he caressed away her fears and distress. "Yes... no," she stuttered and Nicky looked at her, confused. "I only went with 'im as a favour to Carmelita. Madelena an' I rent a small room in a tenement where she also lives. 'E's one of 'er reg'lars. I'd never seen 'im before that night though. She goes out to 'is villa, 'e lives just outside Madrid." The young girl shuddered at the memory. "Carmelita enjoys that sort of man, an' that's what she specialises in," she whispered. "Perversion, pain.... d'you understand?" Nicky nodded distastefully. "One day last month when 'e sent for 'er, she was, um, indisposed, at the time." Rosita shrugged and hurried on, women's monthly problems that broke into their income generation something they simply put up with. "So she asked me to go in 'er place. She didn't wanna lose 'is custom, y'see," she shuddered again and Nicky hugged her closer. "She... she said 'e was a bit perverted, but I never expected nothin' like the things 'e did to me. I thought I'd done most stuff but..." reliving the memory brought tears to her eyes. "That whip, *Dios,* the pain, but the more 'e thrashed me, the more aroused 'e got, an' when 'e took me, I thought 'e would strangle me. It was terrible it was. I don't know 'ow Carmelita puts up with it!" She buried her face in Nicky's warm chest and he hugged her close.

"Who is 'e, Rosita? Tell me an' I'll pay 'im a visit," Nicky bit out. "I'll give 'im a taste of 'is own fuckin' medicine an' see 'ow 'e likes it." He would have no truck with a man like that. Nicky hated perverts and bullies who abused or hit women and children; he'd come across enough evidence of it, even in the upper echelons of the Ton. Affairs with wives who'd revelled in the pleasure of a caring man for a night or a stolen afternoon here or there, one who could make them forget their nightmare existence with a man in an arranged or loveless marriage, especially one who enjoyed beating or forcing them. He'd discovered many gently raised Ladies who'd been extremely ignorant of the wide variety of sexual pleasures or diversions that existed, even if many of their husbands weren't. Often, the marriage bed had come as a distasteful shock to them if their husbands weren't patient, caring or inclined to explain matters to them and introduce their 'idiosyncrasies' gradually.

"I dunno 'is name," Rosita replied. "'E just sent a small carriage for Carmelita with blacked out windows so I've no idea where 'e lives, an' the carriage took me 'ome after... afterwards. Creepy it was. All I know is that 'e's French an' 'e's quite aristocratic like, an' 'e did pay me well. But I swear I'll never go back there again even if 'e offered me double, or triple. 'E's...'e's crazy. Black cold eyes, like 'is hair; gave me the shivers... like the Devil."

The hairs stood up on the back of Nicky's neck. But he carried on caressing Rosita, once more pushing her down into the mattress and running his fingers up and down her thighs and around to her bottom; teasing, tantalising and driving her wild. As she moaned beneath him, he whispered, "Bastard French. Are you sure you didn't get 'is name or 'ave any idea where 'e lives, *Querida*? I'd be 'appy to go an' beat the 'ell out of 'im for you. Now that would give ME pleasure..."

Rosita laughed as she rolled over and pushed him back down, determined to please this handsome and considerate man as much as he was pleasing her. "Aaah, my 'ero," she purred, "but I just wanna forget about 'IM. I don't know 'is name or where 'e lives, south of Madrid I think we went, but 'e had the letter B embroidered on 'is shirt an' kerchief. B for *bastardo* no doubt," and as she laughed again she bent to run her tongue around his navel and then start to kiss her way lower. "Enough of the bloody *francés*. You want pleasure then, my vengeful lion? Why not let Rosita do that for you? My customers tell me I'm very good..." and her mouth opened over him.

Nicky felt his brain and body were split in two. Half was revelling in the pleasure Rosita was giving him while the other half was seized with the information she'd just innocently imparted. An aristocratic Frenchman, with a perverted, cruel and vicious nature, dark hair and dark eyes, living in a secluded villa south of Madrid who obviously wanted to keep his name, location and whereabouts a secret... and his initial was B. It was too much of a coincidence. Finally, finally, after all these months he had a lead.

But there was nothing he could do until the morning, so being Nicky, he simply gave himself over to the pleasure of the night and the seductive young girl who was sharing it with him.

Rosita wailed loudly with intense pleasure as Nicky brought her to a shuddering climax and as she lay back against the dingy pillow, panting, she looked up at him in stunned wonder. "That was quite somethin'" she whispered breathlessly. "You're quite somethin'," and he smiled at her, his eyes twinkling. "Now I really understand why Madalena raved." She put her hand up and caressed his lightly bearded cheek, "Thank you, León. I've... I've never experienced anythin' like that afore. Most men, right from my first, all the men I go with, all they want is their pleasure. I just lay there an' pretend an' make the right noises while they rut away, but you... you... I 'ad no idea it could be so good."

"You mean you didn't pretend to enjoy that?" Nicky laughed and leaned down to kiss the tip of her nose, "*Querida* let me show you just 'ow good it can really be..."

Twice more he brought her to a shimmering, intense climax, laughing at her uninhibited, unbounded enthusiasm, the last remnants of her innocent youth still obvious as she actually blushed at some of the teasing things he did to enhance her pleasure. As Rosita lay back in his arms, sated and sleepily exhausted, she turned to look at him, running her fingers through his tousled mane of thick hair. "You're a very special man, León," she whispered.

"Not really, *Querida*. You just keep meetin' the wrong type of men. I'm nothin' special," he demurred.

"Oh yes, you are, believe me." She looked into his eyes, suddenly older beyond her years and sighed. "Isn't there a woman in your life? I'm amazed there isn't a queue out there fightin' over you."

He grinned at her. "Aaah, *Querida*," he sighed as he thought of Bella and of *Lionesse*, "women just cause me endless problems. Besides, I'm penniless, 'omeless, I've nothin' to offer, other than me an' my guitar."

She laughed back at him. "You fool," she whispered. "You big, soft-'earted fool. As if anyone would care about that if they could 'ave you, all to themself."

The following morning Nicky made love to her again, one final time before they got up to go their separate ways, something about Rosita bringing out the long buried, caring, protective side of him he used to feel for Bella, his little Sooty. He hadn't just fucked her as he did many of the women he'd engaged with, he'd taken care with her, wanting to simply bring some pleasure into her hard and meaningless existence. As she reached up to kiss him goodbye, he pressed a clutch of gold coins in her hand. "Get away from 'ere, *Querida*," he said softly. "You're too good for this life. Go south or east, to the coast; find someone more deserving of you," adding warningly, "an' whatever you do, don't go near that pervert again, no matter what 'e pays you."

Rosita gasped as she saw the money in her hand and tears filled her eyes as she looked up at him. "Whatever are you doin'? You can't afford to give me this..." and she tried to give the coins back to him.

Nicky merely smiled at her and chucked her under the chin, giving her a quick kiss. "Easy come, easy go, *Querida*," he shrugged. "I'll just 'ave to sing a bit louder or for a bit longer, or find a rich widow," and he grinned as he spun her around, swatted her on the bottom and sent her on her way. He'd have given her far more had she but known it, but it would have raised too many suspicious questions. He hoped to God she took his advice.

As Rosita wandered off down the deserted street, Nicky appeared to go back inside the tavern, but as she rounded the next corner, he turned and slowly made his way after her, keeping at a distance and staying in the shelter of shop doorways. He smiled as he watched her stroll along in the morning sunshine, her hips swinging, singing happily to herself. Again he thought of Bella, his Sooty. It had to be the hair, or maybe her general enthusiasm and energy for life, like an exuberant young dog, but there was something about her that reminded him of the young woman back in England who'd been a part of his life for as long as he could remember and who he had no idea what to do with. Maybe that was why he'd been so taken with Rosita, he was nostalgic for home and his family. He shook his head and returned his attention to where she was leading him.

Making her way down a maze of dank alleyways, she eventually arrived at a dingy tenement building and disappeared inside. Finding a deep doorway further back up the alley, he loitered in the entryway to another tenement and leaned back against the wall, watching the entrance to her building and who was coming in and out.

There was little movement over the next hour or so and, finally realising that the women who lived there would probably be sleeping off the excesses of the previous night before venturing out again in the late afternoon or early evening, he returned to the *taberna* to pick up his things and find a room in another inconspicuous inn, from where he could move around without anyone noticing.

For the next few days, Nicky watched Rosita's tenement. He saw her come and go and also spotted Madalena, finally remembering her from his brief time at *El Toro Negro*.

While Rosita and Madalena were out, he approached and casually asked one or two of the other residents if Carmelita was around. One young girl shook her head and told him she was often away for days, sometimes weeks at a time if she'd found a wealthy customer. Having no idea what the woman looked like, he also enquired about that and was told Carmelita could always be recognised by the small scar she carried above one of her dark eyebrows. He also confirmed what Rosita had told him, that she catered for a certain type of client. His senses recoiled at the prospect of involving himself with a woman who enjoyed Bernheim's particular form of entertainment.

Working at *Las Miraflores* several evenings a week, Rosita had hoped Nicky would return there. She even called into all of the other cafés and *tabernas* in the area to see if he was singing there, but there was no sign of him and none of the other working girls in the area had seen a man of his description. She sighed sadly, he seemed to have disappeared into thin air as mysteriously as he'd appeared.

Alone in the damp and dingy room she shared with Madalena, she pulled out the small soft bag she kept stuffed deep inside her thin mattress and counted out the coins saved there. With the gold Nicky had given her, she reckoned she almost had enough to leave Madrid and make a new life for herself somewhere far from there. She thought she would follow his advice and head for the coast, see if she could find herself a place as a house or kitchen maid in some respectable villa or lodging house and escape the sordid life she was currently leading. It was nearly Christmas, so with the extra money she could make from helping in the local bars as well as from drunken punters, she thought she would leave in the new year; a new year and a new start, but she just needed a little bit more money. She needed the cost of transport to the coast, money for a room to live in temporarily and to feed herself, and some sensible, demure clothes...until she found herself some proper employment.

Rosita looked at the coins again and tried to estimate how much more she would need. Not a lot, but still a fair bit. Once she'd left Madrid and finished with selling herself, she vowed she would never return to that way of life again, so she had to make enough to ensure it didn't happen. That meant just a few more punters, and the ones who wanted more than a quick fuck would pay more. Christmas was good as the men tended to get drunk and treat themselves, and spend a bit more indulging their little fantasies and foibles, or idiosyncrasies, or perversions. That was how to get more money. She grimaced in distaste, but it was now a means to an end, and not for much longer. Just a few more punters...

Get the book here and carry on reading.

If you've enjoyed the story so far, and there's a lot more drama to come, I'd love you to leave a review here and tell others about it and the rest of the books in The Pride of Lions series: Hunting Lion, Fighting Lion and Wounded Lion. Nicky's adventures are quite a journey …

This is the second set in the whole **Granville Legacy** series, lots more to come, and don't forget, if you're interested in joining my little group and getting advance reader copies of the books to review as they come out, or to hear about special offers, or read my occasional blog, or get a monthly newsletter, go to my website, https://antoinettegeorge.com/ and join my lists. You'll find out about all the rest of the **Granville Legacy** series there, especially the contemporary stories which are being published next, starting with *Soldier Banker*, all about Francis Granville's direct descendant, Marcus Forsyth.

Thank you so much and… keeeeeep reading!

This is
THE GRANVILLE LEGACY

Coming soon, the full series of The Granville Legacy

18th and 19th century

The life and times of Francis Granville and his friends

Behind The Shadow

Pride of Lions

Publish And Be Damned

To Catch a Thief

21st century

The adventures of Marcus Forsyth, Francis Granville's direct descendant, and his close friends and family.

Soldier Banker

Lions and Feathers

Matilda's Diamonds

Never Left Behind

The Chameleon and The Swan

The Cat's Whiskers

Pins and Noodles

Acknowledgments

Barbara – thank you for your continued enthusiasm and support, endless useful comments on everything, and of course, the editing.

Zivan – thank you for your graphics and covers and grappling with a coat of arms!

Clare – thank you for the formatting and pulling all the content into shape.

www.ingramcontent.com/pod-product-compliance
Lightning Source LLC
Chambersburg PA
CBHW051311250626
47155CB00014B/527